# WAY *of* *the* WARRIOR

A romance anthology to benefit the
Wounded Warrior Project

The publisher acknowledges the copyright holders of the individual works as follows:

*Hot as Hell* © 2015 by Julie Ann Walker
*In Plain Sight* © 2015 by Catherine Mann
*Torn* © 2015 by Kate SeRine
*War Games* © 2015 by Lea Griffith
*Beauty and the Marine* © 2015 by Tina Wainscott
*NSDQ* © 2015 by M.L. Buchman
*SEALed with Passion* © 2015 by Anne Elizabeth
*Home Fire Inferno* © 2015 by Suzanne Brockmann

Published by Sourcebooks Casablanca, an imprint of Sourcebooks, Inc.
P.O. Box 4410, Naperville, Illinois 60567-4410
(630) 961-3900
Fax: (630) 961-2168
www.sourcebooks.com

Printed and bound in Canada.
MBP 10 9 8 7 6 5 4 3 2 1

*"IN WAR, THERE ARE NO UNWOUNDED SOLDIERS."*
—JOSÉ NAROSKY

Those seven simple words say it better than I ever could. This book is dedicated to the men and women who nobly and selflessly answer the call to arms, the brave warriors who fight for our freedom and the way of life we hold so dear, those heroes and heroines who carry the seen and unseen scars of war. We thank you for your valor and sacrifice.

Please know, dear readers, that all author and publisher proceeds from this book have been pledged to the Wounded Warrior Project. The money raised will be used to help fund programs that support the mental and physical health of our nation's wounded fighting men and women.

To learn more about how you can donate directly, please visit www.woundedwarriorproject.org.

Julie Ann Walker

# CONTENTS

# HOT AS HELL

A Deep Six Novella

## JULIE ANN WALKER

# CHAPTER 1

*United States Embassy*
*Islamabad, Pakistan*

*Booooom!*

Harper Searcy's eyes rounded as she grabbed the edge of her desk. It shook in rhythm to the rattle of the bulletproof windows in the large office across the way, and the wheels on her rolling chair chattered against the tile floor like teeth in a bony skull. For a moment, her brain blanked. Just…full stop. Nothing. A big, honking nada. And there she sat with her jaw slung open while the whole world did the shimmy-shake.

Then her synapses started firing—rapid-firing, more like—and she snapped her mouth closed, quickly glancing around the small anteroom that was her workspace as the secretary and all-around right-hand man…er…*woman*… for the U.S. Ambassador to Pakistan. A loud *snapping* sound preceded the appearance of a huge crack zigzagging its way up the plaster wall to her right. It rained salmon-colored paint flecks onto the floor. The metal and glass in the overhead light fixture jangled ominously. Then the closed door leading from her office to the third-floor landing above the grand central staircase suddenly swung wide, its hinges creaking eerily as if opened by ghostly hands.

Her heart froze solid—no easy task considering the average temperature in Islamabad in July was 95°F.

*Gas main explosion? Or…earthquake?*

The latter was certainly possible. The city was built atop five major fault lines. Yup, that's right. Five! *And good gracious! Who the hell decides to construct a capital above somethin' like that?* Of course, the question was purely rhetorical, and she didn't bother answering it as she pulled open the bottom left-hand drawer of her desk and snatched her purse from inside. *Cell phone, cell phone.* If she was about to be buried alive—*hopefully* alive—under a mountain of rubble it would be good to have her cell phone on her, right? *Right.*

"Sir!" she yelled in the general direction of her boss's office as she kicked out of her chair. It slammed against the back wall, causing the framed photograph of the president of the United States to hop off its nail and the glass to shatter against the tiles. She didn't give it a passing thought as she slung her purse over her shoulder. "Mr. Ambassador!" she called again. "We need to evacuate the building as quickly as—"

*Rat-a-tat-tat! Rat-a-tat-tat!*

The words died in the back of her throat when the unmistakable sound of automatic gunfire slammed into her eardrums. It was then she realized the rattle and rumble had suddenly ceased. So…*not* an earthquake? A…bomb, perhaps? Was the embassy under attack?

Her heart was no longer frozen. The thing had turned into a hot fist pounding against her ribs, making it nearly impossible to breathe. Every single one of her hair follicles hoisted their charge upright—*could a person get goose bumps on her scalp?*—until she felt electrified from head to toe.

"Sir!" She scrambled around her desk, banging her

knee—*ow!*—against the edge in the process. Then she was racing into her boss's office.

And holy frick! The silly sonofagun was standing at the window, watching in wide-eyed horror whatever was happening out in the embassy's courtyard. The constant *rat-a-tat-tat* was more pronounced here. And as her dear ol' Georgia born-and-bred momma would say, that man's 'bout as smart as tree bark. The glass was bulletproof, but what were the odds it was also *bazooka* proof?

"Get away from the window!" she yelled, ducking beneath the line of the windowsill and crouch-walking her way toward her boss. When he turned to her, his wrinkled face was slack with disbelief.

"That Intel from the Department of Defense was right after all, Harper," he wheezed, his left eye twitching. "The TTP is attacking us. I never thought they would actually—"

"Get down, Mr. Ambassador!" She grabbed his hand and yanked him into a stoop beside her. "We have to get to the panic room!"

"It's too far away." His aging blue eyes were wide and glassy as he shook his head. The soft yellow light from the overhead chandelier glinted off his cue-ball crown, and while Harper deeply respected Ambassador Douglas O'Leary for his diplomatic acumen, it was obvious the man wasn't much when it came to quick, rational thinking outside the negotiation chambers and inside a life-and-death situation. The shock of the raid had already gotten to him. As if to prove her point, when he gestured out the window she saw his finger was shaking. Nope. Correction. His whole *arm* was shaking. "We'll never make it to the basement before we're overrun!"

Chancing a quick peek above the sill, Harper's breath whooshed from her lungs like she'd taken a one-two punch to the gut. The scene that pierced her eyes was pure chaos...

The high iron gate leading into the compound was completely obliterated, as was a good portion of the fifteen-foot concrete wall surrounding the embassy. What appeared to be the remains of a large truck, the armored kind used for hauling cash or gemstones or some other high-value whatnot, sat smoldering in the breach, nothing but an ugly heap of twisted, scorched metal. A mass of bearded men in pajama-like pants and sporting *pakol* hats swarmed over the rubble and through the thick black smoke like bloodthirsty locusts. Ambassador O'Leary was right. It *was* the *Tehrik-e Taliban Pakistan*—the Pakistani Taliban—otherwise known as the TTP. And with machine guns held tight against their shoulders, they kept up a constant barrage of death-dealing fire while advancing on the outnumbered contingent of Marines tasked with guarding the embassy.

"Holy shiiiiit," she rasped, ducking back beneath the window and swallowing the bile that burned up the back of her throat like sulfuric acid. If she'd been raised Catholic instead of Southern Baptist, she would have crossed herself.

"Harper." Ambassador O'Leary grabbed her wrist, his palm cold and clammy. It left behind a wet imprint when he quickly released her. "I don't think we're getting out of this—"

"Nonsense," she cut him off, hastily reaching into

her purse, scrounging past her wallet and two plastic containers of wild cherry Tic Tacs to pull out her cell phone. "We just need to haul ass down to the panic room and wait for the cavalry to arrive."

And by cavalry she meant Michael "Mad Dog" Wainwright and his badass band of Navy SEALs…

For the last six months, ever since the DOD heard whispers over the airwaves of a possible terrorist attack on the embassy, Michael and six additional members of his SEAL Team had been tasked with providing the ambassador and his diplomatic officers personal protection. But after months of radio silence and zippo indication that an offensive would actually, *factually* occur, the Navy decided they had more important things for the SEALs to do than sit around Pakistan twiddling their thumbs. So Michael and his Team had been given marching orders to report to the South China Sea—for God and JSOC (Joint Special Operations Command) only knew what—on a two-week mission. That had been exactly fourteen days ago, which meant Michael was due back today—a fact she'd been lamenting ever since the embassy party when she'd recklessly engaged him in a round of drunken debauchery. Of course, given the quick left turn her afternoon had taken, now the man couldn't return his fine ass to Islamabad quick enough to suit her.

Latching onto the ambassador's sleeve, she broke into a hunched run, dragging the wiry old diplomat in her wake. She'd just made it out of the offices and to the top of the wide, sweeping stairwell when—*boom!*—another explosion rocked the place. She and the ambassador stumbled into the wall, bracing themselves against the plaster and each other. Luckily, this blast appeared to be much smaller than the first, although it was no less frightening—illustrated by the fact that Harper had to gulp twice, three times, in order to force her heart back down into her chest from where it'd lodged in her throat. Then acrid black smoke began to slowly, almost lazily, drift up from below.

*Hell and damnation!*

Now on a regular day, the embassy would be teeming with staff. But it was the weekend—and a holiday weekend at that—so the landing was blessedly empty. The place was operating with what amounted to the barest bones of a skeleton crew.

*Just me, O'Leary, and the Marines…*

Which, on the one hand, was a point in their favor. It meant there were far fewer people the TTP could use as targets or hostages. On the other hand, it was a point against them. Because it exponentially increased her and O'Leary's *personal* odds of ending up as either… or both.

"They've penetrated the building," the ambassador gasped from behind her, pressing himself against the wall like the floor might up and decide to fall out from under his cordovan-colored loafers.

"Then we take the back steps down," she said matter-of-factly, surprised by the steadiness of her tone when her heart had gone all Carl Lewis on her, breaking into a 100-meter sprint. She'd been scared plenty of times in her twenty-eight years, but this was the first time she'd ever experienced pure, undiluted terror.

"N-no." The ambassador shook his bald head

frantically, inching along the wall back toward the offices. "There's no time. We should lock ourselves inside—"

"We'll be sittin' ducks!" she screamed, the tiny cracks in her composure splitting into wide, steaming fissures. It was her job to look after O'Leary, to take care of his every need. But she couldn't help the man when he was refusing to use his brain and save himself.

Lock themselves inside their offices? The Taliban had managed to overrun the Marines and blow up the front door to the embassy! Did he really think something as simple as a deadbolt would keep them out? Talk about being one or two sandwiches short of a picnic. *I mean, come on!*

The sound of heavy footsteps pounding up the marble staircase was joined by a bevy of raised voices speaking Pashto. She held out a hand to the ambassador, begging him with her eyes and her words. "Please, sir! Come with me. The panic room is our only hope."

He shook his head again, stepping back into the office. Then, to her slack-jawed surprise, he slammed the door in her face. And even despite the pandemonium of sounds echoing from below, she could make out the ominous *click* as the lock slid into place.

She had a brief moment to blink owlishly and think *oh, no he di-int* before prudence, and straight-up heart-pounding, soul-sucking fear, dictated she make a run for the back stairs. In less than two ticks of the clock, she was across the landing and throwing open the door that concealed a narrow, winding metal staircase—she'd been told it was a servants' passage back when the building was the mammoth residence of

some hoity-toity sultan. Quietly closing herself inside
the airless stairwell, she was instantly embraced by the
warm, suffocating arms of darkness. She blew out a
wheezing breath and took her first step down just as
a barrage of pounding fists and shouting voices told
her the Taliban fighters had made it to the third-floor
landing and were demanding the ambassador open the
door to the offices.

*You should've come with me, sir.* Although woulda,
coulda, shoulda…there was nothing she could do for the
ambassador now. But maybe, *hopefully*, there was still
something she could do for herself.

Descending as quietly and quickly as she could,
she thumbed on her iPhone and brought up her recent
call history.

There was his name glowing brightly on the screen.
Twenty times in the past two weeks. Once for every
time she had put him off with a *Busy now. Let's talk
later* text, or a quick *Hello, are ya safe? Okay, good.
Let's chat when ya get back*, response, or—and, yup,
she wasn't too proud of herself for these—those times
when, like a lily-livered ninny, she'd flat-out avoided
him altogether.

Well, by God, you can bet your sweet bippy she
wasn't avoiding him now. Because while she may not
trust him with her heart, she more than trusted him with
her life. And since it was her *life* on the line, it was a
good thing—as those twenty calls would suggest—that
Michael "Mad Dog" Wainwright had absolutely no quit
in him…

~~~

*Minhas Pakistani Air Force Base*
*Fifty miles outside Islamabad*

"Yo! Brad Pittstains! You wanna put away your phone and move your ass?"

Michael stared down at his iPhone's irritatingly blank screen, trying—and *failing*—for about the millionth time to figure that damned woman out. If she'd been any other dame, he would've chalked up the night of the embassy party to a simple wham-bam-thank-you-ma'am. No harm. No foul. Just one hell of a rocking good time.

But this was *Harper Searcy*...

The funny-Internet-dog-photo-sharing *Harper Searcy*. The joke-texting *Harper Searcy*. The ol' fashioned, Southern born-and-bred, good girl *Harper Searcy*. The phrase *one-night stand* probably wasn't even in her vocabulary. But that's sure as shit what he was beginning to suspect had happened. Then again, the way she'd snuggled up to him, so close and tight, kissing him directly over his heart? Well...that certainly hadn't *felt* like *see ya, wouldn't want to be ya*. So what the hell was she—

"I said, *Yo, Brad Pitts*—"

"I heard you the first time, asshole," Michael grumbled, sliding his gaze over to his friend and teammate, Bran Pallidino. "And first off, I happen to know you stole that insult from an episode of *Modern Family*. Secondly, I think you may have mistaken me for yourself. For the love of Christ, man, we're barely wheels-down and you already look like a drowned Atlantic City sewer rat, which, in case you were wondering, are uglier than sewer rats any place else. Drowned or not."

Bran made a face that did nothing to detract from his swarthy Italian-American good looks—the bastard—before adjusting the strap of his army-green duffel over his shoulder. He wiped the back of his hand over his perspiring brow. "No big surprise there considering *everything* that comes from that part of Jersey looks like it's been beaten with the ugly stick." He leveled Michael with a meaningful look. Since Bran hailed from Newark, the two of them had that whole North Jersey versus South Jersey rivalry thing down pat. "And besides, I can't help it if I sweat like a whore in church in this damned Pakistani heat. Who doesn't?"

Standing on the side of the wide loading platform, Michael watched as the hydraulic gears on the C-17 Globemaster transport plane groaned while lowering the huge back ramp to the ground. Hot, dry wind immediately rushed into the massive fuselage, ruffling the hair near his temples. When the ramp kissed the tarmac with a solid *thud* and the hydraulics kicked off, he glanced over at their lieutenant, Leo "The Lion" Anderson, before hooking a thumb in the guy's direction. "LT for one," he told Bran, using the military slang for Leo's rank. "As always, he's cool as a fucking cucumber."

"Yeah, sure. But there's something wrong with that guy," Bran scoffed, taking in LT's bone-dry shirt and crisp, efficient movements as he stood from one of the jump seats mounted to the interior wall of the plane and slid on his ever-present aviator sunglasses. With sun-streaked, sandy-blond hair and a perpetual tan, not to mention his seeming immunity to broiling weather, LT looked the part of a man who'd grown up in the Florida Keys. "I think it's glandular."

"I heard that," LT grumbled, unwrapping a stick of Big Red chewing gum and folding it into his mouth. Then he bent to shoulder his own duffel as the four remaining members of Michael's SEAL Team followed suit, unstrapping and grabbing gear. "Which speaks to the fact that on the flight over today, it occurred to me that you're not a nitwit, Bran. You're a shitwit."

One corner of Michael's mouth twitched. "Nice one, LT."

Bran turned from their lieutenant back to him, brow furrowed. "You thought that was funny, did you, *spostata*?"

Michael winked, ignoring the Italian insult.

"Uh-huh." Bran narrowed his eyes. "Well, considering you've been feverishly dialing and redialing—all to no avail, I might add—that cute redhead's number ever since you two smashed naughty bits, I'd say *you're* the shitwit in this group. Not me."

Michael's face instantly fell at the mention of Harper's ongoing cold...er...at least *cool* shoulder routine. They'd made a *connection*, hadn't they? And the feeling had been like being dealt an ace-high royal flush. Just flat-out unbeatable. "She's a Southern belle. I suspect playing hard to get is just part of her courtship ritual."

At least, that's what he'd been telling himself with every unanswered call.

Bran snorted. "Sure, okay. And I'm gonna file that under Bitch and Please. But, hey, I get it, *paisano*. You managed to break off a piece of something you like, and now you—"

"Bran," LT warned, glancing surreptitiously at

Michael over the top of his sunglasses, accurately reading his not-so-poker face, which, you know, was pretty much the expressional equivalent of a line of Do Not Cross tape. As well as the hot, fighting blood that was prized among the SEALs, the ability to out-quip or out-insult a teammate was held in the highest regard. Usually, Michael was able to mix it up with the best of them. But not when Harper was the subject at hand…

*Fuckin' A. You have* got *to get it together, Wainwright.*

Yeah. That was solid advice. And he'd been trying unsuccessfully to take it ever since that god-damned party.

"Aw, hell. Sorry, Mad Dog," Bran quickly relented after grabbing a clue that his jibes were hitting a little too close to home. Even though Bran was the joker in the deck, there wasn't a malicious bone in the man's body. Now, irritating bones? The guy had those in spades. "I didn't realize it was such a touchy subject. And if it makes you feel any better, I figure the real reason she's pulling that whole *mum's the word* shtick is because she's afraid to go another round with that python you pack in your pants."

And just like that, Michael's frown turned upside down. Leave it to Bran. But before he could respond to that ridiculous bit of alliterative nonsense—*python he packed in his pants? Jesus*—his cell phone came to life in his hand, vibrating and jangling out the tune to "Happy" by Pharrell Williams.

"Oh, for shit's sake," Bran cursed, falling immediately back into his role as good-hearted tormentor. "Is it possible for you to upload a ringtone that *doesn't* make me want to take a bath with a toaster?"

Michael liked snappy pop songs. So sue him. Who—
if they were being completely honest—didn't? "Don't
act like you don't *love* it," he told Bran, grinning broadly.
Of course, when he lifted the phone and saw who was
calling, his expression instantly sobered as his heart
drummed out a rhythm to match the melody's tempo.

*It's about goddamned time!*

"Or maybe I was wrong." Bran smiled down at the
phone until his teeth flashed white against his dark,
scraggly beard. When operating in this part of the world,
it behooved the SEALs to blend into the local popula-
tion as best they could. Which meant facial hair came
part and parcel with the job. All of Alpha platoon was
sporting full-on scruff. And, no, in case you were wondering, it didn't do a damn thing to mitigate the heat.
"About her wanting another shot at your trouser snake,"
Bran clarified. "Not about you being a *spostata*." He
socked Michael on the shoulder before ambling down
the aircraft's long loading ramp in the wake of the rest of
their Team, whistling the tune to "Happy," and leaving
Michael to take the call in private.

Raking in a deep breath—*For the love of Christ,
I've got it bad*. Worse than he'd ever had it before—he
thumbed on the phone and lifted the device to his ear. *Be
cool. Just be cool.* "Harper?"

His voice cracked up at the end like he was pubescent
or something. *Fuuuuck.*

"Michael? Oh, thank God!"

She'd only spoken four words, but he immediately
zeroed in on the sharp spike of panic in her tone. The
hairs along the nape of his neck twanged upright, and
he automatically—almost unconsciously—reached for

the weapon secured in the nylon holster strapped to his thigh. "What is it, Harper? What happened?"

"They did it, Michael," she husked, her Southern accent made stronger by her terror. "The TTP attacked the embassy. I'm on my way down to the safe r—"

She was cut off when a loud *crash* echoed through the phone's receiver, followed immediately by angry voices shouting in a language he only had a passing familiarity with. But he was fluent enough to make out the words *capture* and *kill*.

Then the line went dead.

Which is when Michael "Mad Dog" Wainwright knew, for the first time in his life, what it was to be one hundred percent, no-holds-barred, shit-the-bed terrified...

# CHAPTER 2

*HOW MUCH TIME HAS PASSED? TWO DAYS? TWO WEEKS?*

Harper sat huddled in the corner of the spacious, high-tech panic room—her butt having surely made a permanent imprint on the cool concrete floor—feeling like she'd been waiting an *eternity* for rescue. But in reality, it had only been…she ran a hand through her hair and turned over her cell phone, checking the digital clock for what seemed like the bazillionth time…three and a half hours. Three and a half everlasting hours. Three and a half god-awful, lonely, terrifying hours.

And even though she knew it was a useless endeavor, she hit Redial. Lifting the phone to her ear, she hoped beyond senseless hope that this time her cell signal would penetrate the walls of the safe room and link her to Michael. But after a couple of seconds, the loud *beep, beep, beep* of an unconnected call sounded through the tiny speaker. She powered down the device with a disgusted press of her thumb.

"What in God's name is happenin' out there? Why is it so quiet?" She posed the questions aloud just to hear her own voice. Just to assure herself she really *had* made it into the heavily reinforced chamber, slamming the thick metal door in the angry faces of the Taliban fighters who had been hot on her heels in her madcap dash down the stairs and across the basement.

And, yup. So *that* had happened. She still couldn't

quite believe it. Though the fact that she'd shaken like a junkie for the first sixty minutes of her confinement spoke volumes about the awful reality of her very, *very* close call. There had been such hatred in the men's eyes in that split-second when she'd come face-to-face with them. Such feral, evil *hatred*.

Then, of course, there had been the incessant pounding on the door, followed by a series of muted *pinging* noises that she had to assume meant the terrorists were shooting at the bulletproof steel of the chamber. But all that had ended long ago. And now she was left with… silence. *Deafening* silence. A silence so complete that the deep breath of sterile air she pulled into her lungs— the oxygen in the safe room was pumped in through a separate ventilation system to counteract any possible chemical weapons attack—sounded like she was doing her best impression of Darth Vader.

"Luke," she growled, lowering her voice a few octaves. "*I* am your father."

The sentence reverberated around the room before the thick walls absorbed the words. She snorted, realizing she was straight-up losing her marbles. Going *crazy as a bullbat* as they liked to say back in her lowcountry hometown, a place so small it sometimes forgot its own name. And that whole so-small-it-sometimes-forgot-its-own-name thing was precisely why she'd worked so *hard* to make a name for herself within the pool of diplomatic secretaries. So she could get an overseas assignment. So she could get the hell out of Georgia.

*See the world, they said. It'll be fun, they said.*

"Yeah, right." She'd give her eyeteeth to be back

home right now, sitting on the front porch swing at her folks' house, drinking a tall, sweating glass of sweet tea. And if she happened to make it out of this thing alive, that's exactly what she was going to do—catch the first transport home.

She was done with Pakistan. D.O.N.E. She'd *had* a taste of adventure and, quite honestly, she didn't care for it. It was time to go back to the land of the free and the home of the brave and implement her life plan. Husband. Kids. A job that *didn't* come complete with armed terrorists...

Raking in another fortifying breath, she reached into her purse, pulled out one of the boxes of Tic Tacs, and tossed a couple of the tiny candies into her mouth. Then she glanced around the space and decided two things. Number one: she was thirsty as all get-out, and those gallon jugs of water stacked beside the door were calling her name. And number two: if she was going to be here for a while, she had better get comfy and stop cowering in the corner like a chicken-hearted cur. There was only so much self-pity she could stand. And she'd just about reached her limit.

Pushing up, she rubbed her hands over her mostly numb derriere, grimacing when the muscles came back to life in a rush of pins and needles. "Talk about a *literal* pain in the ass," she said, hobbling toward the water containers.

She'd just unscrewed the plastic top on one, using both hands to tilt the room-temperature water down her throat, when a series of soft *pops* sounded outside. She bobbled the jug, managing to spill a good portion of its contents onto her blouse before she caught it and carefully replaced the cap. Setting the half-empty container back atop its carefully arranged compatriots, she tilted her head toward the door, listening.

*Pop, pop, pop.*

Gunfire. She was sure of it.

But this was different than what she'd heard before. For one thing, it didn't sound like the rounds were hitting the walls of the panic room—*praise be for small miracles*. For another thing, the frequency was steady, almost…calculated. Of their own accord, her feet shuffled her closer to the door. She'd just placed a hand on the cool surface when—*Ring, ring! Ring, ring!*—a phone sounded in the room behind her.

She jumped like a scalded cat, glad the water jug was no longer in her hands. *What the what? A phone?* Where the heck had *that* been for the last three hours? She spun, her eyes searching the ceiling-high shelves stacked against the south side of the room and piled with canned foods and dry goods.

*Ring, ring! Ring, ring!*

Where was it coming from? There was no phone on the shelves. No phone on the lone wooden table in the middle of the space. No phone atop or beneath the half-dozen cots crammed together on the opposite side of the room. No phone—

*Aha!* On the back wall, a yellow light blinked over a small door no bigger than that of a mailbox. She raced toward it, wrenching open the little aperture and revealing a cubbyhole where, sure enough, an old-fashioned corded phone sat nestled all safe and sound.

"Now, why wasn't *this* part of my orientation?" she grumbled as she snatched the receiver from the cradle, running a hand through her hair again. It was a nervous tic. One she'd been working to overcome until today when nervous tics were the least of her worries.

"Hello?" she barked, not surprised when that one word sounded like it'd been broken on a hard edge. She prided herself on being a gutsy gal—after all, she'd spent nearly a year living and working in Pakistan, hadn't she? A country where females, especially American females, weren't all that highly revered—but the last few hours had definitely taken their toll.

"Miss Searcy," an authoritative voice sounded in her ear, "this is General Pete Fuller. Sorry we took so long to contact you. We've been a bit busy around here, but—"

The line crackled and cut out just before another voice, a wonderfully deep, wonderfully familiar voice, rumbled against her eardrums. "…thought I told you to patch me through, goddamnit. She knows me and—"

"Michael?" she wheezed, allowing her forehead to fall against the edge of the cubbyhole. The cool kiss of the metal was a reassuring caress but not nearly as reassuring as Michael's bass-drum New Jersey accent.

"Harper?" His hard exhale sounded like a windstorm coming through the receiver. "Do you copy me? Am I coming in clear?"

If she wasn't mistaken, that burning at the back of her eyeballs was the prick of tears she'd managed, up until now, to hold at bay.

He'd come to save her.

She knew he would.

Her relief was so immense, the muscles in her legs threatened to quit their job of keeping her upright. She blindly reached back, bracing herself with the help of one of the chairs pushed beneath the table. "I-I-I..." Okay. So, now was not the time to fall apart. But try telling that to her st-st-stuttering tongue. She swallowed and finally managed, "Yeah, I can hear you."

"Good. Now open the damned door."

―—·ᴍ—―

It had been one ball-busting, gut-wrenching, head-spinning *hell* of a fight...

As Michael leaned against the door of the safe room, blowing hard, his heart pounding while he waited for Harper to open up, he glanced at the carnage he, LT, and Bran had wrought in the basement. Six Taliban fighters sprawled lifelessly around the dank-smelling room, staining the concrete floor with the growing pools of their deep crimson blood.

After fifteen years in the military, two wars, and over two hundred missions, he was used to seeing death. But when it came by way of a lead round traveling at nearly three thousand feet per second, it was never pretty.

There was a part of him that felt remorse for these men. For the poverty, dejection, and desperation that made them easy targets for brainwashing, radical militants. But that jab of sympathy hadn't stopped him from doing his job and taking them out. Just as it hadn't stopped him from doing his part in helping his teammates and the Marines cut down the more than four dozen—total guess there, since he'd lost count after twenty—Taliban fighters they'd come face-to-face with during their two-and-a-half-hour battle to retake the embassy after they'd fast-roped in from the helicopter they'd grabbed at the Air Force base. When it came to kill or be killed, he chose to kill every damn time.

And speaking of carnage and killing, he glanced over at LT.

"Y'okay?" he asked his lieutenant, tilting his chin toward the deep, bloody furrow in the guy's left arm. If that bullet had been eight inches to the right, Leo "The Lion" Anderson might be pushing up daisies instead of standing beside him. Because even though each man from Alpha platoon was geared up in desert-tan camouflage Kevlar, it was well known that the TTP liked to use armor-piercing rounds. Armor-piercing rounds that had *not* been enough to puncture the reinforced steel skin of the safe room—evidenced by the pockmarks riddling the structure. And Michael had never really considered himself an overly religious man but, all the same, he sent up a silent prayer of thanks for that one glorious miracle. Figured a little ecclesiastical gratitude couldn't hurt.

"Yeah. I'm okay," LT said, lifting his slowly seeping arm while cupping his junk with his other hand. "But the boys may've retreated permanently."

"Ain't that a fact." Michael barked out a laugh before quickly sobering again. Then a *clanking* sound told him Harper was working on the door's locking mechanism, and his heart began pounding for a whole new reason.

Flexing against the sudden tension gripping his shoulders—and, okay, so he fully realized how ridiculous it was to feel tense *now*, in this moment. You know, considering all he'd been required to do in the last couple of hours—he turned to LT. "So I'll wait in there with Harper until command calls and gives me the all-clear?"

"That's affirmative." LT nodded, his jaws pulverizing a piece of chewing gum.

Bran, who'd been busy slamming a new clip into his gas-operated, air-cooled Colt M4 and then checking the bodies of the Taliban fighters for any pesky explosives, walked over to slap a hand on Michael's shoulder. The man's brown eyes sparkled like he had an ace in the hole.

Michael made a face. "Okay, Captain Googly Eyes. Why don't you just go ahead and spit out whatever it is that's causing you to give me that look."

"I'm just imagining what will happen once you're in there with Harper," Bran said.

"Oh, yeah? And what's that?" Although, in all honesty, Michael had a few ideas. All of which included Harper naked, sweaty, and sated. Adrenaline did many things to a man's body, but one of those things was...*schwing!*

"Just that she's going to play you like a fiddle at one of those Blue Ridge Mountain hoedowns she probably went to when she was a kid."

Rolling his eyes—mostly to deflect from the fact that he was scared shitless the guy was probably right—he opened his mouth to retort when, with a *pop* and an airtight *hiss*, the door to the panic room swung open.

And there she was. Harper Searcy. Her face so pale it looked like she'd been snacked on by a horde of vampires. Her big blue eyes as round as the pepperoni pies served at Tony Boloney's on the boardwalk back home. Her thin blouse...*wet? Sweet Jesus*. And her wildly curling cascade of red hair sticking up every which way like she'd repeatedly run her hands through it.

It was that last thing that unglued his boots from the floor. Because he'd noticed months ago that she only fidgeted with her hair when she was nervous or, in the case of today, scared to death.

"I'll be waiting on the call," he told LT, shouldering his way into the sterile-looking space, forcing Harper to take a step back. He heard his lieutenant murmur "Roger that" right before he pulled the door closed behind him, twisting the large spinning lock into place. And just like that, he'd sealed himself inside the safe room with her. With lovely Harper. Smart Harper. Brave Harper.

He wanted so badly to pull her into his arms and tell her everything was going to be all right. That he was here with her now. That she was safe. To kiss her and hold her so tight she wouldn't know one additional *millisecond* of fear. But considering she'd been giving him what he'd come to suspect was the world's most blatant brush off? Well, he figured she might not welcome his overtures. Which is why he decided to go with, "So, what's with you avoiding me the last couple of weeks?"

—◦◦◦—

Harper had never been as happy to see anyone in her entire sorry life as she was to see Michael "Mad Dog" Wainwright. And all geared up in desert-tan camo, his wide chest made even bulkier with the addition of body armor, his deadly M4 machine gun gripped loosely in one big callused hand, he struck her as beautiful in the way warriors were beautiful. Harsh and fierce and furious. Not one hint of delicacy about him, except for maybe the soft curling length of his thick, dark lashes and the full, almost pouty curve of his lower lip visible through the dark-chocolate beard covering the bottom half of his face.

*That man is tougher than woodpecker lips.* It was an old phrase her momma liked to use in reference to her dad. But Harper figured it summed up Michael in one go, too.

Of course, regardless of how happy she was to see him, or how savage and gorgeous he looked standing there in the middle of the room, she felt her brow furrow, her mouth pucker, and her hands jump to her hips, because, "Really? That's what you lead with?"

He turned to set his weapon on the table, one of his beefy shoulders lifting in that supremely unconcerned way that only males of the species could pull off. Talk about *annoying*. But when he yanked his helmet from his head, revealing his thick mink-colored hair and the damp tendrils curling around his temples, her irritation disappeared. Mostly because she became wholly distracted by the fact that her fingers were itching with the memory of what it was to bury themselves into that lush, living mass.

*Oh, for love of ladies' underpants, Harper. Now is not the time.*

"I figured that was as good a question as any," he said, and she tried not to notice how his hard muscles coiled like knotted rope under his fatigues when he shrugged out of his rucksack and undid the Velcro on his body armor. The holster securing the handgun to his thigh came off next, and he set the whole kit and caboodle atop the table.

"Oh, yeah? How about, *How are you, Harper? Everything okay in here?*" she huffed. "Or maybe,

*Want to hear how your boss is doin', Harper?* That's a pretty good one considerin' it's my job to look after the cowardly ol' coot." Yup, she had *not* forgotten the way O'Leary had slammed that door in her face. "Of course, if neither of those do it for you, you could always go with the obvious, *Would you like to know what we're doing lockin' ourselves in here instead of gettin' the hell out of Dodge?* That's a good one, too. I like that one a lot, and…and…and…"

She stuttered to a stop when he took two heavy, yet remarkably fluid steps in her direction. She'd noticed months ago that Michael pretty much embodied the phrase *economy of movement*, because even though he was a hulking mountain of a man, there was also an undeniable grace to him. A nimbleness that spoke of innate coordination and tightly controlled strength.

*Coordination and strength…*

A memory of the smooth, forceful way he'd moved against her, *inside* her, flashed through her mind in crystal-clear Technicolor glory. Sure, she'd been pretty tipsy at the time. But even had she been three king-sized sheets to the wind, she was confident she would still be able to recall the miles upon miles of his tough, tanned, burning-hot skin. The way his mouth and tongue had teased her like nobody's business. How his big, rough hands had been so gentle and so very, *very* knowledgeable. And all that was before you got to the thick, pulsing length of his…well…*you know*. Because a woman would have to be six feet under not to remember something *that* magnificent.

When he stopped no more than a hairsbreadth from her, the toes of his giant, scuffed combat boots almost touching the tips of her black kitten heels, chills cascaded across her flesh. Not because the air inside the safe room was cold. But because with him so close, his heat radiated out to her in an unseen, highly sensual caress.

*Good gracious.*

Doing her best to hide her reaction, she tilted her chin far back to glance into his face. He had the kind of deep-set eyes that made it look like he was always gazing out from under his eyebrows, watching, calculating, studying. But right now, the ocean-blue of his irises revealed a sardonic glint. And if she wasn't mistaken, his lips were pulled into the tiniest of smirks.

"First of all," he said, his voice pitched so low it rumbled through her chest, more felt than heard, "I can see you're okay. Not a scratch on you. And the wet shirt is a really nice touch, by the way."

She glanced down at her white cotton blouse and discovered the dousing she'd given herself a moment ago had rendered the material see-through. The peek-a-boo lace of her bra did nothing to hide the deep red of her areolas or the provocative thrust of her pebbled nipples.

*Yeesh!*

She yanked the sodden fabric away from her body. And now there was no mistaking that, yes, indeedie, those fabulous lips of his were most certainly quirked.

She opened her mouth to tell him to wipe that sardonic grin right off his face, but he beat her to the punch. His expression hardened to living stone.

"Secondly," he said, "your boss is being held hostage by a group of TTP who've barricaded themselves in a room upstairs."

*Oh, holy hell. Why* had the silly man thought he'd be safer in the offices? *Why?*

"My Team is doing their best to either negotiate his release or formulate a plan to go in and grab him," he assured her. "But depending on which scenario command chooses, it's possible you and I could be stuck in here for a while."

Stuck. In a room. One that had various surfaces on which to get horizontal. With Michael.

*Lord, help me.*

She'd managed to protect her heart from him after one night together. But two? That would be pushing it. And not because she was a woman and susceptible to the oxytocin—the bonding hormone—that Mother Nature had decreed should flood her system after orgasm. But because Michael was…well…*Michael*. Sexy and smart. Loyal and courageous. But here was the kicker: in the time she'd known him, she'd come to appreciate the fact that he was just flat-out *likable*. And the more she was around him, the more she wanted to *continue* to be around him. In fact, it would be so stinking easy to just—

*No.* She gifted herself with the mental version of a bitch-slap. *Remember what it was like for your momma lovin' a soldier.*

Right. She couldn't forget that. Not when it'd shaped her entire childhood.

*So, stick to your guns. Stick to the* plan. *And for the love of all that's holy, stick to the conversation!*

"Well, I suppose that's good news," she said quickly, then added, "About the ambassador still bein' alive. Not about us bein' stuck here." And then it occurred to her. "Which brings us to my third point. *Why* are we stuck in here again? Can't we just…I don't know"—she shrugged—"slip out the back door or somethin'?"

"There are still a few remaining Taliban fighters lurking around the building. And since neither I, nor anyone else, is willing to take a chance that a surprise bullet might find you"—*Lordy.* Yup. She could go her whole life without experiencing one of those, thank you very much—"we're staying locked up safe in here until the place has been completely cleared."

Searching his face and seeing the lines of strain around his eyes—not to mention talk of the surprise bullet—it suddenly sank in. He'd come in so brash and cocky, acting like everything was A-okay, but the truth of the matter was, he'd been fighting for his life, for *her* life all afternoon long. And even though she was certain he'd seen and done worse things in his storied military career, that didn't change the fact that this was the first time he'd seen and done those things for *her*.

Her heart immediately swelled up like her lips had done that time she was stung in her grandpa's barn by a whole nest of dirt dobbers. And it was a wonder her ribs were able to contain the silly organ.

"Oh, Michael," she whispered, unconsciously dragging a hand through her hair. With tears of gratitude burning the back of her throat, she started to thank him for…*everything*, for being brave and fierce, for being a warrior in every sense of the word—even though a simple *thanks* seemed like such an insignificant way to acknowledge all he'd undoubtedly done.

But before she could croak out one heartfelt syllable, he demanded, "And now how about you answering *my* question?"

She swallowed the burgeoning tears in one gulp, frowning up at him. "I'm sorry." She shook her head. "Which question was that?"

One of his eyebrows lifted, his expression bland. "You know exactly which question."

*Damnit.* She *did* know. She was just stalling because…well…because she didn't know what to tell him.

*I've been avoiding you because you were so wonderful that night, more wonderful than I ever imagined, and now I'm afraid that fallin' for you would be far too easy* certainly wasn't going to work because… Number one: lame-oh. And number two: she wasn't ready to hash out the reason why she was convinced going head-over-keister for him was not at all copasetic with her current life plan.

"I…I…" She stopped and licked her suddenly dry lips. What bastard had gone and stuffed cotton in her mouth? And when?

Michael's ocean-water eyes flashed down to the flick of her tongue, sharpening instantly. The blood coursing through her veins burst into flames like it was made of gasoline and that look of his, that unmistakably *hungry* look of his, had been a match.

"I just figured I'd make it easy on you," she managed, almost convinced that if she glanced down she'd see little sparks flashing through the air separating their bodies. "You know, considering you Navy boys like to practice the art of one-and-done."

"Bullshit." Okay. Yup. Leave it to him to call her on it. "You should've been relieved of that misconception after I called you the first time much less after I called you the *twentieth* time. Now, maybe I can understand if you're playing a little hard to get. I enjoy a good game of cat and mouse as much as the next guy, but—"

"Hard to get?" She went to cross her arms, but he was standing so close her knuckles brushed against the hard, washboard muscles of his stomach. That one touch, that one accidental contact was enough to send electricity shooting up her arm and across her chest, causing her nipples to furl into sharp, painful buds. She did her best to ignore them. "Michael, you already *got* me. Got me *good*, if memory serves."

At that admission, his teeth blazed blindingly white within the dark scruff of his beard. "That's how I remember it, too," he rumbled, mistaking her confession for an invitation to snake an arm around her waist. He was quick to dispense with the scant few inches separating them, and she was left with no recourse but to put her palms on the hard bulge of his biceps as the front of her just went ahead and reacquainted itself with the front of him. Her whole body instantly lit up like a roman candle, and it was a wonder she didn't go shooting off into the air.

*Sweet, sweet heavenly Jesus…*

Her blood fizzed like the champagne at the embassy party. Her head spun like it had when he'd whirled her around the dance floor. And all this happened because he was already… Whoa. Wait a minute.

"Is that…? Are we talking adrenaline here?" she asked since there was no mistaking the hard, insistent bulge throbbing against her belly. She'd heard the SEALs joking about slinging wood in the midst of battle, and now it seemed she was witness to that very thing.

Or maybe not.

In answer, he spread his wide hand over the small of her back, pressing her closer, rubbing himself against her just the teeniest bit. And now it wasn't her head that was whirling, it was the room. "No, angel. That's all for you."

*Oh, goodness.*

She gulped, vaguely realizing a little voice was screaming something in the back of her brain. Something that sounded a lot like *for the love of all that's holy, Harper! Save yourself the heartache!* But she couldn't be sure. Not with her ears filled by the sound of whooshing blood and most of her mind occupied with cataloging every minute detail of Michael's face. The fine lines radiating out from the corners of his eyes, the ones that spoke of the long years he'd spent squinting through the scope of a rifle or laughing with the SEALs. The ever-so-slight list to his nose that attested to a break that was never properly set. The thick fringe of his dark lashes that almost made him look like he was wearing eyeliner.

And the ludicrousness of *that* thought, of hardcore, rough-and-ready Michael "Mad Dog" Wainwright sporting makeup was enough to jangle some sense into her. "Come on now. We can't." She attempted to push away from him. *Feebly* attempted, if she was being honest. Because nothing was better than being held in his strong embrace.

"Why not?"

"Well, because…because…" Truth was, she was having a hard time remembering. With him so close, touching her, her brain had turned to mush. So she fell back on that ol' tried-and-truism. "This isn't the time. And this isn't the place." *Now drive it home, sister.* "And there's a battle ragin'—"

"The *raging* part of the fight is long over," he interrupted. "Now it's just cleanup, which my boys are pretty
good at." She could see the certainty in his eyes, hear
the confidence in his tone. He truly believed they were
safe here, and that it was simply a matter of sit and wait.
"I'd say we have a good hour left before we're sprung
from this lockup," he continued. "So that takes care of
your *time* issue. And as for this not being the place?"
He glanced over his shoulder, surveying the table...the
cots...the chairs. "Looks pretty suitable to me."

*Save yourse*—

That little voice was cut clean off when he turned
back to her and lifted a hand, gently cupping her jaw
and rubbing a callused thumb against her bottom lip.
Her mouth opened over a catching breath. Inside the
vacuum-silence of the safe room, the sound seemed
to echo.

His beard stretched over a smile that was undeniably
male and blatantly triumphant, as if she had unwittingly
answered a question she hadn't even known he'd asked.
He bent close then, his hot breath whispering against her
lips. "Harper?"

Okay, and this time she recognized his inquiry for
exactly what it was. And despite all reason, despite all
rationale, despite the fact that she knew this was a bad
idea, she couldn't bring herself to deny him. Because
he stood there towering above her, a warrior, a real-life
hero, and she wanted nothing more than to be his spoils,
her body the reward for the battle he'd fought and won
today. Which was why the words that tumbled from her
lips were, "Yes, Michael. *Please*."

# CHAPTER 3

IF IT WOULDN'T HAVE RUINED THE MOOD, MICHAEL would have busted out his happy dance. Because not only did Harper's quick acquiescence tell him he'd been right all along—they *had* made a connection—but it also gave him free rein to continue to hold her in his arms.

Which, if you asked him, was exactly where she belonged.

In the time he'd known her, he'd come to like her like no other. I mean, seriously? What red-blooded male wouldn't? Her appeal was so damned endearingly obvious that a man would have to be blind and deaf not to appreciate her sass, her loyalty and integrity, and her particular brand of homespun Southern wit. And then, as if all that weren't enough, there'd been the night of the party, when she'd dealt him the mother of all winning hands and blown his freakin' mind in the sack.

Truly, he'd never met a woman so abandoned, so willing to take pleasure and give it with equal fervor, equal relish. And when he woke up beside her the morning after—*before* she hustled him out the door to catch his transport plane and *before* she started dancing around his repeated calls—he'd begun to believe that perhaps *like* was far too tepid a word for the feelings she fired in him. Which had both terrified and intrigued him in equal parts.

And speaking of terrified…

Even though command had assured him she'd made it into the safe room before the TTP could catch her—something about heat sensors and an indication that the door had been locked from within; unfortunately, there were no cameras in the room to make absolutely sure—he hadn't been able to draw a full breath until right this second. When he could feel her against him and know she was safe and whole. That she was…*his?*

*Fuckin' A. Is that what I want?*

He looked inside himself, searched through his feelings one-by-one like a dealer counting suits, and decided, yeah. That's exactly what he wanted. *She* was exactly what he wanted and—

"Michael?" She tilted her head, her auburn brows pinching together over her deep blue eyes. *Gorgeous* eyes…that matched the rest of her. And if he'd stop with the introspection, he'd probably get a chance to appreciate the rest of her just like the *python in his pants*—Bran…that guy sure had a way with words—was oh-so-blatantly insisting he do.

"Sorry." He shook his head. "My mind drifted there for a bit. But it's back on track now."

And to prove his point, he dipped his chin, pressing his lips to hers and drinking in her sweet exhalation. He loved how she did that. How every time he kissed her it was like she'd been holding her breath since the last time.

With his heart thudding in his chest, sending all his blood south, he opened his mouth, flicking out his tongue to taste her.

Wild cherry Tic Tacs and Harper…

"Mmm," she hummed, sliding her tongue out to meet his, eager to explore the inside of his mouth, burying her hands in his hair to angle his head and more fully align their lips.

And he loved how she did that, too. How she seemed to go from zero to sixty in five seconds flat. Just...*bam!* Hungry and horny and trying to gobble him up. It made him feel ten feet tall and bulletproof...or maybe that was just his dick.

"Harper." He pulled his mouth from hers. This was on the edge of getting out of control. And considering how flighty she'd been after their last encounter, he didn't want to give her any reason not to come back to him for a third time. And a fourth time. And a fifth time, and a sixth... You get the point. "Slow, angel. We have... Oh, hell yeah. That feels good."

She'd used the desertion of his mouth as an opportunity to kiss the side of his neck, running her tongue along the super-sensitive raised ridge of flesh that was an old scar. His testicles pulled up so high and tight against his body, she might as well have been sucking on the head of him.

"Where did you get this?" she whispered, her breath hot and wet against his skin, reminding him of another part of her that he knew from experience was even hotter, even wetter.

"In an altercation with a hunting knife in a cave near the Khyber Pass," he told her. "The hunting knife nearly won."

She pulled back, searching his eyes, her brow puckered. "How can you joke about something like that?"

Sweet woman. Sweet, clueless woman. "Because in this business, it's either laugh or cry. And I've always preferred the former."

"But—"

He sealed their lips to shut her up. Now *she* was the one threatening to ruin the mood. Some guys liked to work out their demons in the bedroom, use sex as a weapon to fight the terrible memories that plagued them. But not him. He preferred to keep those two things separate.

War was war, terrible and soul-sucking and brutal. And sex was sex, delicious and mind-blowing and wonderful.

*"And never the twain shall meet."* At least as far as he was concerned.

And then she did it. She sighed into his mouth like it'd been years since he last kissed her instead of mere seconds, and he was totally done. Wrecked. Lost in all things Harper Searcy…

———

The low growl at the back of Michael's throat seemed to reverberate in the achy spot between Harper's legs, making her keenly aware of its hollow emptiness. And when his beard rasped her cheeks, she was reminded of how deliciously scratchy his face had been against the inside of her thighs…when he'd licked and sucked her to completion.

Had she really thought once would be enough with this man? Had she seriously contemplated letting her head rule her hormones and saying *no* to another go-around? What was she? Crazy?

Yup. She *was* crazy. Crazy *horny*. Crazy w—

"Jesus, woman," he whispered into her mouth when she pulled his shirttail from the waistband of his cargo pants. "I love the way you taste."

"Mmm," she hummed between kisses. "You taste pretty good yourself, sailor." And he did. The inside of his mouth was a combination of Kill Cliff—the sweet energy drink the SEALs swigged by the gallon—hot desert air, and heroism.

In case you were wondering, heroism had a flavor. And it went by the name of Michael "Mad Dog" Wainwright.

*Warrior...*

Once again the word whispered through her over-heated brain. And she realized that for right now, for this one small moment, he wasn't just any warrior, he was *her* warrior.

Fumbling with the buttons on his shirt, she continued to devour his mouth, sucking, licking, laving, moaning when he met her caress for caress. She pulled back when she could spread the two halves wide. And there it was...

The miles upon miles of his hot, hard, tanned flesh.

Her hands smoothed over the crinkly hair that grew in the space between his bulging pectoral muscles and flat brown nipples, following it as it narrowed into a thin line down his flat belly before disappearing inside his pants. His corrugated stomach muscles flexed and quivered under her fingertips, and she delighted at the sight, could have gone on rubbing her palms over him forever. But there was something else she needed to get her hands on. Right now...

Reaching down, she palmed him through his fatigues. And though she was expecting it, she was still surprised by what a delicious, ridiculous handful he was. It was a good thing she already knew they would fit, or else she might have hesitated.

"Uh-uh. No dice." He manacled her wrist, forcing her to look up at him in question. A muscle ticked in his jaw, making his beard twitch.

"Why?" she whispered, leaning forward to drag her tongue over one delicious nipple. She grinned when it instantly beaded against her lips.

"Because I'm too amped up. I could go off before I'm inside you. And that would be a crying shame. Not to mention the fact that since I pride myself on being a gentleman"—he gently pulled her hand away from the hard throb of his manhood—"it's ladies first."

*Bless him.* She knew he spoke the truth.

Her fingers lamented the loss of his pulsing shaft, but he didn't give her much time to mourn. He grabbed the bottom hem of her wet top and yanked it over her head. Her bra hit the floor next, instantly unfastened by his nimble fingers. And then he was cupping her. Weighing her. His rough thumbs brushing over her distended nipples until her pleasure bordered on pain. Her womb pulsed in that age-old rhythm of arousal, making her toes curl inside her kitten heels, sending her head into another spin, causing her legs to become Jell-O.

Catching her bottom lip between her teeth, she gave her legs a pep talk that began and ended with *don't fail me now*. Then she watched his eyes darken with passion as he closely monitored the changes his caresses made to her body, as he eagerly observed her nipples puckering so tightly the areolas nearly disappeared.

"Table or cot?" he husked, hungrily licking his lips.

She didn't need him to clarify. She knew exactly what he was asking. "Table. Quickly."

One downward jerk of his chin was all the answer

he gave before grabbing her waist and pulling her to him. When the tips of her breasts grazed the hot skin of his chest, she gasped, feeling burned, branded. Then his wonderful, knowledgeable mouth reclaimed hers in a kiss that had her sighing with pleasure.

She didn't realize he had moved, that he'd spun her and nudged her toward the table, until the backs of her thighs hit the edge. With a strength that amazed her, he lifted her onto the flat wooden surface and reached down to pull her skirt up to her thighs. She kicked out of her shoes, feverishly returning his kisses, running her hands over his chest, brushing her fingers over his little nipples, listening avidly to the sounds of approval growling low in his throat.

Her veins had turned to rivers of fire, her heart a furnace that burned in her chest. But the place between her legs flamed the hottest. And when he skated his callused palms up the outside of her thighs, hooking his fingers into the waistband of her panties, she stilled in expectation.

The little scrap of black silk she hadn't given a passing thought to when she'd put it on that morning was whipped off her legs in one smooth, sexy move. Then he backed up, her panties clutched in his big hand, letting his eyes run over her breasts as they bobbed with each panting breath. Over her legs that were spread in invitation. Over her center that was swollen and damp with need for him.

"You're so fucking beautiful, Harper," he rasped, his gaze fierce.

For a moment, she thought about calling *bullshit*. After all, it was her turn, right? And the truth of the matter was, she'd never considered herself beautiful—not with her flyaway mass of curly red hair and her pale skin that required she maintain a daily SPF regimen. As a teenager, she would have sold her soul for sleek, blond tresses and smooth, tan skin. But if Michael looked at her now and saw something beautiful, then she was glad she hadn't made a deal with the devil way back when. And when she bit her lip, searching his face, reading the blatant hunger in his eyes and the way the skin on his high cheekbones was stretched tight, flushed with desire, she had to admit she *felt* beautiful.

"Michael." She reached for him, beckoning him closer. "Make love to me."

He didn't hesitate to come to her, pushing his gear toward the opposite end of the table as he gently laid her back, bathing her neck and chest with kisses. When his lips closed over the beaded peak of her right breast, sucking the bud into his hot mouth, the hard pleasure rushed down an invisible line of nerve endings to explode between her legs. She knew he was preparing her, softening her, loosening her. Readying her to receive him. And she loved every second of it.

"Yes." She buried her fingers in his hair. It was almost enough. Just having his lips on her was almost enough…but not quite. And she was suddenly so achy that the only thought was relief. "Touch me, Michael. Please. I need to feel your—Oh! Yes!"

He cupped her in the palm of his hand, his heated skin suffusing her quivering flesh in luscious fire. Then his thick fingers smoothed up her channel, spreading her silkiness around the little button of nerves he seemed to know how to play like no other. Back and forth. Back and forth. The callused pads of his first two fingers thrummed the delicate nubbin. She lifted her legs to plant her bare heels on the edge of the table, opening herself wider, pressing herself closer.

"How do you want me to make you come this first time, Harper?" he growled against her breast.

Oh, the possibilities were endless. He'd taught her that. But right now all she wanted was him. All of him.

"I want to come with you in me," she rasped, her body so heavy, so achy, she figured she'd go off the minute he pressed home.

And that seemed to be the answer he was hoping for, because he pushed back and attacked the buttons of his fly.

---

If there was a world record for dropping trou, Michael had just beaten it. Because Harper was hot as hell, soft as satin, and wet as rain. But more importantly, she was *ready*.

The cool air inside the panic room rushed over the turgid length of him when he pushed his fatigues down to his knees, eliciting a shiver. Or maybe the goose bumps were a direct result of having Harper spread out before him on the table like a lovely, feminine feast. And if he weren't such a gentleman, always eager to grant a lady's wishes, he *would* feast. Just kiss and lick and lave every wanton inch of her. He hadn't been bullshitting her when he told her she was beautiful. With her boisterous mass of hair, big expressive eyes, and milky skin dotted by the occasional sprinkling of freckles—on her shoulders, across her pert nose—she was everything a man could want. Lush and lovely. Wild and womanly. *Delicious*.

But she had requested he put himself inside her. And who was he to argue?

Grabbing the base of his dick, he angled himself toward her swollen, pink entrance, then hesitated when he realized he'd almost forgotten about protection. With a curse of frustration, he bent to shove a hand into the hip pocket of his pants that were bunched around his ankles. Finding a condom among her wadded up panties and the two spent shells that had somehow wormed their way into his fatigues during the battle—the fog of war was a weird thing, and even weirder things tended to happen when a guy was in the middle of it—he straightened and ripped the foil packet open with his teeth.

A line appeared between Harper's brows. "Were you…" she licked her lips, pressing up on her elbows. The move caused her lovely breasts to bounce ever so slightly. "Were you *plannin'* this?"

"Always," he told her. Then barked out a laugh when her piquant little chin jerked back. "No," he relented. "We use condoms to keep sand out of the barrels of our M4s. But I think you and I have found a better use for this one."

"Oh, yes," she sighed, her shoulders relaxing. Then her gaze drifted down his body, zeroing in on the painfully swollen, angrily red length of him as he rolled on the condom. "Mmm," she murmured, scooting her plump ass to the very edge of the table. "Hurry, Michael."

And by God, she didn't need to tell him twice. He finished with the condom and stepped between her legs, using his thumb to bend himself down to her. Then, fascinated, he watched his swollen head press between her folds, press into her body, stretching her, filling her inch by excruciatingly slow inch.

And just as it had the first time, every pleasurable sensation he'd ever experienced before was instantly forgotten. Because nothing could compare to Harper's soft, silky walls closing around him.

"Don't stop," she begged. And there was no way he was going to. Not unless he wanted to walk funny for the next ten years...

# CHAPTER 4

"OH, GOD," MICHAEL GROANED WHEN HARPER HOOKED her heels behind his ass, jerking him forward and seating him that last inch. She was stretched to capacity but not so much that she couldn't squeeze him, loving the way her nerve endings *zinged* with approval. "Do it again, angel. Just…" He pulled out the tiniest bit before pressing home again. "Squeeze me like… Yeah. Just like that."

He bent to reclaim her mouth, not moving one more inch save for the languid thrust and retreat of his tongue past her teeth. Its cadence matched the pulse of his blood, the pulse of *him* held so securely inside her.

And that was something she'd learned the night of the party. That Michael liked to savor the first moments of joining, revel in the simple act of being buried inside her and feeling her muscles contract around him as he throbbed and ached and grew harder still. She liked it, too. Because in her very limited experience, most men tended to go straight into jackhammer mode. And that was a crying shame, because this moment was…

Decadent.

There was no other word for it.

Skimming her hands beneath the halves of his shirt, she relished the sleek feel of his back under her fingertips. Except for where a scar marred its perfection, his skin was smooth as Tennessee whiskey, hot as an oven, and hard as stone. In a word, he was *man*.

And she? Well, she was woman.

"Now, Michael," she demanded against his mouth. "Make love to me now."

She felt his lips curve into a smile, his beard rasping against her cheeks. "Your wish is my command," he said, and then? Oh, and then he began to *move*. In the way that only Michael could move. With a gentle force that was the epitome of coordination, dexterity, and the deep understanding of how a woman's body worked.

Thrust and retreat. Thrust and retreat. Each smooth glide ratcheted her pleasure up another notch. She wanted to draw it out. She wanted to make it last. And she could tell by the way he held his breath that he was fighting for the same. Fighting against the pleasure. Against release.

But the pleasure wouldn't be denied. And despite her best efforts, she climbed higher and higher. Up and up and *up* until…*boooom!* Her orgasm exploded through her as surely and as forcefully as any of today's detonations.

"Jesus! Harper!" he bellowed, slamming home and following her into the abyss. And then together they throbbed, her flesh clinging and grasping, contracting around him in hungry pulls. His flesh filling her to the brim and caressing her walls with each forceful pulse.

After a couple of minutes, he bent and pressed a dozen soft kisses to her shoulder. "My sweet, delightful Harper," he whispered between caresses.

And right then and there, with his strong arms around her, she could almost make herself believe that she *was* his, that everything she knew to be true was all a big lie, and that maybe, just maybe, she should give him, give *them*, a chance.

But then reality—and the memory of her mother crying herself to sleep night after night—intruded…

———

"You're lookin' pretty proud of yourself, sailor."

Michael realized then, braced as he was on his forearms and hanging above Harper, that his face was split into a huge grin. "Well, I've never been one *not* to congratulate myself on a hand well played," he told her, chuckling and dropping a kiss on her passion-swollen lips.

And even though she returned the gesture, even though their bodies were still joined, there was something about her response—a subtle withdrawal, a minor retreat—that had all his mental bells and whistles blaring. *Goddamnit!* Harper was pulling an emotional escape-and-evade maneuver. *Again!*

He caught her face between his hands, forcing her to hold his gaze and, never being one to pull-his-punches or prevaricate, got straight to the fucking point. "Now, you want to tell me the *real* reason why you've been avoiding me since the embassy party?"

"I told you I thought—"

"Cut the crap, Harper," he interrupted before she could break into that whole *I thought you Navy boys practiced the art of one-and-done* song and dance. "I never took you for a woman who's afraid to speak her mind. Don't you go and prove me wrong."

Her jaw hardened against his palms. And when she placed a hand on the center of his chest, he was left with no recourse but to pull away from her, pull *out* of her. The desertion of her warm body was so unexpectedly devastating, his knees loosened and he was forced to brace a hand against the edge of the table. Sullenly, he watched her hop to her feet, her skirt falling to cover her sweet ass as she bent to retrieve her shirt and bra.

And once it became obvious she had no intention of answering him until she'd clothed herself, until she'd placed a barrier between them, he figured he might as well follow suit. After all, if they were about to have a heart-to-heart, it probably behooved him not to do it with his dick swinging in the breeze.

Pulling the used condom off, he hissed when the ring of latex rasped over his hyper-sensitive skin. Tugging his fatigues up his hips one-handed, he left them undone as he went in search of a trash can.

*Bingo.* Over by the shelves.

Tossing the prophylactic away, he was in the process of re-buttoning his shirt and tucking it into his pants when she asked, "Where are my panties?"

A smile tugged at his mouth as he dug in his pocket. He plucked out the bit of black satin, causing the two spent shells to also emerge. They fell, *pinging* against the concrete floor. And the juxtaposition between the softness of her underwear and the hardness of the casings, between the sweetness of making love to her and the horror of the battle beforehand struck him as totally bizarre.

But he didn't have long to dwell on it. She took two steps in his direction and made a swipe for her panties. As lady luck would have it, his six-foot-three stature meant it was easy for him to hold them out of her reach. "Uh-uh. Not until you answer my question."

Her lips flattened. "You're not seriously holding my underwear hostage, are you?"

"A man has to take any advantage he can."

And there they went—her hands found their way to her hips until she stood in front of him like a flame-haired comic book heroine. But when she ran a shaky hand through her curls, God help him, he relented, handing over her panties.

After she stepped into them, wiggling them up her thighs—and that one small sight was enough to have his blood running hot once again—she stood and blew out a breath. "I like you."

The way his chin jerked back, you'd think she'd popped him one on the jaw. *Uh…* "Well, that's good," he managed, hooking a thumb toward the table. "You know, considering what we were just doing."

"No." She shook her head. "I mean I *really* like you."

He couldn't help the smile that spread across his face. And if he wasn't mistaken, that was his heart turning somersaults inside his chest like one of those Cirque du Soleil performers at the Bellagio. "I *really* like you too, Harper."

She blew out a breath, throwing her hands in the air in disgust. "What I'm tryin' to say is that I think it'd be real easy for me to…um…*more* than like you."

Everything inside him came to a sudden, screeching stop. His heart quit doing flips, his lungs quit sucking in oxygen, and each second that ticked by on his diver's watch became a little eternity.

"Harper…" Was that *his* voice, all tight and rusty? "You better just do a full disclosure here, angel. Because I have a feeling this convo just got really real, really fast. And I want to make sure I understand you."

When she rolled in her lips before running a hand

through her hair again, it took everything in him not to reach for her, not to pull her close. But for whatever reason, the woman was spooked. And he dared not make a single move to send her skittering away from him. Not again.

"I think I could," she began, then stopped and shook her head. "No. That's not true. Because I *know*. I *know* I could fall in love with you if I let myself."

*Tick. Tick. Tick…*

He could hear the second hand on his watch counting the seconds. Which was strange, since it seemed to him that time had stopped.

Now before, when a woman whipped out the L-word, he'd always gotten a little itchy. Like he'd slept on sandy sheets. But this time? Oh, this time there was nothing but bright, tingly warmth spreading over his skin.

"I, uh…" He ran a hand over his beard. Dude, were his fingers shaking? "I suppose if we're throwing all our cards on the table, I should admit I've been thinking I could do a little bit of falling in love with you, too. You know, given the chance."

Her succulent mouth opened. Then closed. Then opened again. But not a peep came out.

"Harper?" He dared to reach forward and brush two fingers over her satiny cheek. He didn't know what he was expecting, probably for her to jerk away from him—she looked fragile enough to break with the slightest touch. So he was surprised when she closed her eyes, leaning into his caress. *Screw it*, he decided. *It's all or nothing*. "Tell me what you're so afraid of."

She pinched her eyes more tightly shut, shaking her head.

"Why not?" he asked, his breath held.

"Because my momma always told me it's better to keep my mouth shut and seem a fool than to open it and remove all doubt."

"I could never think you foolish, Harper."

She opened her eyes then. And if he wasn't mistaken, a sheen of tears gathered on her lower lids. *Fuck me sideways*. If she started crying, he didn't know what he'd do. Probably just break down right alongside her. The thought of brave, boisterous Harper Searcy reduced to tears because of *him* was just too much.

"Could you think me a coward?" she asked, her voice hoarse. "Because that's what I am."

"Why do you say that?"

She dragged in a breath, and he noticed her naturally pale skin was chalk white, making the cinnamon-colored freckles on her nose stand out. "Did you know my father was an Air Force pilot?"

Whoa. *Huh?* The change of subject was so jarring, Michael felt like he suffered from whiplash. "Uh... that's a negative. You never said—"

"Well, he was. He's retired now. But he was active duty for nearly twenty-five years."

"Harper, what are you trying to tell me?"

She searched his eyes. Then shook her head, her shoulders drooping dejectedly. "Just that I listened to my mother cry herself to sleep every night when my father was deployed. Just that I saw them struggle to reform their bond, their *love*, each time he came back home just a little bit different than when he left. Just that being married to an airman was a burden that nearly broke my mom who, by the way, is a much stronger woman than I am."

"Harper—"

She held up a hand to halt his interruption. "And since that's the case, I promised myself early on that I wouldn't make the same mistake she did. That I wouldn't let myself fall for a military man. That instead I'd choose a nice *normal* guy to love. One who wears a tie and comes home for dinner every night instead of one who goes off to war in places I can't even pronounce. I don't *want* to be scared every day that two uniformed officers might knock on my door with their hats in their hands. I don't *want* to go to bed alone more nights than not. I want barbecues in the backyard and baseball in the park and B-rate movies on Sundays. I want a man who will *be* there, Michael. And if you think that's cowardly or foolish, I won't blame you. Because it *is*. It's both of those things. But it's the way I feel."

And there it was. The truth. In all its unvarnished glory.

He started grinning.

—∿—

Harper expected any number of expressions from Michael. A curled lip of disgust, maybe. The narrowed eyes of disapproval, for sure. Which meant his smile had her cocking her head and staring at him. "Um…why are you grinnin' at me like a billy goat in a briar patch?"

To her utter consternation, his smile widened. "Because all those things you say you want, I want, too. The barbecues and the baseball and the B-rate movies."

He snaked an arm around her waist, dragging her forward. And just like they always did, her nerve endings lit up like Fourth of July firecrackers. She couldn't breathe. Either because he was taking up all the air in the room, or because, despite her best efforts to keep her heart uninvolved, she'd failed. And the silly thing was breaking…just a little.

She thought she'd explained herself. She thought she'd made herself inexplicably clear. But he didn't get it. He didn't understand that she—

"In fact," he continued, oblivious to her growing distress, "catching reruns of *Mystery Science Theater* is one of my favorite things. You know what I'm talking about? When the guys sit down front and comment on the B-rate movies that—"

"I know what *Mystery Science Theater* is," she interrupted, exasperated. For such an intelligent man, he sure was pulling that whole *porch light's on but no one's home* gambit here.

"Oh, good." He nodded, hitching her another inch closer, until she was forced to either let her arms dangle uselessly or put her hands on his chest. She chose the latter—poor, misguided woman that she was—and could feel his heart beating beneath her palm. It was so solid. So steady. And the urge to lay her head there and listen to its heavy cadence was overwhelming. Almost as overwhelming as the impulse to throw all her carefully constructed plans right out the window. To give in to him in all ways. Even if it meant a lifetime of frightened tears and lonely nights. "Because here's the thing, Harper. Since the very first day I met you, I've felt certain of something."

She swallowed, staring into his wonderful face, trying *not* to read the blatant affection shining in his eyes. *This would be so much easier if my feelings were one-sided.* "Wh-what's that?"

"That you would change my life."

*Oh, good gracious.* "Michael, I don't want—"

"And not that I ever thought you were a uniform junkie or anything." Unfortunately, there were women out there who chased soldiers just for the thrill or prestige of bagging a guy who bore his nation's medals. Growing up an Air Force brat, she'd met her fair share of them. "But all the same, you have no idea how happy it makes me to hear it's me—*me*, Michael Wainwright— and not the Navy SEAL you like so much." He grabbed her chin between his thumb and forefinger. "Because you see, me and the boys are cashing in our chips after this mission."

Harper's breath hitched. Digging a finger in her ear, she shook her head. "I'm sorry. What did you just say?"

"You heard me. We're bugging out. Finished. Done. Kissing the Navy good-bye and going back to live in Civilian-ville."

No, no. It was just too good to be true. "But…*why?*"

A shadow passed over his face, a subtle muscle flexing in his jaw beneath his beard. He dropped his hand from her face, and her chin immediately missed the contact. "It's a really long story," he sighed. "And I promise to tell you someday. But suffice it to say, there was a bad mission, a vow to a dying friend, and the realization that maybe there is more to life than sorties and submachine guns."

As the words fell from his lips, the small spark of hope that had ignited in her chest at his first mention of cashing in his chips turned into a flame. "So y-you're—" She had to stop and lick her lips before she tried again. "You're really quittin' the Navy?"

"Roger that." And if there'd ever been two more beautiful words in the whole English language, she'd never heard them.

A million questions grew wings and flew through her mind. Which was why she was surprised when the first one she landed on was, "But what'll you all do?"

For the life of her, she couldn't imagine the seven SEALs she'd come to know over the past six months as anything other than gun-slinging, mission-taking, hard-assed frogmen. She cocked her head, trying to envision Michael in a polo shirt. It just didn't work.

"Well, the other guys are headed down to the Florida Keys to take over the marine salvage business LT's father left behind when he died. They think they'll either make a go of it or else find a legendary missing treasure and as Chris Rock would say, *get ree-atch, bee-atch*."

She blinked, did a double take, then blinked some more. "I'm sorry. Did you just say missing treasure? As in, *The Goonies*?"

He laughed. She could feel the deep vibration in her chest, right where that flame of hope was burning bright. "I suppose it's something like that."

"But not you?"

He shook his head. "Nope. Not me. You know I grew up in Atlantic City, yeah?" She nodded. "Well, one thing that place taught me is that the odds are stacked against you when you gamble on the big payout. So, they can go try their hands at treasure hunting. As for me? I figure I'll take some time off first. And then I'll take over my father's job as the head of the family ship-building business. The man has been on my ass for years to come home so he can retire and—"

*Ring, ring!* The phone in the wall jangled emphatically, the little yellow light blinking its interruption.

"Hold that thought," he said, walking over to pull open the door to the cubbyhole. Lifting the phone's receiver to his ear, he barked one word. "Go."

She watched his eyes sharpen as he listened to whatever was being said, still feeling a little numb and disoriented from the bomb he'd just dropped. But she didn't have time to pull her spinning thoughts together, because he quickly hung up and walked to the door. Twisting the lock, the safe room opened up with a *thunk* and a *hiss*. And there was Bran Pallidino standing on the other side of the door.

"All clear?" Michael asked him, turning toward the table to re-arm himself and don the rest of his gear.

"You betcha." Bran nodded, his eyes quickly taking in Harper's bare feet and the fact that Michael's hair was sticking up every which way, proof her fingers had been buried there not too long ago. When the guy's teeth flashed white against his dark beard, she felt her cheeks heat. Luckily, he refrained from commenting on the obvious and instead went with, "The TTP holding O'Leary hostage came out of the offices. I think they thought if they used the ambassador as a human shield, they'd be able to escape the embassy. They were quickly taken down."

He made it sound easy. But Harper was smart enough to know it had probably been anything but.

Michael did, too. Evidenced by his next question. "All the guys okay?"

Bran winked. "No worries. We're all as pretty as we ever were."

"And the ambassador?" she asked. Because even though the yellow-bellied ol' fart had been happy to throw her to the wolves, O'Leary was still her responsibility.

"Safe," Bran said, and she heaved a sigh of relief. "The building is clear. And the wounded Marines are being evaced. It's over."

Michael moved to stand beside her and, as always, his heat reached out to her in a soft caress. "That's good," he said, handing over her shoes. She dropped them to the floor, quickly stepping into them. "So then we're ready to blow this popsicle stand, yeah?"

"More than that." Bran's grin widened. "We're ready to blow this whole friggin' country. Word from Washington says the embassy will be shut down immediately, and all personnel are to report back stateside. You know what that means, *paisano*? We're outta here!"

Michael's smile lit up his whole face, and he and Bran exchanged high fives. Then he turned to her, his expression sobering as he held out his hand. "Harper, I think you might want to keep your eyes closed while we exit, okay?"

She swallowed, knowing there were things out there she didn't want to see—namely, the numerous bodies of the Taliban fighters that the Navy would no doubt take out to sea and deep six, Osama Bin Laden–style. Couldn't leave them behind to be buried so that other radical militants could make shrines of their graves. Lacing her fingers through his, she screwed her eyes shut and nodded her readiness to be led from the room.

But he didn't guide her toward the door. Instead he leaned close, his warm breath ruffling the hair near her temple. "So what do you say? You want to try being civilians together?"

"Are you kiddin' me?" she asked, her heart so full of hope and anticipation it was a wonder the silly, lovesick organ didn't burst wide open. "I say *lord, yes!*"

And when she stepped out of the panic room with Michael at her side, she knew she was stepping into the future she'd always dreamed about...

# ACKNOWLEDGMENTS

I'd like to take a moment to thank all those involved with this, the project of my heart…

First up are the fabulous authors who so graciously donated their time and talent. Thank you all a million times over for sharing your amazing stories with me and with the world.

Next is my publisher, Dominique Raccah, and the wonderful staff at Sourcebooks. Thank you so much, not only for embracing the idea of a charity anthology, but for taking it on and making it your own.

I can't forget the awesome Deb Werksman, my editor. Deb, none of this would have been possible without your tireless efforts during every step of the process. And for that, I'll never be able to thank you enough. Simply put, you rock!

And, finally, there's my agent, the amazing Nicole Resciniti. Nic, my humblest thanks. You helped me realize a lifelong dream.

# ABOUT THE AUTHOR

**Julie Ann Walker** is the *USA Today* and *New York Times* bestselling author of the Black Knights Inc. and Deep Six romantic suspense series. She has won the Book Buyers Best Award and has been nominated for the National Readers Choice Award and the Romance Writers of America's prestigious RITA award. Julie is prone to spouting movie quotes and song lyrics. She'll never say no to sharing a glass of wine or going for a long walk. She prefers impromptu travel over the scheduled kind, and she takes her coffee with milk. You can find her on her bicycle along the lakeshore in Chicago or blasting away at her keyboard, trying to wrangle her capricious imagination into submission. For more information, please visit www.julieannwalker.com or follow her on Facebook, www.facebook.com/jawalkerauthor and/or Twitter @JAWalkerAuthor.

# In **PLAIN SIGHT**

## An Elite Force Novella

## **CATHERINE MANN**

# CHAPTER 1

"THIS IS 9-1-1. WHAT IS YOUR EMERGENCY?" A masculine voice rasped through the cell phone receiver.

"Help me, please," Stacy Currie hissed between her clenched teeth, terrified of revealing her hiding place in the laundry room but needing to ramble out as much information as possible. Her life depended on it. "I live at 21 Goldenrod Lane. My ex-husband is trying to break into my house. I have a restraining order. He's going to kill me."

Even now, she could hear the rattling of the front door knob, the thud of footsteps on her porch when no one had reason to visit this late at night. Jared's footsteps. Jared, the walking nightmare she'd married. Her husband who'd abused her for four years. Her ex-husband who stalked her still.

"Ma'am, where are you in your home?" the male emergency dispatcher asked with a studied calm that struck a familiar chord inside her.

Her heart hitched. It couldn't be... Pain must be making her imagination play tricks with her mind. The man on the phone couldn't possibly be *him*, the strongest man she'd ever known. The man she should have married.

She had to think clearly, focus. "I'm in my laundry room, under the utility sink. There's a curtain around it."

Thank God she'd woken up, unable to go back to

sleep. Restless, she'd gone in search of a midnight snack and caught a glimpse of her ex creeping through her garden, daffodils and bluebells crushed under his boots. She'd snatched up her cell phone and ducked into the laundry room to hide while she called for help. She clutched her knees tightly to her chest, the scent of fabric softener and bleach lingering in the air. "Are you still there?"

"Yes, ma'am, I'm here. Is the intruder still outside or has he entered the house?" the dispatcher asked, his voice gravelly and hoarse.

She listened closer to the tones and realized it wasn't Gavin, the man she should have married, on the line after all. Gavin's voice had been deep but smooth, sweeping away her inhibitions and virginity—before she'd ruined her life by issuing ultimatums that had driven a wedge between them. A decade ago, Gavin had left their small Kentucky town and enlisted in the Air Force, his burly presence and reassuring strength gone from her world.

"He's still outside. He's trying to jimmy the locks. There's no glass to break." When she'd moved across town after her divorce two years ago, she'd bought a solid wood door, triple locks, and grilles for the windows, turning her cottage into a fortress. She'd quit her job as an LPN and supported herself by freelance writing medical articles. "You have to send help quickly. He's tried to kill me before."

He'd almost succeeded six months ago, even though the cops hadn't been able to prove he was the culprit. Her side ached at the memory. She'd kept herself alive thanks to her training as a nurse, pushing her fingers into her own wound. The cops had labeled it another unsolved break-in, since she'd never actually seen his face. He always wore a mask. His anonymous texts and gifts were always untraceable but had hidden meanings she couldn't mistake.

"Ma'am, I've already dispatched a patrol car to your address. I will stay on the line until they arrive. Meanwhile, we're going to get as much information as we can to help the police know what to expect."

What to expect? Anything. Everything. Evil.

Jared had threatened her with a gun, his fists, knives, even a winter scarf pulled tightly around her neck. Her hands shook so hard she almost dropped the phone. The most she'd ever been able to achieve was a restraining order. And that he deftly ignored, terrorizing her without getting caught. At one point, out of desperation, she'd tried relocating to a different state, and he'd found her within two weeks. If she couldn't hide, at least she could be safe in her home.

"Ma'am? Talk to me. Tell me what you hear."

"Yes, I'm…just having…trouble…breathing…" Her toes curled against the tile floor, a gust from the air conditioner rustling the sink curtain against her bare legs.

"When you speak, that will help you breathe. Keep talking to me."

"Okay…Okay…Okay…" She sucked in a shuddering breath. Would she ever be able to smell detergent again without having a panic attack? A thud reverberated and sent a jolt of fear through her. "He's ramming his shoulder against the front door."

"That's important to know, ma'am. Keep talking. Details. It would help to have your names."

"His name is Jared Lewis. I'm Stacy Currie. I took back my maiden name after the divorce."

Silence. No answer from the other end of the line. Nothing at all from the dispatcher for three heartbeats, her pulse as loud as the pounding on the door. But no shouting. Jared never risked his voice being caught on tape. He would be masked and gloved too. The more it happened, the more reclusive she became and the more the town thought she was going off the deep end, paranoid from that first "unsolved break-in."

"Sir? Hello?" Had the call dropped? Bile burned her throat. She looked at her cell phone glowing with only twenty-four percent battery life. "Please don't leave."

He cleared his throat. "I'm here, and you're going to be fine. Help is on the way."

The back porch door crashed open. The crack of splintering wood, the slam against the wall sent icy terror spiking through her. She bit her lip until it bled, holding back a scream. Jared wasn't just toying with her tonight. He was inside her home. The alarm squealed into the night. She'd bought this cottage with safety in mind, but even her best efforts hadn't been enough to keep Jared out.

"Stacy…" The dispatcher stayed calm, but she could have sworn even he had a hint of urgency bleeding through his raspy tones. "Talk to me. Breathe."

"He's in the house." Her voice shook as hard as her hands as she heard him move around the living area, then walk toward the bedrooms. "He broke down the door, and he's looking for me."

"Do you have a weapon?" He stayed calm but authoritative.

"No. The knives are in the kitchen." She'd considered

grabbing one, but the fear of having Jared take it from her again was too real. She had the scar on her side to prove it. Tonight, before racing into the laundry room, she'd shoved the knife block under the kitchen sink.

"Do you have anything aerosol close by? Cleaning supplies?"

She pushed the curtain around the sink aside and studied the small room, lit only by the moonlight streaming through a small high window. "Yes. I have wasp spray."

And an iron. But what if he took it from her? Or God forbid, he took the iron and tormented her, slowly, taking his time to burn her as he'd done once before.

"Get the spray. Now. If he finds you, aim straight for his eyes and run. We need to keep him away from you for just a little while longer. The police are close, Stacy. Hang on. Where is he now?"

"I think he's walking down the hall toward my room, but it's a small cottage, only two bedrooms and everything's so open if I go to the front door he'll see me. The back door leads to my garage, and I don't want to be trapped in there by him." She scrambled from under the sink and walked softly in the small, dark utility room, groping along the shelf over the washer until her fingers wrapped around the can of bug spray for ants, roaches, spiders. Appropriate. "He'll check the kitchen next when he realizes I'm not asleep."

"Help will arrive before then." He sounded so certain she almost believed him.

She scrambled back under the sink, phone in one hand and can in the other. "How are you telling the cops? You're talking to me."

"There's another dispatcher on the line. She's

listening and relaying everything to the police. Two units are on their way, Stacy. Not just one. Now, explain the floor plan. Let us know how to find you fastest."

"He broke in the front door, which brings you into a combo living room and dining room. The bedrooms are to the left. The kitchen is to the right. There are three doors in the kitchen—to the garage, the pantry, the laundry room." His footsteps grew louder. He was back in the living room. "Oh, God, he's walking toward the kitchen. I can't talk anymore."

"Don't hang up." The strength in his voice carried her through. "Listen to me, and be sure to breathe so I know you're there. You're doing great."

Sirens sounded in the distance, growing louder, closer. Help. Maybe this time they would catch him in the act and the nightmare would be over. She dared to whisper, "The police. I hear them."

"You're doing great, Stacy. You've protected yourself. Just a little longer."

"He's stopped." She held her breath, listening. "He's…I think he's leaving. I think he's running away. Because of the sirens."

How strange to be upset over that, but if the police had caught him he would be in violation of the restraining order. He would go to prison, even if only for a short time. She had security cameras, but she held little hope they would reveal anything helpful. He would have thought to cover his face. He was careful. Dangerous. She had to try harder to leave this place again. She couldn't live this way any longer. More than just move, she would buy a whole new identity if she had to, but she couldn't just wait for him to kill her.

She sagged against the pipes under the sink as the police announced themselves at the front door. Tears clogged her eyes and throat. "Please, please tell them to catch him."

"Anastasia." The dispatcher's low rasp of her full name froze her. "I promise, he will never hurt you again."

Anastasia?

Her full name. She sat up straighter, thunking her head on the sink, stunned for more reason than one. Only two people had ever called her Anastasia. Her mother.

And Gavin.

The first man she'd ever loved. The first one to break her heart.

The voice might not sound like him, but somehow, someway, it was Gavin. And how damn ironic that just as she finally decided to cut ties to this town for good...

Gavin Novak was back.

———◦◦◦———

The next afternoon, Tech Sergeant Gavin Novak lounged in a hammock in the backyard of his duplex with his dog Radar on the ground beside him. He wouldn't have long to get his thoughts together before talking to Stacy face to face. He couldn't avoid the inevitable any longer, not after last night.

He'd worked the graveyard shift, so his day had started late, the afternoon sun warm on his face, a breeze rustling the maple tree branches overhead. Not that he'd been able to sleep after taking that 9-1-1 call last night from Stacy Currie, the last person he'd expected to be on the other end of the line. At first, he hadn't realized it was her. She'd been whispering so softly.

Then she'd given her name, and he realized she didn't recognize his voice at all. Possibly because he was just a part of her past. But then he didn't sound the same either, not since the accident that had ended his Air Force career as a pararescueman. The helicopter crash a year ago, the flames, the crushed bones. He was a walking miracle, lucky to be alive and talking at all.

He reached over the side of the hammock and grappled for his water bottle, always thirsty these days, his throat perpetually raw, the pain an ever-present reminder that he'd walked away from that accident when others hadn't. He'd been partnered with Captain Jablonski that day. Jablonksi and the flight crew hadn't stood a chance. Pinned by the wreckage, Gavin hadn't been able to reach them, couldn't see, couldn't move, just heard their last gasps. His hand grazed over Radar's soft fur before wrapping around the plastic bottle. He sucked down a long draw of ice water. He swung one leg off the side and tapped the hammock into motion.

His career credo during his Air Force days as a pararescueman had been "These things we do that others may live," and he'd embraced that mission. He'd expected to die in the line of duty. Finding a way to face growing old without that mission had knocked the props out from under him. He took another long gulp of water. God, he missed being a pararescueman—also known as a parajumper, or a PJ.

The job fielding emergency calls had been a godsend, considering he wasn't good for much of anything since that crash had rattled his brains and damn near crushed his larynx. Ironic really. He'd always been known as the least chatty PJ in their squadron, and he'd almost lost the ability to speak altogether. Yet now his world revolved around words. He'd been a damn good medic in his unit. From antiterrorism missions in the Gulf of Aden in the Middle East to earthquake relief in the Bahamas, he was the one everybody requested in a medical crisis. At least he'd found a way to put some of his emergency responder skills to work. Even if he was going damn near stir-crazy, aching to be in the fight rather than just listening.

Listening last night had taken that frustration to a deep, dark level.

And the cops hadn't even caught the bastard.

Gavin had done some nosing around after the incident. The police hadn't been able to pin anything on Jared Lewis other than some harassing texts. There was a restraining order. And Stacy's insistence that he'd tried to break into her house before. For now, Gavin could only make sure she was safe, so he'd called in some favors locally to have her watched until she made it to his house this afternoon. And more favors long distance to help over the next few days. It had been all Gavin could do not to rush right over to her last night, but he knew his time was better spent coming up with a strategy.

Every day this month since he'd moved back to Kentucky to pick up the pieces of his life as a civilian, he'd been tempted to phone her. And every day he'd made an excuse to wait.

After what happened last night, there could be no more waiting.

He heard the car stop outside his home. Stacy Currie. He'd known his Anastasia wouldn't waste time coming to see him once she knew he'd returned. She'd always been braver than him. Since he'd heard her gasp of recognition on the phone last night, he'd known the confrontation would be inevitable. He'd considered going to her place, but being near her again would be difficult enough. He needed the edge of being on his home turf, so once the police had left her house and reassured him she was safely secured, he'd texted her his address, noted he'd be awake by two, and left it at that. Would she come alone? Or with an escort?

Where was her ex now? The cops said they'd followed a car racing away from Stacy's house to outside the city limits. The cowardly jerk would likely lay low for a while. Gavin intended to use that time to his advantage to prepare.

Radar lifted his head, nudging Gavin's hand. The car door slammed closed.

Gavin scratched his dog's ears. "It's okay, boy. She's…a friend." He took another swallow of water and called out, "I'm in the backyard."

The soft tread of her steps rustled in time with the branches. One set of steps. She'd come alone.

His duplex was on the edge of town, with minimal traffic. His backyard was enclosed with a tall, wooden privacy fence. The gate squeaked open in the quiet afternoon. His gut knotted. He nudged his sunglasses up along the bridge of his nose, his eyes closed as he just breathed in the moment. Was it memory or reality that led him to catch a whiff of her—like strawberries. She'd favored the scent for lotion and shampoo when they'd been together before.

"Gavin?"

That voice was unmistakable now that she wasn't whispering, a hint deeper than when they'd been teenagers. Today, the melodic tones weren't filled with terror.

He gestured to the Adirondack chair beside his hammock. "Have a seat. You'll pardon me if I don't get up. It was a late night at work."

"Of course." She walked closer, the sound of her steps on the thick carpet of grass echoing his heartbeat. Of course she'd come. She'd always had a steely will encased in a five-foot-one body, like a delicate butterfly that withstood the fiercest wind. "I got your text."

"I should have sent it sooner."

"Yes, you should have." She hesitated beside him before sitting with a sigh. "You're really back. It's actually you."

"More or less." He shifted on the hammock, both feet on the ground as he faced her chair, forcing himself not to think about how delicately beautiful she was with her strawberry blond hair, sky-blue eyes, pale skin with freckles all over her body that he'd explored with his mouth. "Are you okay after last night?"

He had to know, wanted to ask a helluva lot more.

"Rattled, but all right. Thank you for your help."

"I was doing my job."

"You did it well."

"I wish we could have caught him." He wished he could have been boots on the ground, tracking the son-of-a-bitch who'd dared threaten her. "Anastasia…"

"Don't call me that. My name is Stacy," she corrected softly but with a hint of anger. "Why haven't you come to see me since you returned?"

Now, wasn't that the million-dollar question? If he'd

wanted to stay away from her altogether, he never should have come back to town. This had been inevitable, yet for a month he'd delayed taking that final step. Would she have been safer last night if he hadn't been such a damn coward these past four weeks?

He settled for the obvious answer rather than the deeper, more complex truth. "You got married. We're not together anymore."

Yeah, he'd been bitter for a long time over how she'd found another man to love rather than leave their small country town with him. How could she have given up on the connection they had? They'd been teenagers in the same group home, become friends, then later they'd become way more than friends. He'd lost everything when she'd turned away from him. But even in that bitterness, he'd wanted her to be happy. The thought of her at the mercy of someone who would harm even a single hair on her strawberry blond head…

His hand fell to his dog, and he took comfort in Radar's soft, short fur, a Dutch shepherd, smart as hell and his lifeline. Funny how not too long ago he'd been freaked out by anything bristly or fuzzy, and now he clung to his dog for comfort in a world turned upside down by war.

"Gavin, I still don't understand why you didn't let me know you're back. I'm divorced. Even if I wasn't or you didn't know, I would want to hear how you're doing." Her chair squeaked as she leaned closer, wind whipping a strand of her wispy, long hair over his wrist. So close, he could have reached out to hold her. "We were friends long before we were lovers. How could you come back and not contact me? Let me know how you're doing? Are you okay?"

Of course she would notice the scar along his forehead, the jagged line and melted patch even a skin graft couldn't erase. He wore his hair long these days now that he was out of the Air Force. Not that it really mattered to him what he looked like. "I'm healthy."

"But no longer in the military?"

"Clearly, I have a new job now. I've been medically discharged."

"And you didn't think I would want to know? Do you hate me so much you can't even share a burger and a beer to catch up?"

He smelled strawberries. Definitely more than a memory, the sweet scent teased him, tempted him. "I don't hate you at all."

"Then I don't understand."

He pulled off his sunglasses and waited. How long would it take her to put together the pieces? To really see and understand that he didn't wear sunglasses to protect his eyes from the sunlight that warmed the scars along his forehead. To realize his dog wasn't just a pet, but also a working companion. To discern he wasn't looking her in the eyes.

Because he couldn't.

He was blind.

# CHAPTER 2

BLIND.

The realization stunned Stacy quiet, holding her stone still as she processed a painful truth in front of her. She looked into Gavin's dark brown eyes, his unfocused gaze settled somewhere to the left of her. His fists rested on his knees as he sat on the edge of the hammock in his backyard. She'd been too distracted by the rest of him to notice things maybe she should have picked up on, her own eyes drawn to mouth-watering muscles and his impressive physical presence. He'd always been a big, bold man, like a wrestler. That strength had turned hotter with age. He'd been good-looking at nineteen.

He was mesmerizing and sexy as sin at twenty-nine.

She pulled her eyes off the hard angles of his face, away from temptation. His dog lay on the grass, body pressed against Gavin's thick, muscled leg. She hadn't paid much attention to the dog before other than noting a large, mellow, brindle-colored mutt of some kind. Now, she realized this was a working canine. A guide dog.

The scars on Gavin's forehead—his service to his country had cost him dearly.

She could still remember the day he'd decided to join the Air Force. She'd been so proud of him and crushed at the same time. They'd spent their teenage years in a group home. He'd landed there as an orphan without any relatives after bouncing through the foster system.

Her mother had died of an overdose, and none of her relatives wanted Stacy. Gavin had looked so lost his first day at the home. She knew the others would prey on that. So she'd stepped up to show him the ropes and offer her friendship. She may have been scrawny, but she was fearless back then. She thought she'd already conquered the worst the world had to dish up.

Their unlikely friendship had stuck, shifting to something more on her sweet-sixteen birthday when he'd impulsively kissed her. That one kiss had changed everything for them.

As teens stargazing on the roof of the group home, she and Gavin had dreamed of making a home together. He was going to train to be an EMT. She would become a nurse. They would have a house with a yard… and children.

Then, after he'd seen a television special on Air Force pararescuemen, she'd lost him. He'd chosen a rootless existence. She'd tried to find a compromise, begging him to join the National Guard or enlist in the reserves instead. But in the end, they'd both issued ultimatums with all the fierce stubbornness of two nineteen-year-olds certain they would get their way.

They were both wrong.

She'd followed his career through town gossip at first. He'd become a pararescueman—some called it a parajumper, a PJ. They were like SEALs: supermen with EMT bonus powers and a mission to rescue.

But also so very human. She clenched her fists to keep from stroking back his dark hair and pressing her mouth to his scarred forehead. "What happened to you over there?"

"I lived." He slid his sunglasses back over his sightless eyes.

Her heart squeezed hard. "You were obviously injured. I wish you had let me know after it happened. I would have—"

"You would have done what? Rushed to my bedside?" He laughed darkly and swung his legs back up, reclining on the hammock. "We didn't exactly part on good terms."

Their differences had seemed so huge when they were young, before she'd known how big trouble could be. "I just wish you'd let me know you were home."

"I didn't make a secret of it."

The stress and tension from last night, hell, from the past six months, came rolling over her. A pain deeper than any knife. "You made it damn hard to find out anything about you once you left town." *Yes, she'd kept track of him those first few years, but after he'd finished PJ training, it was as if he'd fallen off the face of the Earth*. "In case you've forgotten, officials don't give up information on military personnel to nonfamily members, especially when that military person works in a Special Operations job."

At eighteen, they'd exchanged vows by a waterfall in a Kentucky valley. But there'd been no witnesses. No minister. Just the two of them pledging their hearts before losing their virginity. They'd never gotten around to legalizing those vows in the year that followed before they parted ways.

"Worked," he said. "Past tense. I worked in Special Operations."

The maple tree branches rustled in the late afternoon

breeze. The wooden fence protected them from prying eyes. She'd been careful driving over, checking to be sure no one had followed her. And other than quite a few cops on the road today, she'd seen nothing suspicious. Jared usually laid low for weeks after reaching out so directly to terrify her. She had time to plan her escape, time to talk to Gavin before they said goodbye again.

Except she'd never counted on him being so injured. Blind. "Which brings me back to my question, Gavin. What happened to you?"

A half smile pushed a dimple into one side of his rugged face. "A really bad wreck."

"You weren't hurt overseas? I assumed…"

His smile faded. "The wreck happened in Afghanistan a year ago. The helicopter I was in got shot down. I was injured. I lived. I'm blind. I can distinguish light from dark, and sometimes I catch hints of shadows, but that's it. Irreversible damage. End of story."

She reached out to him, almost touching, needing to feel the warmth of him, reassure herself he was alive. Her hand stopped just shy of his shoulder. "Gavin—"

"The pity in your voice is so thick it makes me sick," he snapped. "Stop it."

She pulled her hand away. "It's not pity. It's sympathy. Sadness. What kind of person would I be if I didn't feel those things for all you've been through? But I can understand that you would be bitter."

His head turned toward her, those sunglasses almost making it seem like he held eye contact. "I guess you do. But what about you? How are you after last night? What happened was…"

She considered pushing him on his obvious attempt to change the subject, but the brace of his proud shoulders made her reconsider. "Intense? Terrifying? All of the above?" A sigh shuddered through her. "Now I have a window here where he'll hide out before making a move again."

"Damn it, he needs to be locked up."

"I've never been able to prove he's responsible. I'm surprised two police cars came last night. Half the town thinks I'm paranoid because of what happened six months ago."

"What happened?"

"My house was broken into." She'd been stabbed. Jared had whispered in her ear before slipping out of the house. She'd lost so much blood that her account of what happened had been called into question, considered a possible hallucination. "The police couldn't find any evidence to confirm Jared was responsible. The more I called, the more convinced they became that I have a vendetta against him, trying to get his money because he's wealthy."

"Or he's buying someone off because he's rich."

Her head jerked up. How did he know that about her life? Had he kept track of her after all?

More importantly, his comment told her he believed her about Jared. She'd half expected him to doubt her too, and instead he'd come up with a possible solution to why her cries for help were being ignored. "That could be. At any rate, I've decided to relocate. Hide and start over before he has a chance to come back."

"Men like him don't give up." He swung his feet to the ground again, sitting on the edge of the hammock.

He reached for her arm, only missing by a hint, and God help her, she couldn't stop herself from leaning toward his hand to make contact.

"Gavin, I don't have any other choice."

"Yes, you do." He squeezed her arm. "Let's flush out the bastard and put him in jail."

—⁓—

Just the feel of Stacy's arm threatened to shatter Gavin's self-control.

Since losing his sight, the rest of his senses had gone into hyperdrive. Right now, he wanted nothing more than to soak up everything he could about Stacy to make up for the fact that he couldn't feast his eyes on her. The silky softness of her fingertips set his nerves alive. Her strawberry scent made him want to bury his face in her hair and just breathe.

But the fear in her voice held him back from acting on those impulses. She needed him. The way she talked about having no choice except to move away leveled him. He, of all people, knew how important it was for her to stay here in her hometown. When he'd left, he'd been convinced she would follow him. He'd kept tabs on her, waiting, until the day he'd learned she'd married Jared Lewis, a local rich guy who could offer her the home and stability she'd always craved.

Gavin had thought it best to let her go. If he'd put aside his pride and maintained the friendship, she would have had someone to turn to. Guilt hammered him. He had to keep her safe and to do that, he needed to remove the threat. Permanently.

"Let's go inside and talk. Bring me up to speed on

everything that happened with him, where he's been living, where he might be now."

"Just like that you and I are a team again? It's not that simple." He could picture her shaking her head.

"For me, it is."

"Then why didn't you call me when you came back?"

"Because I didn't want your pity," he said through gritted teeth.

"I thought we covered that already. And if I'm hearing you clearly, you're saying it's not okay for you to need me. But it's fine for me to need you."

"Yep, that's exactly what I'm saying."

"That is such a macho load of crap."

He stood, resting his hand on the handle attached to Radar's collar. He loved his dog and hated that he needed him, especially now, in front of Stacy. "Anastasia, are you coming inside with me or not?"

Without waiting for her to answer since standing around without being able to see her face was tearing him up inside, he started walking toward the back door. After three strides, he heard her follow with a sigh of exasperation. He mentally counted the paver stones on his way to the back door, then the three steps leading into the duplex, including the last step that was shorter than the others. He ducked his head and entered the kitchen, aware of Stacy following.

She stopped in the middle of the tile floor. "I brought the lemonade back inside. It shouldn't go to waste. Do you mind if I get glasses from the cabinet and pour us each a fresh drink?"

Stacy always did babble when she was nervous.

"Sure, go ahead. I have ham and cheese sandwiches in the fridge, already made." He hadn't wanted her to see him fumble around. He was getting better at making his way through the world, but there was so much unpredictability. Knowing he wouldn't be able to read her face put him at a disadvantage. Did she hate him for leaving? Or worse yet, was she indifferent?

So many years wasted holding a grudge over their last fight, the ultimatums issued in their tiny studio apartment. If he'd swallowed his pride, he could have helped her. He could have *seen* her at least one more time before going blind. "We can talk about a plan to prevent a repeat of last night."

"You're serious." Ice clinked from the pitcher into the glasses as he heard her fill two of them.

He paused at the refrigerator. "Do you doubt I can help you? Because I'm blind?"

"No," she said with a quick assurance. "I doubt because I've seen how determined he is. Nothing I do makes a difference. Can we talk about something else instead? Just…catch up? Be two normal friends who haven't seen each other in years?"

Could they pull that off? He might have thought so twenty-four hours ago. Now that she'd touched him, now that he'd heard her voice again? His feelings for her were so much fiercer than friendship.

But he would play along for the moment, if that's what she wanted. "Sure, have a seat and I'll get the sandwiches. Do you still like grapes?"

"I do, thank you." The chair scraped against the floor as she sat at his wooden table.

He used the old furniture from his apartment before the accident. Familiar items helped ground him as he figured out how to build images without sight.

"Your dog is magnificent."

"His name is Radar." Gavin pulled out the Tupperware container of sandwiches. He preferred mayo, but since he remembered she liked spicy mustard, he'd just made them all the same. He set the food in the middle of the table, then picked up the colander of grapes, added two plates, and took a seat beside her. All without tripping or dropping a thing.

He felt the brush of Stacy's fingers an instant before she pressed the glass of lemonade into his hand. The heat of resentment almost matched the heat of desire flaming from that simple touch.

Her hand slid away. "How did you get matched with a service dog?"

He exhaled hard, his body still rigid from wanting her. "One of my teammates has a wife who works with search and rescue dogs. Her name's Rachel. She had connections to partner me with a service dog. My squadron raised the money to pay for the training and transport. I didn't know that part until later. I was told the dog was covered by my insurance. I was too drugged up on pain meds to question it. By the time I found out the truth, Radar and I had…gotten close."

He more than depended on Radar. Their bond was tight.

"Is it okay if I pet him? He's working, right?"

"As long as I give him permission. Radar, boy, this is Stacy, my friend." He patted the dog's rib cage. "Hold out your hand for him to sniff, then you can stroke his ears."

His dog held still, but Gavin could feel the acceptance flow between them.

She angled back. "What a good boy, and clearly so smart. I would imagine a comfort too, back then."

"He was, and he is. But I still don't like charity." He picked up his sandwich.

"Hmmm." The sound of her chewing filled the space between them as they slid into old routines, the years melting away. "You figured out a way to pay them back for Radar, didn't you?"

He stayed silent, biting into his sandwich more for something to do than for food. The spicy mustard filled his taste buds, but he'd eaten worse out in the field on missions.

"Or something else." She paused, and he heard the rustle of her plucking grapes before she continued, "You sponsored someone else's dog."

"Doesn't matter." He shrugged. "And if I did do something charitable anonymously and you guess it, then you take away my altruism."

She laughed softly, so different from the fearful sounds of last night. "You are such an obstinate man."

"Always have been."

"I bet that's what got you through your recovery. That stubborn nature and this great dog. He truly is magnificent." Her chair scraped back. "He looks like a shepherd in the body, but he has a brindle coat. What breed is he?"

"They tell me he's a Dutch shepherd mix. Dutch shepherds have brindle-colored fur." He found himself trusting her, asking her something he hadn't been able to bring himself to say to anyone else. "Tell me what he looks like."

She gasped softly, her hand sliding over his. "What do you want to know?"

"People say brindle, and I know what that means, but there are nuances…" He searched for the words to explain how difficult it was to be so close to Radar and have so little idea what he looked like. That sounded… weak. "Ah, hell, never mind."

She linked their fingers. "His coat's mostly dark brown, with hints of a lighter brown, and then there are these stripes through that are a caramel that's almost reddish. The light plays on those stripes of color so they shift and change." The melody of her voice flowed over him. "His muzzle is black. His ears stand up most of the time, but sometimes one ear flops down."

That image made him smile, and smiling felt damn good. "They told me he was found in a shelter and tested well. They think he has some Labrador retriever in him, too. I've seen working dogs on the job, but I never had any idea how tight the bond could be."

"I can see that. When you talk, his ears always twitch toward you even if his eyes are fixed on a target or task. They're golden colored with a dark brown circle outlining the gold. When you're just sitting and he's beside you, not working, the look in his eyes is incredible. He stares at you as if he was put on this Earth just for you."

He swallowed hard. "I get that. Sometimes though, I'm torn between my connection to Radar and resenting the fact that I need him."

What the hell was it about Stacy that had him sharing so much so fast? It really was as if the years apart had melted away.

"The connection you say you feel to him, trust me, he reciprocates, perhaps even more so." She took his hand and placed it on Radar's side. "Can you feel his heart beating? That pulse is focused on you. That's what I see in his expression. This dog would lay down his life for you. It's there in his brown eyes. And in case you were wondering, right now, his tail is wagging."

"I can feel the breeze."

She slid her hand from his. "I'm so sorry you lost your sight."

"I'm so sorry you have to live in fear." Guilt and anger piled up inside him. If he'd fought harder for what they'd had back then, none of this would have happened to her.

Silence settled between them, and he thought he heard her sniffle. He brushed his hand across the table until his fingers bumped her arm. He squeezed lightly in comfort. His arms ached to haul her against his chest as he would have done in the past. How much had changed between them?

He didn't know how to put that into words, so he settled for the simple start while stroking the inside of her wrist with his thumb. "What color is your hair? Has it changed since I knew you before?"

Her pulse leapt under this touch.

Then definitely a sniffle, a soft cough, and swallow of her drink before she said, "A bit darker strawberry blond than before. I still forget to put on sunscreen and let my nose get burned."

An image formed in his mind of her, more mature, still beautiful. His. He slid his hand up her arm to cup behind her neck, her hair flowing over his fingers with such familiarity it could have been ten years ago, just before they'd both gone so off course. "That's the Anastasia I remember."

He urged her toward him, and she didn't resist. In fact, her hands slid over his shoulders, and she flowed right into his arms. Her mouth to his. Her body every bit as delicate as he remembered.

God, she tasted sweet, of lemonade and Stacy. Her tongue against his, her soft hands touching his neck, his face. Such simple caresses but after so long without her, this kiss, having her so close, was everything.

As teenagers, they'd snuck out and hidden in the hayloft to make out, the fresh, earthy scent all around them. She was his first real kiss at sixteen. The first woman he'd ever touched. They'd done everything except have sex for the next two years because she was terrified of getting pregnant. Scared of being like her mom. Young and trapped, and he would have done anything to protect her.

He'd thought he was giving her what she wanted when he'd walked away. Instead, he'd failed to protect her in the most fundamental way ever. She could have died. She'd been in so much more danger here than he'd ever been in overseas, and that gnawed at his gut. He should have checked up on her. They'd meant too much to each other to have let that go.

The warm swipe of her tongue reminded him of all the times they'd tasted every inch of each other, desperate to ease the ache from wanting each other and holding back from the final consummation. He burned to taste her now, to run his fingers through her whispery fine hair…still strawberry blond, she'd said, but darker… His hands roved her body, searching for changes and similarities, desperate to "see" her as best he could, through his fingertips.

He slid his hands lower, down her back to draw her into his lap—

Radar barked, startling them both.

Stacy laughed self-consciously. "I guess he's jealous."

Or smart, because Gavin knew he was moving too fast with her. But the sound of her rapid breaths against his cheek, the feel of goose bumps on her skin, and that kitten purr in the back of her throat told him she was every bit as aroused as he was.

Could he act on that? Was this a second chance to be with her? He had a helluva lot less to offer her now than he had then, but damn it. Walking away from Stacy, especially now, was not an option.

His hands skimmed up and down her spine before he eased back. He needed to take care of security first before acting further on the passion between them, a desire that hadn't dimmed one bit over the years. Where that would lead? He didn't know. But they had to find out. "I've missed you, Stacy."

"Gavin, I'm confused. Why did you kiss me?"

"Because we needed to clear that up before dealing with anything else," he answered as honestly as he knew how. "Because I needed to know if you still tasted the same. I was wrong."

"What?" she asked breathlessly.

His thumb stroked across her lips. "You taste even better."

# CHAPTER 3

Her head still spinning from the kiss, Stacy sagged back in her chair in Gavin's sparsely decorated kitchen, crossing her arms over her chest in counter-pressure against her breasts that ached for his caress. Her eyes scanned the place, looking anywhere but at him. She took in the accommodations she'd missed at first. Minimal furniture. Clear pathways. Braille labels everywhere. No cabinets left open.

A long white cane in the corner by the door.

He eased back into his seat, broad shoulders stretching the gray T-shirt until she could see the cut of his muscles. His long legs stretched in front of him, making his jeans look mighty damn fine. And there was no missing the press of his arousal.

Her heart hitched. Her body hummed from wanting him. Had she ever stopped? "We can't just pick up where we left off, Gavin. It's been ten years."

"Then why did you come over?" His head tipped to the side, a long, dark lock of hair falling over the scars on his forehead. "You could have ignored my text."

Hah. Not hardly. "I had to find out why you didn't let me know you'd returned."

"I've actually only been back for four weeks." He shrugged. "I was working up my nerve."

She shook her head in disbelief only to remember he couldn't see her. "Since when have you been afraid of anything?"

"Only idiots don't have fears. A healthy dose of caution keeps a person alive." He leaned a muscular elbow on the table, his fingers toying absently along her arm. "So let's talk about what we need to do to keep you safe. Then we'll deal with how damn good that kiss felt."

His words sucked the oxygen from the room. Her arm still tingled from just a simple stroke. "My problems with my ex-husband aren't yours to take on."

"Like hell." His square jaw flexed, his hands clenching. "If last night is anything to go by, you have every reason to fear he'll harm you."

She forced herself to admit the worst, the part she'd held back, a part that she feared could send him over the edge wanting to protect her. She needed to make sure he stayed safe. "Six months ago, when he broke in, I tried to protect myself with a knife. He…he took it from me and cut me, on my side…"

Gavin hissed in unmistakable rage, his fists white-knuckled with restraint, but he let her talk.

"Like last night, when the cops came and he ran. Since he wore a mask and there were no prints, we couldn't prove it was him. I was only able to get a restraining order because of his obsessive texts and phone calls."

"How bad?" he asked between clenched teeth.

"How badly was I cut? I'm still here. No permanent damage. Just some stitches along my side." She'd been fighting, trying to roll away. If she hadn't, he would have hit her heart. She would be dead today. "But it was enough to make me realize he's never going to stop. He will never forgive me for leaving him. Except every time I tried to get away, he always seemed to find me, so I convinced myself at least here I knew the lay of the land."

"He will never hurt you again." The vow hung hoarse and heavy between them with unmistakable intensity.

"Thank you." She wanted to have faith in what he offered, but her ability to trust had eroded over the years. He was here for her. But why hadn't he let her be there for him? "Why didn't you tell me right away that you're blind?"

"Are you insinuating I can't help because I lost my sight?"

She gasped, appalled that she may have wounded his ego. "No, no, that's not what I meant at all. I'm trusting you with so much now. I'm wondering why you held back from trusting me."

His chin tipped, revealing that familiar cleft. "Are you sure you're not every bit as susceptible to pride as I am?"

"Yeah, obviously. That's the reason I never contacted you," she confessed softly. "I couldn't admit what an awful mistake I'd made in marrying Jared, especially after the way I pushed you away."

"We both made mistakes in issuing ultimatums. We can't change the past, only work on the future. I will do my best to keep you safe until they lock your ex up in prison. I wish I could protect you on my own. But I can't."

"Gavin, it's not your fault—"

He held up a hand, and touched her lips to silence her. "I have called in friends who can."

"Gavin, stop." The caress of his finger along her mouth tempted her to collapse into the comfort of his arms. But she couldn't bring her trouble, her danger, to his doorstep, especially not now. "The police can—"

"The police have tried without luck." He clasped her shoulders in his broad palms, massaging gently, enticingly. "You're too important to me. This is a small town with an understaffed force. I contacted two of my pararescue buddies, and they're coming up to help with security while we locate your ex and get a handle on his next move."

Her lashes fluttered closed as she took in the seductive feel of his hands on her shoulders. He wouldn't be able to see the betraying way she shut her eyes. "Your friends will take leave, drop everything and come here to help a stranger?"

"If I ask, yes. We're there for each other." His voice went lower, raspier with regret. "Even if I can't be there for them anymore."

Her body chilled, and she opened her eyes again. "I just want to leave town and start over somewhere I won't have to bar the windows and look over my shoulder."

Gavin shook his head. "From what you've told me and based on the level of violence last night, he will find you."

"But to involve your friends?" As much as she ached for help, she wasn't used to calling on others, trusting others.

"I didn't have to think about it for long. I'm of"—his throat moved in a hard swallow—"limited help to you because of my blindness. But I can't just walk away."

If he was injured further because of her, she couldn't live with herself. "What if I say I'm not your problem or theirs?"

"That won't stop me—or them." His raspy voice was steely with determination. "Call it misplaced machismo or whatever you want, but I feel responsible for leaving you behind. I have to know you're safe. Let me do this for you. I need to do this, and I will, with or without your consent."

She sure as hell couldn't handle this on her own anymore with triple locks and barred windows. For now, she had no choice but to accept help from the only person left on the planet she stood a chance at trusting. "When do your friends arrive?"

"By dinnertime tonight." He shoved to his feet, his hand falling to his dog's harness. "So are you ready for us to go to your house and pack a bag?"

---

He had backup.

Shortly after he and Stacy had returned from picking up a suitcase of clothes at her place, his PJ pals had arrived at his house. His buddies were here for him, just as he would be there for them if he could. He felt like hell for asking his friends to drive up from Florida to Kentucky, but Hugh Franco and Liam McCabe, his former pararescue teammates, hadn't hesitated when he'd woken them in the middle of the night. They'd assured him they had leave time to burn between assignments. Liam's wife, Rachel, had accompanied them as well with one of her search and rescue dogs named Disco. Between Radar and Disco, they had the best the canine world could offer for additional alert support.

He was still getting his bearings after kissing Stacy. One kiss, for God's sake, and he was right back flat on his ass crazy to be with her. She moved him in a way no other woman ever had. He suspected that rattled her as much as it did him. They'd both stayed silent for most of the trip to her place to pack her bag and back to his place. Soon, there would be no avoiding talking.

No more avoiding what they still felt for each other.

He flattened a hand on Liam's Jeep while his buddies unloaded their gear in Gavin's garage. The scent of motor oil hung in the humid air. He could hear Radar and Disco playing in the corner with Rachel, wrestling while they got to know each other. "There's no way I can thank you enough."

Liam clapped him on the shoulder. "You don't have to. Right, Hugh?"

"Truth," Hugh barked, a no-nonsense guy with a huge soft spot when it came to women and kids. "We're just gonna unpack our gear, get some surveillance equipment set up. We'll get this place locked down and secure. Then we'll set out the tech breadcrumbs to draw him right in. Just point us to our quarters, and we'll get to it."

Social media worked both ways. People worried so much about having securities in place to keep people out that they missed the beauty of lowering security to let people in. Jared Lewis would be taunted and shown exactly where to look.

Gavin's place. His turf.

He owned the whole duplex and hadn't rented out the other side, yet, since he'd planned to advertise it as furnished. "The other side of the unit has all the necessities, no frills, but the mattresses on the beds are new. I can't guarantee things match. My color-coordinating skills are pretty much shit these days."

Liam thumped his shoulder again, always thoughtful about keeping Gavin oriented. "Thank God you're alive." His voice hitched for a second before he continued, "That's the only thing that matters."

"I realize that." Gavin slumped back against the Jeep, thinking about all the times they'd gone four-wheeling, feeling invincible. "Every damn day I know I'm here and Jablonski isn't. That doesn't make me feel much better."

Hugh's heavier tread sounded, and he stopped beside them. "I never took you to be a self-pitying sort."

"Easy for you to say." Gavin couldn't keep the bitterness out of his voice, then felt like hell for it. Hugh's first wife and child had died in an accident. The man well understood about dark places.

Liam stepped into the breach, ever the peacemaker. "What about Stacy, what does she mean to you? Clearly a lot for you to call us."

He'd considered these men his best friends, as close as family, and yet he'd never told them about her. "We used to be a couple back in high school. Her ex will try to kill her. I have no doubts about that."

Hugh cracked his knuckles. "And why isn't he in jail?"

"Can't prove anything," Gavin answered, frustrated as hell. "The best she's been able to manage is a restraining order."

Rachel rested a hand on his arm. "Then with luck, we'll flush him out, easy enough to do using the Internet and some strategic leaks. Let this guy set himself up, and we'll be here to keep her safe until the police arrive. You're not in this alone."

A strange concept for him to wrap his brain around. Even as part of the pararescue team, he'd usually held himself apart, the quiet dude. Stacy had always been the one to pull him out of his shell. Like she'd done now, having him reach out to his friends.

"I want him in prison where he belongs." And he wanted to hurt him. Bad. With a rage so intense it threatened to overwhelm him. Maybe that was why he'd brought his friends, too. To make sure he didn't kill the bastard. Because he could. Even blind. He could. Slowly. Painfully.

Yeah, he definitely needed his friends to keep him in check while they pulled this off. Because if he killed Jared Lewis, life would be over for Gavin, too. And for the first time since he'd lost his sight, he considered the possibility of a future.

---

Stacy stacked paper plates and tucked them into the trash can, still a little overwhelmed by the people who'd dropped everything to help her—or rather help Gavin. "Your friends are nice."

"Almost felt like a normal supper." Gavin wiped the kitchen table, feeling with one hand ahead of the damp rag.

A normal supper? Like a normal couple having a dinner party. How things could have been if she'd been brave enough to leave town with him. If she hadn't been so stubborn. If she hadn't been foolish enough to throw away the love of this incredible man for some idea of home and family that had never happened for her anyway.

She shook off the regrets that gained her nothing. Focus on the present. She'd been able to get to know Gavin's friends over pizza and tea, learn a bit about his world since he'd left her. And to her surprise, they'd also spelled out a plan to lure Jared out of hiding sooner rather than later. The prospect made her gut knot with terror, but the thought of living her life in limbo was even more unpalatable. "Lucky turn that you own this whole duplex."

"So you can have your own room here on my side?"

"I didn't say that." She folded down the three pizza boxes and tucked them in the trash as well, only two slices left to store in the refrigerator. During that brief time that she and Gavin had lived together on their own after turning eighteen, they'd shared midnight snacks of leftovers. Those two pieces of pizza called to her to make new memories.

He walked to the sink, his hip brushing hers as he passed, then pitched the rag over the faucet with an almost perfect aim, leaving three-fourths of it trailing off the side. "Why *did* you marry him?"

Her hand went to her side, right over the spot where her skin hummed from his simple touch. She wanted to reach out for more, to hell with being smart, and lose herself in the passion they shared.

But his words gave her pause. Was he judging her? That notion hurt. So much. And dissecting the reasons was tough, how she fell into the battered woman pit. Jared had appeared to worship her, played the adoring husband almost too well, flowers and chocolates and jewelry. The signs had been small at first. He'd started dictating what she wore, but she'd written it off as too much stress at work and taking it out on her. Then he took away the credit cards for "fiscal prudence" and put her on an allowance, a move she'd countered by job-hunting to help their cash flow. Except then he was insulted. Adamant about her not working. So many signs that seemed minor taken individually, then the temper, the explosions and apologies. She didn't realize how truly twisted their relationship had grown until the first time he'd hit her. By then, she was already isolated. No job. No means of support.

And it didn't help that she'd felt so…humiliated. Embarrassed. All the things abusers counted on a woman feeling to keep her silent. She'd walked that victim path and told herself she could fix it, even when the bruises multiplied. But then her lung collapsed while she was grocery shopping.

She'd passed out and woken up in the hospital, knowing she could never go home. "Does it matter now why I married him?"

"To me? Yes, it matters." He turned to face her, one hip resting against the counter, his face taut with intensity. "We loved each other. We exchanged vows and maybe they weren't legal, but we have a connection. History."

She blinked back tears at memories of that waterfall "wedding" where they'd pledged themselves to each other with words…and then their bodies. "I loved you, but you made it clear you were never going to settle down. We were both too stubborn to compromise. But I still wanted a life, a marriage, children. I settled for a man I thought I could have that life with. That was wrong of me, and he knew it."

He shook his head sharply. "Don't even suggest for an instant any of what this bastard has done to you is your fault."

His fierce defense soothed a part of her battered ego. Jared had been an expert at eroding her confidence, and trusting her judgment again had been a damn hard row. "That's a part of the mind game of abuse that's hard to shake."

"But you're going to." He reached for her hands, sliding his fingers along the insides of her palms with a gentle stroke, his sightless brown eyes so close to meeting hers. "You deserve better from life. He's a twisted man who should be in jail."

"I know. I just wonder if I'll ever be free. He's so… obsessed. There's nowhere to hide." She swayed closer to him, her breasts skimming against the rock-solid wall of his chest. She ached with the need to press closer, to put her lips to him, explore the hard planes of his body. "And to think I turned you down because I thought military life would be too difficult."

"You were right," he said darkly. "Look at me now. Your fears came true."

"You look…strong. Handsome." And every bit as dear to her now as he'd been all those years ago.

She surrendered to temptation and leaned the rest of the way in, her mouth to his, holding still, their breaths flowing back and forth between them in a frozen moment in time. Then his hands slid up, bold and sure, palming her back and bringing her body flush against his. She moaned her pleasure and consent, her fingers digging into his shoulders. The ever-present attraction between them flared hot and ready, as if the past decade had never happened. But there was a mature edge to the need, a sense of just how much life could steal from them if they were foolish enough to waste this gift.

"Anastasia," he murmured against her lips, then along her neck, "are you sure this is what you want? I need to be clear you understand where this is going if we don't stop soon."

She cupped his face in her hands, his five o'clock shadow rough against her palms. "I'm hoping it's going to your bedroom."

# CHAPTER 4

Gavin wrapped his arms around Stacy, lifting her against him as he walked toward his bedroom. He didn't need to see to move. He knew every inch of his home, so all his instincts could be focused on kissing her, feeling her gentle curves against him, drawing in the strawberry scent of her hair. A decade without her had left a hunger so deep inside him he didn't know if he could ever fill it.

But he sure as hell intended to try.

He booted his bedroom door the rest of the way open, stroking and walking, then pausing at the foot of the bed. "Here or in the shower?"

She purred her approval, whispering against his mouth, "The shower. Then the bed."

"I like the way you think." He cradled her face and took her mouth again, anticipation, all the pent-up tension of the past twenty-four hours ramping him higher.

She tugged at his T-shirt, pulling it from his jeans, sweeping it up and off. The brush of her cool, soft hands against his skin as she unzipped his jeans made him throb harder. He backed her toward the bathroom, sliding free the buttons on her shirt, parting the fabric and yessss, finally touching her. *Anastasia*.

Even with the lacy rasp of her bra, he could feel her heat, the pebbling of her nipples in response to his touch. He ached to see her so damn much that the loss of his sight threatened to bring tears to his eyes. But he could touch, explore, learn the "look" of her again with his other senses, and he intended to make the most of that. He unhooked her bra and flung it aside before sketching his hands around to reacquaint himself with her gentle curves. Perfection.

Inch by inch, he kissed his way down her chest to her stomach before kneeling to peel her jeans down, his mouth exploring each patch of soft skin, his hands roving down her sides. He felt the raised scar along her side, maybe four inches long. The reality of that sent rage pumping through him.

She stroked her hands over his hair. "I'm okay. We're together. Don't let anything or anyone steal this from us."

Nodding, he pressed a lingering kiss to her scar before standing.

"Shower," she demanded, "together. Now."

"Yes, ma'am." He kicked aside his shoes and jeans, the rustle of hers coming off as well urging him faster toward the overlarge shower stall. Pausing by the medicine cabinet, he patted the shelf until his hand rested on the box of condoms. He pulled out a packet.

She plucked it from his hand and backed into the shower… "Uh, which is the hot, and which is the cold?"

Chuckling, he took her hand and pressed her fingertips to the braille words. "I've got this."

He cranked on the shower, and she squealed at the first splash of cold water an instant before the spray warmed over them. He pulled her flush against him, skin to skin, his erection pressing against her. Her hands speared into his hair, and she tugged him back to her, kissing him, open mouth and emotions. His hand slid between her legs, and he felt her slick core, finding her every bit as ready as he was.

Urgency pumped through him and just when he thought he couldn't wait longer, he heard her tear open the condom packet and slide it over him. With a low growl, he lifted her against the tile wall, and her legs hooked around him.

Finally, finally, he slid inside her, deeper, her hips arching to bring him closer still. She rested her head on his shoulder, her face pressed to his neck, her fingernails digging into his back as she murmured her needs and wants. And how very much he enjoyed giving her that and more. She writhed against him, meeting each thrust as they rediscovered a rhythm they'd perfected back when they'd assumed they had forever together.

Holding her in his arms, being inside her again, he couldn't remember a time his life hadn't been all about Stacy. Her face against his neck, her mouth on him, his on hers, had him bracing a hand to the tile wall to keep his feet under him. Their slick bodies moved in sync, the friction bringing him to the brink, but damned if he would go without her. He stroked and listened, waiting for her husky gasps, the kittenish purrs that told him… yes…her sweet cries of completion and the grip of her orgasm pulsing around him sent him right over the edge with her, his hoarse shout muffled in her hair.

Aftershocks rocked through her, rippling through him as well as they held on to each other, the shower spray hitting his back. The years they'd spent apart evaporated as quickly as the water on their hot flesh. This was right, them together. If only he'd had the sense to come to her.

He could have saved her so much pain. His life might have been different, too.

He pulled her closer. The water on his face. The spray of the shower stinging his skin sent him back in time for an instant. So many missions had started in the water. He'd trained by swimming for miles. Jumped out of planes into rough waters. He'd loved his job, the mission, the adrenaline, and ultimately making a difference in the world. He was somebody. He had a purpose. And that had all been taken from him in a flash.

He'd finally found his way back to this woman at the very time he had so damn little to offer her.

---

Basking in the afterglow of damn good sex, Stacy let the shower flow over her, her eyes closed as Gavin massaged shampoo into her scalp. There was something so seductive about focusing solely on his touch. She didn't want to think about tomorrow or even their past. Right now, here in the shower, they had a narrow window of time to be together.

And she intended to enjoy every second of it.

His hands slicked over her hair, brushing suds down her shoulders and forward over her breasts. "Could you pass me the conditioner?"

She forced her eyes open, the bottles labeled with words as well as stickers in braille. "Even your bottles, they have braille labels."

"Mixing up shampoo and body wash, not to mention cleaners, is not a good idea."

He lifted her hand and rubbed her fingertips along the bumps as he had when they'd stepped into the shower.

"I want to learn," she said before thinking, then realizing that implied a future when she'd been so determined to live in the moment.

"Reading in braille increases the sensitivity of touch." His hot breath flowed over her.

"I like the sound of that." She angled back to kiss his bristly chin and pass him the conditioner. She relaxed against him, nostalgia sweeping through her. "Can we really just step back in time this easily?"

"I don't have the answer to that." He massaged the conditioner into her hair, working it through to the ends. "I only know I've missed you every single day we've been apart, Anastasia."

She didn't even bother blinking away the tears he wouldn't be able to see. The shower hid the evidence. She let herself savor the touch of this man. Gavin. A man who cared about her. It had been so long since she'd had the luxury of love. So many took that for granted.

She never would again.

The patter of the shower echoed in her ears along with her heartbeat, so loudly she almost missed the ringing of the cell phone. *Her cell*. Water chilled on her body with premonition. She knew before even stepping out of the shower.

Somehow Jared had risen to the bait even faster than they'd anticipated.

---

Two hours later, Gavin sat in the spare bedroom, Stacy tucked to his side, her hair still carrying the scent of his shampoo from their shower.

The text from her ex had come in sooner than even he would have expected.

He'd made Stacy read it aloud. *You're going to be sorry, cheating bitch.*

Gavin ground his teeth. He would never forget the quiver of fear in her voice.

He and Stacy had thrown on their clothes. Hugh had been awake next door, taking the first watch while Liam and Rachel slept. They'd expected the reaction to come later. His friends had left technological breadcrumbs for Jared to follow that would lead him to this duplex. They'd allowed one of Stacy's social media accounts to post using map data to pinpoint her whereabouts. The fact that Jared had responded so quickly said he'd escalated. Hell, the fact that he'd texted at all showed he was growing reckless. The text alone was a violation of his restraining order.

*You're going to be sorry, cheating bitch.*

Cheating. Somehow Jared had more than followed breadcrumbs. He'd figured out she was with Gavin. How close had he been? Regardless, now they were all on alert. Including the dogs, Radar on the floor beside Gavin. Disco was in the duplex next door with Rachel.

No matter what, he would keep her safe. Stacy didn't know that they'd set things up so Jared would think she was next door where his friends waited with Rachel acting as a decoy.

Gavin knew Stacy wouldn't like that. But she didn't have to know. She had been told they were simply outside securing the perimeter. But Gavin wanted more than a simple trespass. They needed to catch the bastard breaking in to show the pattern. No one was in law enforcement, so it wasn't entrapment. And what digging

Gavin had been able to accomplish told him the department's hands were tied.

For now.

Hugh and Liam would secure Jared once he broke in. Then the cops would arrive. All would be neatly taken care of. As much as he wanted to be in the action personally, he understood this was the best—safest—plan for Stacy.

Calming her after that text had been a major feat. She'd been so keyed up, so worried about putting others in danger, he'd been afraid the whole plan would backfire and she would recklessly try to leave. Not that he would let that happen. At last, though, she'd calmed and trusted him to take care of this, to help her, and that was soothing to his soul, to feel their bond was still intact.

He stroked her hair, her head tucked against his chest. The spare bedroom was the most secure place in the duplex, fewest windows, farthest from the doors. He had a two-way radio at his side. He and his buddies could alert each other with the touch of a thumb to an alarm.

Each shuddering breath Stacy took told him she wasn't having any luck falling asleep. Not that he could blame her.

He stroked her arm. "Tell me about your life these past ten years. The good parts."

Please, God, let there have been good parts. He wanted the best for her.

Her palm rested on his chest, right over his heart. "After you left, I went to school and trained to be an LPN."

"You're a nurse?" Just like they'd planned. He smiled. "That's awesome."

"I *was* a nurse," she amended. "Jared made me quit my job at the hospital. And since the divorce, I freelance write to pay the bills. Everyone's looking for articles on health issues. Pays well enough. I also do some medical chart transcribing."

He wished he could see her face, gauge her emotions. "Are you happy with that?"

She shrugged, the feel of her against him so familiar and good. "I have flexibility. I can work from home."

"All the time?" He frowned.

"Mostly, yes."

"That sounds…solitary." And like a woman in hiding.

"You've always been known as a quiet man." She drew circles on his chest, the night sounds from outside muffled, bugs buzzing and the rare car driving past. "I'd have thought you would appreciate a job with solitude and instead you're the one working with people all the time. Talking."

"I had to figure out how to support myself and possibly put some of those emergency rescue and medic skills to use." It hadn't been an easy transition, but he was taking life one day at a time.

"That's really admirable how you've built a new life for yourself. Maybe I could interview you for an article."

"Me? I'm just doing a job."

"You've taken a difficult blow and rechanneled your life." She skimmed her fingers over the scars along his forehead, her cool touch healing. "What you've done is every bit as brave as what you accomplished in the field."

Her words brought a lump to his throat. "I had to accommodate if I wanted a life at all."

"If?" Her head shifted, and he could feel her look up at him. "You wouldn't…"

"Kill myself? No, I'm past those thoughts now." Life was still hard but not like those early days when he'd woken in pain in a dark world.

"Oh, God, Gavin, why didn't you call me?" She slid her arms around him and held on tightly. "I would have come to you then. You always were too damn independent."

"Joke's on me then"—he laughed at himself, at the crazy turns of the world—"since I'm dependent on just about everyone now, including my dog."

"I don't know what to say."

"Finding a career choice has been…challenging. I'm a military medic, a pararescueman. Tough as hell to do either of those without eyes." He drew in a breath and admitted to her something he hadn't told anyone else. "I've been working on braille, so I can go back to school and get my degree."

She cupped his face, and he could feel her looking at him. "That's fantastic. What are you planning to study?"

"Social work and counseling." He grinned. "I'll get to listen more, talk less."

She pressed a kiss to his mouth, lingered, then said, "You are an incredible man."

He gathered her closer, cupping the back of her head, wondering how they'd gotten so off track. Wanting to be the man she thought he was but not certain he could be what she needed now any more than he had then. He couldn't even keep her safe on his own. His arms twitched tighter around her.

Just as his radio blared with an alarm next to him.

# CHAPTER 5

HEART POUNDING, STACY LEANED IN TO HEAR THEIR conversation over the two-way radio.

Liam reported, "Jared Lewis parked next door and is approaching the house from the east. He's slipping through the fence gate now."

Stark, efficient words that didn't begin to convey the horror of what was moving toward them. Her mouth went dry.

Stacy's stomach plummeted. She looked at Gavin, trying to gauge his mood, but his face was stone. Focused. He was in some other zone. She wanted to warn him how bad this could be. What if she hadn't made it clear how dangerous Jared could be? How relentless and—

"Roger," Gavin replied. "Am securing Stacy now. Over."

"Gavin?" She felt sick.

He hooked the radio to his jeans. "We're going to lock down in the bathroom with Radar. Jared Lewis will never get anywhere near you."

Radar growled low, as if in agreement.

Oh God, how could she have been so selfish as to put him at risk like this? Once she'd found out he was blind, she should have gone to the cops again or left town. This wasn't fair to him or to his friends.

And something niggled at her. Why hide? His military buddies were outside. This plan had sounded so smart when they'd presented it to her over pizza, but now she wasn't so certain. She slid off the bed, standing. "Are you sure they're okay out there?"

From their radio conversation, it hadn't sounded like they were outdoors at all.

"They'll be fine. And so will you," Gavin assured her, gripping her arm to steer her toward the bathroom just as Radar's growl ramped.

A body hurtled through the window and hit the carpet, shattered glass all around him. For an instant she thought one of Gavin's friends had come in only to realize...

She screamed. "Jared!"

Masked, Jared rolled to his feet, a knife in his hand, tiny glass cuts giving him a blood-speckled, eerie look. Noise rumbled from next door. Gavin's friends? The bark of Rachel's dog pierced the wall.

"Stacy..." Jared called out in a low hiss, "you can't hide in the shadows forever."

Beside her, she felt the muscles in Gavin's body bunch. He and Radar launched as one directly at Jared.

"A knife," she shouted, "he has a knife."

While Radar clamped his teeth around Jared's ankle, Gavin was fighting blind but with instincts no blindness could dim. He locked his arms around her wiry ex-husband, using his bulk to weigh the man down, making himself a human barrier between Jared and Stacy while his fist found Jared's jaw. Neck. Whatever he could reach. Her ex-husband wore his standard stocking cap, but it slid askew in the struggle, showing the evil face she recognized too well. Jared slashed the blade across Gavin's arm. She felt the cut all the way to her soul.

"Why did you have to come back to town? She's mine. She'll always be mine," he rambled madly. "You thought you could lure me next door to your decoy, but I'm smarter than that. How are you going to fight against me, blind man?"

Blood leaked onto Gavin's carpet. Gavin's blood. Damn it, she wasn't going to stand here frozen, doing nothing. She refused to let fear paralyze her. She had too much to lose. She considered racing next door for help, but Gavin could be dead before she got back. So she screamed, and screamed, and screamed again while searching for a weapon.

Gavin's cane.

Still screeching her head off because no one would ever silence her again, she grabbed the thick wooden cane and waited for just the right moment…

Gavin had Jared pinned to the floor, but her ex-husband started to swipe with the knife again.

She swung the cane, smacking full force into his wrist. The sound of cracking bone mixed with Jared's howl of agony.

The knife skittered away, and she swept it up quickly, adrenaline pumping hard. "Gavin, I have his knife and your cane, and trust me, Jared, there's not a chance in hell I'll ever let you use either of them against me."

Jared cradled his shattered wrist to his chest, rolling from side to side, whimpering. Radar released his grip, but let loose a low growl of warning without backing up. Gavin rose cautiously to his feet, blood flowing down his arm, not that he seemed to care or notice. The difference in the two men had never been so stark as now.

Footsteps thundered in the hallway as she realized

his friends were running to the rescue. Somehow, in what had seemed like forever, only a minute or two had passed. Sirens wailed, and this time Jared wouldn't be slipping away. Because she and Gavin had rescued each other, worked as a team, the couple they were always meant to be. She loved him.

And this time, she wasn't going to repeat her mistake in letting him go.

---

Gavin tugged on a clean T-shirt with a wince. Hugh had stitched up his arm while the cops took everyone's statements. The bastard Jared Lewis was in the back of an ambulance under police guard and would never be coming near Stacy again. But God, the bastard had almost won. Stacy's worst nightmare had gotten closer than ever to her even after Gavin's promise that he would never let that happen. Guilt pummeled him over how he'd almost failed to keep her safe.

Things definitely hadn't gone off exactly as planned, but then he'd underestimated Stacy, something he would never do again—if she gave him the chance.

His house was quiet for the first time since Jared had come blasting through that glass. Liam had boarded up the window. The cleanup could wait until later. It was almost daylight. That much he could tell, light and dark. But he would never be the man he was. Would what he had to offer be enough for Stacy? Would he be enough for her?

He sure as hell hoped so, because he loved her so damn much, he didn't know how to say good-bye to her again. But after all she'd been through, the choice had to be hers.

Her future had to be one of her choosing.

The scent of her teased his nose an instant before she touched his shoulder lightly. "How does your arm feel?"

"Just fine. Plenty numb around the stitches, which is a good thing." He closed his closet door. "Hugh's the second best medic I know."

"And the first best would be?" She slid her arms around his neck, her body pressed to his.

"Me, of course," he said with a grin, his hands riding low on her back, bringing her closer to him.

"Ah, you're riding an ego high after your big save there." She toyed with the long hair just brushing the collar of his T-shirt. "Thank you. Truly. You saved my life."

"No, I didn't." More guilt piled on top of the heap inside him. "I failed to keep him away from you."

"How could you even think that? You kept him pinned, risking yourself. If you hadn't done that, I never would have had time to grab your cane. Your friends wouldn't have made it in time for either of us." Her words rang with a fierceness and strength that awed him. "Gavin, I have to confess it felt good to get that swing in for myself. We stopped him, you and I, and that felt amazing."

"We worked together," he realized simply, truthfully. "We saved each other, with some help from Radar."

He felt her nod just before he reached down to scratch his dog's ears. Radar leaned against him, resting his head against Stacy, too. The dog knew. Stacy was a part of his pack now.

"I do love you, Gavin Novak."

"And I love you, Stacy Currie."

"Since the day we met. Now and always. I can trust in that." She arched up on her toes to kiss him, once, twice, holding until she eased back with a sigh.

"Stacy," he said, sweeping her hair back, "can you trust that you're safe now?"

"What do you mean by that?"

"What if I said I want us to leave here, to start over?" He wasn't sure why he was bringing this up now rather than biding his time. But there was a desperation in him to make up for lost years. He couldn't wait another minute after waiting a decade. He knew how precious their love was, and he wouldn't lose another moment with her. "You mentioned wanting to leave, but I want you to be sure. I know this is the only sense of home you've known. Your roots are here. I don't want to take that from you. But if you're sure you want to go, I'm ready to start over."

"I have to admit, leaving the bad memories behind and beginning fresh sounds enticing. But it's familiar here for you in your duplex. Wouldn't it be…difficult for you to adapt? Wherever you are, I'll be happy."

How like her to worry about him. This would have concerned him too a few weeks ago when he'd been struggling with how to find the courage to let her know he'd returned. He hadn't wanted to appear weak in front of this woman. But now, he'd found a new sense of himself and the old confidence returning, even if he couldn't tell the mustard and ketchup bottles apart. That stuff was minor. It didn't matter. He would stumble a few times figuring out a new place, but he'd proven to himself he had something to offer her. "I think we've both lived in the shadows here too long. It's time for us to take our love out into the light."

She wriggled against him enticingly. "What exactly are you proposing?"

"Just that. Proposing. Again." He took her face in his hands, wanting her to feel the intensity in his words, even if he couldn't show her with his eyes. "If you'll have me. I might be physically imperfect, but I've got my head screwed on straight now. I can tell what's most important. In that way, I can see more clearly than ever. And I know I want you in my life, by my side. Always."

"Oh Gavin, you are my first love, my forever love." She held his face right back, the intensity of her words flowing into him every bit as strong. "You are everything I have ever wanted. I was wrong to let you leave without me before. I won't make the mistake of losing you again."

"So that's a yes?" he asked, a smile spreading full out from his face and through him.

"Of course it's a yes." She punctuated her vow with a kiss. "Where should we go?"

"Wherever you choose, as long as we're together. Forever this time." He backed her toward the bed until her knees hooked and they tumbled together onto the mattress. "With you in my life, the future looks bright, my Anastasia."

# ABOUT THE AUTHOR

*USA Today* bestselling author **Catherine Mann** specializes in military romances with over fifty books in print. Catherine's works have also made the WaldenBooks extended list. A RITA winner, she has also won the Bookseller's Best Award. She has finaled in the National Readers' Choice Awards, the Reviewers International Organization Choice Award, the *RT* Reviewers' Choice Award, the Maggie Award, and the RITA Award (six times). Catherine's books have been widely released internationally, including Great Britain, Germany, Spain, France, Portugal, Greece, Turkey, Iceland, Australia, and Japan. She lives with her husband, who is a combat veteran and retired Air Force colonel, near Pensacola in the Florida Panhandle. For more information, visit her website at www.CatherineMann.com.

# TORN

A Protect and Serve Novella

## KATE SERINE

# PROLOGUE

*SADIE*.

Her name flashed through his mind as it had so many times before, his connection to home, to normalcy. She'd been there for him through every high point and low point in his life since she was in pigtails and he was just a little shit who liked to tease her with earthworms until she screamed. Well, until that day she clocked him. That had *definitely* marked a turning point in their friendship.

Ever since then, when shit got crazy, when his dad was bustin' his balls, when his older brothers were being total assholes as only older brothers can be, or, hell— when the world just didn't make any fucking sense—she was there. She was his center. His rock.

And during those long, dark nights in Kandahar when his thoughts caught up with him, when the anxiety and the stress of waiting for a conflict that might never happen came together in a single, crushing weight in the middle of his chest, it was thoughts of Sadie that helped him through it.

*But why now?*

He was supposed to be on patrol, needed to have his head in the game. Why the hell would he be thinking of her now?

He shoved away images of the woman he'd been in love with for as long as he could remember and tried to get his shit together. But even as he forced himself to focus on something other than the memory of her wise, dark eyes sparkling with laughter, he felt dread creeping in and was tempted to settle back into that happy place instead of this godforsaken shithole.

But before he could give in to that urge, he heard his father's rough bark in his head, pushing him as he'd always done, *"Man up, Joseph!"*

*Figures. Leave it to the Old Man to intrude on what little happiness there was to be had in the world…*

Joe tried to chuckle, but the effort sent a wave of fresh hell through his entire body, wringing a guttural cry from him before he could check it. Confused, he blinked rapidly, trying to clear the haze that clouded his vision and to get his bearings. Clumps of dirt rained down around him, while the sunlight streamed through the particles of dust creating tiny rainbows completely incongruous with the chaos that was coming into focus.

Ragged breathing filled his ears, loud but not loud enough to drown out the shrill ringing that made him wince. It took a split second for him to realize the breathing was his own—and it sounded like shit.

Somewhere in the distance, he heard muffled shouting, felt a deep rumble, the vibration transferring through the ground and into his chest.

He was on the *ground*?

*What the fuck?*

Adrenaline shot through his veins. He tried to roll onto his side and push up to his knees, but nothing seemed to function. His arms collapsed under him, his legs wouldn't work. The ground rolled, tilting precariously like the world had been knocked off its axis and was spinning out of control toward the sun.

*Get up or die.*

It was his own voice in his head this time, his survival instincts kicking in when his senses couldn't be trusted. But his body refused to obey. He tried again. Failed. This time, when he fell onto his back, his head lolled to one side and he caught a glimpse of Sadie's photo caught in some of the harsh underbrush that grew sparsely in the region. It was the photo he'd carried on him every day. His stomach sank when he saw it.

Only one reason it wouldn't have been safely tucked away near his heart.

*Ah, shit.*

Panic squeezed his gut in its sickening grasp when he realized what must've happened, but he kept it together. He had to. He'd made a promise.

The breeze caught the edge of the photo, making it flap just enough to taunt him with the threat of dislodging it. Somehow he knew if he didn't get to it first, the harsh desert wind would sweep Sadie away from him forever.

His hand trembled as he extended his arm, straining to reach the photo. But his bloody fingers fell short. He moaned, emotion choking him. He had to reach her, had to get to her.

It wasn't supposed to go down like this, damn it! He'd never told her he loved her, had never held her in his arms. *Fuck.* He was supposed to make it home. He'd promised her.

She was gonna be so pissed…

"Hang in there, Dawson!" someone was yelling as

several pairs of hands suddenly grabbed him, jostling him unmercifully as they tried to assess his wounds. Someone pressed on his abdomen, sending him careening toward darkness even as he shouted, "Stay with me!"

He didn't know who the hell was talking to him, didn't give a shit. There was only one person who mattered. He strained harder, flapping his fingers with a groan of frustration, willing his hand to reach the damned photo. But now they were lifting him up, carrying him, the picture drifting farther and farther away from his grasp. And as he watched, the wind snatched the picture from the grass. It flipped end over end twice and then, for a moment, it was suspended in midair as if time had stopped.

Joe's future seemed to hang in the balance while Fate deliberated. But before he could witness the outcome, darkness wrapped him in its cold embrace and dragged him down.

And there was no war. No blood. No pain. Only Sadie as she was the last time he'd seen her that autumn day before his deployment, her cheeks streaked with tears, her eyes swollen from crying, as she'd pleaded, "Come home to me, Joe."

# CHAPTER 1

*Eighteen months later…*

JOE SNATCHED THE BOTTLE OF AQUAFINA FROM THE shelf and pressed it to his forehead, closing his eyes as the air from the open fridge seeped out and cooled his sweat-slicked skin. He'd finished his run two minutes better than the day before, but it still wasn't anywhere close to what his time had been *before*. Not to mention his lungs were shredded, his leg was killing him, and he had a serious case of swamp ass going.

His rational side kept trying to reassure him that what the hell could he expect after sitting on his ass in the hospital for weeks and then being in rehab for months just to get to the point where he could even *walk* on his left leg again? The fact that he was running at all was a frigging miracle. And he wasn't even going to think about the job that fucking IED had done on his gut.

Joe squeezed his eyes tighter for a moment, pushing away the barrage of images that flooded his brain, a year and a half of therapy not helping a damn bit when it came to keeping them at bay. It'd taken him a couple of weeks after that day before he could actually remember what had happened. He wished he never had. Because then he wouldn't have had to relive the sight of Pete Ryan being blown apart a few yards away from him.

Joe's throat went tight with a mixture of sorrow and

regret. And fear. It could've been him. And by all rights it should've been if Fate had had any sense of justice. Ryan had had a wife and three kids waiting for him stateside, people who needed him. And now those kids would be growing up without their dad while Joe got to come back home to what? A job he was no longer fit to perform and bills he soon wouldn't be able to pay unless he got his ass back to said job.

Joe let fly a string of juicy curses and slammed the fridge door. Irritated with his body's continued limitations, he opened the water bottle and chucked the cap with an enraged groan, then chugged the water, hoping it would cool the fire that raged within him. When that didn't work, he stripped out of his shirt and made harsh swipes over his neck and under his pits before tossing it into the hamper in the adjacent laundry room.

He was just heading toward his bathroom to take a shower when the back door suddenly swung open. Instinctively, he wrapped an arm over his abdomen where the skin was puckered and discolored as he spun around, slightly crouched and at the ready to take on his intruder. When he saw who it was, the tension in his muscles instantly eased.

"Hey," he managed, his breath catching in his lungs for reasons that had nothing to do with being startled. It was the reaction he always had when Sadie walked into a room. "What're you doing here?"

Sadie gave him a wry smile, her flushed cheeks at odds with the playfully reproachful look she gave him. "Well, good morning to you, too, sunshine."

"Sorry," he fumbled with a quick shake of his head. He edged around to the other side of the tiny kitchen island to hide his scars from her view as he continued, "I meant—"

"I knew what you meant," she interrupted with a laugh, the material of her pale pink skirt hugging her killer curves and hitting at just the right spot to accentuate very shapely calves as she drifted toward him to stand on the other side of the island. She tossed her keys on the counter. "Sorry I didn't call—I wasn't sure you'd be awake yet. I just wanted to stop by and give you a present to celebrate your first day back at the department."

Joe grunted before he could check it. His first day back at the sheriff's department wasn't exactly cause to celebrate, in his opinion. Yeah, he'd been a deputy for ten years now, but about half that time had been spent on various deployments with his National Guard unit.

Well, those days were over, that was for damned sure. He'd never be able to serve again, not with his injuries. No matter how hard he pushed himself to get back into shape and return to the peak physical condition he'd been in before everything had gone to shit, he'd received his discharge papers and a purple heart—both of which he'd promptly dropped in the trash bin. Sadie had insisted upon rescuing them and putting them away in a safe deposit box "until he was ready." Ready for what, he wasn't sure. He'd never be ready to accept that he'd lost a damned good friend that day. He'd have to live with that for the rest of his life.

At least the nightmares had started to diminish, and he was finally able to drive without breaking into a cold sweat at the irrational thought that an IED might be buried along the side of the road in rural Northern Indiana. And he could now walk into a crowded room without having a full-blown panic attack that had him doing an about-face to gulp down deep breaths of air and a handful of Tums. The rest of the shit he was still dealing with he'd been able to bury deep enough to convince the review board deciding his case that he could return to duty with the sheriff's department. Well, they'd *seemed* to buy it anyway.

But he had a sneaking suspicion that the only reason he still had a job was because his dad was the sheriff and his two older brothers were pretty much next in command. Their family had been the law in Fairfield County, Indiana, since before it *was* a county. So if Sheriff Mac Dawson wanted his son back in the department, who the hell was going to stop him? He'd proven on more than one occasion to the people of the county that he ran things *his* way and if they didn't like it, they could take their happy asses somewhere else.

Still, for all the outward appearances of acceptance, Joe had heard the whispers when the other deputies didn't think he was listening, had seen the sidelong glances when he'd arrived for his evaluations, and he knew what they were thinking: He wasn't fit for duty. He couldn't be counted on, couldn't be trusted. That he was going to crack at the first sign of stress.

He knew what they were thinking because he was thinking it, too.

Still, when Joe saw the mildly disappointed look in Sadie's eyes at his less than enthusiastic reaction to her gift, he forced a grin and reached out to take the small box wrapped in tissue paper and tied with a red ribbon. "A present for me? Aw, shucks. You shouldn't have."

The charade was worth it when he saw her eyes light

up with anticipation as he worked at the ribbon. She was beaming but seemed a little nervous at the same time, he could tell. She fidgeted, brushed a stray black dog hair from the sleeve of her blouse, grasped the locket she wore—the one he'd given her for her birthday a few years before—and slid it back and forth a little on the chain as she watched him fiddle with the ribbon.

God, she was beautiful. He would've much rather been slowly unbuttoning her white blouse, sliding it from her shoulders, pressing kisses to her creamy skin, her full breasts, than working on the ribbon with fingers that threatened to tremble if he kept letting his thoughts drift to far more pleasurable activities.

When he finally tore open the tissue paper, he was a little startled at what the package held. He had to blink a few times before lifting his gaze to Sadie's. "Bullets?"

When he'd first come home, he'd been so depressed that Sadie had taken all his guns from the house, including his grandfather's revolver. He knew the fact that she had brought him bullets was a sign of her faith in him and his recovery.

Sadie came around the island so that she was standing closer and let her hand rest lightly on his forearm. "You're ready, Joe. You were born to protect and serve the people of this county, and they've been without you for too long."

If his anxiety hadn't been eating away at him, the look in her eyes would've made his chest swell with pride. As it was, the nearness of her was making *other* areas swell. He turned slightly to keep her from noticing, a trick he'd learned back in high school that had served him well over the years. "Thanks, Sade. That means a lot."

She lifted her hand to cup his cheek and forced him to look at her. "I wouldn't say it if it wasn't true, and you know it. I want you to keep that in mind when you go on duty today."

He nodded, swallowing hard and trying not to focus too much on the fact that her palm was so soft against his cheek or that her body was only inches away from his. God, it would've been so easy to wrap his arms around her and whisk her away to his bed.

For a long moment, their gazes met and locked. And something in the air between them shifted, the tension that always flared up whenever they were this close now becoming a palpable force that seemed to build with each breath. Joe's eyes flicked down to her lips, his desire to taste them making his mouth water.

Sadie's thumb lightly caressed his cheek, and she swayed ever so slightly toward him.

Good God, it was torture. He'd wanted her for as long as he could remember. He'd even kissed her once before, when they were fourteen and curious about what exactly a true grown-up kiss was like. It'd been a disaster. He'd gone in too fast, too harsh, and his braces had cut her lips. And that'd been that. He'd never had the balls to try again.

There'd been a few times over the years that they'd come close to kissing again. When he'd held her in his arms while she cried from a recent broken heart after some idiot had dumped her, when she'd comforted him after his mother's death, before he'd left for Afghanistan, and they'd clung to each other, the thought of being parted again too difficult to even put into words. But they'd always held back, afraid that giving in would ruin their friendship.

But this time… Something had changed. There was something *more*, a longing that was impossible to deny.

He slowly slid his hand around to the small of her back, pressing ever so slightly, bringing her just a little closer. He could feel her breath quicken, saw her eyes dilate, growing darker. And to his astonishment, her lids drifted shut.

For a split second he hesitated, their mouths so close the heat of their breath intermingled. But only for an instant. When his lips brushed hers in a tender, lingering kiss, it sent a shot of electricity through every nerve ending in his body. Had he not been drenched in sweat from his run, he would've dragged her against him and finally explored the mystery of those full lips in the way he'd longed to, but knowing she was on her way to work, he had to content himself with gently grasping the nape of her neck, sliding his fingers into the length of the silky chestnut brown hair that fell below her shoulders, and kissing her slowly, languidly, savoring the warmth of her lips as they sought his.

A tiny moan escaped her, buzzing against his lips. Encouraged, he deepened the kiss, his tongue sweeping across the seam of her mouth. It was all he could do not to whoop for joy when her lips parted, inviting him in.

Sadie's hands rested lightly against his chest, her palms a welcome warmth against his already heated skin. He took a half step closer but quickly stepped back when his raging erection threatened to give away just how badly he wanted her. "Ah, God, Sadie," he murmured when her hands began to roam.

"I know," she replied, her voice strained, breathless as she pressed kisses to the corner of his mouth, jaw, chin. "I know."

Then her fingertips brushed against his abdomen, over his scars, and suddenly the spell was broken. He jerked so hard he stumbled backward in his haste to get away from her touch, his back slamming into the counter behind him. He snatched up a discarded dish towel and held it over his ruined skin—among other things.

Sadie's eyes went wide with confusion and concern. "Oh my God, Joe! I'm so sorry!" she gasped, the words tumbling out in a rush. "Did I hurt you? Are you okay?"

She took a step toward him, but he held up his free hand, keeping her from coming any closer. "No, no. I'm fine."

*Uh-huh, riiiight… The woman he'd fantasized about since hitting puberty was finally in his arms and he has a total freak-out. Oh yeah, he was golden.*

Sadie took a deep breath and let it out slowly. Then she tilted her head to one side, her dark eyes boring into his as if she was reading his soul. She took a tentative step toward him. And another. Then she reached out and took hold of the dish towel. For a moment, he thought about tightening his grip, but he let go, allowing her to take it from him.

"You don't have to hide yourself from me, Joe," she assured him softly, clearly sensing the reason behind his response to her touch.

And, hell, why wouldn't she? She'd been at his side during every step of his recovery, taking time off from her job as a high school English teacher to be there for him. She'd seen him through that dark time, had encouraged him to keep going. It was his fear of disappointing her that had gotten him through it all, that would be his driving force to continue getting through it. But he couldn't help but think he'd disappoint her in the end. He was broken, damaged. His body was full of scars—inside and out. She deserved better.

"You should probably go," he managed to grind out. "You'll be late for work."

She immediately drew away and forced a tight smile, then pivoted and strode toward the door—but not before he caught the hurt look in her eyes.

She was already down the steps and striding toward her car by the time he made it out the kitchen door.

—∿∿—

*God, she was an idiot.*

What the hell had she been thinking when she'd given into the temptation to kiss him? The temptation that had plagued her since they were kids, that had filled her dreams every night he'd been on deployment—even when she'd spent those nights next to another man. She'd loved Joe for as long as she could remember; her heart full to bursting every time he smiled or held her close. But they'd always managed to stay "just friends," wary of taking it further for fear of what they might lose. But the realization that she'd almost lost *him* to that IED had rattled her to the core, had forced her brain to finally come to terms with what her heart had always known: She was in love with him.

That knowledge made their platonic promise harder and harder to maintain—especially in moments like this morning when she'd walked into his kitchen using the spare key he'd given her, expecting to just leave the present and go. But there he was, standing in the kitchen in only shorts and running shoes, his bare chest still glistening with manly sweat, his hard-won muscles taut with exhaustion from his workout.

Damn, he was even more gorgeous than she'd remembered! With that mixture of Ryan Reynolds boy-next-door good looks, the sharp edges that stress and experience had added to his face, and the network of scars that marked him as a warrior in every sense of the word, he'd literally made her heart skip a beat. Maybe two. Okay, *definitely* two. And then there were those eyes... The color of whiskey, they used to melt her with a mischievous look, daring her to go along with whatever adventure he'd cooked up.

How many times when they were growing up had he sneaked out his bedroom window at night to come knocking on hers, needing only that look to convince her to go check out the old Conway house where blue lights were supposed to mysteriously dance? Or the old railway cars that had been long abandoned and sat rusting in their haphazard graveyard? Or the church cemetery where the white lady was supposed to walk every Thursday at midnight?

Scared to death and shivering, she'd always go along with his latest scheme for adventure, clinging to his hand—yet knowing that no matter what they came up against, her gallant hero would protect her. Because he'd promised he would. And Joe Dawson never broke a promise.

Now those eyes melted her with the heat she saw there when he looked at her. She'd seen that heat so many times when he thought she wasn't paying attention. She'd seen it when they were standing in his kitchen when she'd walked in unexpectedly to drop off his present. And she'd never wanted him as badly as she had in that moment. Fortunately, she'd been able to quickly recover from the heat that had flooded her cheeks with a flippant remark. If he was going to try to deny the desire that simmered between them, she'd do the same, by God.

*But that kiss…*

It wasn't so easy to recover from *that*. The brush of his lips against hers had sent white-hot heat zipping through her veins to pool in all the right, womanly places. And she'd been sure he felt it, too. But he'd jerked away from her touch, almost ass-planting in his haste to get away from her, for crying out loud. He was embarrassed by his scars, she knew. He thought they made him less desirable. He'd once told her as much after one of his surgeries. It was just a casual remark about how women would be lining up to be with a fine specimen of man like him. But she could see the pain in his eyes when he said it.

And it broke her heart. He'd never had the calm self-assuredness of his eldest brother Tom, whose quiet strength made him the obvious heir-apparent to their family's law enforcement legacy. Nor did he have the cocky swagger of his brother Gabe, who thought he was God's gift to women. And he certainly didn't share the defiant, rebellious streak of his younger brother Kyle, who always felt like he had something to prove. But Joe *had* always had the confident bearing of a man who knew the true meaning of courage. He'd never backed down from a fight, not *once*. To see him lose that confidence now left an agonizing ache in the center of her chest.

"Sadie!" she heard Joe call from the doorway as she hurried to her car. The screen door slammed, echoing down the street in the older residential neighborhood in spite of the heavy shade of the trees that crowded in among the houses, their leaves full and just beginning to turn the bright crimson and gold of autumn. "Let me explain!"

She shook her head, waving his words away with a fluttery motion of her hand. Yeah, like she needed him to make the rejection worse by talking about it…

When she heard him jogging to catch up to her, she jerked open the car door, intent on getting in before he could say another word and add to her humiliation. But the moment she swung open the door, she let out a startled yelp, turning away to avert her eyes and relieved as hell to find Joe's strong arms going around her and pulling her close.

"What the fuck?" he muttered, seeing the wilted, blood-drenched roses lying on the driver's seat. His face was hard when he ordered, "Go back inside."

He didn't wait for her to move, just swept her behind him and edged her quickly back toward the house before she even had the chance to protest. Once they were inside, he peered through the glass panes in the door, eyes narrowed as he scrutinized the surrounding area. "You're calling in sick."

Sadie's heart fluttered at his concern, but she continued, "It's not that easy. I don't have time to find a sub. You don't—"

"How long's this been going on?" he demanded, sending a knowing look over his shoulder. When she opened her mouth to deny prior incidents, he interrupted with, "You're not nearly as upset by this as you should be. So, don't even try to tell me it hasn't happened before. How long's this been going on?"

She hesitated a moment before admitting, "About a year."

The outrage in his eyes was exactly why she hadn't said a word. "Are you *shitting* me?"

Sadie huffed, frustrated with his anger when she'd only been trying to protect him. "Joe, all the books I read on PTSD said—"

"Piss on the books!" he shouted, closing the gap between them in one long stride to take hold of her upper arms. "You should've come to me."

Sadie lifted her gaze to meet his, momentarily mesmerized by the way the morning sunshine streaming in through the kitchen window made the flecks of gold in his whiskey-colored eyes dance with light. "I didn't want you to worry," she murmured, damning the way her heartbeat was thundering in her ears, the tempo picking up the longer he stood this close.

He abruptly released her to run a frustrated hand over his golden brown hair, newly shorn high and tight. "Do you have any idea who it is?"

She shook her head. "It started out with just a few poems left on my desk at school, then explicit notes, telling me what he wanted to do to me. I thought it might've been a student, so I reported it to my principal. But the notes got more intense, violent. A couple of weeks ago, the roses started showing up."

"Do you still have the notes?" Joe asked.

She shook her head. "No, I turned them over to the police."

This brought Joe up short, and his eyes went stormy as he demanded, "Which police, *specifically*?"

Sadie closed her eyes, instantly realizing her mistake. "Your brother. Tom."

Joe's face went rigid at the mention of his eldest brother, his jaw clenched so hard she half expected to hear his molars crack. "I'm driving you to work," he announced. "And then I'm going to have a word with my big brother."

# CHAPTER 2

Tom Dawson glanced up from his paperwork and frowned. "You're early for your shift."

"Yeah, well, I'm clockin' in," Joe retorted as he stormed into Tom's office. He tossed the bag full of bloody roses onto the desk.

"What the hell?" Tom demanded.

Joe jerked his chin at the bag. "You tell me. This was left in Sadie's car when she dropped by my house this morning. Why didn't you tell me some asshole was leaving presents for her?"

Tom glanced toward the open door to his office then got to his feet with a sigh and shut it before resuming his seat behind his desk. "Maybe because I knew how you'd react—and so did Sadie."

Joe raked a hand over his hair, pacing as much as Tom's cramped office would allow. "This is bullshit, Tom. Bullshit! I can't believe you'd keep this from me."

"There's nothing useful to tell you," Tom admitted, spreading his hands. "The notes didn't have any fingerprints on them except Sadie's. And there were too many prints on the flower boxes and cards to get anything useful."

"And that's it?" Joe snapped.

Tom sighed again, this time with an edge of pity. "Whoever is stalking Sadie hasn't done anything more than send her bloody roses and shitty poetry. I don't even have a suspect to investigate."

Joe pulled a hand down his face, hating how helpless he felt. The asshole had been right outside his fucking house, a couple of yards from his door. And he'd moved fast. Sadie had only been inside for a few minutes. And Joe hadn't noticed, hadn't heard anything. Not the car door opening or closing, not another car's motor. Which meant the guy had probably parked his car down the street and walked to Joe's house from wherever he'd parked. Hell, for all he knew, the guy had left his little present and then waited in the bushes, hoping to get a glimpse of Sadie's reaction, taking off only after Joe had ushered Sadie back inside. What if he hadn't followed her outside? What would've happened then?

"You know how these kinds of things work, Tom," he said. "From everything Sadie's told me, it sounds like the guy's upping his game. He's been content to send her poetry, notes until recently. But they're growing more explicit, more violent. And now he's leaving bloody flowers in her fucking car? What's next?"

Tom spread his arms. "What do you want me to do, Joey?"

"What do I want?" He tossed the other bag he carried onto Tom's desk.

"Jesus Christ!" Tom cried, his chair rolling back several inches with the force of his startled reaction.

"I want you to help me find this asshole before Sadie ends up like this!" Joe ground out, jabbing a finger at the mutilated rabbit inside the gallon-sized Ziploc bag. "That's the source of the blood on the roses. I found it in my fucking mailbox, Tom."

Yeah, that'd been a nice surprise. Joe had noticed that his mailbox was ajar when he was backing out of the driveway to take Sadie to work and stopped to check it out. Clearly, the stalker had *wanted* it to be found, had wanted to send a message to Joe, a separate threat just for him that underpinned the one he'd left in Sadie's car. And the best part? The rabbit's head had been ripped off. Not *cut* off. That would've been humane by comparison. This sick bastard had *ripped* the *motherfucking* head off.

And he hadn't been content with that. Oh, no. He'd also gutted it, probably with a pocketknife, and a dull one at that. It was this kind of savage violence that spoke of something more than just a secret admirer who'd taken things too far. He was dangerous, unstable. And it was only a matter of time before he was no longer content to gut rabbits.

"This bastard is off his fucking nut," Joe assured his brother. "Considering there was no blood on my driveway or in the grass around the house, I'm guessing he caught the rabbit and gutted it to bloody up the flowers ahead of time and brought the corpse with him."

Tom nodded, his brows furrowed. "As careful as he's been up until now, preparing everything ahead of time to leave for Sadie makes sense. But my guess is ripping off its head and leaving it in the mailbox for you to find seems like an impulse of rage, probably because she was with another man. You need to be careful, Joe."

"I'm not worried about me," Joe informed him. "I'll take the bastard out if he wants to try something with me. But I can't just sit here with my thumb up my ass and wait for him to make a move on Sadie." What he didn't need to say was that when this guy finally *did* show himself, he knew it would be because he couldn't control himself anymore, couldn't restrain his obsession with Sadie any longer. And after seeing the guy's handiwork on the rabbit, the thought of this sicko getting his hands on Sadie scared the shit out of him.

"I know how much Sadie means to you," Tom told him, his tone infuriatingly calm. "She means a lot to all of us. Hell, she's like the kid sister we never had."

*Kid sister. Right…*

"But I can't assign a deputy to be her personal bodyguard for who knows how long," Tom continued. "Aside from sending out a couple of guys to process Sadie's car and take prints off your mailbox to see if we get anything, there's not shit I can do, and you know it."

"Put me on it," Joe suggested without hesitation. He'd been mulling over just this kind of solution on the drive over to the department. When Tom opened his mouth to protest, Joe said in a rush, "You know the guys are nervous about me coming back on duty, but the Old Man wants me back on the job. So assign me to the case. You're car two. Who's going to argue with you about it?"

Tom frowned at the slang term for the sheriff's second in command. "I might be executive deputy, but I still can't put you on the case," he insisted. "It's personal. You couldn't be objective."

"Bullshit," Joe shot back. "I know I've been through a hell of a lot, Tom, but I need you to trust me. So pull strings, kiss asses—whatever you have to do in order to make this happen. I'm not letting something happen to Sadie because of red tape."

"I can't assign you, Joe," Tom reiterated, holding

up his hand, halting the furious protest that immediately rose to Joe's lips. "But I can't control what you do on your own time either—like look over the case file. And if you offer up any suggestions based on your own observations…"

Joe gave him a terse nod. That was good enough for him. Now, he just needed this asshole to make a mistake. One mistake. And then he was going down.

———— ∿ ————

"Hey, Ms. Keaton."

Sadie glanced up from grading quizzes on Charlotte Perkins Gilman's *The Yellow Wallpaper* and offered Sam Hittle a smile. "Hey, Sam. Did you forget something?"

The tall, powerfully built senior grunted. "Left my book." He held up his bulky *Norton Anthology*. "Again."

Sadie gave him an amused grin and folded her hands on her desk. "This is becoming a habit. Something tells me you're forgetting it on purpose. Not subconsciously trying to avoid the unit on women's literature, are you, Sam?"

"Of course not, Ms. Keaton," he drawled with a hint of sarcasm, giving her a disarming smile that brought dimples to his cheeks, a smile that was no doubt the reason for the throngs of high school girls that flocked to every single one of his football practices to sigh and giggle over the handsome boy.

When she gave him a knowing look, the impudent cad winked at her and brandished the anthology like a trophy before pivoting and jogging toward the door. But he came to an abrupt halt at the doorway when he found it blocked.

"Sorry, dude," Sam said in a rush, holding up his free hand.

Sadie struggled to stifle the gasp of surprise—and desire—that escaped her when she saw Joe standing in the doorway, dressed in his Class A's and looking hot as hell. She'd never thought of herself as a holster sniffer—the term the deputies used to refer to the law enforcement groupies who threw themselves at anything and everything with a badge—but she had to admit, raw masculinity and fierce authority looked seriously freaking good on Joe.

"Dude?" Joe repeated, giving Sam a stern look. "That's 'Deputy Dawson' or 'sir' to you, son."

Sam cast a glance over his shoulder at Sadie. "Oh, hey—is this *the guy*?"

She flushed for the second time that day when Joe sent her a questioning glance. Oh, good. More humiliation. Because she hadn't been tormenting herself with memories of their kiss and his subsequent backpedaling all day or anything…

"You've heard about me?" Joe asked, not moving his gaze away from her face.

"Oh, yeah," Sam told him, ever helpful. "When you were on deployment, we did a big care package project for honor society. And thank-you letters at Thanksgiving and stuff. It was pretty cool. Thanks for your service, man—uh, I mean, *sir*."

Joe's brows lifted slightly. Then he finally turned his attention to Sam and shook his extended hand, giving him a terse nod. An awkward silence fell in the room for a few seconds before Sam jerked his thumb over his shoulder. "Well, I guess I better get to practice before coach kicks my ass."

Sadie gave him a disapproving look. "Language, Sam."

He just grinned and slipped through the doorway when Joe took a step inside.

"You told your students about me?" Joe asked as soon as Sam was gone.

Sadie busied herself with her papers, gathering everything together now that her ride was here—and to keep from having to look at him too long for fear of breaking out into spontaneous drooling. "Of course," she said with a shrug. "I thought it would be great for the students to support our troops as part of their service projects."

Joe's smug grin grew. "There are plenty of servicemen and -women in the county you could've mentioned."

*Yeah, but I wasn't in love with any of* them…

"It helps if they can make a personal connection," she evaded. "Several of the students knew someone deployed, but most didn't. I gave them a name and a face, a real person, to make the project more meaningful."

He nodded, strolling toward her, a hint of his grin still tugging at the corners of his full mouth, making her wonder what he was thinking, for he was clearly preoccupied as he visually inspected the room, taking in her surroundings with his scrutinizing gaze.

"So," she said, trying to keep her tone light, "how's your shift going?"

He grunted. "I haven't even had so much as a traffic violation. I'm sure Tom thought he was doing me a favor by putting me in a slow area, but it was boring as hell. On the upside, it gave me time to go over your file."

She swallowed hard, waiting for another admonishment for not telling him about her stalker, but when it didn't come, she was glad to change the subject. "Did you hear from Kyle?"

At the mention of his younger brother who'd broken family tradition—and their father's heart—by joining the FBI instead of the sheriff's department, Joe's smile actually reached his eyes. "Yeah. Called to tell me I was a total loser and that I'd probably fuck up my first day back."

She laughed. "Nice. Dare I ask how you responded?"

He chuckled. "There was more than a little profanity involved. And I might've invited him to bite my ass."

*Brothers.*

Being an only child, she'd never quite understood the Dawson brothers' brand of affection for one another. But having grown up next door to the houseful of rowdy boys, she'd always had a front-row seat to the brawls in the front yard that often ended in bloody noses, black eyes, and more than a little laughter. They might talk tough and give each other a hard time, but they'd always have each other's backs.

"Any chance he'll be coming back to town soon?" she asked, trying not to focus too much on the way his uniform hugged his broad shoulders and toned pecs.

Joe shook his head. "Nah. He's determined to stay pissed at the Old Man. And you know my dad—no way in hell is he going to admit *he* was wrong."

She caught the bitter note in Joe's voice and decided to change the subject once again, "Any word on my car?"

"The guys towed it in for processing," he told her, turning his back and giving her a good look at a ridiculously fine ass as he skimmed the student poetry she had hanging on the bulletin board. "You can borrow mine until they're finished." Before she could ask about its return, he turned back to her and jerked his thumb over his shoulder. "How recent are these poems?"

She shook her head, a little confused as to why he'd be asking. "Uh…they were from an assignment we did a few weeks ago in my creative writing class. I do a poetry unit at the beginning of the school year."

She could practically see him mentally sorting through the data as he tried to put the pieces together—and the frustration when the pieces didn't fit. "Any of the students last year have a similar writing style to your stalker?"

Her eyebrows came together in a frown. "I didn't really try comparing any of them."

He jerked his head toward the doorway. "Who was *that* kid?"

Her brows shot up. "*Sam?* He's one of my best and brightest. Honor student, star athlete."

Joe heaved a sigh, clearly having hoped she'd have something else to say. "Any other students come to mind? Pissed off about grades? Any bullies—or kids being bullied—who'd be trying to get your attention?"

She shook her head. "No one comes to mind. Just the same teenage angst and attitude I always get."

"You said that the notes were showing up on your desk at first, right?" he asked, his brows knit together tightly in a dark frown. "Whoever was leaving the notes had to have access to your office. And the school's doors are always locked during the day."

"But not after school," she argued. "Too many activities going on. And even though I lock my classroom before I leave, all the building locks are keyed the same.

So anyone with a key could still get in—staff, teachers, student assistants, cleaning crews... It's hardly Fort Knox after you get inside the building."

He put his hands on his hips in frustration, the position making his biceps bulge beneath the fabric of his shirt. "What about parents or colleagues? Any of them unusually friendly? Or *un*friendly?"

She'd certainly had her fair share of irate parents over the past few years, but she honestly couldn't think of anyone who held a grudge or what would be considered an unhealthy obsession. Was she being too naive? Had she missed something somewhere? Had she overlooked some vital clue? "No," she told him, wishing she could give him something to work with.

"What about that ex of yours?" Joe asked, an edge in his voice that was unmistakable. Her heart fluttered at the thought that he might actually be jealous. "The beefcake."

She winced a little, hoping he didn't catch it. She'd had a hard and fast rule about not dating coworkers, but she'd suffered a serious lapse in judgment when it came to Sean Jackson. She'd been lonely after Joe's deployment, missed him desperately. Hell, if truth be told, she'd been lonely long before then, even during those brief periods when she'd been in a relationship, trying to convince herself that she could be happy with someone other than the man she was already in love with.

True to her dating form, she'd only dated Sean for a couple of months before she'd broken things off. At first, she'd worried about how he'd take it, seeing as how Sean's ego had proven to be *his* true love. But he hadn't seemed perturbed in the least.

"That ended amicably," she said.

Joe jerked his chin at her. "Says you. I want to talk to him."

<center>~~~</center>

Sean Jackson was a tool. That was the nicest way Joe could put it. The guy stood there with his bodybuilder muscles, in his tight athletic shorts and too-tight T-shirt that clearly showed off his bulging biceps and spray tan, chomping his gum like a teenager, wearing his whistle like a medal. Dude needed to let go of his high school glory days. And lay off the 'roids.

"Welcome back, buddy," Jackson managed through the *smack, smack, smack* of his chewing gum, extending his hand to Joe. "Glad to see you're back up on your feet."

Joe shook the offered hand and sent a glance Sadie's way, wondering just how much people knew about him. "Thanks."

"So…what? You two together now?" the coach asked, gesturing back and forth between the two of them.

But before either of them could respond, Jackson suddenly blew his whistle before barking out instructions at his players, berating them rather colorfully for screwing up the last play. When he'd finished, he turned his overly white grin on Joe and Sadie. "What brings ya by?"

Joe narrowed his eyes a little at the coach, marveling at how the guy could just turn his anger on and off like a switch. "You know anything about the notes someone's been leaving Sadie?" he asked pointedly, not liking the way Jackson's gaze kept flicking down to Sadie's cleavage.

"What kind of notes?" Jackson asked. He grunted. "Another parent pissed that their precious snowflake flunked a test?"

"Parents are always getting upset if they think their children were graded unfairly," Sadie explained, shrugging it off. "The notes I've been receiving are far more… *personal* in nature."

Jackson pulled back just a little, glancing back and forth between Joe and Sadie before his lips curled up in a wide grin that didn't quite reach his eyes. "Oh, I get it. And you think 'cause Sadie and I had a thing for a while that I might be leaving her these notes."

Joe lifted a shoulder in a half shrug. "Gotta ask."

Jackson suddenly caught a glimpse of the play going to hell on the field and blew sharply into his whistle. "What the hell was *that*?" he demanded. "Get your heads out of your asses!"

Joe shook his head. *Oh yeah, total tool*.

Jackson's face was still flushed from his outburst when he turned back to Joe, puffing out his chest. "Well, it ain't me. I've got babes linin' up to have a go. I sure as hell don't need to chase after some chick who doesn't know what she's missin'." He jerked his chin at Sadie. "No offense."

Sadie laughed drily and shook her head. "None taken. Trust me."

That was Joe's cue to wrap it up. "Thanks for chatting with us, Coach. I'll be in touch if I have any other questions."

Jackson gave him an absent nod before yelling, "Seriously, Parker? What the hell was that? You got a sister? Maybe *she* can throw worth a damn!"

As Joe led Sadie back to his patrol car, he rested his hands on his gun belt, vaguely noting how good it felt to have the heft of it around his waist again, even if it did pull at the still-sensitive skin on his stomach. "Charming guy."

"I seem to recall more than one questionable choice in your dating history, Joe Dawson," she shot back.

Couldn't argue there. The biggest one being that he'd never asked *her* out. "Yeah, well," he chuckled, "they all had their finer points."

"Oh, uh-huh," Sadie said, nodding with mock agreement. "And if I'm not mistaken, most of those 'finer points' were right about"—she brought her fists up near her breasts and made a popping sound as she shot out her index fingers—"here."

Joe threw his head back with a laugh and draped an arm around her shoulder, hugging her close for a moment before he remembered he was still on duty. His arm dropped back to his side, and he edged to his left, putting a little space between them.

After a moment of tense silence, Sadie linked her arm through his, leaning on him to keep the heels of her pumps from sinking into the grass, and asked, "So what now?"

He took a deep breath and blew it out in a frustrated burst. "Hell if I know. I guess we wait until he makes another move. I just wish you'd told me about this sooner."

Her gaze flicked guiltily up to his as they reached the car, but she quickly looked away when he opened the door for her to get in. "You were a little busy getting your life back together, Joe," she muttered. "I didn't really want to burden you with my problems."

He wanted to argue with her, insist he hadn't been such a fucking wreck that she couldn't have confided in him. But the truth was, he *had* been. And it was her love and support that had gotten him through it. Now it was his turn to be there for *her*, unconditionally. He chucked her gently on the chin. "Let's worry a little less about me and more about you, whaddya say?"

She rested her hand on the top of the door, brushing her fingers briefly over his. "I can't make any promises there."

Taking a chance and knowing he was a total idiot even as he did it, he slid his hand forward just enough that their fingers were laced together. "Try," he pleaded, his voice low.

She glanced at their intertwined fingers, then lifted her eyes to him. "Okay," she relented. "For you."

He smiled down at her, loving the way her eyes danced when she looked at him that way. And, like an idiot, he burst out with, "Sadie, I..." But his voice trailed off, the words that sat on the end of his tongue, still too heavy to give voice to.

And there it was—that sudden tension that filled the air between them, that unspoken desire that simmered just below the surface. She must've felt it too, because she quickly turned away and got in the car, slamming the door shut and nearly nailing his fingers in the process.

Joe closed his eyes for a moment. The back and forth between them was torture. Complete and utter torture. He wasn't sure if he was a dumbass or a chicken shit for not just telling her how he felt and putting it out there, confessing what was becoming harder and harder to suppress. And considering how he'd been reliving their kiss over and over again throughout the day only to have to divert his thoughts to keep Little Joe from popping up with an ill-timed "Hi, how are ya!" he was inclined to add *pathetic loser* as an option...

# CHAPTER 3

SADIE POURED ANOTHER GLASS OF CHARDONNAY, hoping it would help her wash down the chicken that was sticking in her throat like ash. She glanced up at Joe where he sat across the table, eating in awkward silence. He'd showered after getting home from his shift and changed into low-slung jeans and a loose-fitting Army T-shirt, looking far too hot for his own good. As usual.

The rock band Snow Patrol was playing on the stereo in her living room, the soothing music the only thing filling the silence. The tension between them had never been this heavy. In fact, there'd been a time when sitting in companionable silence was comfortable, welcome. Back when they were in high school, they'd just lie on a blanket in the meadow behind their houses, staring up at the clouds and dreaming about what the future might hold. There'd been no need for words then. They'd known each other so well. There was no mystery in a glance, a sigh. Not like now. With everything going on, she'd never longed for those days as badly as she did at that moment.

She had to admit to having a bit of a panic attack when he told her he'd be staying at her house for a couple of days in an effort to make it look like they were together, show the stalker that she had a male presence in the house. It also would give him the chance to give her parents' old house the once-over and make sure it was safe for her to be there on her own when he couldn't be with her. Had his father still been living in one of the only other houses on the secluded street, he would've felt a lot better, but Mac Dawson had sold the home after the death of his wife, and the current owners were veritable strangers, rarely home.

Sadie hadn't realized just how little she knew about her neighbors until Joe had quizzed her on their names and daily habits. When they were growing up, it had always been a tightly knit rural community where neighborhood kids could stay out after dark catching fireflies without their parents worrying about where they were or if they were safe. She'd taken for granted that it still was that way. She'd certainly never worried about her *own* safety before now.

Oh, sure, she'd considered having an alarm system installed on the old house after her parents retired to Charleston, but she'd quickly dismissed the idea. This was a community where people left their doors unlocked at night, their keys in their cars. She'd never imagined she might actually have reason to worry. But recent events—and Joe's litany of questions—made her realize just how wrong she'd been.

That said, it'd been a week now and nothing had happened. Nothing. At. All. Not with her stalker and not with Joe. And him sleeping in the guest room just down the hall every night made her want to scream in frustration. To have him right there, so close, with nothing but a wall and an antiquated promise to remain *friends* separating them, had become a special kind of torture. Not to mention seeing how worried he was for her safety didn't do much to calm her nerves.

It was the PTSD. That's what she kept telling herself. She'd read in all the books that soldiers suffering from post-traumatic stress could exaggerate threats to those they cared about, would be hypersensitive to the safety of their family and friends. That had to be it. Because, jealous or not, that sicko who'd been stalking her wouldn't really get to the point of trying to do her harm. *Would he?* Not when she'd taken every possible precaution she could think of and now a sheriff's car was parked out front. *Right?*

She cleared her throat, no longer able to stand the silence. If Joe was going to be there all night, they'd have to talk at some point. "So," she began, clearing her throat again when the word stuck. "Have you found anything in the file that we might've missed?"

Joe took a swig of his beer before answering. "No. Nothing."

She studied him for a moment, knowing that frown well. "And that worries you."

He nodded. "I've gone over everything a dozen times. Tom was right—the guy's meticulous, not a single piece of evidence. He hasn't called or emailed or anything traceable. There're no fingerprints to work with. And I checked with the local florists—they don't have any deliveries on record for you. And the roses were just generic flowers you could find at any gas station or grocery store. There was nothing unusual about them at all. Nothing to tell us where he got them."

"He's thought of everything," Sadie said, unable to keep the worry out of her voice. "God, Joe, what the hell are we going to do? I saw how you looked at that rabbit the other morning. This is more than just some obsessed secret admirer, isn't it?"

Joe set aside his fork and got to his feet, coming around to her side of the table. Without a word, he took her hand and pulled her to her feet…and into his arms. She slipped her arms around his waist just above where she could feel the bulge of the weapon concealed at the small of his back and rested her head on his chest. For several moments, they just stood there, holding on to each other. But then she felt him take a deep breath and let it out slowly and knew the perfect moment of peace was about to end.

"Sadie," he said, his voice hesitant. "About that morning—"

A sudden crash in the kitchen cut off his words. Before she even realized what'd happened, he'd abruptly set her away from him and pulled his Glock, every muscle in his body taut, on alert and ready for a fight.

She opened her mouth to ask what the hell was going on, but he held a finger to his lips and motioned for her to stay where she was. Sadie's heart raced, her blood pounding in her ears, every instinct urging her to run, but she nodded.

Joe crept toward the swinging door that led from the dining room to the kitchen, the only escape from the tiny dining room in the old Victorian home. He took a deep breath, then threw open the door, his gaze sweeping the room. Finding it clear, he darted away from the wall, peeking through the gap between the door and the frame, getting a quick look at that side of the room as well. Still not seeing the source of the noise, he motioned once more for Sadie to stay back and pivoted away from the wall and into the room, gun outstretched. A few seconds later, he cursed and stormed back into the dining room, gun down at his side.

"What was it?" Sadie asked, her heart in her throat.

Joe ran a hand over his hair. Then, with a quirked eyebrow, he held open the door and whistled. In response, a very guilty-looking black Lab slunk into the room, his muzzle slathered with sauce. "Looks like Jasper decided to do a little counter surfing for his dinner this evening."

Sadie gasped then laughed, snorting with the force of her relieved mirth, which only served to make her laugh harder. She doubled over as the tension melted away. Finally, when her stomach muscles began to ache, she straightened, wiping tears from her cheeks, hoping to see Joe laughing too and maybe catch a glimpse of the smile she so adored. But instead, he was leaning against the dining room wall, his head back, eyes squeezed shut.

Her laughter instantly died. "Joe?"

He heaved a sigh. "I don't know how I'm going to do this, Sadie."

She went to him, cupping his cheek. "Do what?"

"Go back to being a deputy." He opened his eyes, meeting her gaze. "Yeah, this week has been fine. Uneventful. But when Jasper knocked that damned pan off the counter, I nearly hit the frigging deck. How am I going to deal with it when I'm actually up against some asshole who's trying to hurt me?" His brow furrowed, his gaze growing more intense as he searched her face. "Or hurt someone I love."

*Someone he loved? Did that mean…? Was he saying…?*

Sadie smoothed her thumb over his cheek, her heart

thundering with tentative hope that was growing more certain as their gazes held. She almost pulled back, afraid of another humiliating rejection like she'd experienced a few days ago, but then Joe's arm slid around her waist, drawing her to him. And then his lips were brushing against hers, so warm, so gentle.

Her arms went around his neck, not about to let him back out of their kiss this time. She pressed her body into his, their kiss growing more insistent, frenzied, their breath coming in gasps as he pushed off the wall and walked her a few steps backward. For one crazy second, she thought maybe he was going to sweep their dinner from the table and take her right there, but then she heard the heavy thud of his gun as he set it down to free up his hands.

And—*oh, dear God*—those hands were magical. Rough, callused, powerful...*manly*. They slid under the hem of her T-shirt, lightly caressing her back until reaching the clasp of her bra. A quick flick of his fingers. She gasped, breaking their kiss as he cupped her breast, his thumb brushing over her nipple and making her shiver.

"I want you, Sadie," he breathed against the curve of her throat, pinching her aching nipple, rolling it, making it impossible for her to do more than nod. "I always have."

In the next instant, he was pulling her shirt over her head and tossing it aside. Her bra followed. For a millisecond, she almost brought her arms up to cover her chest to hide herself from his gaze, but then he was pulling her back to him, claiming her mouth in a harsh kiss. And his hand was sliding past the waistband of her jeans, cupping her ass with rough, demanding hands. And there was only one thing on her mind…

―――∞∞―――

This was wrong. Joe knew it even as he and Sadie slammed into the wall of the upstairs hallway in their blind desperation to make it to her bedroom. He bent, taking one of her perfect breasts into his mouth, the little moan in the back of her throat making his already painfully hard cock throb even harder. Christ, if he didn't bury himself in her soon, he was gonna blow like some virgin teenager.

He groaned, sliding his hand down between them, his heart somersaulting with joy when he found her burning up with need, already slick and ready for him. She cried out a little as his fingertip brushed against the sensitive bud of nerves.

"Oh no," he murmured with a low chuckle. "Not yet."

She writhed against his hand with a little whimper. "Please, Joe," she gasped, tearing at his fly. "I want you inside me. Now."

*Holy hell. Okay, then.* So much for his *go slow* strategy. He just hoped like hell she had a condom somewhere because he sure as shit hadn't bought any in the last couple of years… But before they could take another step, Sadie was pulling him down to the ground, her hands pushing his jeans over his hips and freeing his swollen cock, taking him in her hand. She stroked him, gentle but purposeful, making his head spin.

*Sweet Jesus.*

Why in the hell had they waited so damned long? He shuddered, perilously close to losing it, and cursed under his breath. "Sadie," he rasped out, grasping her wrist to still her hand. When she frowned, confused, he offered her as much of a grin as he could muster, then slid her jeans and panties over her hips, along those luscious thighs, down her shapely calves. He kissed his way back up, his mouth and tongue tasting every inch of her. When he reached her swollen sex, she lifted that sweet ass, urging him on with a strangled sound of need that sent a shudder through him. How could he resist?

She shattered apart the second his tongue flicked. But he grasped her hips and pushed her through her climax until she gasped his name and clawed at his shoulders, desperately trying to drag him back up into her arms. At last, he relented—if for no other reason than her gasps and moans of pleasure were making his cock weep with need, and he was hanging on by a very thin, very taut thread.

He was panting with the effort to hold back, his voice strained and rough when he gasped, "I don't have a condom with me."

But even as he said it, he was lowering himself between her legs, and she was guiding him to her sweet heat, arching into him. He'd always been safe—even when he was a stupid teenager who'd bang anything with a pulse. He always knew he'd only have unprotected sex with the woman he married. And there was only one woman he'd ever pictured in that role. And she was lying naked beneath him on the hallway floor, beautiful, sexy, and wanting *him*, too.

He plunged deep, sheathing himself completely, making them both gasp.

"Oh, God, Joe," Sadie moaned, breathless as she rose to meet each thrust of his pelvis. "I love you."

He instantly went still, the words knocking the air from his lungs. He blinked down at her, hardly daring to believe what she'd said. "What?"

---

Sadie wrapped her legs over Joe's ass, the look in his eyes making her fear he was about to bolt again. "I love you," she whispered, rolling her hips against him, not wanting him to stop. Their bodies had been joined mere moments, and Sadie was already perilously close to coming again. "Every time I've said it… This is how I meant it."

He peered down at her for a long moment. "Sadie," he breathed finally. "I don't want you to say that because you think you have to…"

She took his face in her hands, searching his gaze. "I *do* have to," she insisted. "Because it's the way I feel. I always have. And I don't want you to stop making love to me. Not ever."

Joe held her gaze for a moment longer, but then something in his expression changed. And he claimed her mouth, savagely, hungry and demanding. And then he was thrusting hard, deep, claiming every ounce of pleasure that was theirs to share. Sadie rocked with each hard thrust, loving the way he filled her.

And as her pleasure reached its climax, starting at the center of her and exploding outward, she cried out, curling into him, clinging to him as he continued to rock her through it. And then when she felt his muscles begin to tense, she slid her hands up the shirt he'd refused to remove, dug her fingernails into his back as another climax built, urging him on and screaming his name when the next one shook her even more than the first. And when he finally let go, she wrapped her arms around his neck and held him close, pressed kisses to his shoulder, his cheek, and then his lips.

This time their kiss was slow, tender, unhurried. When it ended, she pulled on the edge of his shirt, pushing it up until, after a moment's hesitation, he pulled back enough so that she could pull it over his head.

"I want all of you, Joe Dawson," she told him when his gaze shuttered and he seemed on the verge of closing down on her. "For always."

His expression softened then as he smoothed her hair. "Then I suppose I should get you off this floor and make love to you properly. Because I don't plan on going anywhere."

His words filled her with joy so intense that it was all she could do not to break into tears. But she somehow managed to just lift a brow and give him a flirtatious grin. "You mean it gets better than *that*? I'm not sure how that's even possible. Because—sweetheart—that was un-*freaking*-believable."

A smug smirk curled his lips. "Oh, baby... You ain't seen nothin' yet."

# CHAPTER 4

SADIE CURLED UP ON HER SIDE, WATCHING THE shadows play over Joe's face as he slept on his back, arms over his head, only a sheet covering him from the waist down. They'd made love twice more that night before taking a long, steamy shower together that had ended up in yet another intimate tangle.

She'd never considered herself a prude by any stretch of the imagination, but the level of pleasure and abandon she'd experienced with Joe far surpassed anything she'd experienced before. Whether that was more a testament to his mind-blowing skills in the bedroom or to the depth of her love was hard to say. She didn't care. All that mattered was that he was there beside her, that they'd at last found their way into each other's arms—and the result had been a level of bliss she'd never imagined possible.

Sadie traced a fingertip down the center of his chest to the network of scars on his abdomen that she'd glimpsed earlier. He'd been self-conscious about them even in the shower—until she'd kissed her way down to them and then over to the erection that had swiftly risen in response. She was pretty sure at that point he wasn't concerned about *anything*…

A slow grin grew on Joe's lips as if he were reading her thoughts, and his arm snaked around her, pulling her close. "Why aren't you sleeping?" he murmured, rolling onto his side to face her.

"Couldn't." She grinned, shifting a little so that her breasts were pressed against his chest. Then she snaked an arm around his neck and pulled him to her for a long, sultry kiss. God, she'd never get enough of him. Every touch, every kiss ignited a fire in her.

Things were really starting to get interesting again when a loud crash brought Joe's head up. Every muscle in his body went tense, on alert.

"It's probably just Jasper," Sadie assured him. "We didn't exactly get around to cleaning up the kitchen. Besides, Jasper would bark if there was something to worry about."

"Probably," Joe said, slipping from the bed. "But I'm gonna take a look. Stay here."

Sadie threw off the covers and grabbed a pair of black yoga pants and a bright pink Butler University T-shirt from her dresser drawer, listening intently as Joe crept through the house. She heard a soft rustle—probably him pulling on his discarded clothes.

She moved to the bedroom doorway, holding her breath as she waited. Joe's cache of weapons was in a box under her bed, but, except for the box she'd gifted to Joe, she'd given all the bullets to his brother Tom for safekeeping. Aside from throwing one of the guns at an intruder, they weren't going to do a whole lot of good.

She waited, heart pounding for who knows how long, every second that ticked by ratcheting her anxiety for Joe's safety a notch higher. She heard Joe opening and closing her front door. And then the back door. And for a long moment she held her breath, listening intently.

Suddenly, a shuffle down the hall startled a gasp from her, but the shadowy figure's loping gait made her heave a sigh of relief. "Jasper!" she scolded, shaking her head. "What have you been into this time?"

Then she brought her gaze back up to see another hulking shadow at the end of the hall. "Oh, God, Joe!" she laughed. "You scared the crap out of me!"

—⁓—

Joe stuck to the shadows as he crept along the perimeter of the house. He was just making his way to the side yard, when he caught movement out of the corner of his eye and turned just in time to catch a glimpse of a tall figure booking it toward the meadow.

Fury burned in Joe's veins. He raced after the sick perv, glad he'd taken the last few months to work up his strength and endurance again after his recovery because the fucker was fast, especially given his size.

"Stop!" Joe ordered, patting his pocket for his cell phone and finding it missing. Belatedly, he realized it must've fallen out on the floor of the hallway, either when he and Sadie had been ripping off each other's clothes or in his mad scramble to pull them back on.

*Shit.*

The guy darted right, bolting toward the tree line. But Joe shifted direction just as quickly, his legs pumping, swiftly gaining ground in spite of the searing pain in his leg as the damned thing began to protest.

During his search of the house, he'd grabbed his gun from the dining room table where he'd left it earlier that night, but he couldn't shoot at that asshole, no matter how tempted he was. Not unless his life or Sadie's was in danger. "Stop!" he ordered again. "Police!"

The guy surged forward with a sudden burst of speed,

but then he began to slow. Joe was panting as he slowed his own pace and brought his gun up, aiming it at the guy's center of mass. "Turn around. Slowly."

The guy held up his hands and did as he was told.

Joe frowned when he realized who it was. "You?" he blurted. "*You're* the one stalking Sadie?"

"I can explain!" Sam said in a rush. "It's not what you think!"

"Says you," Joe shot back. "You're under arrest, you little bastard."

"Dude!" Sam pleaded, taking a step forward before halting again. "Okay, yeah, I was looking into Ms. Keaton's windows." He paused, his expression agonized in the moonlight as he glanced around as if expecting others to suddenly appear. He leaned forward a little and lowered his voice when he said, "I saw your car parked out front on my way home from my girlfriend's house, okay? She lives about two miles down the road. And, you know—I was curious. I mean, Ms. Keaton is *seriously* hot, man. Why the hell do you think I keep forgetting my shit in her class? But I was just hoping to catch a glimpse of her tits or something. I'm not *stalking* her!"

"Yeah?" Joe eyed the kid for a moment longer before gesturing at him to head back to the house. "We'll see about that. Let's go."

Sam started back toward Sadie's house, his head hanging, his feet dragging with each step. "This is *so* messed up," he muttered. "My dad's going to have a total freak out if he finds out I was looking in somebody's window. I swear to God I've never done that before…"

Joe grunted. "Sure you haven't."

"I'm telling the truth!" Sam insisted, speaking in

such a rush Joe had to work to keep up with what he was saying. "I didn't even see *anything*! It's not like I climbed the tree to look in the upstairs windows or some shit. Hell, I was just getting ready to leave when I heard you knock over Ms. Keaton's trash can and hid out in the bushes until the coast was clear. But you showed up again when I was coming out to head back to where I'd parked my car on the road, and—"

Joe stopped dead, shaking his head. "I didn't knock over the trash can." Dread sucker-punched him in the gut, making his stomach heave. He bolted toward the house, yelling over his shoulder, "Call the police!"

---

"What the hell are you doing in my house?" Sadie demanded, moving a little closer to where Jasper sat at her side, panting merrily at seeing their visitor. Of course, maybe he'd have been a little more unsettled if he hadn't known her intruder.

"Well," Sean drawled, strolling toward her, his broad shoulders slightly hunched over, "my present to you earlier this week didn't seem to get my message across, so I figured it was time to deliver one in person. Little easier, this time around, though. Didn't have to hide my car down the block like I had to do at your little boy-friend's house—just parked in the neighbors' driveway. I remembered you telling me once that they're never home. Thanks for that info, babe."

Her eyes went wide. She remembered that conversation! It'd taken place months before they'd even started dating. She'd been lamenting her lack of neighbors at a staff cookout, wishing they could have neighborhood get-togethers like some of her colleagues described. He'd obviously tucked that info away for future reference. The arrogant asshole had been plotting even back then!

"Get out of my house, you son of a bitch," she hissed. She edged down the hall as she spoke, trying to put more distance between them as he continued to advance and wondering if she could make it to the bathroom and lock herself in, maybe crawl out the window, before the bastard could get to her. "We were through months ago. You weren't even upset!"

Sean smirked, continuing forward. "'Cause I knew you'd come around. It was just going to take some persuasion. But then that fucking gimp came home, and he was all you cared about. Well, don't worry, babe." He held up his hand, flashing the gun he held. "Soon, it'll just be the two of us again."

*Holy shit.*

Sadie swallowed past the growing panic, her mind racing. "So help me God, Sean, if you hurt Joe—"

"You'll what? Kick my ass?" Sean laughed derisively and flexed, growling, then cackled again, enjoying his own joke. "Yeah, I'd like to see that one. But you go ahead and fight me right up until I go balls deep. Make it more fun for me."

Sadie's gaze flicked toward the open bathroom door, debating her odds. Deciding to take a chance, she pivoted and lunged, grabbing the door and trying to slam it shut, but Sean was already there. He shoved, sending her stumbling backward, her head striking the edge of the bathtub. She was laying on her back, fighting against the darkness that momentarily threatened to descend, when Sean's face came into view, his cruel smirk chilling her to the bone.

---

Joe's instinct was to barrel in when he reached the back door, take out the motherfucker, but his training quickly overrode his instinct. It wasn't going to do Sadie a damned bit of good if he got them both killed. He took a deep breath and let it out slowly, quietly turning the knob and throwing open the door. He sidestepped in a swift arc just outside the doorway, his Glock at the ready, clearing the kitchen in a glance.

He'd just cleared the dining room, assuring the asshole wasn't in there when he heard Jasper barking up a storm overhead.

*Gotcha.*

Joe moved quickly but quietly, his steps nearly silent as he crept along the wall. The initial panic he'd felt outside when he realized Sadie's stalker was inside the house had settled to a deadly calm. The bastard was going down. It was up to that asshole if he left the house in handcuffs or a body bag.

---

Darkness threatened again as Sadie tried to push out of Sean's chokehold, struggling for air and trying her damnedest to stay conscious. Jasper was snarling at Sean, barking furiously, the sound echoing strangely in her head. She blinked rapidly, trying to clear the blur from her vision to no avail. She just had to hang on a few more minutes. Joe would be there soon. But as soon as she thought it, her fear reared its ugly head, taunting, *And would walk right into his death…*

She shoved the thought away. *No. No way. Not Joe. He was her hero. Had been since they were children.*

"Shut the fuck up, you stupid mutt," Sean spat. He swung his leg, catching Jasper in the head, then kicked him again. This time Jasper lunged forward, sinking his teeth into Sean's leg and shaking his head, growling furiously. Sean yowled with pain. But the sound quickly morphed to rage. And too late Sadie saw him raise the gun and point it at her dog. She brought her fist down hard, nailing him in the nuts, her heart lifting a little when he cried out in pain, but her triumph was short-lived as the gun went off at the same instant. The sound of Jasper's yelp brought tears to her eyes, but in the dim light she could see her dog as he scurried away into the shadows.

He was wounded, but still alive, thank God! At least, he was for now.

She renewed her struggle, tucking her chin into the chokehold to try to lessen Sean's compression on her windpipe and would've cursed the asshole a blue streak for hurting her dog if she could've gotten any air in her lungs.

Enraged, Sean shoved her away from him, slamming her into the wall. "You stupid bitch!" he growled. "I'll fucking kill you!" He grabbed her by the hair, jerking her back to him and shoving the barrel of the gun up under her chin. "Is this what you want? Huh? You want me to blow your fucking head off?"

Sadie ground her teeth together, fighting back the tears of anger and fear, not about to let him see how scared she was. "Go to hell."

He chuckled. "Later," he said, his lips near her ear. "First, I think we need to have a little fun…"

# CHAPTER 5

JOE'S HEART WAS POUNDING AS HE SILENTLY MADE his way up the stairs. He winced as one of the stairs creaked, but the voices upstairs continued without interruption. His muscles ached from the tension; his head throbbed from the adrenaline rush that was pumping through his veins. And he felt that initial tingling at the back of his neck, the anxiety that clawed at his stomach, making its way up his esophagus, branching out into his lungs and making it impossible to breathe...

He shook his head, fighting the panic attack that was threatening to overtake him. He had to soldier through it, stay frosty. Sadie's life depended on him keeping his shit together, and there was no way he was gonna let her down. Not now. Not ever.

Yeah, so he was damaged goods. He'd never be the same man he was *before*. But Sadie was right—he'd been born to protect and serve. And if that was as a soldier, or a deputy, or a man hell-bent on protecting the woman he loved, he'd do his duty until his final breath.

Setting his jaw with a steely resolve, Joe adjusted his grip on the gun, steadied his shaking hands, ignored the perspiration on his forehead and the bead of sweat snaking down his back. And moved forward.

---

Sadie dug in her heels, trying unsuccessfully to prevent Sean from dragging her back to her bedroom. There was no question what he intended to do to her. The thought of him taking her on the very bed that she'd just shared with Joe infuriated her. She'd sooner die than let him defile the beautiful memories of making love to Joe, of his softly whispered endearments, her name on his lips while in the throes of passion.

"Please don't do this," she pleaded, trying a different tack with Sean. "It's not worth it!"

He grunted a laugh. "You got that right, you frigid little bitch! We dated for *months*, and you didn't give it up even once! You're sure as hell not worthy to suck my cock, but once you get a taste of this"—he ground his bulging erection against her ass—"you'll know what you've been missing."

"Let her go."

Sadie nearly melted with relief. Yep. A big puddle of goo right there on the hallway carpet. The tears she'd been holding back scalded a path down her cheeks as she gasped on a sob, "*Joe*."

But Joe didn't even spare her a glance. His deadly glare was fixed on Sean, his gun trained on the man holding her captive. Or, hell, she hoped it was. Because right now the coward was using her as a human shield, and there was precisely zero margin for error.

Sean pressed his gun harder into her chin and cackled, his voice taking on a hysterical edge that scared the shit out of her. She suppressed a revolted shiver, afraid that even the slightest movement might result in him pulling the trigger...

"Sadie," Joe said, keeping his gaze trained on Sean as he spoke. "You okay, baby?"

"I think so," she said, her voice thin, strained, and thick with tears.

"She's mine, you fucking prick!" Sean Jackson roared. "*I'm* the one who tosses my whores to the curb when I'm tired of them. Bitches don't break up with *me*. And she never would've broken things off if you hadn't come back. You should've just died back in Afghanistan and saved the taxpayers a few bucks!"

"Well, why don't you rectify that, pretty boy," Joe replied, his tone even, deadly calm. "Take your best shot."

*Oh God, oh God, oh God…*

"Joe, what the hell are you doing?" Sadie beseeched, her pounding heart making her already throbbing head ache so badly her stomach rolled with nausea.

"Go ahead, sweet cheeks," Joe taunted, ignoring her. "Bring it on. Show Sadie what a total badass you are. Just let her go first. Don't want her interfering with your shot, right?"

In the distance, Sadie heard sirens. A lot of them. Joe had called for backup, thank God! And if there was one thing she knew after growing up next door to the Dawsons, they took care of their own.

Now they just had to live long enough for the cavalry to arrive…

—m—

Joe could barely hear over the blood pounding in his ears, but he wasn't about to let on to Jackson that he was nervous at all. This whole plan depended on him persuading the asshole to let Sadie go, defuse the situation like he'd been trained. But his instincts told him there was no use asking Jackson for demands or trying to reason with him, tell him it'd be easier for him if he gave himself up. That train had left the station, and it was pretty damned clear it was on a one-way trip to Crazy Town. Right now his biggest concern was getting that gun out from under Sadie's chin. And as soon as he accomplished that, all bets were off.

"Look," Joe said, raising his hands and letting his gun hang from his finger. "You want to have a go at me, fine. But Sadie can't see what a big tough guy you are if she's wounded—or dead. So let her go, or you'll have an audience of one. And where's the fun in that? Who's going to tell everyone what a badass you are if no one's here to see it?"

He could see Jackson mulling it over. Then the guy suddenly shoved Sadie away from him, sending her stumbling down the hallway toward Joe.

Joe grabbed Sadie's forearm as soon as she was within reach and flung her behind him, using his body to shield her from harm even though he desperately longed to kiss her hard and deep, lose himself in her arms, assure himself that she was safe. But she wasn't. Not yet.

"Go, baby!" he ordered, bringing his gun back up and training it on Jackson's chest as he spoke. "Get out of here!"

He half expected her to protest. But she didn't. Not his brave, beautiful Sadie. She raced down the stairs, allowing him to keep his focus on Jackson. God, he loved her! And he was going to tell her so every single day for the rest of his life…

—◆◆◆—

Sadie stumbled down the stairs at what felt like slow motion, gripping the railing to keep from pitching forward and taking a header. To her surprise, her dog was right at her heels, limping from the blows he'd taken and the wound he'd sustained trying to protect her. Poor Jasper. Add his injuries to the list of reasons to despise that worthless son of a bitch upstairs.

She hated to leave Joe up there alone, but she knew if she'd stayed she would've just been a distraction. So she'd taken off as fast as her feet and her spinning head could manage. She just had to get to the front door, let the arriving officers know what was going on, what Joe was up against. But the distance between her and the front door seemed to stretch out, lengthening and getting farther away with each step toward it. And somewhere there was a rhythmic pounding that seemed to emanate from within and without her head at the same time.

*What the hell?*

It took her a moment to realize it was someone banging on the front door. "Sheriff's Department! Open up!"

Before she could respond, the door burst inward, and she was falling forward into the arms of Joe's brother Tom as he rushed to her. His brother Gabe was right behind him. And—*good God*—was that Mac Dawson? Joe's father, in all his impassive ferocity, strode in, gun drawn, his heavy brows furrowed. And there were about half a dozen other deputies behind him.

Mac pegged Sadie with a look that had been known to make even the most hardened criminals wither and demanded, "Where's my boy?"

—*vv*—

"There are only two ways this can end," Joe said, keeping an eye on the gun hanging down at Jackson's side and working to keep the rage out of his voice. There was really only *one* way he *wanted* to end this and that involved him tearing the bastard apart with his bare hands for terrorizing Sadie. But his honor prevented him from doing anything he'd regret. So, instead, he offered a choice. "You give me the gun and walk out of here in handcuffs, or I drop you. You pick."

Jackson puffed out his chest and for a split second looked like he might actually come at Joe, but a cacophony of voices and thundering footfalls downstairs brought him up short.

"Hear that?" Joe asked, his focus laser sharp. "That's probably half the Fairfield County Sheriff's Department. Now, drop the gun, and let's end this."

"You'd like that, wouldn't you?" Jackson sneered. "Make it look like you're some kind of hero?"

"It's over, Jackson," Joe informed him. "Don't be an idiot."

That's when Joe heard the footstep behind him, noticed the enraged expression on Jackson's face, saw the bastard's arm come up to take aim.

Joe didn't hesitate.

—*vv*—

The report of the gunshot echoed through Sadie's house, startling her heart into her throat. "Joe!"

She wriggled with what strength she had, trying to get free of Tom's hold, but he refused to release her, no matter how many times she pounded at him with her fist and kicked, landing several blows that made him grunt as he carried her outside to the waiting ambulance.

"Goddammit, Tom!" she screamed. "Let me go!"

But he just calmly set her down on the edge of the ambulance's open bay, keeping a firm hand on her shoulder as the paramedics rushed to check her out. Sadie blinked and batted away the penlight they shoved into her face, leaning out around them to watch the front door of her house, praying fervently that the man she loved would come walking out at any minute.

Several agonizing moments passed. Tom's hand reflexively squeezed her shoulder, and she turned her eyes up to him, the stress and concern in his face a reflection of her own.

"Tom?" she choked through barely suppressed tears. But then his expression suddenly relaxed, his entire body sagging with relief. Her head whipped back to the door so fast, the world swam before her eyes, the exiting deputies a blur of faces.

But there was one face that was perfectly clear. The only one she needed to see.

The paramedics who'd been tending to her jogged toward the house at Mac Dawson's beckoning, and she felt Tom leaving her side as his brother approached.

Joe strode toward her, limping a little but otherwise unharmed, a few of the other deputies clapping him on the back or nodding toward him as he passed. And even as an outsider, Sadie could see that these were gestures of acknowledgment, of acceptance of Joe as their equal. In their eyes, he had proven himself worthy to be among them.

And that's when the dam broke. The tears she'd been fighting burst forth in strangled sobs as Joe's arms came around her, grasping her so tightly she could hardly breathe. "I love you," he whispered, pulling back enough that he could take her face in his hands. And then his lips captured hers in a hard, deep kiss that left her breathless.

———※———

Joe kissed Sadie long and hard, not giving a damn if the whole frigging department got a good look at them. All that mattered was that she was alive. And safe.

Finally, the rattle of the gurney brought his head up, and he and Sadie shuffled out of the way so that the paramedics could load Jackson into the ambulance. Odds were good he'd survive the gunshot wound to his shoulder that had taken him down and probably saved the life of Joe's brother Gabe who'd just entered the hallway to back him up.

Joe's arm tightened around Sadie when she buried her face into his chest to avoid having to look at Jackson, and he pressed a kiss to the top of her hair, knowing that the nightmares she'd probably have from the experience were going to be rough. But he'd get her through it— just as she'd helped him through his.

"You all right, sweetheart?"

Joe and Sadie both glanced up, surprised to see Joe's father standing there, his normally hard expression curiously tender as he gazed on them. Joe felt Sadie's slight nod but said, "I'm taking her to the hospital to have her checked out, just to make sure."

"No!" Sadie protested. "I can't go to the hospital. I need to get Jasper to the vet, and—"

Mac jerked his chin toward Joe's car. "You go on with Joe," he interrupted. "I've got this under control." Joe gave his father a nod of gratitude, then started to lead Sadie away but stopped short when Mac called, "Joseph?"

Joe turned to him, brows raised, knowing his father wasn't exactly one for conversation—especially at a crime scene. "Yes, sir?"

The sheriff dipped his head ever so slightly in a terse nod, then headed back to the house.

"What was that all about?" Sadie asked.

Joe hugged her closer, his throat growing tight. He knew exactly what that nod meant. He also knew it wasn't something any of Mac Dawson's sons had received often in their lives. He had to swallow past his emotions before he said, "I'm pretty sure it meant he's proud of me."

# EPILOGUE

Joe ADJUSTED THE BLINDS IN HIS BEDROOM, BLOCKING out as much of the early afternoon sunlight as possible, then stripped out of his clothes and climbed into his bed beside Sadie, pulling her into the curve of his body. After leaving the hospital and making a quick visit to Jasper at the vet's office where he was expected to fully recover, Joe had brought Sadie back to his house, not wanting her to have to deal with going back to her own just yet. She'd go back when she was ready to face what had happened. And knowing his brave Sadie, it wouldn't take her long.

She murmured something incoherent in her sleep as she nuzzled close, seeking his warmth. He smoothed her hair, careful not to disturb the knot on her head where she'd struck the bathtub. The hospital had confirmed that she had a mild concussion but would be fine. But when he thought about how much worse things might have gone, how close he'd come to losing her…

He tried to suppress the shudder that rippled through him, but it was enough that Sadie's eyes fluttered open.

"Hey, you," she muttered, turning in his arms so that she was facing him. "I was worried you'd be gone when I woke up."

He shook his head. "I took the day off. Turns out I have an 'in' with my boss."

She chuckled, then winced, her hand going reflexively to her head. "Damn, this hurts."

Joe pressed a tender kiss to her hair. "Better?"

She shook her head, grinning. "Maybe it was the wrong spot."

He rolled her onto her back, then his mouth found hers in a slow, lingering kiss. "How about that?" he murmured against her lips. "Was that any better?"

She gave him a playful grin. "You're getting there…" She shifted, urging him into the cradle of her hips, and wrapped her arms and legs around him, keeping him close.

Joe peered down at her, marveling at the love in her eyes as she met his gaze. He gently brushed a lock of hair from her eyes then kissed her again. "My God, Sadie," he whispered when the kiss ended, pressing his forehead to hers for a moment, "when I saw you there last night with that gun under your chin—"

She stopped his words with a brief kiss. "I'm fine. Don't give it another thought."

He shook his head. "But—"

"Do you know what I kept thinking when Sean had that gun on me?" she interrupted. "I just kept telling myself, *Joe will come for me*. I know you've been worried about your ability to do your job, but you saved my life last night, Joe. You're a hero—*my* hero."

"I'm no hero," he argued, caressing her cheek with the back of his hand. "I was just doing what had to be done."

"And putting yourself at risk in the process," she reminded him.

"You're everything to me, Sadie," he told her softly. "There's nothing I wouldn't do to protect you. I love you. I always will."

A slow grin curved her lips. "Well, then, Joe Dawson. I'd say you'd better get to showing me how much."

He chuckled. "You need to rest."

"I can rest later," she told him, snaking her arms around his neck. "Right now, all I need is you."

And as she pulled him down to receive her kiss, Joe realized he'd finally kept the promise he'd made to her over two years ago on that sun-drenched autumn afternoon before his deployment when they'd tearfully clung to one another, reluctant to part, too afraid to confess the truth in their hearts.

He'd come home.

Home to Sadie's arms and to the love that had always been his beacon of light in the darkness. And no matter what the future might hold for them, Joe knew that it was her love that would sustain him, keep him true, and always—*always*—guide him home.

# ABOUT THE AUTHOR

**Kate SeRine** (pronounced "serene") has been telling stories since before she could hold a pen. When she's not writing, you'll find Kate watching low-budget horror movies or geeking out over pretty much any movie adaptation of a comic book. As long as action and suspense are involved, she's in!

Kate lives in a smallish, quintessentially Midwestern town with her husband and two sons, who share her love of storytelling. She never tires of creating new worlds to share and is even now working on her next project—probably while consuming way too much coffee.

Connect with Kate at www.kateserine.com, Facebook.com/kateserine, or on Twitter @KateSeRine.

# WAR GAMES

An Endgame Ops Novella

## LEA GRIFFITH

# CHAPTER 1

*2100 hours, January 15, 2011*

ANTHONY "ROOK" GRANGER WAS A BIG DUDE. FROM the top of his shorn head to the bottom of his…well, his foot and blade prosthesis, he was one of the largest men she'd ever encountered. And that was sitting down. If he were standing, he'd tower over her by at least a foot, maybe more. His shoulders were broad, looking like they could carry the weight of the world and not falter. The hands he fisted on his muscled thighs clenched and unclenched, a warning in the gesture.

Vivi shivered. A steel door clanged shut behind her. One more cage door to go, and she'd be in the same room with him. His only visitor in three months. The man had been in solitary confinement since his sentencing, not allowed even a meeting with his lawyers. He'd been moved into this holding wing of the prison on orders from Brigadier General Kennedy Johansen of the U.S. Joint Special Operations Command.

The guard escorting her turned as they came to the door and smirked. "Wonder what kind of strings you pulled for this?"

Vivi arched a single brow and narrowed her gaze on the man. "We don't have to talk for you to do your job, do we?"

His face went red, but he caught himself before he

popped off in anger. "Turn around, please." He may have said please, but it was an order nonetheless.

Vivi bristled and shoved the phone she'd been allowed to keep in her pocket. The phone was a concession, much like this meeting in the first place. Vivi had most definitely pulled strings, but so had the brigadier general.

The guard huffed. "Today?"

Her jaw tightened, but she turned, raising her arms and preparing for the feel of his hands on her body. She was glad she'd worn pants. God knows the bastard might have tried to cop a feel between her legs if she'd worn a skirt. As it was, he lingered too damn long.

The sound of metal sliding against concrete invaded the silence. Vivi turned her head toward the noise. Her quarry had wrapped his hands around the chains tethering him to the floor, knuckles bleeding to white at the grip he had on them.

His head was bowed, gaze on the floor beneath the metal folding chair he sat on. His stillness made goose bumps dance along her skin. He knew everything going on around him. No doubt about it.

She glared over her shoulder at the guard. "If you touch me there once more, I'm going to rip your arms off and beat you with them."

The guard laughed but removed his hands from her ass. "I'd like to see you try, little girl."

Vivi ignored him. She had no choice because the man she'd come to see, Prisoner R5762, the infamous Sergeant First Class Rook Granger, raised his head, narrowing his gaze on the guard's hands, jaw clenching.

Vivi inhaled sharply. She had no frame of reference

to compare the beauty of Rook's face. The symmetry of his broad forehead, high cheekbones, and square jaw was breathtaking. His eyebrows were wide swaths of ebony against the bronze of his skin. The bridge of his nose was slightly crooked but did nothing to detract from the otherwise striking canvas of his features. His lower lip was fuller than the top, but the curve of his mouth gave him a mocking, almost rakish appearance. It actually took that face from beautiful to downright sinful.

But it was his eyes that took her breath, hell, her *mind*, away and replaced them with an emotion so foreign to Vivi she couldn't name it. Coal black, bright with malice but shadowed with secrets, his gaze was both a silken caress and the burning promise of retribution.

His stare unsettled her so much that she simply stood there for several seconds, unaware of her surroundings. The guard pushed her forward and she stumbled, righting herself before she sprawled face-first into the cell. The chains rattled again, and malevolence poured off Rook.

*Honor*, her brother had said as he lay dying in the hospital. Rook Granger had more honor in a single breath than most men could claim their entire life.

Yet here he was—a prisoner of the U.S. Disciplinary Barracks at Fort Leavenworth, Kansas. Honorable men didn't go to prison, did they?

Sometimes, she mused. Prisoner R5762 was living proof.

"You don't like it when I touch her, blade runner?" the guard taunted. The reference to the prosthetic on Rook's left leg fell like a gauntlet.

He remained silent, but the vow in his eyes was unmistakable. With that look, it wasn't hard to believe he was the killer his Army superiors made him out to be. Vivi held her breath, willing the fear to subside. She wasn't his target.

Not yet.

She straightened her shoulders and glanced at the guard. "You can leave."

He smirked. "I'll be right outside if you need me, little girl." It was a taunt, plain and simple.

If only she'd met him outside these walls...

*Yeah, Vivi? What would you do? Hack into his email account and send his wife pictures of him having sex with her sister? Hack into his bank account and send all his money to a charity in Africa? Flip him the bird and stomp off?*

She ground her back teeth together. She might be CIA, but she wasn't quite as physically intimidating as she'd like. She'd love to hand him his ass. She'd love some revenge for the feels he'd copped, but there were rules in this setting and she had a goal that wouldn't be met sitting around jonesing for payback. Maybe she'd hack into his email next week.

Vivi smiled serenely, affecting a look of tranquillity like she'd been born to it. She'd damn well practiced it her entire life. As a woman in a man's profession, she'd had to swallow more than her fair share of shit. This was small potatoes. She could do this.

She walked to the only other chair in the room, located approximately five feet in front of her quarry, and sat down. It didn't escape her notice that Rook's eyes fixed on her once the guard left. His gaze was a tactile stroke, leaving no part of her untouched. Vivi took another deep, cleansing breath and raised her head.

She met his gaze, and the air in her lungs froze. Panic sliced through her as the black ice of his eyes effectively trapped her thoughts, bypassing her intent and worming through her veins. Stone. Cold. Killer. It seemed there was no life behind those eyes, nothing but a veiled intent to destroy anyone who got in his path.

She was now all up in that path—a direct target. And she'd put herself there intentionally. She glanced at the chains that shackled him to huge bolts in the floor. Yes, he was a big, strong Delta Force officer. Yes, he was one scary dude. Yes, he'd been convicted in the deaths of his entire Delta Force unit. But the chains were overkill. He'd pissed somebody off so badly they'd determined to make every second of his life behind bars miserable.

She smiled and lifted a shaking hand to push a wayward curl behind her ear. "My name is Olivia Bentwood. I believe you knew my brother, Michael."

She left her words hanging in the air. She'd made the initial foray and waited for him to either pick it up or leave it lying there. He did as she expected and said nothing.

She didn't drop her gaze but cocked her head and made it glacial. "You knew my brother, served with him in Iraq, Afghanistan, Syria, and Lebanon, along with a few incursions into Indonesia. According to Michael, you pulled his ass out of so many cracks during the time you served with him that he could never repay you. On July 3, 2007, you saved him from a burning helo after it crashed in Helmand Province. On September 3, 2008, you pulled him, shot and bleeding, from a firefight in

Kunar Province. And on February 24, 2010, you saved his life when your Delta Force unit and two CIA paramilitary operatives were ambushed at a security checkpoint outside Mogadishu, Somalia. He had more respect for you than anyone he'd ever met, and your name was the last thing he said before he died from the wounds sustained on that op."

She paused, searching for any flicker of recognition, any hint of emotion. As Michael had told her he would, he remained ice cold. He had no way of knowing, would probably not understand, but one day she'd thank him for that iciness. It gave her strength.

She sighed and plastered the smile on her face again. "It's a pleasure to meet you, Sergeant Granger. My brother spoke highly of you, swore the gods of war had created you as the perfect soldier. Said that although you lost your leg in the Second Battle of Fallujah, you were the best damn warrior he'd ever known. He passed nine months ago, in a hospital bed at Walter Reed. They said you were responsible. My brother knew different. You saved his life, and I'm here to repay the debt."

The silence in the room was absolute, an empty void waiting to be filled. He didn't disappoint her.

"Leave."

One word, so simple, yet complex all at once.

"I cannot do that, Sergeant Granger. You're in trouble. You'll rot here if I don't get you out. And actually, the point is moot because the wheels are already turning." The clanging of a door down the hall resounded in the sudden silence. Determined footsteps headed their way. "Here comes our first salvo now."

She reached into her pocket and pulled out her

phone. Her thumb caressed the screen, hovering over a particular button. *Almost time*. She stared at him, trying with her demeanor to calm the beast she knew writhed beneath his skin. He stared back, promising hell if she didn't do as he'd commanded.

"We will be leaving here tonight, Sergeant. I have information I believe you've needed for almost a year now. That information would have saved your men's lives and negated the need for your imprisonment. It's important you listen to me very carefully."

His face was blank. His eyes, filled with cold temerity moments earlier, shut down flat. He slouched in the chair now, leaning back negligently. But Vivi had the upper hand here. He couldn't bluff her because she knew the truth and she knew he wanted that truth. Badly.

"Leave," he said again. Oh, the look on his face was calm, bored even, but his voice was horrible. Yet the deep baritone moved her, settling her nerves.

He was a strong man. An honorable man. He'd been done wrong. And Vivi had made a promise to her brother. Rook Granger would not prevent her from keeping it.

She shook her head, crossed her legs, and stared at him, waiting for the next phase of his denial to begin. He stood so abruptly the chair skated backward, hitting the wall behind him with a banging screech of metal. The guard behind the glass to their left stood up as well, walking around to the door to unlock it and get her out of there. She held up a hand and thanked her lucky stars Brigadier General Johansen had seen fit to help her, greasing the wheels for this venture so everything went smoothly. The guard stopped and returned to his seat.

Vivi remained seated, though now she looked up to where he stood, arms stretched to his side by the metal chains bolted to the floor. "You don't scare me, Sergeant."

"I should fucking *terrify* you."

She ignored him, keeping her voice even but low, almost a whisper. "You are going to walk out of here with me, and we are going to do whatever must be done to get to the truth. I made a promise. I have called in favors owed to me by men in some of the highest positions of our government. If you do not go with me, my life is forfeit. My inquiries have no doubt met the ears of the very people responsible for your incarceration—the ones responsible for the death of your Delta Force unit and my brother. In an effort to hide their very ugly truth, they will eliminate whomever they need to. Neither my position in the CIA, nor the people indebted to me, will be able to stop the bad guys. Do you understand what I'm saying?"

He said nothing, maintaining that stony silence.

The door to the visitation cell opened. "It is time, Ms. Bentwood," the new guard said.

She stood to her feet, keeping her gaze on Rook, daring him to naysay her. The guard walked over to stand next to Rook. He was an average-sized man and the difference between him and Rook was startling.

The war truly began in that next moment. The first skirmish was one Rook had with himself, and it showed in small ways. The tensing of his jaw, the muscles there bunching and relaxing. His narrowed gaze and flaring nostrils. He was a wild thing, and Vivi irrationally wanted to soothe him.

She smiled once more, aware it may be her last for a

while. Michael had told her Rook Granger was a mean son of a bitch when riled. But he hadn't met Vivi. She was the most stubborn woman in the world. Badass Delta Force commander or not, she could take his mean and counter it a million different ways, tipping the scales in her favor.

The first guard, the one with the touchy-feely hands, glared at her through the doors. He was her biggest obstacle at the moment, but not for long. Her thumb pressed the screen and within moments the lights of the holding wing of the prison began to flicker.

Vivi trained her gaze on Rook.

"What the hell are you doing?" Rook asked in disbelief.

Long seconds passed, and she arched a single brow. He bit off a curse but raised his arms. The guard unlocked his shackles and stepped back as the lights went out completely. As soon as the lights extinguished, every guard with the exception of the one in the room with them scattered to assure the prison remained locked down.

"This way," the guard said and moved for the door, placing a key in the lock and opening the cell.

The backup generator kicked in, the lights flickered back on, and Rook Granger was in her face before she took a breath. "I don't know you. I don't know why you're here. But if this is some kind of trick, it won't matter that you're Michael's sister. I'll snap your skinny neck and keep moving."

His heat wrapped around her, and she wanted to sink into him, let that warmth chase away the chill his gaze had spread.

"You would have to catch me first, Sergeant. I feel it only fair to tell you that I'm pretty fast," she murmured.

"You think because I've got a prosthetic I can't catch you?"

She wouldn't even dignify that with an answer.

"Ms. Bentwood," the guard urged.

Vivi turned away from Rook, away from that sensual, mocking curve of his lips and that bitterly cold ebony gaze. His hands landed on her shoulders, preventing movement but not painful. A shiver worked through her.

Even as she recognized he was affecting her, Vivi pressed one more button on her phone. The entire holding wing of the prison went dark once more. Security protocols were overridden, and the backup generator was disabled. Vivi had hacked the prison's system, infiltrating it two weeks ago with an ease that made her stomach cramp. She'd established a program that allowed her to remotely manipulate the lights, cameras, and security grid for this wing with her smartphone. The doors to the cells would remain locked unless a key was inserted to override. She'd shut the entire wing of a federal maximum security prison down with the touch of a button.

Rook leaned against her back, lowering his mouth to her ear. He inhaled deeply, the air he moved with that breath slithering against her skin, heating her in ways she'd never been heated. "Michael told me about you. How much he loved you, how he helped raise you when your parents died."

She snorted as the darkness pressed on them. "There's a reason for this?"

"Just one and I want you to listen to it closely," he said.

Another shiver caused by a voice that was gravelly but delicious nonetheless. "I'm waiting."

"Don't make me kill you. I don't have much of a conscience left. Killing Michael's little sister would destroy it," he whispered.

He stepped past her, and then they were hurrying down the hall, following the faint yellow glow thrown by the guard's flashlight.

*I don't have much of a conscience.* The phrase rang in her ear the entire way through the holding wing. The sounds of the prison moving into lockdown mode came from a distance. Vivi had built in a twenty-four-hour window to allow for their truth-finding mission. It would take another A-rated hacker that long to discover the virus she'd placed in the system and potentially correct it.

Her hope was they'd be too busy chasing their own asses, making sure the prison was safe from any further infiltration, to chase his. After that twenty-four-hour bubble, a full-scale, nationwide search would begin and nowhere would be safe for Rook or Vivi. It might be a fruitless hope, but it was all she could offer.

They exited a side entrance normally used by officials and prison personnel.

The vehicle was waiting where she'd left it. The guard opened the passenger door, and she bypassed him, walking to the driver's side and opening the door. Rook shook his head, refusing to get in.

She sighed. "I'm a good driver."

He shook his head again. The guard tried to cover his laugh.

"Get in the car. Me driving is nonnegotiable," she said and got behind the wheel of the blacked-out Suburban.

It took a solid minute for him to come to grips with the fact that he was at the mercy of a female driver. She couldn't see him, but she felt him glaring at her. Finally, he got in and slammed the door. Vivi bit off her smile and pulled away.

"We now have twenty-three hours left of your temporary reprieve from prison," she told him.

"Why twenty-three?"

"I'm giving them twenty-four hours to find and override my virus in their security system. After that, all bets are off. That whole song and dance we just went through at the prison used up one hour. Are you ready, Sergeant, to discover the truth?" she asked.

"I know the truth. I was framed," he bit out.

She shrugged. "Yes, well, finding the proof is the problem, isn't it?"

Vivi pulled out of the prison facility. She took a right on State Route 73 and then a left onto Twentieth Street. From there she took another left onto Seneca and pulled into a liquor store parking lot.

"I'm not thirsty, but I'll watch the car for you," he said in a hard voice.

She laughed, couldn't help it. Somewhere under that painfully gruff exterior was the man he'd once been—the man her brother admired so much his name had been the last word he'd uttered. "No need. We're switching cars."

She turned the engine off, sat back, and waved her hand in front of her. "Pick."

He remained silent, and she sighed again, getting seriously put out by his reticence.

"We have no choice but to change vehicles. This one

was tagged before it was dropped off for my use. While I'm sincerely appreciative for the efforts of Brigadier General Johansen, we don't need him to know all our secrets, now do we?"

He turned his gaze to her, and her breath locked in her throat. "You just told him."

She forced her serene smile back in place and reached into her pocket. He went on alert, in her face and grabbing her hand in one of his while wrapping his other hand around her throat before she could pull out what was in that pocket.

"You are so suspicious," she said with that same smile plastered to her face.

He grunted. She was starting to realize that was his rote response to most things.

"Let me go," she ordered calmly.

"Don't try me." But he released her.

She pulled a tiny black box out of her pocket and set it on the dash. "Jammer," she said softly.

His gaze never left hers, but eventually he sat back on his side of the vehicle. The goose bumps were back in full force. Being the recipient of his full attention was both exhilarating and unnerving. He finally, *finally*, looked out the windshield.

"I don't trust you."

She could understand that. "My brother prepared me for that. I think I can give you something that will help a little."

"Yeah?" He looked at her again, raven eyebrow raised. "What's that?"

"It's a single word. Michael said you'd understand. After all, it's the reason you're in the position you're in."

More silence. Her nerves were stretched. She really needed a damn break from all the damn quiet.

"I'm waiting," he said softly.

She made sure her gaze connected with his before she said the single word. "Endgame."

His eyes didn't flicker, his face remained impassive— there was nothing to betray he'd even heard her. The silence stretched again, taut, deafening, and filled with all manner of things she never wanted to know about. It was as close to death as she wanted to skate and had her brother been there, she would have seriously ripped him a new one.

"The black Honda," he said.

She blew out a breath and nodded. "Good choice, since it's the one I had delivered for us. Looks rather sad and inconspicuous, right?"

His jaw tightened and his hands clenched. "Was that some kind of test?"

She shook her head. "Nah, I just wanted to make sure I picked a decent getaway car."

Had she not been looking at him, she wouldn't have seen the slight lift at the corner of his mouth. It happened so fast, there and gone, but she had seen it and relief made her want to dance a victory jig. Badass Delta Force commander indeed.

He shrugged. "Let's do it then."

Vivi pulled the large duffel bag out of the back of the Suburban, ran a device detector over it before pulling everything out and running the detector over those as well. She found seven more bugs, ripped them out of the seams of the clothing and the bag, and headed to the Honda.

They made the switch quickly and were on the road three minutes later. She hated that it was smaller because that put her much closer to Rook.

"Where are we going?" he asked as he looked out the window.

"We'll be traveling to Warrenton, Oregon." She let that sink in. "You're familiar with Warrenton, right?"

He nodded sharply before he took a deep breath.

"Are you okay?"

He flexed his hands on his thighs, so very obviously not okay. He remained silent. "I'm right as rain, Olivia Bentwood."

And with that, she headed in the direction of Manhattan, Kansas, a convicted killer at her side, and a boatload of trouble in her lap.

# CHAPTER 2

OLIVIA BENTWOOD WAS A TINY WOMAN. PROBABLY NO taller than five-two, she was slender, delicate, but curved in all the right places. Big brown eyes dominated a heart-shaped face and her skin, so smooth and creamy, made his palms itch. Her high cheekbones rouged when she was angry, frustrated, or embarrassed.

Rook didn't want to notice these things. Hated that he did. But the goddamn woman was a siren, luring him in with her gamine features and soft, husky tone.

And she'd broken him out of prison.

She'd surprised him. Beyond her reason for being there, her audacity, her *bravado* had struck a chord in Rook. She seemed just as stubborn as her brother, Michael. But she'd stood up to that shithead guard and then Rook. Not backing down when he'd threatened and done his level best to intimidate the sexy-as-hell woman. With her long, curly brown hair and fuck-me eyes, she was trouble on two legs—stubborn trouble.

He rubbed his own eyes, fatigue pulling at him. Her smell, something elusive, feminine, and reminding him of wildflowers, permeated the tiny car. He laid his head back, tried to breathe through the sudden case of lust and, yeah, fear. How the hell had he ended up in this place? Who had pegged him as the fall guy for an op his troop should never have been involved in? The truth was there, but in jail he'd had no resources to ferret them out.

His lawyers thought him delusional. The judge at his trial thought him a killer. The families of his men hated him with a passion. All, apparently, except for one.

*Endgame.* The word whispered through Rook's mind, finding purchase in a past he'd thought buried for nearly two years. Only one other person besides Rook had known the truth of that single day in the mountains of the Hindu Kush outside of Kunar Province, and he'd not made it out alive. *Knight.*

"You should rest," she said softly.

He took a deep breath, felt the isolation of the last nine months press in on him, then release. He wasn't alone now. *Fuck.* "Who sent you?"

"I told you my brother sent me."

"Your brother was always a pain in the ass." He watched the cars pass on the other side of the highway, wanting to punch and hit something. Michael had been a devoted soldier. He'd loved his sister, loved his country, and had wanted to start a family of his own when he finished his fourth and final tour. Now, he was dust in the wind. "He sent you on a fool's errand."

She shrugged but kept her gaze pinned on the road ahead of them. "I'm a big girl. Michael was the most honorable man I've ever known. The truth was so embedded in his DNA that to separate him from it would have killed him long before the bomb that blew up your unit did."

Her words were confirmation that Michael knew much more than he'd ever let on. "What truth?"

She glanced at him then, her eyes pinning him like a butterfly to a collection. "All truth. But in your case, you know exactly what truth I'm talking about, Sergeant."

"We each have our own truths. And sometimes they are all a lie." Five men, all gone in a single instant. Greed was at the root of their deaths. But there was also a much more sinuous snake that slithered along the periphery. Rook needed to find the head of that snake.

"Michael came to me over two years ago," she began, voice full of pain and something else Rook couldn't place. Love? Possibly. "His command sergeant major had gotten drunk after a particularly bad firefight. I believe your unit lost Sgt. First Class Jonah Knight in that battle of Kunar Province. You took Jonah Knight's loss hard."

For a split second, Rook was back in that firefight, mired down once again in the hell that was the Battle of Ganjgal.

The sun had been so fucking hot and bright that day, and fire had burned everywhere. Chunks of debris rained down, and he smelled the blood, heard the cries for help, felt the bite as pieces of concrete gouged by bullets tore through his skin. Rook shook his head, pushing the memories down. There was no time for them now. Because if he were to be truthful with this woman who'd come on her crazy-ass venture of finding said truth, he'd have to tell her he not only lost Knight that day, he'd lost himself too. They'd been through hell together. So many battles they'd pulled each other alive from and then Knight wasn't there anymore.

She took his silence for encouragement to continue. "You said things that night that led my brother to certain conclusions. You spoke of betrayal and righting wrongs—how your team was in the wrong place at the wrong time. My brother spoke of you often, but after that incident, he decided he would do whatever he could to find out what happened in Kunar Province. 'There's a truth somewhere in there that will set him free, Vivi. I've got to find it,' he said. You were his family at that point, and Michael always took care of his family."

He wanted to rail at her to shut up. Freedom was so close. He didn't need to hear about honorable Michael and his insane crusade to save the un-savable. He could ditch her and take off, just disappear where nobody would ever find him.

But the truth. Where would that leave the truth? He owed Knight. He owed Michael and the four other men who'd given their lives in a fight two years after that fuck-up in Kunar. That last battle in Mogadishu hadn't been for God and country but rather a self-serving entity that wanted the secrets of Kunar kept silent.

"My brother's last words to me were, 'Find the truth, Vivi. He saved me. Help me save him.' I have the tools, the connections to get you in front of who did this. But we need verification. Because if it's who all the roads lead to, we could be signing our own death warrants."

He laughed, surprised at the sound that felt like rusty nails scraping his throat. "Here's a truth for you. My death warrant was signed in Kunar over two years ago. I've been living on borrowed time, Olivia Bentwood."

"Time is finite for us all, Rook Granger," she said, mimicking his use of her full name. "But I made a promise to my brother as the air left his body. And by God, not you, the men responsible, or any-fucking-body else will keep me from seeing it through."

The woman was as batshit as her brother. "Even if it means your life?"

She nodded. "Even then."

He laid his head back against the headrest. Her words were another nail in his coffin. He knew damn good and well what Michael Bentwood had discovered about the incident in Kunar, and he wished he'd never gotten drunk after he'd seen Knight's body loaded into the plane for transport back to the States.

Nothing he could do now. Whoever was responsible for that battle two years ago had decided it was time to take Rook out. And they'd done it in Mogadishu, Somalia, nine months ago. Best guess, Michael's poking had prodded the beast, and that beast had destroyed Rook's entire unit, then pinned it on him when he'd been the only one to survive. Case closed. Loose ends tied up.

"I've got questions I must have answered," he bit out.

She glanced at him. "Soon," she said and focused back on the road.

He closed his eyes and waited for soon to come around.

# CHAPTER 3

It took them a little over an hour and a half to make it to their destination in Manhattan, Kansas. Her contact at the airfield had left the gate open and a light on. She pulled into the main gate, got out of the car, and locked the gate behind them.

Vivi breathed a sigh of relief as she pulled up to the main building and put the car in park. After the intensity of their earlier conversation, she'd needed the break and was glad things were going so smoothly. She got out and retrieved the duffel from the back, setting it on the hood of the car.

"Here," she said as she threw him a change of clothes and a single boot in his size. "I'd suggest you change out of that lovely prison orange. The door to the building is open, and there's a bathroom in the back." She threw him a small packet wrapped in gray plastic. "Put this in the toilet tank once you've showered and cleaned up. I need you to wipe it all down, no prints, please. Put the prison suit in the dumpster out back."

He caught the packet, looked at her with a raised brow, and headed into the building. The man didn't walk—he stalked. The prosthetic wasn't a hindrance in any way. If anything, it made him even more badass. It was eerie how he was so in control of his space and how the environment around him morphed to his presence. She took her first deep breath in well over four hours once the door shut behind him. Then she stripped, right there in the darkness of the parking lot, changing into black cargos, a black hoodie, and combat boots.

They were going to have to hike once they made it to their ultimate destination in Warrenton. The former Delta Force member living on that property didn't play, and while he was expecting them, pulling up to his front door wasn't an option.

Vivi pulled out her laptop. It was an off-market computer, though no less high-end, and she'd spec'd it out last week for this job. In the Company one week. Rogue the next. Who would have thought Olivia Bentwood capable of such a thing?

She booted up the device and stroked it as if it were her lover. Lots of RAM, 32GB, an SSD hard drive, and a 64-bit quad-core processor completed the unit. She'd installed a Linux operating system because of the security. She'd also installed an in-device Wi-Fi system that would allow her to piggyback off CIA satellites. She would remain untraceable because she'd created the program that allowed her to mask her presence on the originating IP address. There was a certain irony in using her employer's resources to perpetrate this crime. She booted up, brought the encryption software online and shot out the first email to the man she was going to owe big-time for his help.

*ALL IN*, she typed before she shot off the email and shut down the device. The recipient of the information had the mate to her sender's key for the encryption. He'd be able to unlock her messages with a series of letters and numbers she'd designed. If he shared her information, she and Rook were screwed. But right now, the man sitting in Washington was her only hope.

"What are you doing?"

Vivi froze as his voice stroked over her eardrums, sank into her skin, and forced her heart to beat faster. She shut off the computer and stuffed it back in her duffel. "Things," she responded as she turned around.

This put her back to the car and Rook at her front. Much closer than she expected. He cocked his head and stared at her, the night around them making his eyes appear endlessly deep. God, he was such a big man. Dressed now in the same type of garb she wore, he appeared every inch the spec-ops soldier he was. He'd donned the black skull cap she'd stuffed in his pack earlier today. Worried he might get cold, she'd put it in on a whim. It was snowing in Oregon right now. Why she'd been thinking of him, she had no idea.

Except that he was hers now. Yeah, once her brother had painted his picture of Rook in her mind, he'd become hers. Michael had saved Vivi's life. Rook had saved Michael's. Debts had to be paid. She'd never been so glad the CIA had recruited her out of high school as she was when Michael had asked for her help. It had nearly destroyed Vivi when she'd gotten the call he was injured.

He'd had massive internal injuries. They'd operated and managed to extend his life for two days. Long enough for Vivi to get there, speak with him, and say good-bye.

Tears clouded her vision, falling over the precipice of her eyelid and drifting down her cheek. Rook raised his hand, and she flinched. He halted, his look going from concerned to closed. But his hand continued to move and before she could blink, he wiped the tears from her face. She sobbed then, overwhelmed by the tenderness.

"Michael was one of the finest men I ever served with. He loved you. I'm sorry he's gone," Rook said in a gruff voice.

Vivi glanced up then and became caught in his pitch-black gaze. The moment stretched taut, a yawning chasm between them with the promise of something neither needed nor were looking for. She inhaled, and he moved closer. He tipped her head back with nothing more than his finger at her chin.

Vivi reached for his hand, grabbing it, but he took control, meshing their palms and entwining their fingers.

Then he took her lips and her mind in one fell swoop. And it was a taking, no doubt about it. She lost herself as his tongue licked into her mouth, finding every heated hollow while his lips sipped at her, tasting, commanding her tongue to dance with his.

If his body was heat, his mouth was a supernova, firing every synapse in her brain, forcing her against him. He accepted her, pulling her closer, wrapping his hands in her hair and tugging until he had her right where he wanted her. How long it went on, she didn't know. She was lost to the mastery of him, the undeniable pull that was Rook Granger. She gorged on the taste of mint and male, and he breathed fire into her, making her wanton.

He rolled his hips into her stomach, and the feel of his hard cock made her moan. Her hands dug into the firm skin that covered the steel muscles of his back. Another roll of his hips and she was lifting her legs, wrapping them around his hips as he pushed her against the Honda.

The cold of the glass on her now exposed back had her gasping, bringing reality crashing down. She went stiff against him, disbelief cooling the fire that he'd built inside her. His hands were on her skin, and holy shit, it was heaven.

Vivi pulled her mouth away, pushing his head back and lowering her legs. "Stop."

He growled. Honest to God *growled*, and Vivi wanted nothing more than to climb back up his body and start all over.

"We can't do this," she said. "Not until we get you cleared."

He pulled in a deep breath and stepped away from her. Her hands fisted. She missed his skin beneath her fingers. Missed his hands on hers.

"That might never happen," he said, his face hard, eyes glittering in the meager light.

"We must focus. Right is right. This," she said, gesturing between them, "isn't imperative."

He smiled then, and she damn near melted into a puddle at his feet. She'd seen the wry twist of his lips, the sexy sneer and the flat line of irritation on his scrumptious mouth. But his full-blown smile blew her away.

She put a fist to her stomach and held up a hand. She was so screwed. His gaze moved over her face, cataloging every nuance of her expression. That smile never waned.

He glanced down her body, a single glance, but it was enough to convey intent she didn't know if she was ready to meet. "I think it's very imperative."

The click of her jaw as her mouth fell open was loud in the sudden silence. She stared up at him like a moron. His face in relief was beautiful. Lit by his smile, it was drool-worthy.

They gazed at each other for long moments, the intensity of what flared between them settling into a simmer. She realized she was in way over her head. But she hadn't been kidding with him. They had to move, and fast. Vivi pulled away from the car, straightening her spine and tossing her hair over her shoulder. Rook crossed his arms over his massive chest and waited.

He didn't even look affected anymore. Except for that very large, very intimidating bulge in his pants.

"We have to get to Warrenton. Time's wasting."

He grunted. So they were back on relatively safe footing again. She breathed in a sigh of relief.

"How are we getting there?" he asked.

She smiled then, and his gaze narrowed. Under his stare, she knew what it was to feel hunted. She pointed in the direction of the lone hanger.

He shook his head, but before he could voice a negative response, she picked up her duffel and set off in the direction of the plane.

"Seriously, I haven't flown in years," he called out.

She stopped. "Since you lost your leg?"

Silence met her question. Then a harsh breath followed by, "Yeah."

Again, the need to comfort him curled through her, warming her heart. But he wouldn't appreciate it, and they didn't have time for it anyway. So Vivi hardened her heart, made it cold. He was rated to fly them and had flown for pleasure long before the loss of his leg. This was about getting him cleared. Whatever it was about for him, he had to get over it. Quickly.

"Well, Sergeant First Class Rook Granger, it's time you got reacquainted. Because we've got to get to

Oregon. I can do a whole helluva lot of things, but flying a plane ain't one of them." She took off again, hoping he'd follow.

# CHAPTER 4

Rook breathed in the bitterly cold air of Warrenton, Oregon, and felt the vicious talons of fear release their hold. She'd made his ass fly, and the entire time his palms had sweat and his neck had prickled. He'd wondered if they were being tracked. If they'd be blown out of the sky. If he'd kill them with his lack of experience. So many things had run through his mind, but right now, in this place of cold Pacific winds and snow, he felt safe.

"Here," Olivia said, handing him a long plastic case.

He turned to her and took it. She smiled shyly, and he felt something move in his chest. Another release but this one caused a different sort of alarm to replace the fear of death. He was attracted to Michael's sister. And it had nothing to do with the fact that it'd been well over a year since he'd had a woman.

If only it were. Then he'd be able to live with what he knew was going to happen between them. Because as sure as hell was hot, he was going to have the woman with the chocolate-brown eyes, soft lips, and enough bravery for an entire company of soldiers.

"What is this?" He took it from her and snapped open the closures.

What met his gaze had him going into panic mode. She'd brought him a brand-new carbon fiber–reinforced polymer blade prosthetic. The lightweight material was multifunctional and would allow him an ease of movement the one he normally wore didn't. It even had traction plates on the bottom of the blade. He hadn't had a new prosthetic in over five years. Such a simple thing and yet it stole a heart he didn't think even beat anymore.

Rook had gone through hell getting back to active status. After an RPG had taken his leg in Fallujah, he'd suffered depression. Losing his leg hadn't been the half of it. He'd been a soldier his entire adult life. It defined him as nothing else. The loss of his active status, not being able to be out there with his teammates, had destroyed him.

So he'd worked at making himself invaluable. He'd been one of the first men ever reinstated to active duty with a prosthetic. Sure, it had been active duty as a Delta Force *liaison*, but he'd been back in. He'd regained who he was. Then he'd lost it again when he lost his unit in Mogadishu. And here was this woman, this crazy, gorgeous as all hell woman, trying to give it back to him?

He glanced up at her, noticing how the low lights of the plane highlighted the cream of her skin. "You're mine."

The words were pulled from him. It was insanity. He couldn't have her. More than likely, he'd die on whatever this mission of hers was. But if he managed to keep her alive, he wouldn't shackle her to him. He had nothing to offer but duty. Yet those words solidified his objective. And when Rook focused on something hard enough, completely enough, it became his.

"Nope. I'm mine, but you're welcome for the new blade," she said saucily. "You might want to go ahead and change. We've got a fifteen-minute drive from here, and then we'll hike in."

He set aside his lust. Business it would be then. "Soon is now."

Her brows lowered, and it was the cutest fucking thing he'd ever seen. "Huh?"

"I need those answers," he said.

"Change first, and then we'll talk," she urged.

He bit off his reply and sat down to change his leg. Her delays had his instincts roaring at him, but he'd walked out of Leavenworth with her. He had to see this through to the end. If it meant his life, so be it. Plus, she'd given him the single word that above all others led him to believe her motives, while crazy, were altruistic. *Endgame*. The secretive spec-ops entity that had been courting Rook for well over a year now. Good guys dressed in shadows and willing to do whatever was necessary to win any and all wars in the name of freedom.

"The car is secured," she said as she stuck her head back in the plane.

He followed her out, testing the movement of the new prosthetic. These limbs had to be fitted perfectly. How she'd managed to get one made to his specifications he had no idea. He needed to thank her, but the cold wind took his words and flung them to the sea writhing yards beyond the airfield where they'd landed.

"I'm driving," he said above the wind.

She shrugged and got in the passenger seat. He smiled. It was his first victory with her, unless you counted the kiss in Kansas.

He got in, turned up the heat, and sat there.

"We really need to move. Small window of time here. Lots of shit to get done," she reminded him.

"Who are you, Olivia Bentwood?"

She didn't answer right away, obviously weighing what she would give him and what she would hold back. His neck prickled again, and he recognized it as the fear taking hold. He was a soldier, hardened in battle, but his nightmares caused his waking hours to be filled with horror. He'd done and been the recipient of unimaginably bad things. Fear held his hand and kept him sane. It was a comforting friend in the midst of a world gone mad.

"Don't bullshit me. You know who I am. You know what I've done. I want it all, Olivia, or I'll leave you the first time you turn your back," he told her, making sure to keep his voice as deadened as his intent.

She glanced at him, eyes wide, mouth falling open. "You would leave? After everything I've gone through to get you this meeting, you would leave?" Her disgust at the prospect reverberated through the car.

He opened his hands and clenched them again. "You made the decision to do this. Not me."

"Is that how you sleep at night? You didn't make the decisions so that absolves you from responsibility? Michael told me all about you, Rook, but never that you were a coward."

He grabbed her neck then, wrapping his big, scarred hand around her throat, holding her loosely as he stroked the soft skin of her chin with his thumb. His threat was implied. He controlled the situation, not her. "Who are you? You told me CIA. I've no doubt you're probably a desk jockey cyber spook with that fancy, blacked-out computer, but I'm just not sure."

"Why not a badass CIA field operative?"

He snorted, barely cutting off the laugh that threatened to escape. "Seriously?"

"Not entirely out of the realm of feasibility. Maybe I'm as hardcore as you?"

He narrowed his gaze and squeezed his hand infinitesimally. "I have your throat in my hand. You wield a mean computer virus, but if you were with the Company, I'd be digging a knife out of my side right now. CIA field operatives are the very best killers, almost as good as Delta Force."

Her eyes went wide, sucking the air from his lungs. He didn't want to scare her, but at the end of the day, he'd been trained to do just that and he did it really well.

"You don't scare me," she whispered.

He almost laughed. She'd read his mind. "Yes, I do. You were scared from the moment you saw me sitting there, chained to the floor. You were scared when that goddamn guard touched you over and over. And you were scared when I got in your face. You hid it well, but yes, it was fear. I smelled it all over you, tasted it when I kissed you. Now tell me, who are you?"

"Cyber spook," she said with a sigh. "I was recruited right out of high school. I went to school at MIT, dual majored in computer science and programming, and entered the field of cyber spying at the age of twenty-one. I've worked at Langley for six years, in all areas of interest for the agency."

It made sense now, how Michael had managed to find out so much. He'd had his sister do his research for him. "You make a habit of dipping into classified information for personal use?"

She didn't deny it. That same core of honor that ran through Michael hadn't missed his sister. "Michael needed me. I answered the call. You have no idea what I would have done for my brother."

"Oh, I think I most definitely know. After all, you're here, aren't you?"

She nodded, but her eyes were drooping.

"How long since you slept?"

She licked her lips. His dick went hard.

"Two, maybe three days now?"

"We're headed to see General Arbor?"

Surprise flared in her eyes. Fatigue was making her slow.

"You knew I knew where we were headed," he reminded her. "You need sleep."

She licked her lips again. "I can sleep when I'm dead," she pointed out.

He stroked his thumb over her lips now, taking the wetness and spreading it. He ached, couldn't remember ever wanting a woman as badly as he did Michael's sister. "I'm going to make sure you don't die, Vivi."

She smiled. "Michael always called me Vivi."

He almost groaned. "I know." Rook pulled his hand away, palm itching to stay against her warm skin. "Who gave the order for the clusterfuck in Mogadishu?" he asked.

Her gaze met his, direct and without any hint of subterfuge. "Deputy Director of the CIA Grant Horner along with former Joint Special Operations Commander Gordon Channel."

Rook nodded. The CIA worked closely with JSOC, so it wasn't unusual for Delta to be involved in their

# CHAPTER 5

A KNOCK ON THE WINDOW PULLED VIVI FROM SLEEP. IT was a rough slide that ended with her heart in her throat. She snorted. Some CIA operative she was. Rook's face was highlighted by the moon as it peeked from behind a cloud, but Vivi noticed the snow continued to fall softly. She opened the door and got out.

"Shit, it's cold," she muttered.

He grunted.

"Hey, that grunting thing you do? Yeah, it really gets on my nerves."

He laughed. "Not a morning person?"

"It's the middle of the night, so I guess not," she bit out acerbically.

"Look at me," he demanded.

She did but just couldn't muster the energy to get mad at herself for obeying. "Yeah?"

"Now's the time to cut bait and run, Vivi."

She shook her head. "I made a—"

He held up a hand. "I know, I know. You promised Michael. But the truth is ugly, Olivia, and I'd rather not expose you to it."

"Not your decision to make. I pulled this meet for you. He's expecting both of us," she reasoned.

"No, he isn't. He's expecting me." He rubbed his chest. "Michael was a good man. You've done what his crazy ass asked. I don't want you involved in this," he said in a hard voice.

operations. Fucking spooks. When they weren't lying, they were lying. He put the car in gear.

Horner was a name, a place to start. But Rook knew that Horner was the fall guy. So was Channel. The game had begun in the mountains of the Hindu Kush of Kunar Province. Rook's unit being inserted into the shithole that was Mogadishu two years later had been another move on the game board. Ultimately, Horner was simply a pawn for the main players as they sought checkmate.

*Endgame.*

"Here are the directions," Vivi said in a voice that sang with weariness.

He wanted to leave her here. Take up this campaign on his own, but he knew she'd follow and cause problems. "I know how to get there."

She nodded. "I thought so. Seems like you know everything."

He ignored her jab. "Get some rest. I'll pull up, do some scouting and come back for you before we meet up with him."

She yawned, and before he could say another word, she was out.

So many unknowns in this game. So many entities vying for the ultimate prize of power. The waters were murky, and while Rook had struggled to maintain a position on the fence, he was being forced to align with a side.

He just hoped he picked the right one.

How had this man managed to weasel under her skin so quickly? What was it about him that made her want to throw away everything she'd worked for to save him?

She cocked her head, remembering her brother's words, his plea. "My brother told me how you pulled him from the hut when the bullets started flying. You gave him your weapon, propped him against the outer wall of the compound your unit was scouting, and went back in for more men. He said he remembered seeing you flying out of the front door of that hut in Mogadishu, the world exploding around you. He remembered every bite of the shrapnel entering his body. He remembered you reaching him, finding his comm device and calling for help. He remembered the blood pouring from your head and your cries into his device for extraction."

Vivi paused, her brother's words ringing in her ears. She breathed in and smelled the antiseptic—that unmistakable hospital scent that never quite left you. "You saved him, and even though he died from his wounds, you gave him enough time for me to say good-bye."

Her eyes blurred, but she met his gaze, tears rolling down her cheeks. "Do you have any idea what that meant to me? My brother was my world. He was all I had, and he knew I'd need something to keep me going. So he gave me you. He was the most honorable man I've ever known. The strongest man I've ever known. And I will see this through so that you live free because my brother couldn't."

He shook his head, reaching over and once again whisking away her tears. "Michael wouldn't want you to give your life for me. I'm not worth that, Vivi."

Her heart was back in her throat. "You are worth that. My brother believed it, and after everything I've learned about you, so do I."

"When I see General Arbor, it will be over. If he's not who you seem to think he is, he'll report that he's seen me. From that point on, your name will be locked with mine—"

"I've got this. I wear big-girl thongs and everything," she said with a smile.

He grunted. She lowered her brows. He laughed. She sighed.

He finally relented. "Let's go. You sure those scrawny legs can handle this terrain?"

She crossed her arms over her chest and cocked a hip. "Scrawny legs? Your mama's got scrawny legs, Beret Boy."

Those delightful lips of his tugged upward. "I don't wear berets, baby."

She shrugged. "I'm a cyber spy. I don't really pay too much attention to what badass spec-ops boys wear. Also? I've got this. And contrary to your belief, Arbor is expecting me."

He shook his head. "You're armed?"

She raised a brow and rolled her eyes. "To the gills."

"I found your stash," he told her.

"Wasn't hard considering I left it on the backseat in plain view."

"For the record, I really don't want you going in here."

She nodded. "Yeah, I noticed. For the record? I'm going."

He rolled his shoulders and looked up at the dark sky.

Snow fell on his face, dotting his lashes, and she wanted to lick that snow, kiss his brow, hold him in her arms and tell him it would all be okay. Instead, she straightened her shoulders. "Fifteen hours, Rook."

He breathed deep and glanced at her, gaze hard, face blank. "It'll only take one."

She didn't know what to make of that. General Arbor was the first step, not the last. "Do you know something I don't?"

His lips curved, and his face warmed. "Nobody knows more than you, Vivi. That's what Michael always said. He showed me your picture once."

She cocked her head. "I hope it was a good one."

That panty-dropping smile was back in place, and she actually took a step toward him.

"You were wearing a teeny-tiny red bikini." He licked his lips. Vivi went liquid. "I never knew red was my favorite color."

Desire curled low in her body, loosening her muscles and flowing through her like a luxurious wave. "Maybe I'll wear it for you one day."

She wanted to slap her hand over her mouth. What the hell?

"Goddamn, I hope so."

Four words and he stole her heart. It was insanity. Along with all the intelligence her brother had lauded her for, all the stubbornness he bemoaned, Vivi was an all-in kinda gal. And in the space of nine hours, she'd gone all in with Rook Granger.

She hoped so, too. She really hoped she got to spend some time with SFC Rook Granger, either with or without the teeny-tiny red bikini.

"Wish I knew what was going on in that brain of yours." He tapped her nose. "But we need to move."

She nodded, shoving down her desires and forcing herself into business mode.

"You'll take my flank. I go in first. Watch for my signal before you make entrance," he said.

"Got it. Um, Rook?"

He had turned away from her, grabbing up the backpack she'd brought for him. "Yeah?"

"What do you think I'd have to do to become a fullfledged CIA field operative?"

He shrugged those massive shoulders, but a grin played about his lips. "I don't know. Get shot or some crazy shit like that?"

She nodded and bit her lip. He turned away.

"Um, Rook? One more thing?"

He stopped and looked at her over his shoulder. "Yeah?"

"What's the signal?"

"You'll know," he told her before he took off in the direction of General Arbor's place.

"Great," she muttered as she watched him disappear into the copse of cedars at the edge of the clearing where she'd parked.

It took them thirty minutes instead of the fifteen she'd prepped for. The heavy snow, wind, and darkness took their toll on her pretty quickly, so when Rook raised his fist in the air, she was grateful for the reprieve.

Ahead of them was a lone cabin, no lights, only the occasional moonbeam dancing between the towering trees and shadows. Something stirred to her right, and she pulled her pistol, training it on the spot before she noticed it was just a low-hanging branch.

She glanced back to where she'd last seen Rook, sifting through the darkness but only finding more darkness. Fear tripped through her belly, knocking her heart like a pinball against her ribs. The silence was deafening, not even the shushing fall of snow on top of more snow could be heard.

A twig snapped, and she turned in a circle, searching for the source. Muted footfalls echoed, then complete quiet.

"Turn around, Ms. Bentwood."

She knew that voice. Had spoken to the man just yesterday, outlining her plans. All except for coming to Warrenton. That she'd told no one except the man in Washington.

She searched the shadows once more, seeing no sign of Rook. They'd not made a contingency plan, though she had no doubt he'd be fine on his own.

Vivi, however, was toast. She raised her hands, knowing before she turned there was a gun held on her.

"Brigadier General Johansen," she said aloud, hearing her voice echo back to her.

To her left, lights speared the darkness.

"Tell him to come out," Johansen bit out.

He pushed the barrel of the gun against her cheek.

Johansen had once been a fine-looking man. Nearing fifty, he still had the regal bearing of a soldier, but his face was lined now. Stress and regret carved a map in harsh relief on his handsome features.

"Don't try me, Ms. Bentwood."

"I didn't have you pegged as a traitor, Brigadier General."

He pressed harder, and Vivi wanted to beg him to remove the gun. The cold of the barrel against her face was like acid.

"I'm no goddamn traitor!" Spittle lined his lips, some of it landing on Vivi's cheek. Disgust curled through her then. She'd played right into his hands.

"Who's pulling your strings?" she asked, not bothering to veil her rage. She was shaking. Not with cold but with a volcanic anger.

"Have him come out, Ms. Bentwood," he said again. In his voice was the promise of something really bad should she not obey.

Vivi had known the price she might pay. Her brother had been worth it. Then she'd looked into Rook Granger's pitch-black eyes, and he'd become worth it. So Vivi straightened her shoulders, tipped her head back in spite of the gun digging into her cheek and she said two words, "Run, Rook!"

Johansen's face hardened though his eyes widened in what Vivi imagined was disbelief. She saw his hand rise, felt the barrel of his weapon leave her cheek, heard the sharp report of a weapon discharging, winced as the hot slide of a bullet kissed her neck, and then…darkness.

# CHAPTER 6

HE'D SHOT HER!

Rage poured through Rook, a superheated frenzy that threatened to snap his hold on sanity. She fell at the man's feet, a crumpled rag doll, dark hair a shadow on the snow. He almost stepped into the moonlight, lifting his gun and aiming between Johansen's eyes but something held him back.

He focused on Vivi, watching as two men stepped forward to pick her up by her arms. She groaned, and it was a precious sound against the backdrop of the ocean in the distance. There was a long mark on her neck, and the snow at her feet was dotted with dark stains. His vision hazed the color of her blood.

Then Rook shut down—just gave himself over to the soldier who ruled his mind. He counted five men, all black-ops soldiers by their bearing. One hung back at the tree line, but Rook took in the others' eyes, memorizing them in a split second, recognizing none but realizing he'd kill them all if Vivi was more than just winged by that shot. *Run*, she'd said. *Goddammit*. She'd trusted Johansen, not realizing she shouldn't have trusted anyone.

He watched them drag her through the snow into General Arbor's house. He hoped Arbor was still alive. Rook had known when they'd come up on the house that something was off. Arbor had been moving around his kitchen when he'd scoped the place earlier. In the time it had taken him to get back to Vivi then back here, Johansen and his men had shown up.

Vivi had been surprised. Rook hadn't. The signs were all there—this was too big for the men gunning for him not to have their hand in everything. This type of presence here was proof.

Rook waited, keeping to the darkness and watching as the lone man moved in from the edge of the woods while the rest entered the cabin. He moved like a wraith—in his space one minute, gone the next. Rook had only ever seen one person do it quite like that. And that person was dead. *Knight.*

Rook headed for the back door of the cabin, plans forming instantly. He'd been trained to plan, execute that plan, and kill. He did them all really well. Anyone who'd touched her had become a target for him.

Rook slowed his breathing, fought the need to get to her, and wasn't shocked when the man who'd hung back attacked him from the rear. He turned, catching the man with a short right cross to the jaw, then wrapping his arm around his neck.

"Calm the fuck down, Rook."

Rook froze. The voice belonged to Knight. The man moved like Knight. But Knight was buried in Virginia, a single cross marking the place he'd finally come to rest.

Rook released him, turning him around quickly, striking out and taking him down with a single punch to the solar plexus. He followed him to the ground, his forearm to the other man's throat and his gun to the man's forehead.

The moon peeked from behind a cloud, and Rook

watched as it revealed a face he'd never expected to see. "What the fuck?"

Knight smiled. "Good to see you, brother."

Rook pressed harder. "You're dead."

"Get that fucking gun outta my face, dude. I'd hate to have to kill you with it," Jonah Knight said, smile gone, eyes hard.

It still sounded like Knight. That mocking smile looked like Knight. "You're dead."

"And you're a broken fucking record. Look, we don't have time for this. Johansen will kill both Bentwood and Arbor if we don't get in there. The men with him are freelance. They're ready to take off at my signal. Then it will be you, me, Johansen, and maybe some answers."

"I don't believe this. How do I know it's you?" Rook demanded, not lifting up off the gun at all.

"Because it looks like me?" Sarcasm hung in the air, and then Knight's face blanked but the truth was in his black eyes. "Endgame."

Rook rolled off his best friend and stood. "Why?" he asked.

Knight stood, brushed off the snow, and looked at the sky. "Had to be done. The truth caught up with me before it did you. But we've got a way now to settle this. A way to make it right."

"There's no way to make what happened on the side of that fucking mountain two years ago *right*," Rook ground out.

Raised voices from inside the cabin had Rook moving. A hand on his shoulder stopped him.

"She's important?" Knight asked.

Rook took a deep breath, sifted through his mind for the answer, feeling it notch in his throat. "Yeah."

"What the fuck, dude? Only *you* could find a woman in prison," Knight said caustically.

Rook ignored the bait. He hadn't found her. She'd found him. "Call those spec-ops boys off, Knight. You make entry first. I'll tag Johansen, and we'll play, yeah?"

"On it." Knight was gone then, a breeze and then nothing.

Rook entered the cabin, checking the shadows and listening. A thud sounded from the area of the den, and then a large black shape entered the kitchen. Rook aimed, the man held up a hand. Rook let him leave the way he'd come in.

Knight had done what he'd said he'd do. Rook pushed the disbelief aside. He and Knight had been a unit for so long that it was easy to fall back into the pattern of trust. The fucker would have questions to answer later, but right now, Rook had no choice but to depend on him.

He entered the den, took in the blood dripping onto the floor beneath Vivi's chair and then the gun Johansen had trained on her. Her head was forward, chin touching her chest and her breaths were choppy. Vivi's eyes were closed, but she winced and he knew then she was aware of what was going on.

"Wake the fuck up, Agent Bentwood," Johansen yelled as he kicked her chair.

It nearly toppled, but Johansen reached out to steady it and that's when Rook struck. He shot the gun out of the general's hand and was on him in the next second.

He punched him in the face, clocked him in the ribs,

and turned him over, wrapping both the general's hands in one of his before he stood him up.

"Ties," he demanded, and Knight was there.

He used the zip ties to bind Johansen's hands in front of him before pushing the man to the sofa and forcing him to sit. Blood dripped from his nose and hate burned in his eyes. Rook shrugged and turned to Vivi.

Knight was there, wrapping gauze around her throat. "She's good. He winged her," Knight reported.

Arbor roused then, cursing. He'd been hit several times in the face, but his wounds weren't serious. The general looked pissed. "Johansen, I'll have your fucking ass in a sling for this," he spit out, along with some blood, maybe a tooth or two.

Johansen had gone silent.

"Goddammit," Knight yelled as he rushed to Johansen.

Rook turned and panic rushed through him. Johansen was foaming at the mouth, a single plastic packet falling from his dying hands. He fell over on the sofa, and Rook saw his chances at redemption fading away along with the life in the brigadier general's eyes.

Cyanide. *Goddamn*. What was so bad you wanted to kill yourself to keep it from getting out?

"You Delta boys are always in the middle of some serious shit," Arbor said wearily. "Now untie my ass, soldier."

Knight did as Arbor requested.

Rook was busy with Vivi. Her eyes were open, but she refused to meet his gaze. "Olivia?"

"Yeah?"

"What's wrong?"

"I got shot, Rook," she said, and a small smile curved those full lips he wanted to spend his life licking and kissing. Fuck that. A lifetime might not be long enough.

"Are you smiling?"

"This makes me a full-fledged field operative now, right?"

He rubbed his eyes and laughed. This was another clusterfuck all the way around. He and Knight could still pump Arbor for information, but their most solid lead, Johansen, had killed himself. And here he was fucking laughing. "Sure, Vivi. Full fledged."

"Boys," Arbor said into the silence. "I think it's time Agent Bentwood was returned home."

She shook her head as she rubbed her wrists. "Um, hello? All this started because of the research I did. I contacted General Arbor, and I got you out of prison, Rook."

Her voice wavered. Rook wanted to hold her. There was no time. Rook hardened his softening heart. "You did good, Vivi. You led me to General Arbor, and you've given me the deputy director's name. But this is shit you don't need to be involved in."

"I'm in this. They know I've been asking questions, delving into files," she managed to get out in a raspy voice. "You can't just go after the deputy director of the CIA with no evidence."

Arbor walked over to her then and got down on his haunches in front of her. "You did good, Agent Bentwood. Go home. You covered your tracks. I can't believe your brother involved you in this, but you've done everything you could. Don't ruin your life for a fight you weren't meant for. I'm going to fill these men in on everything you told me, okay? Go back to D.C., live your life, and know that you honored your brother in the very best way possible."

She nodded, but around her mouth were the lines Rook had begun to associate with stubbornness. "They'll be searching for Rook. They'll take him back to Leavenworth. This was supposed to be over in twenty-four hours. We were supposed to verify the truth and let justice prevail."

Rook rubbed his chest at her forlorn tone.

Arbor shook his head. "Rook won't be going back to Leavenworth."

Unspoken communication hovered in the air between him, Arbor, and Knight—Johansen's unforeseen suicide played into the very large picture.

That day in the Hindu Kush two years ago had been the beginning. But the roots of it all were embedded so deep it would take more than twenty-four hours to unravel it all. He and Knight had taken their unit into those mountains and been forced to fight their way out. Rook thought he'd lost his best friend.

That he hadn't, that Knight was here, obviously alive and well, told Rook things were murky and ominous. The packet Rook had placed in a safety deposit box in Oklahoma City held the answers. But it was encrypted. He'd taken it off their communications specialist, Private E. R. Coombs, when he'd found his body. Coombs had been shot point-blank when he'd walked into a copse of trees, leaving his unit behind as he ran a subversive mission within their mission.

Who had sent him on that death errand? Who was to be the recipient of that information that now lay hidden in an Oklahoma City bank under an assumed name? Who the fuck wanted to destroy an entire unit two years later because of that information?

It was all on the disk. But he wouldn't involve Vivi. He refused.

"You need me," she stated as she lifted her chin. "The information in that safety deposit box you opened two years ago is encrypted. You need me."

Shock made him cold. Olivia Bentwood was dangerous. Beautiful and dangerous. A deadly combo. Long moments passed, but he finally shook his head. "No."

"He's right, Agent Bentwood," Knight chimed in. "We really need you back inside."

"You aren't locking me out of this?" she asked, spearing Rook with her gaze. Warmth replaced the cold from seconds ago.

"No. You've done more for me than anyone else. I won't lock you out of this. But it'll be need-to-know, Vivi."

"Endgame is real," she said firmly.

Arbor raised his hand, demanding silence. "Not now, Agent Bentwood."

"I know it's real, Vivi," Rook said. "The packet I took off Coombs was labeled with a single name—Endgame."

She raised her gaze to his. It took his breath. "You'll be safe?"

"Yeah."

"You'll let me know what you need?" she asked, and a single tear dropped down her cheek.

Knight and Arbor disappeared into another room. Rook was grateful. He went to a knee in front of her then. "I could tell you now what I need, Vivi."

She cocked her head and stared at him intently. Slowly, she lifted a hand and traced his eyebrows. Her fingers were gossamer silk over his skin. She would unman him with a single touch.

"I'm worried. What if they come after you? Me?"

He raised his hand then, wrapping it around her neck and pulling her to him. "Don't worry about me. They've already tried. They had no idea I'd have a rogue CIA cyber spy on my side. And I'll be watching out for you. But I need everything you have, and that means you going back in. Arbor will fill me in on this end. But at the first sign of anything off, you tuck tail and use the phone I'm about to give you to call me. Watch your back."

She nodded and licked her lips.

He took her offer and sank into her heat, twining his tongue with hers, telling her with his actions everything he wanted to say with his words. She tasted of promises he'd denied himself. And sex. She tasted of sex and want and need.

He pulled away when his cock beat at him to take her to the floor and cement her to him with his body. Now wasn't the time. He needed to get her on her way back to D.C.

"I don't understand this," she whispered as she stroked her fingers over her lips now.

"I don't either. But I'm coming for you, Vivi. You came for me, and I won't let you go."

Rook stroked a thumb over her cheek, letting the softness of her ground the hardness in him.

Her brother was a smart man. Because Rook had been drifting, lost in a sea of desperation and betrayal and then there'd been Vivi. He owed Michael Bentwood and would pay the man back by making sure Vivi was always kept safe.

Rook stood and turned. Knight was there, holding out a sat phone. Rook took it and gave it to Vivi. "Check it," he said to her while never removing his gaze from Knight.

Knight smiled and shrugged. "I understand."

"It's clean," Vivi said and stood to her feet. To Knight she said, "Do I need stitches?"

"Nah, Johansen was a horrible shot."

She snorted. "Or a great one." She averted her gaze from the deceased man on the couch.

"Agent Bentwood?" General Arbor called her name from the doorway. "One of my friends is going to fly you back to wherever that jet of yours came from. I'll take you back to the airstrip now."

She nodded and glanced at Rook, then turned.

"Jonah Knight? I traced you to Syria after the transport plane supposedly carrying your body landed in Germany. From there, you were off-grid. When I first started digging, I thought you were in on framing him. When I realized you weren't, I decided your secrets were your own. You'll tell him now though. Or I'll make your life very uncomfortable."

Rook wanted to grab her and run, take them far away from this insanity. It didn't even shock him that she'd known Knight was alive.

Knight held up his hands. "Understood."

She nodded and turned to follow Arbor. Rook wanted to call after her, but when she looked back at him, all he could do was nod.

He'd known her mere hours, but she'd stolen a vital piece of him. It pissed him off but more than that it made him nervous. It wasn't about Rook alone anymore. She'd taken something from him, but she'd replaced it with something invaluable. Her.

Then she was gone, and by the time the dawn broke the night sky open wide, he knew that Endgame was much more than he'd ever suspected. He knew Coombs had told Knight what was going on, and before Knight had a chance to tell Rook, the game had been in play so he'd had no choice but to disappear, faking his death and sending an empty coffin up the on-ramp to the transpo flight to Germany. He'd been on the plane, but he'd been very much alive, and searching for the ones behind the clusterfuck on the side of that mountain.

Arbor urged Rook and Knight to seek out the help of a man more powerful than most but one who had something the other men in power didn't have—honor. He gave them a single name, The Piper, and a number. Arbor told Rook that The Piper would be very interested in the information both Rook and Vivi had.

Rook knew what he was setting in motion was going to tip the balance of power for some of the most powerful people in his government.

And it was all good. Because Rook was in for a penny, in for a pound. He'd destroy them, and if he gave his life in the process, so be it.

# CHAPTER 7

VIVI OPENED HER APARTMENT DOOR AND WALKED IN, dodging her cat and throwing her keys on the table. It'd been two weeks. Two weeks with no calls from Rook and a level of diligence she'd not thought herself capable of. She hated looking over her shoulder and knew beyond a shadow of a doubt she wasn't cut out for field operative work.

Her cat meowed loudly, and Vivi sighed, unbuttoning her dress shirt and shrugging it off. She flipped on her bedside lamp and a whisper of fear danced over her flesh, catching her off guard even though she'd damn well knew better than to let her mind wander.

Someone was in her room. She turned, and there he was, casually leaning against her bedroom door frame, hands in the pocket of his jeans, head cocked arrogantly to the side and a knowing smile on his face.

She lifted a hand to her chest and tried to catch her fleeing breath. "How'd you get in my apartment?"

He raised an eyebrow.

"Damn it, Rook Granger. You scared the shit out of me," she whispered.

He grunted. "I can see that. So much for watching your back."

She shrugged and let her shirt fall to the floor before unzipping her skirt and letting it fall too. His indrawn breath had her smiling. His "Goddamn, woman," had her heart tripping.

"I need a shower. You gonna leave, or you here for a while?" She held her breath. What would it be? She'd been digging for two weeks, but she'd not heard from him. Not a peep, and she'd worried. But she'd never picked up that damn sat phone to call him. It was for emergencies, though she'd been tempted as hell.

"Oh, I'm here for a while, baby," he said softly.

Chills danced along her skin.

"I really like you in red, Olivia."

"Yeah. I kinda thought you might." Then she went all in once more. "I've worn it every day since I left Oregon."

He hissed in a breath, and she closed the bathroom door and proceeded to take the shortest shower in history. She wrapped her hair in a towel, wrapped another one around her body, and stepped out, right into Rook.

Her gaze rose, meeting his. His black eyes, normally filled with ice, were hot. So hot they singed her skin, their heat sinking deep and wrapping around her heart.

He traced the healing wound at her neck, face hard, mouth in a flat line. "You know I want you," he said in a growl.

She nodded.

"I'm an all-in kinda guy, Vivi. It'll be you for me and me for you as long as we're together. You get me?"

Vivi got it. She got it so much she had to squeeze her legs together to ease the ache between them. "All in how?"

He smiled, that full-blown, sexier-than-hell curving of his lips that took her mind and scattered it. He reached for the towel on her head and tore it off. A shiver rocked her at the intent on his chiseled face. Her wet hair was cold against her quickly heating flesh. Then he reached for the towel covering her body, and she went liquid.

"Right here, right now, Vivi, all in *you*," he murmured as he lowered his head.

She thought he'd kiss her, but he bypassed her mouth and stroked his lips over the healing mark on her flesh. Her hands rose of their own accord, sinking into his hair and tugging on the short strands. She sighed, and he chuckled.

"You taste really good, Vivi. I wonder how you'll feel?"

She moaned as he licked over the shell of her ear, peppering kisses along her jaw until he hovered over her mouth. Their breaths mingled, and her lips parted. "I feel pretty good right now, Rook."

"Just good?" he asked, and his thumbs stroked over her cheeks.

She smiled, feeling wanton and needy. "Well, yeah, right now I feel pretty good. But I'm sure, Sergeant, that once you go all in, I'll be feeling much better than that."

"Oh, Olivia." He paused, dropping his lips even closer to hers. "I can guarantee it'll be much, much better."

Then he picked her up, turned, and deposited her gently on her bed. He stepped back, toeing off his boots, pulling off his black T-shirt, and very slowly lowering his jeans. That left him in a pair of black boxer briefs that lovingly cupped his impressive erection. The tip peeked out the waistband, and Vivi wondered what he tasted like. Spicy? Sweet?

Vivi licked her lips.

He groaned. She smiled.

"You're going to take it all off, right?" she asked.

His body tensed, and his gaze narrowed on her. "I said all in, yeah?"

"Yes, you did. So get to it…*yeah*?"

He growled, and she giggled, but then he was on top of her, sucking all the energy out of the room and giving it back to her with his mouth. He poured his need for her down her throat, leaving nothing but the taste of him on her lips. Desire coiled inside of Vivi, flaring and burning everything it touched, leaving her brand new.

Rook took her higher with every touch, every kiss. Along her collarbone, between her breasts, over her nipples, and across her belly.

"Goddamn, Vivi, you're so sweet," he murmured against her flesh.

He whispered a kiss at the top of her pubis before he spread her legs and wedged his broad shoulders between them.

"Look at me," he ordered.

She did. The sight of him there, at the entrance of her body, made her thighs quiver. His black eyes burned, and her hips lifted. He grinned, then spread her pussy open and sank inside with his tongue. He drank from her, teasing with nuzzles then dipping deeper as he stroked her clit with his thumb. She spiraled. Up, up, up she flew before the lights behind her eyelids coalesced and burst. He caressed her through her orgasm, wringing every drop from her until his hands became more purposeful once again. He slid up her body, palming her breasts and kissing her neck, her lips, her shoulders. Nowhere was safe. He was devouring her, and she burned for him.

"Please, Rook," she begged. Her release moments

earlier had only banked the roaring blaze inside her. His hands on her body rekindled it, making it flame even brighter.

She heard the rip of a foil packet and opened her eyes. "I'm safe. We don't need it," she said. Whose voice was that, she wondered. A wanton seductress's.

"Are you sure you're ready for this? For me?" he asked, face strained at holding back.

She nodded and rose to her knees. "I've never been more sure." Her hands wound with his hands, palm to palm, fingers curled with his—a lover's embrace. "All in," she whispered.

She unleashed the beast then. The same beast she'd seen writhing under his skin in the prison. She'd known then that she wanted him. Something in his eyes had called to her. Now she'd have him.

He pushed her back gently, coming over her and seating his cock at her entrance. He pushed into her slowly. His jaw tensed, and she stroked her hand over it, smiling.

"I'm so glad I came for you," she said softly.

His eyes closed, then opened, and she knew…she'd be his until time ended. His body went still above her, and then he pushed in to the hilt.

He was so big, and she was a tiny woman, but as he settled his hips against hers, stroking her from the inside out, she knew he fit her just right.

"What you do to me," he said harshly.

Then he ushered her to a place she'd never been before, thrusting into her body, taking everything she was and returning it to her a hundred times over.

"So good," he said as he lifted away and put a pillow under her bottom.

"So mine," he reiterated as his hands traced her curves then grabbed her hips, holding her still.

He shifted as he thrust deep and stole her soul, wrapping it up in his own and sheltering her in the midst of his storm.

"Vivi?" he demanded.

"Rook?" Their eyes were as connected as their bodies. He refused to let her close them, anchoring her mind as he ravaged her body.

"I'm not letting you go."

"That's good, because I'd hunt your ass down," she murmured.

Then he showed her his intent, pounding into her body, making her keen in desire and finally forcing them both over the edge in a white-hot wave of release.

"All in," he muttered again before he tucked her into his side and covered her legs with one of his.

She relaxed against him, replete, complete, like she'd never been before. Then she slept.

# CHAPTER 8

VIVI WOKE AT HIS SIDE SLOWLY. ROOK HAD WATCHED her sleeping, cursing himself for coming here but knowing she was in his blood and he'd never be able to resist her lure. She was both the last and only thing he needed. Olivia Bentwood was a huge complication in a life already so FUBAR it was hard to process.

"You're thinking really hard," she muttered as she snuggled into his body, licking his skin before she placed her chin on his chest.

He wiggled his eyebrows. "That's not all that's hard."

He'd always been known as a rough and mean son of a bitch. This tiny woman made him soft. The imp smiled. He cupped her luscious ass and then smacked it. She moaned, and he almost, *almost* rolled her over and sank into her heat. "Get dressed and come into the living room," he said as he pulled away from her and sat on the side of the bed.

Rook needed to tell her, but it was going to be hard. He was never going to be a free man. He'd signed on with the devil in order to capture the ones who'd done this to him. And Vivi wasn't part of the deal. He'd been allowed forty-eight hours with her to make sure she was safe, and then he had to head back to his new headquarters in Port Royal, Virginia.

He reached for his backpack and pulled out some sweats, glancing at his watch and bemoaning the fact that he only had about six hours left with her. It wasn't enough time to make a lifetime of memories. But it was all he had until this business was finished.

She got up and threw on some sweats and the T-shirt he'd discarded last night. She tossed him a shy smile, and he rubbed his chest. He hoped he made it to heaven, so he could first thank her brother for sending Vivi his way, then choke the life out of him for the same reason.

"Come on," she said. "I'll make us some coffee."

He followed her into the kitchen, watching her prepare the coffee, enjoying her naturally seductive movements. She'd once been a dancer. She loved the beach. She made love like a goddess. She tasted like sin.

He hoped he lived long enough to claim her. She set the coffee, creamer, and sugar in front of him and watched as he pushed everything but the coffee away.

"Black? Eww," she complained with a laugh.

"I'm a soldier, Vivi. Not some frou-frou CIA field operative."

She laughed. He smiled and rubbed his chest again. The skin over his heart would be raw before all was said and done.

"Tell me," she said as she hopped up on the stool beside him.

"This shit is deep, Vivi. I can't give you any more than what you already know. You're in the clear right now. Arbor managed to talk the warden at Leavenworth into keeping your presence there a secret. He's former Army, knew Arbor really well, so we got lucky. Johansen's death was chalked up as a suicide due to the stress of his job. But right now, you're safe. Being with me puts you in the crosshairs. They're hunting me and Knight, Vivi, and they won't stop."

"Did you bring me the disk?" she asked as she sipped her own coffee.

Rook wanted to wipe the frown from between her brows. "No. You're not touching that disk."

"So what you're saying is that when you leave here, you'll not be back?" Her voice was mild—the energy drifting from her was anything but.

He blew out a rough breath. "Yeah, that's what I'm saying."

"No."

A simple refusal full of her intent.

"You weren't cut out for this, Vivi—"

She held up a hand and cut him off. The woman was a constant surprise and obviously had no fear of Rook. His cock went brick hard. She was perfect for him.

"You didn't call me for two weeks, and you think I wasn't busy researching my cyber-spy ass off? Oh, Rook, for such a smart man, you're incredibly stupid."

Rook smiled. Vivi frowned.

She set her cup down hard. "I know who you've aligned with. I wish there were another way, but there isn't. And now I, too, have cast my lot with your new boss. I believe he likes to be called The Piper. You see, he's been my contact since the beginning."

Rage made his gut roil. "You cannot do this," he said in a hard voice. "No goddamn way am I letting you into this, Vivi, you're too... Wait. Since the beginning?"

She raised a brow. "Too what?"

Rook wasn't taking her bait. He was a man, built for war. She was a woman, built for loving. "It's not happening," he damn near yelled.

"You're a sexist pig, Rook Granger. I'm good

enough to fuck but not to stand beside you in this fight? Have you forgotten what they cost me? My brother died because of their damn war games!"

He reached for her, but she hopped off the stool and sidestepped him, moving around to the other side of the counter.

"And then you're forgetting the most important thing," she muttered.

"Yeah? What's that, Vivi?"

She narrowed her gaze on him. "They also brought me to you. I want to find them and thank them properly."

He snorted. "You're a vicious one, aren't you?"

She cocked her head. "You have no idea. Besides, your new uber-secret black-ops group needs a cyber spy with CIA contacts and mad computer programming and hacking skills. Knight vouched for me."

He was going to run right through Knight when he saw him next time. The fear he thought he'd shed was back in full force. It wasn't as comforting as it normally was because now he had his woman to worry about. His brain halted. His. Woman.

His woman.

Holy…*his woman*.

"I meant what I said on that plane in Warrenton, Vivi."

She nodded. "I know you never say anything you don't mean, Rook."

"You're mine."

"And you're mine, Rook Granger. I won't let you go without a huge fight. You became mine when Michael brought your story to me two years ago. Then I saw you chained in prison, and you made me realize what honor was. So you remain mine."

"The men perpetrating these war games are powerful. We still don't know how high this reaches. And there are other governments involved. We're talking world order kind of shit, Vivi. You'll have no choice but to come to Port Royal. If you signed on with Endgame Ops, then you know that."

"Yes. We sharing quarters there?" she asked.

"If I can't talk you out of this then goddamn straight. What about 'you're mine' didn't you understand?"

"Just making sure."

He rubbed his chest.

"Why do you do that?" she queried.

He ground his back teeth. *All in, Granger.* "You make my heart hurt. You have from the moment I saw you in that goddamn prison."

"It's only fair," she responded.

"Why's that?"

"Because you do the same to me."

He calmly got up and walked to her, pulling her against him and holding her close. "I don't want you there, but I can't let you be anywhere else. Endgame Ops was formed specifically to fight these guys. That we're using their code name for their war games is thumbing our noses at them, but they'll find out eventually. We have no idea who this is, who's pulling these strings, setting the moves into play, killing our men and putting our country in jeopardy by selling secrets and weapons. Are you sure you want in on this? I can talk to—"

She looked up at him, and he knew. She was all in.

It made his heart beat fast and hard, the drum echoing in his cock. Her eyes widened, and he lifted her up.

She wrapped her legs around his waist, and he pressed into her.

She hissed in a breath. He lowered his mouth and suckled her breast through his T-shirt. She moaned and he gloried in the sound.

He pulled away and lifted his head, gazing deep into her eyes, willing her to understand.

"I know," she said. "I feel it too."

"He knows you're coming back with me?" Rook referred to the head of Endgame Ops. The man sitting in a cushy office up on Capitol Hill, controlling things for this entire operation. The Piper. The man Vivi had been corresponding with from the very beginning. They'd have to talk about that soon—all three of them, together.

She nodded solemnly.

He pushed down his panic, let the fear grab him by the throat, and relaxed. Then he walked them to the bedroom, laid her on the bed, pulled their sweats off, and proceeded to make love to her every way he knew how.

When morning came, he checked in at Port Royal and helped her pack her clothes and her cat.

"This is it, Vivi," he said as he kissed the tip of her nose.

"All in," she said with a bright smile.

"Let's do this," he said, taking her hand, picking up her cat's crate and heading out the door.

He had no idea what they were entering into, but he'd keep his woman safe. He'd give everything he was to keep her safe. She glanced back at him as she got in the waiting vehicle and he saw it in her gaze.

She would follow him into hell and hold his hand

while they burned together. What she didn't understand yet was that he'd protect her with his dying breath.

No half measures. All in.

*Hooah.*

# ABOUT THE AUTHOR

**Lea Griffith** began sneaking to read her mother's romance novels at a young age. She cut her teeth on the greats: McNaught, Woodiwiss, and Garwood. She still consumes every romance book she can put her hands on, but now she writes her own.

Lea lives in rural Georgia (GO DAWGS!) with her husband, three teenage daughters, two dogs, three cats, and a betta fish named Coddy George. If she isn't running her teenagers hither and yon, you'll find her at her keyboard giving life to the stories in her mind. She loves all genres of romance, and nothing is off-limits when it comes to her muse. For more information, please visit www.leagriffith.com or follow her on Facebook at www.facebook.com/LeaGriffithWrites and/or Twitter @LeaGriffith.

# BEAUTY AND THE MARINE

## TINA WAINSCOTT

# CHAPTER 1

THE BEAST WAS ABOUT TO MEET BEAUTY. THAT'S HOW Griff Tate saw it, anyway. And not just a pretty lady but a freakin' *model*. The only people who saw his scarred face were his family and the hunting or fishing parties he took out on Tate acreage. Many were vets like him who didn't flinch at his war wounds.

Griff opened the fridge in the guest lounge, known as the "Mud Room," and poured a glass of iced tea. Footsteps echoed in the hallway, the only noise besides the country song playing on the intercom system. The entire two hundred acres of his family's property had been reserved for this special op, so the footsteps had to belong to Chase Justiss.

Griff leaned into the hallway and greeted the man he'd only met twice before. While recovering in the hospital, Chase had offered him a job with his so-called private security agency. Griff had respectfully declined, wondering why Chase wanted to hire a man who might scare small children. Or pretty women. Didn't matter. Griff had already decided on holing up at his family's "resort," offering skills he'd been honing since he was knee-high to a mudbug. Then, last week, Chase had called him again, remembering the particulars about Griff's remote sanctuary. For this op, MUD'N HUNT, unofficially dubbed the "Redneck Playground," was the ideal locale. So were Griff's qualifications to instruct on hunting and handfishing.

Chase, in his linen slacks and expensive dress shirt, could have passed for a movie star. He held himself with the kind of confidence Griff once possessed.

Chase pumped Griff's hand. "Good to see you, my friend. Looks like we're all set."

"Yep. Most of my family headed down to Disney World." Even though this part of the op wasn't supposed to be dangerous, Chase didn't want to take any chances. "They sure appreciated the free vacation playing in the civilized world, as they call it. My cousin and uncle are on call to help as needed."

"I'm happy to give them a break." Chase gestured behind him. "The film crew is in the parking area, and two of my J-Men—my operatives—are doing recon. Risk and Julian brought their fiancées, capable women who will play the models competing with Kristy."

Kristy...the beauty. And the reason for this op. The Atlanta-bred model had drawn the attention of a vicious stalker whom the police were unable to identify.

Griff had signed on without hesitation when Chase told him why he wanted to rent the property: to stage a phony "reality" show about models competing to be the best redneck chick in order to lure the stalker. Griff acting as Kristy's on-camera guide, now that had taken some convincing.

"You ready to rock and roll?" Chase asked.

"Oorah," Griff said, what his Marine comrades shouted before heading out on a mission.

A memory of their faces flashed in his head, their cocky smiles after a dirty joke shared in the Humvee. Right before the explosion...

"You all right?" Chase asked, the man's eyes assessing him.

*Note to self: do not use military jargon. You're not in the military anymore.*

Griff gave a stiff nod. "I'm aces."

Chase clapped him on the back as they headed toward the front door. "There won't be any danger while you're in the scene. No one knows where we are or what we're doing except for a couple key Atlanta Police personnel. They'll come in once we've released the commercials, and you'll be long gone by then."

And staying at his cousin's place in Tennessee. "Not worried about danger, sir. In fact, a little excitement would do me some good. I'm fine with sticking around."

"Only if you're an employee." Chase arched an eyebrow. "I do have room for another J-Man."

Griff stepped outside and waved his arm to encompass the woods surrounding the lodge. "This is where I belong." Hidden from society. Out in nature, where the animals didn't care that he was scarred.

Away from the kind of beautiful women like the one who stood with the film crew talking about the camera she held. But Griff's gaze was hardly on that fancy camera with the foot-long lens. It was riveted to the tall woman with the straight blond hair and lithe figure. When she spotted him and Chase, she handed the camera back to the man next to her and walked over. Griff waited for her eyes to settle on his face, ready for the flinch. Everyone had some kind of reaction, though most tried to hide it. She didn't even blink as she approached, but her light blue eyes gave away a smidge of pity.

Chase said, "Kristy Marsden, this is Griff Tate."

She was clearly making an effort to keep those

gorgeous eyes on his and not let them drift over his ruined face as she held out her hand. "Thank you so much for doing this."

Her fingers slid over his palm before connecting in a handshake. Her touch was gentle, probably deferring to his condition. He firmed his grip to let her know he wasn't fragile. Then he released her, because her hand felt a little too good enveloped in his. "I'm happy to do whatever it takes to wrap up this sick son of a...gun. I understand this was your idea?"

"The concept of a setup was. Chase helped me disappear after Eye, the name my stalker uses, broke into my apartment and attacked me. For eight months, Eye couldn't find me. I guess that pissed him off."

"So he threatened your friend."

Kristy nodded, guilt pushing her mouth into a frown now. "Aisha didn't deserve to be dragged into my mess. I should have known he'd figure out a way to monitor my Facebook and Instagram pages. He saw a lot of pictures and selfies with me and my bestie."

The beautiful black model had received a threatening call: if he couldn't find Kristy within the next two weeks, he would shift his attention to Aisha. He was probably betting that Kristy wouldn't let that happen.

"Chase and I went to the police, but we were faced with the same problem we've had from the beginning. We don't know who this guy is. That's when I came up with the idea of luring him to someplace where we could at least photograph him and maybe capture him. The police were trying to figure out the logistics."

Chase shook his head. "But we don't have time to wade through the red tape. The compromise is that we're starting the op now with their guidance. Detective Burns will bring in his team if they get clearance in time. If not, he'll at least come when we're ready to pull the plug and make sure it'll stand up in court."

"And Kristy will be out of here before the first ad airs," Griff confirmed.

"Back in my safe house," she said with a sigh.

Chase put his hand on Kristy's shoulder. "Which must feel like a prison, though I know you're too kind to say it in front of me. Once we get this guy, you and Aisha will be able to live in the open again."

*Live in the open.* The words resonated. Not something Griff could ever do. It wasn't fair that this gentle woman had to hide, to live in fear. Griff, well, he'd signed on for that shit the moment he put his signature on the enlistment paperwork.

Kristy flattened her hand against her collarbone. "Living out loud," she said on a sigh. "After almost two years of hiding, I can go shopping and have lunch with friends and see a play!" She spun around but came to an abrupt stop. "I'm almost afraid to hope that it can be over. I used to think he'd lost interest when I hadn't heard from him in a week or so. But he always came back."

Now Griff could see the vulnerability and weariness Kristy masked with her brave smile. Probably the way she'd masked her horror at his scarred skin, his misshapen nose, and crooked mouth.

"We'll get him, one way or the other," Chase said. "If the police don't get approval in time, I have a decoy to pose as Kristy. My former Navy SEALs will secure the scene."

Griff caught Kristy looking at him, though she quickly averted her gaze. "Let's head on over to the bog." He winked at her as best as he could with the tighter skin around his right eye. "You ready to get muddy?"

She gestured to her black shorts, bathing suit top, and the net shirt she wore over it. "Ready as I'll ever be."

He figured she'd be prissy and maybe a bit superior, and some part of him was relishing seeing her all covered in mud. But damn, her trepidation and determination twisted him up inside. *Be careful, Griff.*

He hadn't been remotely interested in sex since the explosion. The warning in his head seemed unwarranted.

"Let's head over and situate the film crew," Chase said. "Then we'll bring in the supposed competition."

Griff pointed at a large SUV. "Take that one. It should fit the crew and equipment." He tossed a key ring toward Chase.

Chase caught it with a flick of his wrist. "Kristy, why don't you ride with Griff? Since you're going to be working together, you can get to know each other."

Kristy brushed a strand of hair from her face as she gave Griff a nervous smile. "You're going to have your hands full. I've never fished or hunted or anything. I'm a total city girl."

"I'll ease you in, though I'm supposed to create some commercial hooks. Which, unfortunately, means putting you in some uncomfortable situations."

She pulled her lower lip between her teeth. "I trust that you'll be as gentle as possible."

And just like that, he wanted to do his best to keep her safe and comfortable. By necessity, they would be in close proximity these next few days. He pulled the numbness that cocooned him close just in case he got any crazy ideas.

"We're ready," Chase called out. "My J-Men will give me a shout when they're done and meet us there."

"Just follow me." Griff led Kristy to the mud-splattered truck with big tires. He stepped up on the foot rail, opened the door, and held out his hand to her.

She allowed him to help her up to the first big step and settled in, looking like a flower in a pile of rubbish. The truck was fairly new, but it already sported the wear and tear of numerous hunting and fishing parties.

He closed the door and walked to the driver's side. As the engine started rumbling, Florida Georgia Line blared from the radio, and he quickly turned it down. "Sorry 'bout that. I keep it loud when I'm by myself." To keep the thoughts at bay. The memories.

"It's fine." She was already strapped in with the seat belt, her hands searching for a place to perch.

"You like country music?" He headed down the dirt road, checking to make sure Chase was behind him.

"Not particularly, but I don't dislike it either."

He kept the volume low, wishing he could amp it up and fill the awkward silence. In the corner of his eye, he could see her glancing his way, then turning toward the window. He hated that the scarred side faced her. All she could see was the beast.

"It's all right to look at me," he said quietly.

"I'm sorry, I don't mean to…"

"I know. It's hard not to look. Kinda like when you pass a car crash. You just can't help yourself. Took me a while to get used to it myself."

She narrowed her eyebrows at him. "You're not a crash."

Damn, was she taking him to task? He smiled, feeling the tug of the right side of his mouth. "It was just an analogy." But it wasn't, and by her silence, she wasn't buying it.

Even faced forward, he could see her surreptitiously glancing his way. He remembered the gruesome sights in Afghanistan, things you didn't want to look at, tried not to, but did anyway: severed body parts, exposed brains, the dead lying in the streets. He didn't want the sight of him seared into her head the way those images were seared into his.

"If you want, you could sit in the back," he offered. "If that makes you more comfortable. I know I'm not a pretty sight."

Her mouth dropped open, and her eyes widened as she obviously searched for the right—the diplomatic— thing to say. "Do you seriously think I would sit in the back just so I wouldn't have to see you?"

"I wouldn't blame you."

"You think I'm that shallow?"

"I didn't say that." He glanced in the rearview mirror to make sure Chase was still behind them. His eye, surrounded by scar tissue and what was left of his eyebrow stared back. "Hell, I don't like looking at myself, and you've got the ugly part of me facing you. I'm just offering you an escape, is all."

"I'm not sitting in the back. And your face isn't that bad."

"I look like a monster, but thank you. It's not just the unsightliness. I've been through all this with my family and the few people I've seen. They see me and feel bad. Sad."

She gripped the door handle as the truck hit a rut and lurched. "We always see ourselves as worse than we are."

"Not when you're beautiful." He smiled. "Why, I couldn't find one flaw on you, even if I tried." He let his gaze sweep over her creamy complexion, her golden hair that fell in a cascade over her shoulders. He drank her in, the perfection he could never have. He could see no sign of the knife attack she'd suffered. Thank God the psycho hadn't cut her face.

Her hand went to her collarbone. "There's plenty." She believed that, too, by the shadow that crossed her eyes. "I never set out to be a model, you know. I fell into it. I wanted to be an editor. After college, I got a job at a New York City publisher. But I had college loans to pay and I wasn't making a lot of money as an editorial assistant. You have to work your way up. My roommate's sister was a model, and when she told me how much she made, I think I salivated. She got me an appointment with her agency, they signed me on, and pretty soon I was too busy to work at the publisher."

He navigated around a large, mud-filled rut, so that his side took the brunt of the dip. "What made you return to Atlanta?"

"My parents. They were freaked out about my moving to New York to begin with. When I—quote— 'abandoned' my career, and my degree, they were worried for my safety and disappointed in my choices. So I compromised. I continued modeling but moved back to relatively safe Atlanta. Ironic, huh?"

He wanted to know more, but he rolled up to the parking area next to the mud bog. "I'm sorry that happened to you."

She turned to him. "I'm sorry that happened to you, too." Not pity in her eyes but a kindred sense of life's unfairness. Of overcoming tragedy.

He felt an inflating sensation in his chest, as though his heart was reaching toward her. He pulled it back and swaddled it in that cocoon. "Hang on a sec, and I'll help you out." She might be perfectly capable of getting out on her own, but something inside him wanted to make this as easy as possible. Wanted to take care of her.

*She's not yours to take care of. That's why Chase and his Navy SEALs are here.*

Kristy leaned forward, her hair spilling over her shoulders in a curtain, and Griff braced his hands at her waist and lowered her to the ground in front of him. He didn't want to release her. He stood there like an idiot for the longest three seconds of his life—well, the second longest—before he made himself drop his hands and look to where Chase and the crew were stepping out of their vehicle.

He had to force himself to head over to the men, though he couldn't help glance back to see her following. She was taking in that big, delicious mud puddle, with her lower lip pulled between her teeth again.

"Does anything live in there?" she asked. "Like fish or other slimy creatures?"

"Just the bog slugs. But they're real easy to pull off if they latch onto you. Kidding," he added quickly at the horror on her face. "No, this is a man-made bog. Nothing in there but a lot of lost egos when the big talkers get bogged down."

"I'm not actually going in there, right?"

The slight, effeminate cameraman aimed his lens at Kristy and whispered, "Go ahead and tell her what she's going to do."

"You're gonna get muddy," Griff called to her, unable to hide the grin or the teasing of his voice. He pointed to three Jeeps beneath a stand of maple trees. "And you're gonna do it while driving one of those."

"I'll be driving?"

"Yep. You and the girls are going to race in this bog. We run races here all the time, and lots of women bring their own trucks or ATVs." He usually watched from the judging grandstand, unwilling to join in. He'd only been home for ten months. He wasn't ready to face the weekend crowds, especially since they included a lot of locals. They waved and shouted up to him, but Griff talked to them from a distance. This would be a nice taste of mud racing, like dipping his toe in.

But for now, he was enjoying the startled expression on Kristy's face. "They're probably manual shift, right?" she asked. "I only do automatic. And I won't know what to do if I get stuck. I'll probably tip the whole thing over."

"They are manual, and I can teach you to drive it in about fifteen minutes. You will get stuck, but you'll know how to get unstuck because I'm going to be in the Jeep with you. So you won't tip it over." Relief saturated her expression, and damn did that bring back that twisting in his chest. "You in?"

She lifted her hand in a high five. "I'm in."

He met her palm with his. Only then did they realize the cameraman had been filming the whole thing.

The guy lowered the camera and gave them a wink. "Damn, I wish this was a real show. You two have fabulous chemistry." He skipped back to the vehicle.

Griff glanced to see if that statement had horrified her.

Her half grin held a hint of sheepishness. "Well, Griff, now you have the same expression I probably had when I was taking in that mud bog. You sure you're in?"

"Too far in to back out now." He offered her his bent arm. "Let's do this mud bog thing."

# CHAPTER 2

GRIFF LOOKED DECIDEDLY DISTURBED BY TRENT'S assessment of their chemistry. Kristy might have been amused, if he hadn't brought down a wall between them with a resounding *crash*. The statement surprised her. She didn't think she could have chemistry with anyone. Not after all she'd been through and was going through now. But there was...well, *something* between her and Griff.

He excused himself to prepare the Jeeps, turning down her offer to help, which left her standing amid all the activity, watching him. Griff thought he was a monster. It made her want to pull him into her arms and coax him into telling her all his fears and pain and hopes.

Griff was no child who would succumb to coddling. He was six foot two and over two hundred pounds of solid muscle. Though his shirt covered his chest and back, his biceps bulged, and his camo khakis tightened over muscular thighs. She wondered if he kept his left side facing her on purpose, given his concerns in the truck.

Which, damn, had really made her want to just lay her head on his shoulder and tell him that it didn't matter what he looked like on the outside. It did. To him, to the world.

*To you?*

She was in no position to get involved with someone. She couldn't even remember the last time she'd entertained a romantic thought, much less partook in the act itself. But there she was watching him, and the sight of all that male power spiraled heat in her belly. Before the explosion, he'd been gorgeous. She could see his high cheekbone and strong jaw that scar tissue buried on the other side of his face. His light brown hair shone in the sun, thick, with a slight wave where it curled against his neck.

He glanced up at her, and she quickly averted her attention to the guys discussing camera angles. Everyone raised their heads when two vehicles ambled down the gravel road. Kristy had only briefly met the couples who exited the vehicles. She felt a twinge of jealousy—*or was it merely longing?*—when the women gave their handsome men sweet kisses, took a duffel bag, and walked over to Chase. The two men stripped off their shirts as they began to fill Chase in on their surveillance and update them on the progress of the guys setting up cameras and motion detectors.

Kristy watched Griff as he tossed the last canvas onto a pile beneath a tree, turning when she heard the women coming up behind her.

Mollie, the dark-haired one, was taking in the trees all around with delight. "We don't get to see the changing of the leaves in Florida. This is amazing!"

Addie, a fair-skinned blond, had a decidedly different expression on her face as she rubbed her arms. "It's lovely, but it reminds me too much of that canned hunting property down in southern Georgia."

Griff's voice behind Kristy was a surprise. "You involved in that takedown?"

Addie's expression went from fearful to proud. "Yep.

Me and an unnamed former military guy who saved my fanny more than once." The way she glanced at Risk rather gave that away, though.

Chase and the two men came over. "Griff, this is Risk, and this is Julian."

Griff exchanged handshakes with the light-haired man first, then the dark-haired Latino. Neither showed any reaction to Griff's damaged face. No doubt they'd seen worse.

"Thanks for giving us the place to pull this off," Risk said. "We have a soft spot for women in trouble." His hazel eyes took in his fiancée, then landed on Kristy.

"Glad to help," Griff said. "I don't cotton to anyone harassing a woman."

Risk chuckled. "Cotton? Haven't heard that word in a long time."

"It's one of my grandpa's favorite expressions. Funny how it kinda slips out once in a while."

Addie and Mollie pulled off their tops and shucked shorts to reveal bikinis and shapely figures. Addie raised her arms and called out to Chase, "I hope this is skimpy enough. I'm not going any tinier."

Chase gave her a thumbs-up. "You both look perfect."

While the two women stuffed their clothes in their duffel bags, Kristy shuffled out of her shorts. The net top was staying on, though. She wasn't as brave as Griff was. And she could hear Eye's voice in her head, dammit. *Stop showing your skin, sinful woman! You are for my Eyes only. Get it? Eyes????*

When Griff turned to her, he must have seen the angst in her eyes and the way she was gripping the bottom edge of her shirt. Thankfully, he didn't call her on it. "Who else needs some instruction on driving a manual shift?"

Mollie raised her hand, and Addie said, "I drive one at my ranch. But I'll watch, since I've never driven a Jeep before. Especially one with big ole wheels."

These were definitely no ordinary Jeeps. Besides their huge wheels and higher profile, they were fitted with roll cages. Griff gave them the rundown on shifting gears, wrapping his hand over Kristy's on the gearshift a couple of times when she was too slow in shifting. After about twenty minutes, she and the other gals had a pretty good handle on the process.

Griff leaned against the vehicle, instructing clearly one of his talents. "Muddin' is a popular activity among the redneck crowd. At its core, it's about driving around in the mud, spraying it everywhere, and gettin' all dirty just for the fun of it. Sometimes we make it a formal race, like today."

"Why, exactly, do people like to get all muddy?" Kristy asked.

It was the first time she saw a genuine smile on Griff's face. "'Cause we can." The scarred side of his mouth didn't tilt up as far as the other, and it gave him an endearingly crooked smile. When he caught her staring at his mouth, it vanished. That wall came down again as he took in everyone and pasted on a pleasant expression. "You all ready to rock the mud bog?"

Risk hollered, "Hell, yeah!" and grabbed Addie's hand, hauling her over toward the Jeeps. Julian shook his head at his friend's unbridled enthusiasm, threaded his fingers through Mollie's, and led her over.

Griff turned to Kristy, and she wanted to tell him that

she liked his smile and to please not dim it just because she was looking at him. The words jammed in her mouth, and then Griff looked beyond her to ask Chase if the camera crew was ready. When he answered that they were, Griff nodded toward the Jeeps.

She followed him, taking in the width of his shoulders and the way his chest tapered to narrow hips. Despite his scars and everything he'd been through, he walked with pride and confidence. His T-shirt was so faded that she couldn't make out what had once been on it. But it looked so soft that she fought the insane urge to touch his back, to run her hand down his spine.

"Where are the doors?" she asked. There was only a gaping hole where the doors should be.

"Don't need 'em." He gave her a reassuring smile. "And, no, you won't fall out. You'll be strapped in nice and tight."

And he'd be sitting there right beside her.

Griff helped her climb into the driver's seat, then went around the front and hopped in beside her. "Start her up like I showed you, and pull over to the line."

The vehicle lurched, nearly stalled, but she managed to steer it to the starting line where Addie was already waiting. Mollie was the last to get her pitching Jeep into position.

"Remember," Griff said, "once the mud starts flying, you won't be able to see much. Just keep going straight until you feel the incline as you come out. Don't worry; I'm here if you need me. You can do this."

She gave him a grateful look for his reassurance. Trent, who was perched on a stand in the back of a truck, gave them another thumbs-up.

As Griff had instructed earlier, she returned the gesture. Once the other two women did the same, Chase stepped up to the line, raised his hand, and brought it down.

"Easy does it," Griff said.

She eased the gas pedal down instead of punching it, and the Jeep slogged into the bog. Mud flew everywhere, from their tires as well as the Jeep on the right. Cool splats of it landed on her arms, her cheek, and everywhere inside the vehicle.

Griff touched her elbow. "Relax. You're going to strain your joints."

She focused ahead, finding less and less clear glass as mud covered it. In her peripheral vision, she saw the mobile cameraman racing along capturing it all. The Jeep tilted but righted itself just as a scream escaped her mouth. Then she reached the incline and rolled out of the bog.

"You did it!" Griff said with that amazing, crooked smile. "And you won!" He held up his hand, and she slapped it, sending more bits of mud everywhere.

Their palms connected, and so did their gazes. His face was so mud-splattered that she could hardly tell he was scarred. Only his mouth showed any evidence, and when he saw her gaze zero in on that, his smile vanished again.

She reached out, and he inhaled when her fingers made contact with his cheek. She rubbed her thumb at the corner of his mouth. "Please don't stop smiling. It's—"

"We have our winner!" a voice shouted from beside her. She jerked around to find Trent shoving the lens her way. "How was it?"

"I, uh…dirty." She wiped the mud clinging to her cheek. The memory of touching Griff's face, his surprised expression, flashed into her mind. "And amazing."

"Good. Let's do it again. I need to make sure I have plenty of footage."

For the next two hours, they raced. Griff's guidance, along with his gentle corrections, helped her manage the course over and over.

"We don't have a lot of light left, so we need to go on to the next event," Trent said.

"What's that? I thought this was it for the day." She glanced at Griff, who was obviously in on this by his sheepish smile.

Trent positioned his camera to catch her reaction. "You and your competitors are slogging through the mud bog…on foot this time."

---

"That was utterly humiliating," Kristy said as she trudged out of the mud thirty minutes later. She jabbed a finger at the gathered men, ending at Griff. "And you all enjoyed it."

"Was it the guffawing that tipped you off?" Addie had her blue eyes narrowed at her man. "The snorting laughter?" She advanced on Risk, who realized she had nefarious intentions concerning his dry and relatively clean person and her muddy one. And when she gave him a full-body hug and big kiss, everyone laughed. Even Risk.

Mollie gave her man the same treatment, which left Kristy facing off with Griff and feeling awkward with all that loving going on. And a tiny bit naughty, too.

Griff took her in with faux wariness and a spark of that same impishness. "You gonna get me back, too?"

"Was this your idea?"

He grinned. "Yep."

He was daring her! Kristy had given up enough in her life, forgone parties and events and jobs. She was not giving this a pass. She stomped closer, deciding how far she'd actually go. He tucked his fingers in his front pockets and rocked back on his heels. No, he definitely didn't think she'd do it.

So she did. She smeared mud all over his clean face, down his neck, and into that soft hair.

His hands automatically clamped down onto hers as he ducked his head and squirmed. "I don't mind the mud, but I'm ticklish as all get out."

The sound of his laughter nearly undid her. Deep, full laughs not unlike the ones she'd heard when she'd been a mudbug for his amusement. Those scratchy, rusty laughs filled her chest like helium. So she bent down, scooped up a handful of bright orange mud, and threw it at him like a snowball.

He didn't duck fast enough, and it hit him in the chest. His face flared in mock indignation, and he scooped her up and threw her over his shoulder. Her screams weren't exactly mock, even if they were peppered with laughter. He sloshed into the bog and moved to drop her in. She'd been plenty familiar with that bog, thank you very much!

"All right, I give, I give!" she shouted, clutching his shoulders. God, she hoped she didn't hurt him. She had no idea how sensitive his skin was.

He was breathing heavily, his face inches from hers

as he leaned over her. "I didn't hear an 'I'm sorry I got mud all over you' in there anywhere."

He was having fun with her, teasing her, giving her a glimpse of the man he'd been before...she pushed the rest away. "It's your fault I have mud all over me!"

"Hey, it's all for the show. You looked great out there. Lots of those hook moments they're after. Say you're really, very, terribly sorry, and I might not drop you."

She loved the Southern honey of his voice, now so clear in his teasing command. She pasted on a contrite expression. "I'm very, terribly sorry—" And tilted just enough to throw him off balance. With her clinging to him like a burr, he couldn't right himself, and down they went, her on top of him.

Mud splattered all over them. She was laughing too hard to even finish her sentence, falling flat on his chest as she fought to catch her breath.

He was shaking his head, his eyes narrowed. "You're in big trouble now."

She leaned close, her muddy hair drifting down over his face. "What are you going to do about it?" The flirtatious words were out before she could even consider them. When was the last time she'd flirted, for God's sake?

His mouth opened, perhaps with unbidden words of his own ready to roll out.

Suddenly, she became aware of a presence to her right. Trent had his camera aimed right at them. Whatever Griff had been about to say, he changed his mind, taking advantage of the distractions to flip her over and squish her into the mud beneath him. His thighs tightened against her hips, pinning her thoroughly.

"That," he said, the playfulness gone even as his crooked smile was still in place. He glanced at Trent. "Good hook?"

Trent was all smiles as he pressed a button and lowered the camera. "Awesome sauce."

Griff got to his feet and gave her his hand to help her up. As Trent sloshed through the mud to the bank, she said, "So that was all about the hook?"

Damn if he didn't give her a guileless look. "Of course. We have to sell this if we're going to lure this sicko in."

She was so mad at his lie—*it was a lie, wasn't it?*— that she took one lunging step and fell forward.

He caught her around the waist, lifting her easily and carrying her toward the bank, her body flush against his. Her hands had gone to his shoulders, and she was high enough in his hold to look down on his head. His hair was a wet, muddy mess, revealing the ruined shell of his ear that was usually hidden beneath it.

And since her chest was at his face level, if he looked through the netting, beneath the mud, he'd see her scars. He held her with one arm, the other out for balance. He lost his footing, making them wobble, before regaining it as he reached the bank. The other couples were over by the showers, and she realized she'd forgotten about everyone else there.

Damn Trent. But yes, that's what they were there for. Not to fall in love or like or anything even close to it.

But right now, she was in Griff's arms, both of them now that he'd reached solid ground, and it felt darned good. He looked up at her, no trace of a smile now.

"Sorry 'bout that," he said, all contrite. "I got carried away. I shouldn't have—"

She placed her finger against his lips, feeling the ridge of scar tissue. "When I look at you, I don't think, 'Aw, poor guy, how sad for him.' I think, 'What a strong man to endure what you did and still be here.'"

His breath hitched, and she felt his arms loosen enough for her to slide down his body to her feet. She could see his struggle: shut her out or let her in?

"I thought the same about you," he said at last. "I read the articles about what this guy put you through." He swallowed. "I want to do everything I can to help you go back to your life." He released her, and she nearly stumbled.

Julian, Risk, Addie, and Mollie returned, the women swathed in towels. "We're going to hit that BBQ restaurant down the road after we get properly showered. You guys in?"

Griff shook his head. "I don't go out much. But ya'll go on, enjoy. Try the pulled pork. It's good. I have it delivered every Friday." He'd included Kristy in that send-off as he swept them all with his gaze.

She watched him head over to where the muddy Jeeps were parked. Her heart tugged in his direction. She turned back to the group as Chase reached it, trying to find a diplomatic way to make her request.

"Chase, can Kristy hang here with Griff while we hit that BBQ place we saw on the way in?" Addie gave her a conspiratorial wink. "Are the sensors wired yet?"

"Yes, they're in place." Chase met Kristy's gaze. "You don't want to get out of here for dinner?"

She lifted a shoulder, trying to play it casual. Despite the fact that it must be friggin' obvious that she wanted to spend time alone with Griff. Sheesh. "I'd like to talk to Griff a little more. I have a friend whose cousin is a plastic surgeon. Maybe he could, you know, do some pro bono work."

"Already tried," Chase said. "I told Griff I'd made some arrangements in repayment for his help here, but he turned me down." He gave her a curious look. "Maybe you could provide him with different motivation. I'll be at the lodge in case the sensors go off, but I don't anticipate any problems." He looked at his people. "Let me know when you leave and when you get back."

"You bet, chief," Risk said. "Let's go. I'm famished." He glanced back at Kristy, trying to maintain a serious expression. "Must have been all that laughing."

She flung her hand, sending tiny bits of mud at him. "Brat."

Addie thunked him in the back of his head. "Big time. You ought to live with him!"

Kristy watched the four depart, Risk taking Addie to task for her quip with a mock abusive kiss. She couldn't help but smile at their playfulness. Their joie de vivre. She wanted that. She wanted affection, too, aching for it as she watched Julian pull Mollie against his side and plant a kiss at her temple.

Wait a minute. She'd shut desire down a long time ago, when Eye had threatened the guy with whom she'd gone on a first date. Who could want romance when a stalker continually called with his threats and orders and admonitions? Where had this gut-wrenching ache come from?

Kristy turned to Griff, who was hosing himself down. He ruffled his fingers through his hair and soaked down his shirt. Like her, he wasn't exposing more than he had to. His shirt, though, clung to his muscular build, and his khakis molded to his ass and legs. She swallowed a sigh.

She bet he'd shut down that part of himself, too. They'd had that moment, and then he'd yanked down the wall and said he was flirting with her for the camera. The film crew was packing up, making plans to join the other four for dinner. Griff wouldn't be able to use that excuse if he slipped into the playful mode again.

She needed to get him there.

He looked up as she approached. "Here comes trouble."

She suspected he meant that in more than one way. "And don't you forget it."

He met her gaze, looking all too serious. "I won't." Then the serious mask slipped as she kept advancing, and he held the nozzle out like a pistol. "Back off, woman. I see that predatory gleam in your eye."

She froze for a second, thinking he'd seen her desire. Then she realized she was still covered in mud, and he thought she was going to slime him. She raised her arms to her sides. "You could hose me off, neutralize the threat."

"Mmm, don't tempt me."

Was he tempted? She hoped so, because something about Griff pulled and tugged at her. She wanted to make him laugh again, to smile a lot. She wanted him.

He used his chin to point to the outdoor showers. "There are showers, you know."

"I know." But she remained in position, amazed at her brazenness. She simply wasn't like this around men. Even before Eye.

He put a kink in the hose, unscrewed the nozzle, and let the water flow again. "All right, come here, trouble."

He held the hose above her head, and the water poured over her face and down the front of her. She tilted her head, closed her eyes, and sank into the sensation of the cool water. The day had been warm, but now the early fall evening was cooling down as the sun sank in the sky. Griff ruffled his fingers through her hair as he'd done for his own. *Heaven.* Gently, tentatively, he worked the mud out of the strands. His fingers brushed her back through the net.

"Kristy."

"Hmm?"

"Er, you should probably…"

She opened her eyes to see him gesturing to her body. "Oh. Yes, of course." She thought about taking off the net cover-up, which would make washing off the mud easier. But she worked out the dirt the best she could, sticking the hose beneath her bikini top and even down into the bottoms to get everything out. When she glanced up, Griff averted his gaze.

"Here." She handed him the hose. "Is there another one? I could help you hose these Jeeps down. It's getting dark fast."

"You should probably get on back to the lodge. The camera guys are about to head out. Get yourself some dinner with the rest of the group. I'll see you in the morning."

He didn't want to spend time with her. Old insecurities

reared their head, pushing her to turn and leave. "Should I bring you something?"

"No, but thanks. I'm going to throw some burgers on the fire pit."

"That sounds nice. Mind if I just stay here with you? I'm not really up for a lot of socializing."

A sound rumbled from deep in his throat. Agony? Hunger? He handed her the hose and headed over to the showers to pull out another hose, then went to work on the next Jeep.

Okay. Well, he hadn't said no. That was a start, anyway. *But what is it the start of?*

# CHAPTER 3

GRIFF WATCHED THE MARSHMALLOW AT THE END OF his stick bubble and burn and eventually drip into the fire pit's flames. Dumb idea to roast marshmallows. At first, all he could think about was his charred skin. At least these smelled good.

It had been worth it to see the delight on Kristy's face when he'd suggested it. "Like a campfire!" she'd said, clapping her hands together.

They'd cooked burgers, and he'd scrounged up carrots for her 'cause she wanted a healthy side. She wasn't one of those women who picked and ate like a bird though. She'd eaten two burgers, a handful of the fries he'd thrown in the oven, and half the bag of carrots.

Now she was working on her third marshmallow. He liked a woman who ate. In fact, he'd had to pull his gaze away time and again before she caught him. Before she got the wrong idea.

*And you have enough wrong ideas for the both of you.*

Hell of a time to get his libido back. Well, it was knocking at his door anyway, reminding him that he hadn't so much as taken a hand to himself since the explosion. She was going to be gone before long. And it was very likely he'd misinterpreted her flirting. Of course he had.

And now Lady Antebellum was on the radio, singing "Just a Kiss."

"You just lost it," she said.

He blinked in surprise. Had she read his thoughts? "What?"

She nodded toward his stick, now with just a smear of marshmallow at the tip. "Or you're just lost in your thoughts."

He took in the way the flames flickered across her face, gilding her like an angel. Yeah, he was lost all right. "Thinking about tomorrow, is all."

"What are we doing tomorrow?"

"Can't say. They want to capture your expression when I tell you."

Her marshmallow dropped into the flame. "Oh, hell. On both accounts."

He couldn't help chuckling. "You'll be fine. You did great today."

"Hmph." She speared another marshmallow, looking endearingly indignant. "Glad I could be so entertaining." Her mouth turned into a smile in one second flat. "You know what I liked best?"

"What?"

"You laughing."

He sat back. "What do you mean?"

She tilted her head, giving him her full attention. "You have a great laugh. And a nice smile."

He forced himself to look away from her beautiful face, staring into the fire. He'd heard that plenty…before. "Now I know you're yanking my chain. My smile's messed up. But it's nice of you to say." He'd purposely sat on her left tonight, so she'd only see the worst side.

"You think I'm yanking your chain? Griff, you're a handsome man."

He reached over and took hold of her bottle of water, sniffing it. "Hmm. I don't smell any alcohol."

She smacked his arm, pulling the bottle away. But she kept a grip on his arm so he couldn't sit back. Her eyes searched his. "I'm serious. When you smile, your mouth tugs in this adorable way. Like this." She tried to emulate this supposed adorable smile. "Haven't you seen yourself smile?"

"I don't look in the mirror much. Only enough to shave." He rubbed the normal side, wondering what she'd think of the broken mirrors in his bathroom that revealed just his jaw and cheek.

She touched the side of his face, as she'd done earlier. He wanted to pull away, needed to for his own sanity. But hell if he could. "Why are you doing this? Touching me, telling me this?" His voice came out hoarse.

She feathered her fingers over his scarred cheek. "Because I want to."

"Why?" he asked again, uncomfortable with the raw need to know so clear in his voice.

She placed her other hand on the good side of his face. "I feel a connection to you, Griff. Maybe because we both have scars."

He couldn't help the scoffing sound. "You're perfect. You don't have a lick of makeup on, and you're so damned beautiful, it hurts to look at you."

She gave him a soft smile, still brushing her fingers across his skin. He wanted to grab onto her hand and stop her because he was about to fall into the sensation. So simple, so innocent, and so powerful all at once. He hadn't been touched by anyone but a doctor or nurse in over two years. That she was touching his scarred skin with such tenderness and reverence, he could barely stand it.

She unzipped her jacket, slowly, and pulled the two sides apart. The top beneath it dipped low, showing a hint of cleavage. But that's not what riveted his attention. Faded red slashes marred her chest nearly up to her neck.

"I've been hiding from the world, too," she whispered after a few moments. "Not just because of Eye." Another few moments passed, and she said, "Say something."

He'd forgotten to breathe. But even a long breath didn't ease the ache in his chest. "He did this to you?" He had to hold back a string of curses unfit for a lady's ears.

She nodded. "He was hiding in my apartment. When I came home from a night of partying with friends, he attacked me with a knife from my own kitchen. He'd called two days earlier—he always managed to get my phone number—furious because he'd seen an advertisement I'd done in a bra and underwear. That's as undressed as I ever got, but it infuriated him. I called him a bully and a coward and hung up. That really pissed him off."

Griff wanted to touch her the way she'd done to him, but he held his hands still on his thighs. "He tried to kill you?"

"No, he said he didn't want to kill me. He wanted to give me scars so I couldn't model anymore. So I wouldn't 'show off my body like a whore.'" She showed him the side of her hand where two more slash marks showed, then tilted her chin up to reveal another scar just beneath. "This is as far as he got. Then my roommate rushed in, after hearing my screams, and threw a lamp at Eye. That gave me the diversion I needed to get away, and Eye took off. He wore a mask, so I still couldn't identify him."

She pulled her knees up and hugged her legs close. "He got his way, and that's what makes me the maddest. I'm not modeling. I'm hiding. I hate that he won."

Griff felt the same anger burn inside him. "We definitely need to take this son of a bitch out."

"So you see, Griff, we both suffered bodily injury at someone else's hand. We're both hiding because of it."

He flattened his hand on his chest. "But the suicide bomber did what he did because of some ideal, as screwed up as it is. He wasn't tormenting us for some sick pleasure."

"Can you tell me what happened?" The question floated in the air, gentle as mist.

He'd stopped telling the story months ago, but her expression wasn't of morbid curiosity. It held genuine interest. "I was part of a scouting convoy, three Humvees. I was the gunner in the turret." He stared into the flames as they licked the darkness. "It was my job to spot attacks. I didn't see him until he was right on us, and I couldn't get the gun around in time to…" Guilt infused him. He swallowed hard. "The guy detonated himself. I remember the fireball, and then I was lying on the ground, staring up at the sky. I'd been blown right out the door." He had to push out the words, "I was the only survivor. Four men died." Because he'd failed.

She touched his arm. "It wasn't your fault. You did the best you could. You, a lot of those soldiers, they're only kids. You're what, twenty-two?"

"Twenty-four."

"Damn, Griff. You're still carrying that Humvee and all those guys on your shoulders, aren't you?"

He met her eyes, seeing only compassion. He didn't need to answer, though; she could see. But instead of trying to talk him out of his guilt, she only said, "Guilt's a bitch, isn't it?" She gave his arm a squeeze. "You've gone through enough on the outside. I can't even imagine what that was like." She let that hang, not quite a question and yet…

"I was put into a coma for three weeks right afterward. When I woke up in Brooke Army Medical Center, they told me I was burned over twenty-five percent of my body. The first few times I saw my reflection, I didn't believe it was me. It felt like I was seeing a stranger. Then I'd turn and look at the good side of my face. And yeah, it was me, all right. I had thirty surgeries and put in two years of rehab before I was able to come home ten months ago."

She was looking at him with compassion, and because it wasn't pity—because she'd been brave enough to share her scars—he pulled off his shirt. It was easier to look at his body than his face, so he knew well the line of scarring across his chest, down his side.

Her eyes roamed over his body, a slow sweep that returned to his face. "At least you had this place. And your family, I imagine."

"Thank God for them." Sometimes he didn't feel he deserved their support. "I suffered from what the hospital therapist called survivor's guilt. There were times in those first few months of recovery that I wish I'd died that day with my friends. It's hard, knowing I lived and they didn't. Why me? Why them? But every time I think of my family's reaction when I came home or when they visited me at the hospital, their relief that I was alive… I couldn't wish I had died. I'm here. I have to live enough for my fallen comrades." He fought the urge to pull on his shirt again.

"When will you venture out into the world?"

The thought of it tightened his gut. "I've only just begun taking out hunting parties. Mostly men, a lot of vets, so they don't pay a lot of mind to my face. I saw the way people looked at me while I was at the hospital, the short outings I did in San Antonio. Horror. Pity." He shook his head. "I'm happy here."

"Are you?"

The gentle challenge on her face made him uncomfortable. He stared into the flames again. "Yes. It must seem unfair, me holing up here on purpose when you've been stuck in hiding."

"Only unfair to you."

The crack of a twig in the woods shot her to her feet, sending her whirling around staring into the darkness. "What was that?"

"Critter. Maybe a coon."

She zipped up her jacket, her eyes wide. "Are you sure?"

He hated the fear that tightened her pretty mouth. "I grew up on this land. I know the difference between a human's footstep and an animal's. But we can go in."

She nodded, meeting his gaze. He pulled his shirt back on, but his eyes went right back to her. The words wanted to come out: *you could stay with me, if it makes you feel safer. No expectations of anything, 'cause I don't even have that inclination…*

But he did, and his body stirred at the thought of
lying in bed with her. Holding her. She swallowed hard,
and her eyes pleaded with him to kiss her. Maybe he
was misreading her. Maybe he was crazy. No, he was
definitely crazy, because he brought his hand up to her
cheek. She moved closer, tilting up her chin, softening
her mouth. He leaned down...

Another sound, coming from the front of the lodge,
stopped him. Tires on gravel.

"They're back," he said. Relief and regret warred
inside him for not having pushed out the offer. But she
would feel safe now with everyone back. And it was
better that he and Kristy didn't start something they
couldn't finish. He couldn't condemn her to a life of
hiding out here.

He waited inside with her until the group filled the
lodge with the sounds of laughter. The BBQ place was
a hit, the sawdust covered floors quaint and the band
raucous. Griff pushed past the longing to experience the
latter two elements and bid everyone good night.

It only hit him later, as he stretched out alone in his
bed, that the word he'd used to describe his life here
was *condemned*.

# CHAPTER 4

KRISTY SAT WITH THE OTHERS IN THE MUD ROOM, eating a hearty breakfast before their mystery event. Addie and Mollie looked as nervous as Kristy felt, but at least they had their guys to encourage and egg them on. Griff was nowhere in sight. It was annoying how disappointing that was. Just because they'd almost shared a kiss, and showed their scars, didn't mean they'd bonded or anything.

She let out a soft sigh. Except she did feel a bond that she couldn't quite explain. Not one of the guys she'd dated in college or met during her brief dalliance with the party scene had made her feel like this. Yet, what kind of future could they have? Griff didn't seem inclined to leave here, and she couldn't blame him. She needed the excitement of city life, meeting new people, living out loud.

And she only had one more day, one more night, before being escorted back to Atlanta. They lived three hours away from each other but worlds apart.

Once she was done with her oatmeal and banana, she wandered the room, studying the pictures on the walls. Yeah, she was looking for Griff. She knew his uncle had started MUD'N HUNT right after Griff enlisted, so he wasn't in many of the pictures showing guests holding up huge fish, strings of rabbits, and trophies while standing in front of mud-covered trucks. But she found one of Griff as a teenager with a buck draped over his shoulders. He'd been gorgeous, with a carefree glint in his eyes. He was no doubt different now than that cocky young guy in a Marines T-shirt who raised a beer with a bunch of friends all perched on a hulking truck. She probably would have never connected with that Griff.

Footsteps clomped down the hallway, and she turned to the door. Holding her breath, for Pete's sake. Something shifted in her chest when Griff came in, followed by Trent. Trent filled the room with his effervescence, and Griff filled it with his masculinity. And his smile.

His gaze landed on her first but quickly skipped to the others. "Cleared today's area of snakes and snapping turtles." He gave Kristy a wink. "Don't want one of 'em taking off a finger."

Kristy surged to her feet. "Are you serious?" She glanced at the other two women—*should she call them victims?*—before turning back to Griff. "What are we doing?"

"Wait!" Trent whipped the camera into position, hit some buttons, and said, "Go ahead and tell them."

Griff paused for dramatic effect. "You're going ticklin'. Or grabblin'. Or what's better known as noodlin'."

Kristy crossed her arms over her chest. "Sounds like a porn movie." She would have enjoyed the chuckles at her assessment if she weren't so worried.

Griff grinned. "You're going to be handfishin' catfish in the river. I got licenses for you ladies, and special permission, since we're out of season. But we're just doing catch and release."

Addie stepped closer. "When you use the words *hand*

and *fishing* together, do you mean we're catching fish…
by hand?"

Griff gave her a deep nod. "Yes, ma'am. I suggest
you remove all jewelry, 'cause it might end up in a catfish's gut."

Kristy wiggled her fingers. "Will our fingers end up
there, too?"

Oh, yeah, Griff was enjoying this. Which would have
been nice if it hadn't been at their expense. "No, ma'am,
as long as you follow my instructions."

Kristy indicated a couple of inches between her finger
and thumb. "Fish this big?"

He held his hands several yards apart. Okay, not
yards, exactly, but close enough. "This big. You ladies
will be competing to catch the biggest fish. Noodlin' is
easy. You stick your hand into a hole and wait for the
fish to grab hold. Then you pull it out and hold on so that
whoever's assisting you can weigh it."

"We're sticking our hands into a hole?" Kristy
squeaked out.

"You'll be sticking your whole arm in most of the
time. Or your foot. Basically, you're luring the fish out
of its hole with some part of your body. You'll each
have one of us right next to you, so you have nothing to
worry about."

"Nothing to worry about," Kristy echoed as they
headed out. "Yeah, right."

They piled into the Jeeps, Chase and the cameramen
in the SUV at the end of the caravan. Kristy held onto
the bar as they lurched over the uneven ground. Every
time she started to say something, a rut stole the words
out of her mouth. Griff was in guide mode, confident

and easy. She liked him this way, but she loved the way he'd opened up to her last night. There would be none of that happening during this ride.

The river was nearly as muddy as the bog, only a lot wetter. And things lived in it. Fish and creepy crawlies and maybe even those slugs Griff had mentioned yesterday. Panic spiraled through her. "How are we going to catch a fish when the water's the consistency of coffee?"

He pulled to a stop and hopped out. "It's all by feel."

Once everyone was assembled, waist-deep in brown water, Griff led them over to the bank. He sank in up to his chin. "First you find the hole, and then you stick your arm into it. The fish is going to bite your hand."

"B-bite?" Kristy uttered.

His eyes were narrowed in concentration as he maneuvered beneath the surface. "It doesn't have sharp teeth. Once it clamps on, you clamp on back and pull it out. It'll fight you, but hang on."

He was clearly wrestling something. The scarred side of his face was in the water, and she watched his jaw muscles tighten as he fought, then jerked a huge, slimy fish out of the water. He held the wriggling monster over his head. "See, nothin' to it." That garnered groans from Kristy's competitors. He lowered the fish to the water and released it. "Let's roll, ladies."

Griff's uncle and cousin led the other gals down the river, and Griff pulled Kristy by the hand to the opposite side of the bank. There were several fallen tree limbs, washed smooth brown by the water and time, and all she could think about were snakes or beavers or some other horrid creature lurking beneath.

"I'm really sorry I ever watched that *River Monsters*

show. The host hangs out in water just like this searching for crazy-huge creatures. And piranha."

Griff chuckled. "There are no piranha 'round here. Or gators. Just snapping turtles and snakes."

"Which you said you cleared out."

"As of forty minutes ago, anyway."

"You're not helping!"

The vexing man chuckled again, clearly not the least bit worried. "You'll be fine."

Trent hovered with his camera as they approached the bank, but the idea of that hole garnered all her attention.

Griff kept hold of her hand. "I'm going to guide you to the opening. As soon as you pull out the fish, I'll string it up and weigh it." He took her by the chin and gently turned her to face him. "I'll be right here."

That comforted her, right up until he guided her hand inside a hole and said, "You'll be more startled than anything when it grabs you. Be ready to grab it back."

"I don't want to—ah!" It attacked, just like he'd warned. "It's on me, it's on me!"

"Hold on." Griff came up behind her, reaching down her arm, and pulled up a fish by the rope in its mouth. "You did it!" The fish flopped and fought as he handed the rope to her.

She'd done it. A gooey sense of pride and relief washed through her. "I did it. I did it!"

He pulled a mesh bag around the fish and held it up with a ruler-like thing. "You caught a thirty-two pounder!"

A woman's piercing scream sailed through the air. One of her competitors had obviously caught a fish, too. Kristy hoped it wasn't bigger than hers. Even if this wasn't a real contest.

Griff released the fish, but his gaze was on her. "Nice job, Kristy."

His proud smile was an even bigger rush.

Trent checked something on the screen. "Perfect." He tilted the camera to show her the replay of her terrified expression when the fish took hold of her. And there was Griff, his good side toward the camera, watching her, not the fish. She saw something in his eyes, in the way that he looked at her…

She turned to him as he hovered just behind her. He cleared his throat and turned to Trent, whose expression was filled with glee. "That should be a great hook. You both gave me a huge helping of awesome sauce!"

Kristy couldn't help giggling at Trent's unbridled enthusiasm. Even Griff was chuckling. Trent headed toward the bank, where Mollie and Julian waited, and Griff's cousin led them around the bend. Kristy turned to face Griff. "That was amazing. Freaky, slimy, and a bit painful, but amazing."

She inspected her hand, and Griff took hold of it for a closer look at the bleeding scratches. He lifted it to his mouth and planted tender kisses on each one. Her heart dropped right out of her chest.

"Do you do this to all your noodling clients?" she asked, her voice a hoarse whisper.

"Nah. Most of 'em have hairy hands." Even though he was making a joke, his expression remained serious.

"And I bet most of them don't tip like this." She freed her hand from his and laced them behind his neck. Up on tiptoe, sinking slightly in the mud, she pressed her body against his and kissed him.

His breath caught in surprise, but he responded

with kisses that were sweet and soft and chaste. His hands came up to slide into her hair, and his breathing quickened. He paused, his nose brushing against hers. "I haven't kissed a woman since before the explosion."

Her smile probably gave away that she liked the idea of being the first. "Then I think it's high time you did."

He studied her with hazel eyes so serious that she feared he might step back. But a smile tugged at the corner of his mouth. "Why, ma'am, I do believe you're right."

He braced her face and kissed her again, his mouth covering hers, brushing back and forth in sensual sweeps, and then opening to deepen the kiss. She invited him in, touching the tip of her tongue to the ridged skin of his lower lip, then running it along the entire length. He let out a soft groan as their tongues came together, as he moved even closer and explored her mouth. She could feel all of him pressed up against the front of her body, his hard muscles, and his even harder erection. Her hands slid up the sides of his chest and down his broad back as she'd longed to do earlier. She traced the tips of her fingers down the indent of his spine all the way to the top of his waistband.

"It's been a while for me, too," she whispered between kisses. "This feels like my first kiss." Had she felt this pulse-pounding rush of blood with that first kiss? She couldn't even remember it now. All she could see in her mind was Griff, his face, his smile. She threaded her fingers through his hair, brushing the ridges of his damaged ear.

He pulled back, looking thrown off.

"Did I hurt you?" she asked.

"No, it's..." He ran his hand back over his hair. "I forgot. For a few seconds, I forgot what I look like."

"I don't care what you look like."

All of that beautiful openness was now hidden behind a wall. "I don't know how you can want me. No woman deserves to look at my ugly mug every morning."

"I have scars, too."

He reached out and dragged his thumb down her jawline. "You are amazingly beautiful. Once this is all over, you can go back to modeling. Keep pursuing your dream. Go to fancy parties and find a guy who will look good at your side."

"Griff, I don't want a guy who *looks* good. I want a guy who *is* good."

Voices pulled their attention to Addie, Risk, and the other cameraman, along with Griff's uncle, trudging back along the bank. Addie was saying, "I hope we didn't hurt the fish. Didn't it look lethargic when we tossed it back in?"

Risk shook his head, giving her a conciliatory pat on her shoulder. "I'm sure it'll be fine, my big-hearted little animal hugger."

"We got a twenty-nine pounder," his uncle called out. His gaze zeroed in on her and Griff. "What'cha still doing in the water? You wanna catch another one?"

Kristy shook her head vehemently. "One's plenty, thank you."

Griff helped her to the shore, his hand tight on hers. But his words hurt more than that catfish ever could, how no woman deserved looking at his face. "What about what you deserve?" she asked quietly.

He gestured to include everything around him. "I have all this. It's everything I need. It's where I belong."

A part of her longed to refute his hollow words. *No, Griff. You belong with me.*

# CHAPTER 5

Kristy tiptoed down the hallway at two in the morning. She couldn't sleep, and she knew why. Griff. She would tap on his door. If he answered, that meant he was awake, too. Maybe feeling as restless as she did. If he didn't, either he was asleep or ignoring her.

He answered the door after one tap, standing in dim light wearing only a pair of black jersey pants. His eyes were shadowed, so she couldn't see whether her presence was welcome, but he stepped back as an invitation to enter.

As soon as the door closed, they came together, bodies and mouths, hands touching and sliding down each other. His fingers seemed to drink her in, slowly moving down her back and up beneath her loose nightshirt. She desperately needed to feel him, all of him, so she pulled it off and let it drop to the wood floor with a soft whoosh.

"You're beautiful," he whispered, taking in her naked body as though she were a goddess. He slid his hands over her shoulders, the scars on her chest, and gently cupped her breasts. She released a long breath and leaned into a touch that filled a hunger she hadn't even been aware of. She rocked her head back, losing herself in the feel of those big, callused hands caressing her. He circled his thumbs around her nipples, spiraling heat from her stomach all the way down to her apex. God, to feel desire again. To have a man like Griff, so honorable and real, touching her…

"I want you, Griff." She drew her hands over his shoulders to his neck, kissing the rough skin on his chest. "I don't care if we're two out-of-practice fools. I want this with you."

She heard an answering rumble in his chest, something between a growl and a groan. "I don't have any condoms. I wasn't planning…had no intention…"

She reached down to her shirt and pulled the package out of the tiny pocket on the front. "I borrowed one from Trent, just in case. He was happy to contribute to our sin."

Griff captured her mouth in a soul-searing kiss, his tongue sweeping slowly, sensually, against hers. "See, I knew you were trouble." She could hear his smile, feel it in the stretch of his mouth.

He scooped her up into his arms and gently set her down on the rumpled sheets. She pulled his pants down his hips and thighs, and he kicked them off before lowering himself over her. He was big, in body and in erection, and she relished the feel of both as he held the bulk of his weight off her.

He kissed and touched her like a man who treasured every inch, and she could see him taking her in with his eyes. In the near dark, they were two perfect people. Right here, right now, nothing else mattered but finding each other. Connecting.

He was tender and passionate at the same time, dragging his hands down her hips as he left a trail of hot kisses across her breasts, then her stomach. He nuzzled between her legs, and his tongue touched her clit with toe-curling flicks and gentle sucking motions. As her fingers drove through his soft hair, he made love to her with his mouth, bringing her to two delicious orgasms.

"Like riding a bike," she managed when she caught her breath.

"Like we've been making love for years," he said, kissing his way back up to her neck.

Yes, that's exactly how it felt, she realized, as she curled her hand around the back of his neck. Exciting and new, yet incredibly easy. She pulled him close for a kiss, then pushed him back onto the bed, straddled him, and gave him all the affection he'd lavished on her. She nibbled his smooth skin and brushed her lips softly over the scarred sections. His breath hitched and huffed, his stomach quivered.

"Kristy, I don't know what you're doing to me."

"Well, I'm kissing my way down your stomach, and now I'm wrapping my hand around your shaft and—"

"I know what you're doing to my body." He groaned as her hand tightened at the base. "It's the insides that are all confused. I was dead. Hell, I haven't even given myself a hand job. I had no sex drive, and I didn't even care. Then you came along and woke me up."

She kissed the tip of his cock. "Good. I hope you stay awake." *And keep wanting me.* To help that endeavor, she took him into her mouth and brought him to the brink of orgasm.

His breath was sawing in and out. "Oh, darlin', if you keep doing that, we won't need that condom."

"Then let's use it tomorrow morning." And she sent him over the edge.

—◦—

Griff thought he was dreaming when he slowly rose to consciousness and felt the warm weight of a woman snuggled up against him. Then it all came back, how Kristy had come to his room just as he'd stood inches from his door wrestling with doing the same to her. How they'd come together so naturally that it made his chest feel like it was filled with helium. And when he remembered that they had the condom, another part of him filled, too.

She opened her eyes and gave him a sleepy smile, which just about undid him. He kissed her, his hand slipping down between her thighs, then to her sweet folds. She was soon wet, but he made sure she was good and ready by bringing her to orgasm. And when she arched into his touch and exhaled loudly, he captured that breath with a kiss.

They weren't out-of-practice fools. Like earlier, they fell right into a natural rhythm as he eased into her tight canal. God, this woman, what she did to him. He was lost in her, in the feel of her in his arms, in the way thrusting into her felt like home. He knew it was dangerous territory, but he couldn't manage to care at the moment.

"Griff," she whispered, then panted as her body tightened. She gripped his shoulders and looked into his eyes as she came, and he'd never seen a more beautiful sight. Except maybe finding her at his door in the first place.

His orgasm shuddered through him a minute later, and he buried his face in the crook of her neck and held on tight. He rode it out, more powerful than the one the night before. She throbbed all around his cock, and damn, it made him feel as though he were going to come again.

As he relaxed around her, he memorized the feel of her. The smell of her. The way her hair caught the light coming in through the window and the silky feel of it across his shoulder.

Sounds drew their attention to the door as a couple of people passed by his room. They didn't knock, thank God, but it was an indication that the morning was upon them.

He cupped the side of her face. "I wish we could stay here all day."

She had a worried expression. "I have to go back to Atlanta this morning."

The prospect made his chest hurt. But he couldn't keep her here. He and this place would feel like another prison to her. "I remember how excited you were about living out loud. You looked so happy at the thought of it. Pretty soon you'll be free."

She placed her hand against his chest. "I wish you could come with me."

He took her hand and pressed it against his mouth. "The thought of going to a city, walking around in public…" He shook his head. "I can't."

She slowly nodded, her mouth stretching into a frown. "I understand. But if you change your mind, I have this little deck off the back of my apartment. It's a ledge really. I sometimes sit out there at night and listen to the wind chimes. When this is all over, you could come around the back of the building, use the ground floor table behind my neighbors' apartment and climb up to the ledge by my bedroom window." She gave him a hopeful smile. "Throw pebbles. Except that might freak me out, so call first. But the point is, no one would see you."

"Isn't that a security problem, having a deck by your window?"

"Chase thought so, too. First of all, it's on the third floor, and you have to be in really good shape to climb up, like you are. Eye isn't. I could tell that much about him. Chase installed a security system, with the windows wired, and bars as well. If the window opens, the alarm beeps." She gave him a small smile. "It'd be kind of romantic, like that Melissa Etheridge song, 'Come to My Window.'"

And pathetic. He planted a kiss on her palm and set her hand down. "Once this bastard is behind bars, you have to get on with your life. You don't need someone like me keeping you in the dark."

She placed her hands on his face, leaning close, looking like she was about to implore him. Then she tilted her head. "You don't think you deserve to be happy, do you? Because you think you let your comrades down?"

The truth of that speared him right in the chest. "I don't know what I deserve. I'm too messed up to even consider it. And you don't need to be involved in the mess that's me." He gently disengaged, kissing her on the forehead before going into the bathroom.

She was dressed in her long T-shirt when he came out a couple minutes later, brushing her hair with her fingers. He picked up his pants and pulled them on. "I'll walk you to your room."

"I got here all right; I can get back on my own." She

paused at the door, her hand on his over the doorknob. "I wouldn't mind waking up to your ugly mug every morning, by the way. Just sayin'." She went to her room.

He leaned against the closed door, gripping his temples. Those words tightened and pulled and twisted inside him. The selfish part of him wanted to explore this connection between them. And the amazing physical aspect, too. But it wasn't fair to her.

He quickly dressed and headed to the Mud Room, where Chase and a man in his mid- to late-twenties were talking about surveillance cameras.

Chase introduced him to Detective Adam Burns. "Burns has looked over everything and says we should have an iron-clad case when we catch Eye."

Griff asked, "You're that sure he's going to come here?"

Burns nodded. "The guy's obsessed with her, and he's mad as hell that he can't find her. He threatened her friend, for God's sake. What a coward."

Griff had nothing but respect for what Kristy was doing. But he didn't much like putting her on display to get the sicko's attention.

"And you're sure she'll be safe?" Griff asked. "Maybe I should go—"

"I don't want any more civilians involved in this than there already are," Burns cut in. "I assure you, she'll be fine. I'm going to clear her apartment when she gets home. We'll have a patrol car keeping an eye on her place, and I'll be checking in on her. But the less commotion and strangers hanging around to pique attention the better."

"I don't like involving civvies either," Chase said.

"But I have to admit, we've had a few cases where they've proven invaluable. Kristy's cooperation along with Griff's property were perfect. And they aren't going to be here when the show is publicized, so they're perfectly safe. So, what made the police cut through the red tape and mobilize so fast?"

Burns gave him a sheepish smile. "If this blows wide open, there's going to be a lot of publicity. The captain didn't want a private firm getting all the credit while the Atlanta police were sitting on their thumbs waiting for approval."

Griff swore he felt Kristy before he even heard her footsteps coming down the hall. He turned to see her carrying her duffel bag, her gaze on him. Damn, she looked sad. Didn't she realize he was doing her a favor? She'd get tired of seeing his face every day, and then there were his nightmares, having to sleep with a night-light on…

"Good morning," Kristy said as she joined the men. "Detective Burns," she greeted with a nod. "Guess you're here to take me home."

"Yep. As soon as you're safe and sound, Chase's crew is going to release the first clips."

She set down her bag and walked over to Griff. "Thank you for everything." She placed her hands on either side of his face, her palms cool against his skin. "Remember what I said. I meant it." She gave him a soft, sweet kiss, then stepped back and pressed a folded piece of paper in his hand.

Burns was watching, but he shifted his gaze when he saw Griff's eyes on him. "Ready?"

She nodded, gave Griff one last bittersweet smile, and walked out. He felt a piece of his heart leave with her.

Chase clapped him softly on the arm. "Time for you to head out, too. Here's a DVD of some of the footage." He gave him a knowing smile as he handed him an envelope. "Trent wanted me to make sure you got it."

Within ten minutes, Griff was in his truck heading to his cousin's house in Tennessee. No sign of Burns's unmarked car anywhere. Why was he even looking? They were headed in opposite directions. Which was true in more ways than one.

He glanced at the DVD in its soft plastic sleeve, and the note lying on top of it. She'd given him her phone number and address, and drawn a diagram of how he could go around to the back and sneak in like a thief. Because he was a coward, too.

# CHAPTER 6

KRISTY KEPT CHECKING HER PHONE, HOPING HE'D CALL. Every hour, holed up in her apartment, felt like a day. She tortured herself even further by watching the DVD Trent had given her as she'd walked to the car with Burns, whispering, "Chemistry," in his singsong voice.

As she watched the footage, she could see what Trent saw. Yes, she and Griff had tons of it. She hadn't smiled so much in two years, maybe longer than that. But mostly she loved seeing Griff's smile. And the way he watched her when she hadn't realized it. The way he hovered protectively as he guided her toward a hole in the muddy water.

As it turned out, she hadn't needed the DVD. Chase had flooded the Internet with promos of the phony show, even getting it to trend on Twitter.

The sun had long ago set, which meant several hours had passed since she'd given Griff that note. She turned off the television with a sigh and headed into the kitchen to fix something for dinner, even though she wasn't hungry. As she'd been doing all day, she glanced out the front window to see the patrol car parked across the street. Every now and then the officer inside would walk around the building.

When her phone rang, her heart shot into her throat. Griff! But the screen read Detective Burns's number. True to his word, he'd checked in on her earlier in the day. And was apparently doing so again, though this time in a soft, low voice.

"Hello, Detective Burns," she answered. "Everything's fine."

Though Burns wasn't the detective originally assigned to her stalking case, he had requested to work with her and Chase because, as he'd admitted, he felt bad that the police hadn't been able to help her.

"I'm glad to hear that, but I have a concern. I was just by to check in with my officer and saw a shadow around back. I don't think it's Eye, but I want to be sure. And while I'm at it, you know I had issues with that ledge outside your window. Even if it is wired. I'm going to try to climb up and make sure it's secure."

"Chase already did that."

"Look, I'm sure you paid him a lot of money to set you up here, but to be honest, I don't know much about him or his company. Please let me put my concerns to rest. I want to test the security cameras, too, so go to your computer and see if you can spot me on the video feeds. If I make it to your window, I'll tap."

Chase had installed three discreet cameras to cover the back of the building and side. She'd gone over everything with Burns when he'd expressed his concerns. She suspected it had more to do with his dislike of Chase butting in on police territory.

"And turn off your lights," Burns went on. "If someone is skulking around, I don't want him to see you or me."

Now her heart was beating for a different reason. "I'll do that now." After thrusting her apartment into the dark, she sat at her computer and pulled up the security software. Three views filled the screen. She searched among the shadows, trying to discern whether they were shifting because of the wind or not. The view of the ledge was wide open, as she'd removed the potted plants per Chase's instructions.

Suddenly, it flickered off. She reached for the phone to call Burns but halted. What if Eye was out there? If Burns's phone went off, it would alert him.

*No, he can't have found me. He's supposed to be at Griff's property.*

So she waited in the silent darkness and listened. A few seconds later, she heard a tapping. Thank God.

Except, not really. It meant that Burns had been able to climb up on the deck. Maybe Eye couldn't break in, with the additional security measures, but he could crouch there and watch her. The thought shuddered through her.

She made her way through the bedroom, glad for Burns's directive to turn off the lights. She could see him, though she made absolutely sure it was him before disarming the window alarm, opening the bars, and then the window.

He climbed inside and closed the window. "Sorry, but you see that it was entirely possible for someone my size and strength to get up here."

She nodded. "I'm glad you checked."

"Maybe I should look the rest of the place over." He headed toward the living area. "Could you see me on the video?"

"No, but the one on the deck stopped working."

"That's odd. Let me take a look." He sat down at her computer and studied the images. "It shut off right about the time I was up there. I wonder if I accidently broke a wire." He clicked on some of the software settings, then stood. "I'll go back out and take a look. Got a flashlight?"

She went to the kitchen. When she turned, flashlight in hand, he was standing right behind her with an odd expression.

"You don't remember me, do you?" he asked. "You really don't."

There was a tiny line of anger at his mouth and in his dark blue eyes. She studied him, thinking that he was older by a couple of years. "No, I'm sorry. We've met?"

His laugh held no humor. "We went to Jonas Middle School together. I was in your seventh-grade homeroom. Mrs. Skull, as we used to call her."

"Oh." She studied his face but still couldn't place him. He looked so very ordinary, with brown hair, brown eyes, medium build. "Well, that was a long time ago. I'm sure you've changed a lot since then."

"I had a crush on you. All it took was one smile, when we were standing in the lunch line together. My parents, they thought I was gay, and my father was always harassing me about being more athletic and getting a girlfriend. The thought must have terrified him, homophobic bastard that he is. So I told him you were my girl and that you were going to the dance with me. They were thrilled. Relieved more than anything, I imagine. I worked on the yearbook committee and took some pictures of you to show my parents. They bought me a suit for the dance and a corsage to give you. And I did ask you, but you turned me down."

Why was he telling her this? She awkwardly held

the flashlight, rubbing her thumb across the ridges of the handle. "I wasn't really into boys much then." She'd been insecure, too tall and gawky. "It was nothing personal."

"My father beat the living daylights out of me when he found out I lied. Maybe you remember the kid who winced for a week every time he sat down."

She grimaced at the thought of such a beating but held back another apology. That wasn't her fault. Then a vague memory surfaced, a boy who was shorter than her telling her that she was going to the dance with him. He'd been angry when she turned him down, and he'd given her creepy stares for the next several weeks. Then the school session had ended, and she couldn't remember seeing him the next year.

"Sorry, didn't mean to make you feel awkward," he said, waving it away. "Give me the flashlight, and I'll check the camera."

When she reached out, he grabbed her arm instead. In a flash, he'd spun her against his chest and slapped his hand over her mouth. When she tried to scream, he pressed a finger to the front of her throat, nearly making her choke.

"I didn't ask another girl out for years," he went on, as though he wasn't holding her against her will. He walked them to the counter where he pulled a knife from the butcher block. He fiddled with something in his pocket and produced a cloth that smelled like ether.

Chloroform! He was going to knock her out. She fought him, uttering as much of a scream as she could manage with his hand smashed over her mouth. He brought the cloth over her nose, and the acrid smell filled her nostrils.

*No! I can't let him do this!*

"My father called me faggot and other vile names until he died when I was seventeen." She struggled, but he continued talking in an eerily calm voice. "I watched you over the next couple of years. You filled in, became more beautiful. And you didn't see me at all. Then you moved away, and I tried to forget you. Until I saw the ads. You in skimpy bathing suits showing off your flesh. An article in the *Atlanta Constitution* about the home-town girl who'd become a successful New York model and then, aw, moved back because her parents were worried about her. And everything I'd done to better myself, achieving detective at an early age, the cases I'd solved, all melted away to leave me as that invisible kid again. It's your fault, Kristy. It's your fault that deep inside I feel like a nothing. I wanted to make you feel bad, too."

She was struggling, holding him off enough to grab a breath of fresh air and keep darkness from falling. "You're… Eye?" she managed.

He shoved the cloth hard against her face, clamping down over her nose. "Yes, Kristy. And while the cops and your security expert are waiting for me to take the bait, you and I are finally going to get some quality time together."

Darkness pulsed in and out. She knew his name. He was a cop. No way was he going to let her live to tell. And then she fell into the abyss.

# CHAPTER 7

GRIFF HAD SPENT THE AFTERNOON WATCHING THE DVD. He'd hardly recognized the man helping Kristy drive through the bog or catch fish. That man laughed. Smiled. Forgot he was a beast. And she never looked at him with anything but acceptance. Trent had included footage of their kiss, too, right at the end. Griff had caved at the sight, bodies pressed together, his hands at her waist.

And he'd heard her voice as clear as a bell: "Griff, I don't want a guy who looks good. I want a guy who is good."

Was he a good man? Good enough for her? He had to take the opportunity to find out. He'd been given the gift of life, of surviving. She'd given him the gift of her heart. And when he'd made love to her, he'd felt like a man for the first time in years. He'd felt alive.

So he'd been driving to Atlanta all evening. He even decided that he was going to come in the normal way, right through the foyer she'd described. It was after ten when he drove into the area of the city where she lived. He imagined that people in the cars next to his stared over at him. He didn't have to imagine the piteous stares of the man pumping gas across from him, or the kids who gawked.

*What am I doing here? I need to be in my comfort zone, in a couple hundred acres of woods.*

He dropped into the seat of his truck, hidden again by

tinted windows. Maybe her affection was all about the fact that he was helping her. He rested his head against the seat with a loud sigh. He'd grown so insecure. Afraid. Not of physical pain—he'd endured plenty of that—but the kind that took even longer to heal.

All right, so he'd call her. If she sounded happy to hear from him, he'd see her. If she sounded hesitant or unpleasantly surprised, he'd go back to Tennessee.

He called the number she'd written on the note. It rang several times before someone picked up, and then another three seconds passed before he heard her tentative, "Hello?"

"Hey, it's Griff."

Damn, another second of silence. Then, "Oh, hey."

"I didn't wake you up, did I?" Yeah, he was digging for a reason she didn't sound enthusiastic.

"No, I…I'm awake."

"You okay? You sound kinda funny."

"I'm…fine. I just woke up from…a nap." There was another sound, though he couldn't place it. "Griff, I have to go. It's not a good time to talk."

She was blowing him off. He gripped the phone, the edges biting into his palm. But he wouldn't slink away in silence. No, he was going to put himself out there. "Did you change your mind? About us?"

The silence said it all. He was about to say goodbye, wish her well, when she whispered, "I meant what I said when you were showing me how to shoot the rifle. Please remember that, Griff. I have to go."

The phone went dead. He stared at it, nearly dizzy from rejection. He didn't want to remember anything now. He didn't—

Wait a minute. He'd never taught her to shoot. What had she meant by that? She'd said it very deliberately, with more conviction than she'd said anything else.

*Because she was trying to tell you something.*

Hell. Was he just digging for a reason for her dismissal? When he pushed past his sensitive ego, he felt something dark in his gut. He'd rather her have a change of heart than be in trouble. He glanced at the note again. No way would she have changed her mind about being with him in the course of a day. Seeing her diagram, remembering her sadness at leaving him, Griff believed she meant everything she'd said. Which meant something was terribly wrong.

He drove the final four blocks to the address, passing a patrol car parked by the curb across the street. The guy inside was looking down, probably playing some game on his phone. Griff didn't want to ask him to check on her, only to find an awkward situation. He parked along the side street and pulled his thirty-eight special from the glove box. He knew there were cameras outside the building, so with his gun tucked into his waistband, he strolled down the sidewalk and looked as casual as possible. He spotted the first camera, ducking around a bush and cutting around the back way. He used the neighbor's table to climb to the second level, then sidestepped around some railing to climb to the third floor. The ledge was just above him, the wind chimes his assurance that it was her bedroom window.

Once he reached the deck, he couldn't avoid the camera aimed right at him. He approached the darkened window, seeing that the bars weren't latched. That sent his spider-sense into overtime. No way would she leave this open. He followed a loose wire, which brought his attention to the section leading up to the camera. It was cut.

*Hell.*

That's when he heard the plaintive sound. Not words, but a cry. He couldn't see inside, but the light was on in a room beyond her bedroom. He pulled the bar grate open, then tested the window. It was unlocked. Someone had come in this way. But how had he opened the bars?

Griff climbed in, scraping his back against the top of the window, and felt carefully for a place to land without making noise. His marine training came right back as he landed soundlessly.

A man's voice floated in from the living area. "Aren't you going to beg for mercy, Kristy? Aren't you afraid?" he taunted. "You're a model. Give me some fear. How about some tears? Work it."

Son of a bitch! Griff shifted enough to see the most terrifying scene he'd ever taken in, worse than anything he'd encountered in the war. Kristy was tied to a chair, her mouth bound with a gag. She was bleeding from tiny cuts on her shoulders, neck, and cheeks, but her face was a cold mask.

He went into soldier mode, a deadly calm replacing the rage threatening to roar through him. The man's back was to him, and he stood directly in front of Kristy, making for a dangerous angle to shoot. Not some grungy psycho. He was dressed in business attire, even had his shoes shined.

"And you call yourself a model," he sneered.

Griff knew that voice. From where? He held the gun in a ready position and assessed the situation. If he moved out of the shadows, she would see him, and the flick of her gaze would give him away to her tormenter.

The man lifted a knife. "Maybe a deeper cut will make you cry? I bet you won't ignore me now."

Griff stepped out, Kristy looked up, and the man spun around. Which shifted him two inches from Kristy. Griff only had a second to reconcile the disbelief of seeing the detective's face. When the man started to swing the knife down toward her, Griff pulled the trigger twice.

Blood splattered across Burns's chest, his face now registering shock. He kept bringing the knife down. Griff couldn't shoot at his arm; it was too close to Kristy. But she saw the knife coming her way and threw herself to the side, sending the chair crashing to the floor. Griff shot Burns again.

The knife dropped, and so did Burns. Griff scooped Kristy up as he kept the gun aimed at Burns. He was gasping, holding his chest while blood spurted out between his fingers.

"I'm the youngest detective on the force," he whispered, grimacing in pain. "I have a spotless record. But you still didn't see me."

Griff wanted to shoot him again, but he knew the legal system wouldn't see it as self-defense. He kept an eye on the man as he tugged on the gag and took inventory of Kristy. "Are you all right?"

She nodded, her breaths coming fast. Relief washed over him, nearly sending him to his knees. He tugged the ropes to free her.

Someone was banging on the door. The cop from the car, hollering about opening up. Griff didn't want to leave Kristy, nor did he want to take his gun off

Burns. "Call an ambulance!" he shouted, just as the door smashed open and the officer rushed in, weapon pointed. "Drop the gun!"

The fresh-faced guy was barely a kid, and he clearly couldn't begin to make sense of the scene in front of him. Griff set the gun down. "Burns is Eye."

Kristy clung to Griff, her body trembling, tears flowing.

"*Now* you cry," Burns whispered, one last bittersweet statement before his mouth went slack and his head rolled to the side.

---

Griff stood vigil as the paramedics checked Kristy and treated cuts that were, thank God, superficial. Her gaze kept going to him, which was good because she didn't see Burns get carried out of the apartment on a covered stretcher. She also didn't see the five obvious members of law enforcement who were waiting to hear her official statement.

"I let him in, Griff," she said, her voice strained. "I let Eye into my home. He said he wanted to test the cameras, the back way in. And I believed him."

The medic gave Griff a nod, and he stepped forward and pulled her into his arms. "Of course you did, honey. The man was a police officer." At least that answered how the bars had ended up open. The rest, he could wait for. He kissed her forehead. She was alive. And free. But he knew better than anyone that the injuries of war took longer to heal on the inside than they did on the outside.

She melted into him, her hands gripping his back. "I was so afraid you thought I was rejecting you." She looked up at him, her eyes wide and damp. "You came to Atlanta. I just realized that. You were already here when you called."

He brushed a strand of bloodied hair from her cheek. "Four blocks away. I decided I had a lot more to lose by staying in my comfort zone. I had you to lose. And I almost did." God, he wanted to squeeze her tight, but he held back so he wouldn't hurt her. When he sensed the officers approaching, he tilted her chin up. "The police need to talk to you. But I'm going to be here holding your hand, just like I did with the noodlin'. And if you can still stand to see my ugly mug in the morning, I'm going to be here all night. All day. For as long as you can stand me."

She smiled through her tears. "I have a feeling I can stand you for a good long time."

# ABOUT THE AUTHOR

**Tina Wainscott** has always loved the combination of suspenseful chills and romantic thrills. She's published fifteen romantic suspense novels, as well as fourteen paranormal romances as Jaime Rush. Losing her nephew, a Marine, in the war made her realize that our military men are the perfect heroes. Not only during the war but afterward as they try to stitch their lives and souls together once they're home. And so was born her series for Random House about five Navy SEALs who take the fall for a covert mission gone wrong and join The Justiss Alliance, a private agency that exacts justice outside the law.

As Jaime Rush, she is the author of the Hidden series, featuring humans with the essence of dragons, angels, and magic, and the award-winning Offspring series, about psychic abilities and government conspiracies.

Tina lives in southwest Florida with her husband, daughter, and cat.

For sneak peeks and more, visit www.TinaWainscott .com. For more on her paranormal romances, go to www.JaimeRush.com.

# NSDQ

## A Night Stalkers Novella

# M.L. BUCHMAN

U.S. Army Captain Lois Lang circled her Black Hawk helicopter five miles outside the battle zone and ten thousand feet up. Usually height equaled safety in countries like Afghanistan where the Taliban had no air power, especially in the middle of the night. Get above the reach of most of the cheaper weapons—rifles, rocket-propelled grenades, and the like—and you were generally safe.

But the Lataband Pass, visible as a thousand shades of green in her night-vision gear, deep in the heart of the Hindu Kush Mountains, was at eight thousand feet and the surrounding peaks cleared ten easily. Even at night in the mountains, ten thousand was pushing the high-hot limit of the helicopters. The high altitude and mid-summer temperatures gave her chopper's rotor blades thinner air to push against. To get higher, she'd have to really burn fuel; never a good bet on a long mission.

So, she and her crew circled wide and low, and watched their threat displays closely. Not a soul this far from the pass, not even a goatherd. Nothing to do but wait. Their job was CSAR—she always thought of a seesaw whenever she heard the acronym for Combat Search and Rescue, every time—which meant their night would be quiet and routine, unless something went wrong with the attack the U.S. Army's 160th was about to unleash at the heart of the pass.

A ground team, probably from the 75th Rangers, had been dumped in this barren wasteland a week before to do recon. And for tonight, they'd reported a massive convoy of munitions crossing this disused pass from Jalalabad, Pakistan, to supply the Taliban forces inside Afghanistan. With the drawdown of U.S. troops, the Taliban were gearing up to hit the Afghani government forces and hit them hard. Special Ops Forces' job tonight was to make sure they didn't have the supplies from the ever-so-innocent Pakistanis to do so.

"Keeping chill?" she asked her crew.

"Chill," Dusty replied from his copilot's seat beside her. He'd been a backender, only recently jumped from a back-seat gunner crew chief to front-seat copilot, and they were rotating him through the different choppers for cross-training. He normally flew troop transport but had logged time in the heavy weapons DAP version of the Black Hawk, as well. Now that it was nearing his last flight in CSAR, she'd definitely miss him. It was tradition to scoff at backenders who aspired to be pilots, but Dusty definitely had what it took.

"We be very cool, Superwoman," Chuff and Hi-Gear answered from their crew chief positions right behind the pilots' seats.

Her nickname had been inevitable. Being named for both of Superman's girlfriends, Lois Lane and Lana Lang, had labeled her for life. Her mother had always been a crack up, right to her last comment from her death bed, "Flying out now, honey." The fact that Lois had the same light build, narrow face, and straight dark hair as Margot Kidder—who'd played Lois in the old *Superman* movies—didn't help matters.

The two crew chiefs sat in back-to-back seats facing sideways out either side of the chopper. Steerable M134 miniguns were mounted right in front of them.

The days of the UH-1 Huey medical choppers with the big white square and red cross painted on their unarmed bellies were long gone. Bad guys now thought the red crosses made for good targets. And in the modern world of strike-and-retreat tactics, there was no quiet after-the-battle moment when it would be safe to go in and gather the wounded.

Rescue ops now happened right in the heart of the fray, and a medical chopper arrived ready to both save lives and deliver death. Some of the old guard guys complained about that but not SOAR. The 160th Special Operations Aviation Regiment had flown into Takur Ghar, bin Laden's compound, and a thousand other hell-holes, and CSAR crews like hers had been there to pull the lead crews back out when things went bad.

The two medics, a couple of new guys, checked in with her, as well. They were the real crazies: Chuck and a new woman named Noreen. They went into a hot battle zone armed with a stretcher and a medical bag. Beyond crazy.

"Thirty seconds," she called as the mission clock continued counting down to 0200. The Night Stalkers, as everyone called the 160th SOAR, ruled the night. "Death Waits in the Dark" was their main motto, and it did. They were the most highly trained chopper pilots on the planet, and she'd busted her ass for eight years to fly with them, spent two more years in training, and had now been in the air with them for two more. It was her single finest achievement.

Even five miles out, the flash of the first strike was a clear streak across the infrared night-vision image projected on her helmet's visor. The resulting explosion was small. The night's mission brief had said to stop the convoy, gather intelligence, then destroy the munitions. So, first strike had been merely to stop the gun runners' forward progress and get their attention.

The latter part definitely worked. Fire raked skyward, and not just little stuff. She could see anti-aircraft tracers arcing upward in a white-hot trail of glowing phosphors and hoped that no one was in the way.

"Stay sharp," she warned herself and her crew. The fire show was a distraction for others to worry about. Their worry was—

"CSAR 4. Immediate extract. Grid 37," Archie, the air mission commander, called in. He was back at their helibase a hundred miles into Pakistan, watching their world from an MQ-1C Gray Eagle drone circling another fifteen thousand feet above them.

She acknowledged and dove for the roadway. Grid 37 was right in the gut of the pass, so coming in high was just asking for trouble with the ongoing battle she could see still in progress. At five feet above Lataband Pass, she unleashed the five thousand horsepower of the twin GE turbine engines. Fifteen thousand pounds of Black Hawk helicopter flung itself toward the battle at two hundred miles an hour. Even with the twists and turns of the narrow gravel road winding between the steep peaks, they were just two minutes out.

These were always the fastest and the slowest two minutes of her life. At her present altitude and the narrow valley she was flying in, even a stray boulder was a life-threatening hazard. Constant adjustments were needed to crest every rise and take advantage of every little dip. This is what SOAR trained for: flying nap-of-the-Earth to come out of nowhere, in the dead of night, exactly on target and on time.

Yet every second that ticked by, someone lay on the battlefield fighting to stay alive long enough to be rescued. She drove the turbines another couple RPMs closer to yellow-line on the engine's tachometers.

This time the faster feeling won out, and they were on the battlefield with a shocking abruptness. And battle was definitely the operative word. Her tactical display showed two Black Hawks and two of the vicious Little Birds dancing across the sky. But there had been three Little Bird helicopters when they left the airbase.

Grid 37.

Pull back on the cyclic control between her knees for a hard flare to dump speed; pull up on the collective along the left side of her seat to gain just enough altitude to keep her tail rotor out of the dirt as she slowed. She hammered them down less than a hundred feet from the crumpled remains of the Little Bird helicopter.

Everything was happening at once. Chuff and Hi-Gear were already laying down covering fire, their miniguns blazing with a dragon's deep-throated roar. At three thousand rounds a minute, they scorched the earth anywhere they spotted a bad guy. Chuck and Noreen were already out at a dead sprint toward the crumpled chopper.

She debated pulling back aloft to offer them better cover, but the intensity of the overhead air battle told her if she went aloft, she'd have to move well out of the area to be of any use. Her people stood a better chance if she stayed on the ground.

So instead, she remained a sitting duck on the ground and intensely counted the seconds. A hundred-foot sprint, with heavy gear, but high adrenaline: ten seconds. If the injured weren't trapped but perhaps delirious enough with pain to fight against rescue: thirty seconds to get them strapped down. A hundred-foot return carrying deadweight on a stretcher or slow-limping someone back to the chopper: twenty seconds more. If they were bloody lucky, they only had to survive one minute on the ground.

Rather than watch the medics, she watched the tactical displays. She was getting heavy cover from above. A technical appeared from nowhere around an outcrop: a Toyota pickup with a heavy-caliber machine gun mounted on the bed—serious nightmare vehicle. But Hi-Gear was on it, and in moments the truck was adding its own fireball plume to the light and confusion of the night.

"Ten," one of the medics shouted.

Lois began counting down seconds and eased up on the collective until the chopper was dancing on the dirt in its eagerness to be aloft.

She ignored the bright sparks of bullets pinging off her forward windscreen, hoping nothing was a big enough caliber to punch through. Her audio-based threat detector filling her ears with muted squeals indicating only small-arms fire; the big stuff was still hunting the SOAR attackers overhead. The directional microphones translated each bullet's trajectory into fire-return data, and her crew chiefs were pounding back on those positions.

At five seconds to go, a crowd came out of the roiling dust kicked up by her rotors.

She glanced over for just an instant and then returned her attention to tactical while her mind unraveled what she'd just seen. One medic carrying a man over his shoulder, dead-man style. The second medic pulled one end of a stretcher, the other end dragging on the road's gravel surface with a body strapped to it; good, both of her crew accounted for. Two other guys limping in with their arms around each others' shoulders, clearly nothing else keeping them upright.

The last two deserved a second glance. MICH helmets and HK416 rifles rather than the FN SCARs that all of SOAR carried across their chests. Delta Operators. If Delta were on the ground here, it meant this action was much heavier duty than she'd thought. That explained the unexpected scale of the firefight.

At zero on her countdown, she could feel the shift in her two-inch high hover as the team slammed aboard. She gave the stretcher bearer an extra three seconds to load.

The "GO!" came just as she racked up on the collective, getting her off the dirt and airborne without a wasted instant.

Whatever was happening in the cargo bay was no longer her problem. They could do everything that most field hospitals could do. If you were alive when CSAR got you, your life expectancy was very high. And sometimes even if you weren't.

Lois punched through the dust brownout kicked up by her own rotors and headed back the way she'd come. She slewed hard to clear the first turn in the road as the battle behind her moved toward the other end of the pass.

She climbed enough to keep her rotor blades clear of the ground and leaned into the first turn in the ravine.

She barely had time to see the white-hot streak coming in her direction. "RPG!" the warbling tone of the threat detector screeched out. The rocket-propelled grenade impacted her Number One turbine engine with no chance of an evasive maneuver. Dusty pulled the overhead Fire Suppress T-handle as Chuff's minigun announced he was taking care of whoever had gotten them. That was no longer the problem.

The problem was she was in a turn that needed four-thousand horsepower to recover from, and she now only had twenty-six hundred. She cranked the Number Two engine right into redline and yanked up hard on the collective.

Not enough. The steep rock wall of the pass loomed before them. The night-vision gear gave her a perfect, crystalline view—as well-lit as if it were broad daylight—of the boulder field that was going to kill her Hawk.

And her crew.

No! There!

Normally, she'd pull up on the collective and let the tail hit first and then belly flop the bird down—worked well on a flat landing area. The Hawk could take a lot of abuse that way and could often be bounced off its wheels and they'd be on their way.

But not with these boulders. The very worst of the damage path would be right through the center of the cargo bay where she had four injured, two medics, and two crew chiefs.

She slammed over the collective and rammed down hard on the right rudder pedal, intentionally driving the pilot's side rotor blade into the cliff wall.

They would tumble in a hard roll, but it offered the best chance of the crew's survival.

Only one problem.

She'd known it even before she'd slammed over the collective and didn't shy away.

U.S. Army Captain Lois Lang's position was the very first point of contact in the developing crash.

---

Lois jerked awake in a cold sweat.

No cockpit!

Crisp white sheets. Soft pillow.

She let out a long, slow sigh of relief. If the damn dream insisted on waking her every single morning, why did it have to be so utterly accurate. And real. Her adrenaline was through the roof, her heart rate only now cascading down through stratospheric flight levels.

She was in her own apartment in Fort Lewis post housing. She was still here, housed with the rest of the SOAR 5th Battalion. Like most single soldiers in post housing, her possessions were not a major burden. Most of them were hanging on the white walls: the line of pictures of people she'd served with, the ones she'd dragged out of hell and the pictures of them back in the air or back with their families, and most importantly, her different crews over the years—the ones she'd shed blood and sweat with. Her ROTC graduation certificate and the letter signed by the president to commission her as an officer in the U.S. Special

Forces were framed at the center of the wall. She belonged here.

At least this time she'd woken before the final crash, which she often relived in agonizingly slow motion. She'd count that as a good start to the day.

She swung up to a sitting position and stared at her options. Start the day on crutches or crutches with the prosthetic. She wanted to ignore the damn foot, but reminded herself that "Night Stalkers Don't Quit." NSDQ was a motto commonly heard during tough times, and she'd been saying it a lot lately. Well, if they didn't quit, that also meant they didn't shy away from the hard choices.

Fine. As of this moment, no matter what the medicos said, she was done with the crutches. She reached for the foot and began putting it on.

Two layers of anti-abrasion sock that rolled up over her knee, at least *that* was still hers. She'd always been told she had great legs, had enjoyed wearing shorts to the inevitable volleyball or beach gatherings to show them off. Now, not so much.

She slid on the socket and strapped it into place. She'd tried the suction mount but never liked the slick feel of it. So, socks and straps. They'd offered her two different right-foot prostheses, but she'd only taken the one. She didn't need some dandied-up version of cosmesis. Her right foot was gone; a transtibial shear-off right at mid-calf as she'd kept the rudder pedal rammed down throughout the entire crash to buy every last ounce of safety she could for her crew. And it had worked. Other than a few broken ribs and a concussion, hers was the only injury. If she had to deal with a false foot, then people would have to accept her as she was.

For the first time since the crash, she didn't pull on pants, but chose a skirt instead. *If you're gonna do it, girl, you're gonna do it all the way.* So, no false camouflage either.

The leg came with a fake, skin-toned covering shaped like a human foot. She considered throwing that in the garbage disposal for good measure, but it would just clog the thing up. Hell, lettuce would clog her damned disposal. She chucked the offending plastic covering—with its fake big-toe gap so she could wear a sandal—in the garbage. She had a custom sneaker that would hide most of the prosthetic's mechanics, but she bypassed that as well, opting to clip on just the rubber toe and heel pads that left the mechanical foot exposed.

They'd released her from the WTU yesterday. Thank goodness Joint Base Lewis-McChord had one of the Warrior Transition Units right on the base. That meant she'd been able to go through much of her recovery in her own apartment. Well, if the WTU had decided to declare her healthy, then she'd start acting healthy.

She was still awkward without the crutches. Once dressed, she walked back and forth across the apartment several times. With a curse, she assessed herself as not stable enough to go out without at least a cane. She'd long since discovered just how badly it hurt when she took an unexpected tumble, and this wasn't a good day for that.

They'd promised that this foot with its aluminum core and titanium fittings was solid and durable enough for her to run on, but she still found that hard to credit.

The nerve sensations she received from her missing foot had nothing to do with what her new one was doing. She actually did better if she didn't keep looking down to see when it was on the ground and when it was in the air, but it was hard to break the habit when she couldn't actually feel the ground. Every step was a surprise when ground contact actually occurred—especially because she felt it in her calf and knee, not her foot.

At the door, she really, really wished she didn't have to hold onto the knob for a good ten minutes before she could force herself to go through, but she did. That, too, was part of her new reality.

Head finally high, she made it out the door and through the small lobby. Thankfully, she had a ground floor unit, as the complex had no elevators. Refusing the ADA-compliant access ramp, between her cane and the railing she did manage the three steps out front. The Medical Evaluation Board offices were only a half mile away. She could have called for a car, but for a woman used to twenty-mile runs, it was too demeaning. *NSDQ. NSDQ.*

Summer had given way to fall in the Pacific Northwest while she'd recovered. The blazing arid heat of the high passes of the Hindu Kush would be switching to freezing temperatures and impassible snow. She'd always been a Northwest gal and could smell that fresh snap left by an overnight rain, which would have been snow atop the nearby fourteen-thousand-foot peak of Mount Rainier. The thick smell of evergreen and undertone of moss. She could practically taste the apple cider season on the air. The hint of the ocean from the waters of Puget Sound. The sunlight cool as it shone off the wet paving of the walkway. This was home. At least until the Army medically retired her and said it wasn't anymore.

"Hey, Lois. How's life on the *Daily Planet* today?"

"Hey, Clark. Doing just *super*!" And she was doing a little better for Kendall Clark's presence. She'd allowed herself an hour to cross the half mile to the MEB building, so she could afford to stop and rest a moment after the first hundred yards. "How about you?"

"Super, now that I've run into you." And he really did look super. Always a little standoffish but a pleasure to look at.

"Haven't seen you in a bit." Not since before her accident.

"Was at the Sikorsky home office in Connecticut for some upgrade training the last couple months. Didn't know you were back until just yesterday."

"Back." Nice way to put it. Nicest she'd heard yet.

Clark was the Black Hawk specialist embedded at Fort Lewis by Sikorsky—the Hawk's manufacturer. Part engineer, part instructor, and all around good egg. It was inevitable that they'd been thrown together, aside from the training he provided. With him being almost the Clark Kent mild-mannered alias of the superhero, it had been inevitable.

Others had picked up on it even before they met. Crazy Tim had started it, of course, going way out of his way to introduce them. Then he'd set off on a quest to find a Jimmy and a Perry to form the "ultimate team against evil." He hadn't reported any results yet. Of course, Crazy Tim was still aloft in Afghanistan, and she was permanently grounded in Washington State, a bitter pill she did her best to spit out rather than swallow.

—⁓—

Kendall's eyes kept tracking down to Lois's uncovered prosthetic foot. He'd pull them away and look back up at her eyes, but it was clearly giving him trouble.

"It's okay, Clark. I'm going to just have to get used to it." She wasn't happy about it but tried not to sound too upset either; she was the one who'd chosen the skirt after all. "Go ahead, give it the good once-over." She leaned on her cane and turned it sideways for him to see.

He squatted down to look, then had the decency to glance back up at her to make sure it was okay. He was such a geek, one of his more charming features. Actually, one of his many charming features. She'd always liked him once Tim had bumped them together.

"The Soleus Tactical," she filled him in. "They designed it specifically for a double amputee named Dale Beatty. National Guard guy who hit an IED over in the Dustbowl." Iraq and Afghanistan lacked many things, but they had plenty of dust. Six months out and she could still feel it clogging her pores.

"Slick. The springs are adjustable?"

It was the first time anyone other than a doctor or physical therapist had even been allowed to see it. If there was anyone to be her "first time," she liked that it was Kendall. For reasons she didn't care to contemplate, she was ridiculously tempted to run her hand through his black hair not so different from Clark Kent's. Was she that desperate for company?

"Yeah," was the answer to both questions. "They keep retuning the springs as I get used to it, though they're pretty well done with changes now. The harder

I push down, the more reaction back I get. They say I can run on it. That won't be anytime soon, I can promise you. Even with the socket, it weighs less than my real foot. Great weight loss plan, huh?"

The engineer in him came out as he tapped a finger against a couple parts of the armature. It was so personal—almost as if he'd just stroked his hand down her bare foot. She must have reacted somehow, because he suddenly jerked his hand back, looked up at her in shocked apology, and proceeded to tip back onto his butt in an effort to withdraw.

"Crap!" He'd landed on the wet grass, which responded with a distinct squishing sound. Then he looked up at her again. "I'm so sorry. I shouldn't have… Sorry. I wasn't thinking."

He was trying to get up without placing his hands in the mud, as well.

She braced herself and offered her hand to help him up. He took it and, after testing that she could take the load, managed to get back to his feet and stand.

He twisted to inspect the damage, his hand still in hers. She gave his hand a slight tug, causing him to expose his wet and muddy behind. He had big hands, good ones. She'd witnessed a thousand times how delicate they were on the controls and how powerful when taking a chopper apart to inspect it for wear and tear.

"Superman with a wet butt." She could feel the laugh bubbling up inside her. It came out slow and rough. Her voice was long out of practice with making such a sound, but it did come out. She clamped down on it for fear it would go a little hysterical on her. She retrieved her hand, a bit reluctantly. It was her first non-medical contact in six months, and it was surprisingly powerful. So starved for human contact that even clasping hands for a moment had roared through her nervous system and left her jittery. *Pitiful, Lois, really damn pitiful*.

He flexed his hand as if terribly conscious of their contact, as well.

"Pretty super move there, Clark," she ribbed him to cover her own unease.

"Damn! I've got a meeting in about twenty minutes. I don't have a change of clothes in the car."

And he lived off post. She remembered a nice party at his house, a bunch of Black Hawk pilots from the 4th and 5th Battalions, a summer's eve barbecue in a suburban backyard. She and Clark had spent much of the evening chatting quietly beneath the arching branches of an old cherry tree. It was a good memory.

"Here." She dug out her key. "Unit 32. Don't make too much of a mess. Towels and a hair dryer under the bathroom sink. You can bring me the key after your meeting. I'll be over at the MEB offices. Have to do all the Eval Board paperwork about no longer being medically qualified for active duty." She rapped her cane against her foot with a dull clank for emphasis, then wished she hadn't.

"Sorry about that, Lois. You were damned good."

She had been, but it felt different having the resident Sikorsky guy say it. "Thanks. Real fun begins after they boot me over to the PEB. The Physical Evaluation Board is going to medically retire my ass no matter what I say. You better scoot if you want to make your meeting."

"Right." He held up the key. "Thanks."

"No problem." She turned and began clomping off

toward the MEB office. This was not what she planned to be doing with her life. A pair of the big twin-rotor Chinooks lumbered by low overhead, hammering their way aloft on a training flight. That's what she wanted to be doing. Flying. They faded away.

"Hey, Superwoman!" she turned at Clark's call and almost ate dirt. Only a quick stab with her cane kept her upright after the unexpected motion.

He should be halfway to the apartment by now, but he still stood where they'd talked; she'd made a good dozen paces from there. He'd been watching her walk like a total Terminator machine, not like the woman she'd once been. She hoped they were far enough apart for him to not see her blush. She kept her chin up so that her embarrassment wouldn't show.

"Unit 32," she told him, risking a point with her cane, the Chinooks moved off enough that she only had to shout a little to be heard. With someone so sharp, he always forgot the strangest things.

"Knew that." He inspected his feet for a moment as if to see if they were prosthetic or as if he didn't want to look at hers.

Fine. She didn't need anyone's symp—

He looked up. "Are you free for dinner tonight?"

"I'm free the rest of my damned life."

"That's a yes then?"

Was she low enough to take a sympathy date? After she was done with the Medical Eval Board, she'd be low enough for anything to look good. It didn't really seem fair to a guy as nice as Kendall to use him to cheer herself up, but he had asked.

"That's a yes."

"Great! I'll get your key back before then." He spun around, stepped off the edge of the concrete walkway, and almost went down in the grass again. Then he righted himself, waved, and rushed off. Odd, he wasn't a clumsy guy, not at all.

Lois turned herself carefully and aimed back along the path. She was surprised to discover that her step was a little lighter than it had been when she started out.

—◆—

"So, did the MEB go like you expected?"

Lois looked around the restaurant. She figured they'd grab dinner at the post's mess hall, she'd gather her twenty minutes of sympathy, and he'd be done with her safe in the knowledge he'd performed a kindness. Instead, he'd taken her on a real splurge up to Stanley and Seafort's, perched on the hillside above the city of Tacoma.

First, it was off post.

Second, it had an amazing view of the harbor with its big container ships plying the shining waterways of southern Puget Sound. The Olympic Mountains to the west had just gobbled the sun and earned a stunning blood-orange aura for their trouble.

Third, it wasn't the sort of place you had a twenty-minute dinner. It was the sort of place you had a two-hour dinner in nice clothes. She hadn't worn her dress blues or her ACU—Army Combat Uniform—fatigues. Both reminded her too much of the end of her military career, but now she wished she had for the "armor" it would have given her, the explanation of her amputation. Instead, she'd opted for a nice blouse and the same knee-length skirt she'd worn this morning.

Damn Clark for not telling her where they were going. Of course if he had told her, she probably would have balked, and the man wasn't stupid. She hadn't thought to ask, merely hanked her shoulder-length hair back in a ponytail and called it good. Her dog tags were her only ornament, she'd worn those for strength, but with civilian clothes they now felt ridiculous. She slipped them inside her blouse.

Lois wouldn't have minded being dressed this way on post. Looking like a civilian except for the damned peg leg. But here in public, she really hadn't been ready for the exposure. If only she'd worn slacks, at least the cane alone would be unremarkable. She looked longingly at the exit but didn't want to let Clark down.

She could feel every eye in the place follow her still uneven walk to the window table. Not the kind of looks she was used to having follow her across a room. Once seated, the tablecloth was long enough that she felt a little less self-conscious. A little.

"Hello. Lois. Someone hit your hearing with a dose of Kryptonite?"

She tried for a dutiful laugh but had trouble dredging one up.

"I haven't really been off post since…well. It's been a while."

"That's kind of what I figured, thought I'd give you a pleasant night out."

"Well, this is certainly pleasant." White tablecloths, candlelight at each table, immaculate waitress, and a one-page menu that looked so good an additional page would have been overwhelming. Then she glanced at the prices. This was definitely outside a soldier's budget except for something really special. She eyed Kendall suspiciously.

"What?" He closed his menu and set it aside. She could never decide what to get, and he was already done.

"What's going on, Clark? Why are we here?"

He laughed, "You always speak the same way you fly, straight shooter."

"It's what we women of steel do"—she pointed down toward her foot to make her point—"even if we're only partly made of steel. Now, answer the question."

"Actually, I read up on your foot, and it's all aluminum and titanium, so I'm not sure it counts."

"Modern materials, modern woman of steel. Besides, 'woman of aluminum and titanium' doesn't have quite the ring I was looking for when I did this."

He propped his chin on a hand and aimed those dark eyes at her. They caught the candlelight and were warm and friendly.

She resisted the urge to reach out and brush the hair out of his eyes where it had slipped down. What the hell was he doing to her?

"Maybe I just like looking at a beautiful woman while I eat."

"Asked the wrong girl then."

"Says you."

"I'm—" then she stopped herself. The WTU psychologist had given her a list of trigger words to avoid. Words that would be "negative reinforcers for her emotional frame of mind." *Damaged* was way high on the list. She toyed with her water glass to buy some time. The waitress arrived with a long list of memorized specials, which bought her some more time but not enough.

She went with a Dungeness crab-stuffed salmon, Kendall ordered jumbo shrimp and steak.

Damaged. She had a few other scars besides her leg but nothing hideous. Her foot was far and away the worst of it. Kendall had seen that, inspected it, and still somehow saw her as she'd been before the accident. He made her feel ridiculous for attaching her self-image to something as small as a foot. Well, if he wasn't going to see her that way, maybe she should stop doing so herself. Or at least try.

"Well." She sipped her first glass of wine in a very long time and let the deep red Merlot warm her insides. She circled back to his earlier question as that now seemed to be a much safer topic. "The MEB was about what you'd expect. A lot of paperwork and a lot of sympathy—neither of which I wanted—but because I'm injured past possible recovery to full status, I'm not their problem. Tomorrow, I tackle the Physical Eval Board. That's going to take a while. I really don't want to leave the service, but they're gonna shuffle me out anyway."

"Aren't there plenty of things for you to do?"

"Yeah, great. Army Wounded Warrior program. Talked to the AW2 advocate, but stay in and do what? Fly a desk? The only thing I love to do is fly choppers. Well, I sure lost my superpowers on that one."

Kendall reached across the table and took her hand. She let him because it felt so good and it kept the fears at bay.

"There's lots—"

"Let's talk about something else. Anything else."

He squeezed her hand, then he did. Most guys would push and shove. Kendall Clark had apparently decided it was his duty to fly to her rescue and at the moment she wasn't complaining. He started with a funny story from a training mission that somehow involved a standard poodle with the name Underdog and a paper chain of cut-out Santas.

"I swear, I'm not making this up."

She didn't care if he was. As long as he kept holding her hand, she felt as if she somehow belonged.

—◆◆◆—

Kendall escorted her to her front door. It was long past dark by the time they returned to post. Most of the apartments would be empty, any Night Stalkers not on deployment would be night flying. She found it disorienting to be done with her day while the rest of the company was just starting theirs.

After holding the front door for her and making sure she had her keys, Kendall turned to leave. She was done in, it had been her longest day in a long time, but she still didn't want it to end.

"Hey, Clark. Where are your manners?"

He stopped with one hand on the lobby door and furrowed his brow at her.

"C'mere." She waved him over when he hesitated.

He approached cautiously.

"It's rude to hold a woman's hand half the night, tell her she's beautiful when she's feeling like shit, and then you don't at least try for a good-night kiss. What's up with that?"

"You want me to kiss you?"

"I wouldn't complain if you at least tried. Don't tell me you haven't been thinking about it." Because she knew *she* had, and it surprised her no end. And not just human-male contact. She wanted some Kendall Clark contact.

He stepped until he was so close that she actually backed up the last half-step against her locked apartment door.

"I…" His voice was soft and deep. They were so close she could feel the vibrations as much from his chest as she could with her ears. "I've been thinking about it since that day two years ago when we sat under the cherry tree in my backyard."

Then, before she could begin to process her shock, he kissed her. Not some friendly thanks-for-the-nice-date kiss. Not even a testing kiss from a handsome and geeky guy.

He wrapped his soldier-strong arms around her and pulled her in against his surprisingly hard body. She'd never really quite paid attention to how often he'd joined in when they were doing physical training workouts. Now, she certainly could appreciate that he had. The heat of the kiss built until all she could do was wrap her arms around him and hold on for the ride. And it was a wild one.

He plundered, and she gave until her entire body heated turbine hot. The adrenal roar so loud it drowned out everything except how Kendall felt in her arms, his lips and tongue offering no hint of gentle in their need, and his hands—those wonderful hands—one dug deep into her hair and the other at the small of her back, pulling their bodies tight together. Somewhere in the distance she heard the clunk and rattle of her cane falling to the tile floor.

Then, just as abruptly as he'd taken her, he stopped and took a step back. Her hands, so recently clenched in that black wavy hair that was even softer than it looked, now rested on his chest. And his rested comfortably on her waist as if they'd been there a hundred times before.

"Been wanting to do that for a long time, Captain Lang. Even better than I imagined. Way better." He offered a very self-satisfied grin, then kissed her on the tip of the nose. "Sleep well, Superwoman." He retrieved her cane, slid it into her nerveless fingers, and was gone.

She didn't manage a good-bye or even a wave. Her body buzzed very happily as she let herself into her apartment.

Lois lay down in her bed knowing there was no way she'd find sleep anytime soon. Eight hours later she startled awake—startled because for the first time since the accident, she'd woken up after she'd extracted the injured but before the crash had begun to unfold.

———

Lois spent a grinding morning with the Physical Eval Board. All paperwork. "Do you need any help keying this in? No? Okay. Go to computer station B-24 and fill out forms…" and the interminable list had begun. Army thinking, the fact that all the information was on file for the Medical Eval Board didn't mean it was in the right format for the PEB. Thankfully, she'd been smart enough to bring the paper copy of the MEB stuff, so it was mostly transcription.

That had left her plenty of time to think about Kendall while typing. A lot of little pieces began to fit into place. She thought all the way back to that party he'd had out at his place. He knew who he was dealing with so he had some beer, a lot of soda, and an impressive amount of meat for the grill. SOAR pilots were on-call 24/7. They also had a rule of twenty-four hours bottle-to-throttle, so having the chance for a drink didn't happen very often. Some of the ground crew who'd tagged along took a beer, but SOAR was a pretty straight crowd.

But before the party, Kendall had made a point of finding out her preferred beverage. She'd given him two answers, because she could never decide about food. There'd been a significant stock of both the caffeine-free Diet Coke and a giant pitcher of fresh-made iced tea. He'd served her a double cheeseburger on a toasted bun with only stone-ground mustard, without her having to ask. He'd probably gotten that from watching her at cookouts by the hangar and noting that's what she always ate.

With her new perspective of last night's very pleasant memory, that still raised her pulse each time she thought about it, some of the older memories were painting a picture she'd never seen.

So, she sat and remembered and keyed down her family status: none—mother deceased and dad bailed when she was six. Medical status: BK—below the knee transtibial amputation. Procedure: amputation by five tons of crashing helicopter. The medics, who had survived the crash mostly intact, had patched her up before she bled out, but it had been a close thing. The hard rattle of gunfire back and forth as Dusty and Hi-Gear guarded their position was a constant backdrop until one of the big DAP Black Hawks had come over and laid down some serious fire from above. Chief Warrant

LaRue had really torn up the landscape to protect the downed CSAR craft.

Lois had learned to roll through these flashbacks, offering little outward sign other than a shake of her head to clear it off. Just part of the "new life."

Clara, the one-armed AW2 Advocate, met her for lunch. No, she'd snuck up beside the PEB computer station number B-24 and launched a tactical strike.

Lois could see the woman's determination, so she rolled with it. But that didn't mean she was above complaining over a BLT.

"I'm getting pretty sick of the 'new life.'" Lois snagged a potato chip from the bag on her tray. "Where can I put in a requisition for the old one back? Never mind, I know it's not going to happen, but I don't want the new life."

"If you proceed with medical retirement, what are your plans?"

"Well, I sure don't have the patience you're showing in dealing with a jerk like me."

"Then what are your plans?" Clara was tenacious.

That's why she hated talking to the advocate. If Lois couldn't fly, she didn't have a clue.

---

"Hey, Superboy." Lois had tracked Kendall down in neutral territory. It hadn't been hard. He was usually at the hangars or the simulators, and the simulator building was close enough that she could trust herself to walk there despite the long day at PEB.

"Hey, woman of steel. Give me a minute. Got one more run to do."

She considered going up to the controller's console

and sitting in the observer's seat, but that felt a little presumptuous, so she found a plastic chair, sat, and propped her cane between her knees.

This glaring white room and its ugly fluorescent lighting was as close to a second home as she had. First was the hangars and sitting in a Black Hawk, but she'd also spent a lot of time in here with the flight simulators. It was a lot cheaper to crash a simulator than a twenty-million-dollar helicopter. They'd cleaned up the remains of her chopper with a set of destruct charges that left behind nothing bigger than a notepad. Thankfully, she'd been under the drugs by then and hadn't seen her bird go up in a roar of C4 and flames.

The simulator building itself was unremarkable. Outside was standard Fort Lewis white with a steel roof. Inside was white-painted concrete. It was the three tall stations that were the whole point. Looking as strange and clunky as two-legged *Star Wars* Imperial scout walkers, the simulators were boxy affairs atop spindly hydraulic pistons a dozen feet high. They allowed the simulator's cockpit to pitch, roll, yaw, and buck hard unexpectedly, just like a real chopper.

Little Bird, Black Hawk, and Chinook—the three choppers of SOAR turned into the three best video games on the planet. She pretended for a moment that everything was normal, and she just sat in the hard plastic chair by the Black Hawk simulator waiting her turn. She tried to recall the casual boredom she must have felt the last time she had sat here, but couldn't find it.

Training was a constant in SOAR. Thousands of hours in flight and thousands more in the trainer. Old Master Sergeant Jake Hamlin had a vicious bent, like he had it in for all SOAR pilots. She used to wonder if he especially had it in for her: flameouts, engine fires, hydraulic failures. All in the midst of a turbulent thunderstorm that had replaced the sunny day on her windscreen just moments before.

Now, all she felt was a loss as some chief warrant she didn't know clambered up into the "box." She should just leave. She really should. But she was tired, her leg—her real one—hurt from being on it all day, and she really did want some words with Kendall. So, she just sat and waited, occasionally looking up when the simulator gave a particularly violent wheeze of hydraulic pistons and a hard lurch. Not a comfortable ride. She closed her eyes and settled in to wait.

"You're up, missy."

"I wish." Lois smiled even before she opened her eyes to see Jake now standing in front of her. He was as big as Kendall. Despite a couple more decades, he was still Army strong, though his hair was now a gray crew cut.

"You're in my chairs, then you're up next. Move your behind, Captain. Your trainer says he's waiting for you."

More amused than anything else, she climbed up the steep metal stairs to the simulator's entry level. She could feel Jake close behind her and see that he was carefully gripping the rails on either side. If she stumbled, he'd be braced to catch her. She'd worn slacks today but left the armature exposed. If he had any thoughts about her new foot, he kept them to himself. She made it to the top clean and offered him a nod of thanks.

Kendall was strapped in left-side copilot. She climbed in as right-side pilot, glad she had gone back to pants.

Lois braced for nostalgia, sadness, tears… It had been a long six months since she'd been aboard a Hawk, even a simulated one. Instead, it just felt right. This is where she belonged. Through her thin civilian clothes rather than the normal flightsuit, the seat felt closer, more real, more personal against her body. Not even really thinking about it, she buckled on the harness that lay heavy against her skin through the cotton blouse.

"You remember the way of it?" She ignored Jake's sly comment. Kendall had watched her settle in but hadn't said a word. They traded surreptitious smiles that were just the beginning of a whole conversation they wouldn't be having in front of Jake. She pulled on a headset and adjusted the microphone. Her helmet was in her closet covered with six months of dust, so this would have to do, though it felt ridiculously light.

She cycled up the simulator. *One more flight. Just one more.* She didn't bother reaching for the manual, even after six months, the steps of the engine start-up procedure were still a part of her nervous system. The turbines lit off with a simulated roar through her headset. Falling into his copilot role, Kendall fed her engine temp data and RPMs as she continued down the list flipping the Blade De-icing switch to auto and all the other twenty steps of engine run-up.

The Black Hawk cockpit in the simulator was so real that she could almost believe it, if she weren't in civilian dress. She was the only anomaly in the space. The radio and comm gear ran between her seat and Kendall's, with all the engine controls and electrical system mounted in the ceiling above them. The main console stretched side to side at chest level. At the center, a few key instruments that needed no electricity. Altitude, attitude, and compass would all keep working even if everything else failed. Above them, a large shared screen that might show terrain or weapons status depending on the mission.

In front of Kendall and her were two large glass screens each. The screens had a couple dozen modes so that the displays could be customized as needed. She toggled through the settings using the switch on the collective in her left hand and set up for standard flight information.

Above the console was a wraparound windscreen that showed Fort Lewis airfield, realistically enough to believe she just might be out on the tarmac, sweating in the last heat of the setting sun before a night flight. Down by her feet—foot—was an additional view of the terrain below, just a projection of pavement at the moment. She couldn't feel the right rudder so had to visually check that her foot was on the pedal…it was. She could even get some feel of how much pressure she was applying through her calf and knee.

She called the tower for clearance to depart. Jake Hamlin answered from his control console at the back of the simulator. She eased up on the collective with her left hand and nudged the cyclic forward to get a little nosedown attitude and forward motion. She talked her way out of the flight pattern until she was up over Puget Sound.

Lois was flying. It was only a simulator, but she was up and flying. Her eyes were burning, she had to blink away the incipient tears. She didn't want to brush at her eyes; Kendall would notice when she had him take the collective to free up her hand to do so. Instead, she blinked hard and banked right so that she'd have an excuse to look out the side window away from him. The simulator's pistons canted the cockpit to match her control motions and the video projected on the windows showed the land rotating below her.

Kendall and Jake left her alone and just let her fly. She shook it out a bit, testing her reactions, testing her foot. The control wasn't as bad as she'd feared. The nerve sensations coming up her right leg were different, but she learned to interpret what they were telling her fairly quickly.

Jake threw a small thunderstorm up on the screen, not much more than a squall line, and she climbed for safety and rode out the turbulence. Her gut informed her that her tail rotor control of the rudder pedals wasn't great, but it wasn't bad either. Maybe she could get a civilian job, flying tourists around or something.

After she took them "back to the field," landed, and shut down, she had to just sit there for a long time before she remembered how to breathe. She heard Jake shut down his control station and head down the stairs. When Kendall peeled her left hand off the now inactive collective and held it in his, that's when the pain really began to flow. It took everything she had left in her to keep the tears on the inside.

—⁓—

"I lost so much." Lois hadn't really been functional after the simulated flight. She'd let herself be led by Kendall. Down the stairs, to his car, back to her apartment. There she'd simply handed him her keys, and he'd let them in.

She'd kept her composure through delivery pizza. Held it together while they spoke of nothing at all really. At least not that she could remember.

"Well, I should—"

"Will you stay?" She could hear his "it's time to leave tone," and she really didn't want to be alone.

Kendall looked at her as if not quite believing what he was hearing.

"Okay, I know I'm a bad bet. I'm"—*to hell with the WTU's words-to-avoid list*—"crippled. I'm an emotional train wreck. And I can't promise I won't be a worse one tomorrow."

"I could sit with you—"

"I'm no longer an invalid in a hospital bed." She stopped herself before it turned into a shout. Getting to her feet, she clomped away from where they'd been sitting ever so carefully on opposite ends of the couch. She came to a stop facing the unlit kitchen, her back to Kendall. Taking a deep breath, she braced her hands on the counter for support but didn't turn as she spoke.

"I've been thinking about what you said. You've been stuck in my head the whole damn day. I finally get that you liked me…"—she thought about last night's dinner and kiss—"like me. I don't know why you never said anything. I can't figure that part out. I was single. I never slept around in the unit or much outside it. Why two years—"

"Because you flew." Kendall had come up behind her without her noticing. His voice was barely a whisper. So close she could feel him there now, though he didn't touch her.

"Because I flew?" But that's everything she was…

had been. "You didn't clue me in about how you felt, because I flew."

"Yes."

She spun to face him so fast that he took a quick step back. "Oh, but now that I can't fly, now that the sky has been ripped away from me, now it's okay to kiss me like you want to take me to bed? Well, to hell with you." She tried to storm away, but he stopped her. He was far more powerful than she was, could have caged her against the counter, done anything, and she couldn't have stopped him.

All Kendall did was rest his hand lightly on her arm, and suddenly all of her momentum failed her.

"Why?" She couldn't look up to meet those dark eyes. "Can you at least tell me why?"

He nodded slowly, then led her back to the couch. His hand was strong and warm as he supported her through the still awkward transition from standing to sitting. She wanted to curl her legs under her, but the cool metal creeped her out each time it brushed her other leg.

"It's not that you flew—"

"But you just said—"

He held up his hand to stop her. His face was unreadable. She might not remember much of their last hour together, but she had remembered watching the mobility of his features. His easy smile, the laugh that started in his eyes long before it reached his lips or his voice. There was something behind his eyes now, a darkness she recognized and now wished she didn't. Kendall had become her beacon of light somewhere along the way. Two dinners and a kiss hadn't been what did it.

The flight. The gift of flight, even if it was a simulated

one. She couldn't see where the hope led, but she could feel it lying somewhere just out of reach.

Well, the light had gone out, and now the man sitting across from her was frowning with a seriousness she didn't recognize, didn't know he had in him.

"My dad flew Desert Storm." His voice with thick and slow. "He's one of the ones who didn't make it home."

"I'm so sorry." She reached out and took his hand. Why hadn't she known? Because he hadn't told her, *duh*! But as she watched how hard it was, she understood that not only hadn't he told her, he'd never told anyone.

"My mom broke that day." He stared down at their clasped hands, began massaging her hand as if it weren't connected to her, just an object to keep himself distracted. "She was great, everything a kid could ask for in a single mom, but she's never even dated again. 'No point,' is all she says to anyone who asks. I swore as a kid that I'd never be with a serving soldier."

Then he looked up at her. Those deep brown eyes so close and intense. "No one. And I mean no one ever came close to making me break that vow, except you. So I need you to be really sure that you want me in your bed for more than a one-night rehab therapy session. Because to me, it's a hell of a lot more important than that."

—◦◦◦—

Lois stood at the living room window, lit only by the distant field lights that found their way here, for a long time after she sent Kendall away into the cool spring night. She'd sent him with half a pizza and the best kiss of her life, but she'd sent him nonetheless.

"I don't dare risk hurting you as much as I expect I will," she'd told him. He was too important, though she was unclear how or when that had happened.

He'd tried to protest that he could take care of his own hurt, but she'd refused.

"Time. Give me some time." That's when he'd hit her with that kiss. It hadn't scorched and burned like last night's. Instead, it had asked and promised. She had wrapped her leg—her missing leg—behind him to keep him close and neither of them had reacted to that. She'd wanted and needed, but she hadn't taken. Hadn't taken him to her bed or taken him on the couch.

Instead, she had shown him the door and, without a word, released him into the night.

From her front window, she could see the airfield lights shining beyond the next set of barracks. Dozens of choppers were parked there, the more specialized ones tucked safely out of sight in hangars. That's where her heart had been, tucked safely out of sight. The question she couldn't answer was how safe it would be if it got out.

—⁓—

For a week, Lois went to the PEB offices to check if there was any information on her paperwork processing. More often than not she met Clara the AW2 advocate for lunch. Clara didn't push anymore. Instead, as they slowly became friends, she told Lois her own story.

"I was part of Team Lioness. We were temporarily attached to Army and Marine units, meaning we were dropped into combat teams without heavy combat training. Our job was to frisk the women so as not to violate their religious laws against any man other than their husbands touching them. You tell me how we go in with a gung-ho Marine team and don't end up in the thick of it."

"Pixie dust? I hear the Pentagon is making that standard issue now."

Clara laughed. "Could have used some. I got this one woman cleared of guns, and she had several. But my teammate hadn't secured this damn big kitchen knife just sitting out in the open. She missed my heart by that much." She raised her artificial arm. Her prosthetic began just below the shoulder. She'd chosen a cosmetic arm controlled by wires in a harness attached to her opposite shoulder. It was good enough that it would have passed for real at a casual glance, if she hadn't chosen a short-sleeved blouse to go with it.

Lois could only admire the ease with which Clara moved through the world. But she could never be a paper pusher, nor a hand holder. She was a combat pilot who could no longer fly with her team. The near daily emails they kicked her from the front were both precious and painful. Their lives were going on, and hers had stopped. But they were flying, that was something she'd done for them that they'd never know. Her crew was still up in the air...even if she wasn't.

Lois saw plenty of Clara, but she didn't see much of Kendall. She stayed away from the hangar and simulator building. He, in turn, didn't come calling. It didn't feel as if he was avoiding her so much as giving her space to think.

Damn him for being decent. It just made her think about him all the more. His compliment, which had rankled at first, had shifted over time. "Didn't want her while she flew" had shifted into the background. "Had almost made him break his own promise to himself," shifted forward.

Why had she never hooked up with him? He was funny, handsome, smart, and a damned fine pilot for a civilian. She had high standards, but he flew past all those easily. Also on the plus side, he was a civilian, so no fraternization issues would have come up.

Over the second week, she eventually reached the conclusion that the reason Lois Lang and Kendall Clark had never become an item was that she was as stupid as a brick. Which was about how she'd always ranked Clark Kent for never bedding Lois in the movies.

---

Neutral ground again, she was waiting outside the main hangar as he returned from a training flight. She'd been building up her walks, stretching the half mile to the PEB offices out to a mile, then two.

For today, she had taken the risk and left her cane behind. She'd gone back to a skirt again for the first time since their Stanley and Seafort's date and was relaxing on a bench on the service side of the hangar. The afternoon sun had almost lulled her to sleep by the time he flew back in. Daylight training today.

"Great leg!" He stood in a full flight suit, his helmet under one arm, and the lowering sun lighting him up from behind.

"Which one?"

"I'm an engineer."

She laughed, she couldn't help herself. He simply

made her feel good about herself. "You done for the day?"

He nodded.

"How about I take you to dinner?"

For an answer all he did was smile.

She'd actually cooked. Nothing fancy, but she'd made the lasagna from scratch, except for the red sauce, which was jarred because life really was too short. The post commissary also had some great baguettes, so she'd snagged one and a bag of salad.

The meal hadn't been hurried. At first, they were avoiding that she'd propositioned him, and he'd pretty much said he loved her. But soon it fell by the wayside as they each told mom stories and flying tall tales. Much of the evening had passed before a comfortable silence fell between them.

She stood. "I'm not much for romantic gestures," and she reached out a hand.

Without a word, he rose, scooped her up in his arms over her cry of protest, and carried her into the bedroom. He neither made a point of nor ignored her leg. Undressing each other was a slow, mutual, and nerve-tingling experience.

And still he didn't address her leg. Not until her skirt was off and little remained—just panties, bra, and prosthesis—did he mention it. He no longer boasted any clothes at all, and she wondered why she had avoided him so long. Kendall's body wasn't soldier strong, it was more than that. He had the strength without the overstressed leanness that so often accompanied the military lifestyle. Runs, weight room, constant training made for excellent conditioning and endurance, but the physical stresses showed—even worse after a forward deployment. Kendall's physique had all the advantages and none of the drawbacks.

"Show me how," he whispered as he nuzzled her breast through the bra's fabric.

"Not if it means you're going to stop doing that."

He obliged her until long after that bit of clothing no longer hindered his investigations.

She sat up on the edge of the bed. He sat beside her. When she reached for a buckle, it felt as if she was about to expose herself far more than merely removing her clothes.

Sensing her apprehension, he slid his fingers beneath hers and undid the first one. She guided his hand to the second. With a slight shake and a push, it came free.

He knelt before her. This beautiful, naked, gentle man knelt before her, and slid the leg off. Setting it carefully aside, he peeled off one abrasion sock and then the other.

Lois had never in her life been so exposed or felt so vulnerable. And then he kissed the inside of her bare thigh, and the sensation rocketed into her so hard and sharp that she cried out, not knowing if it was pleasure or pain.

Kendall took his time proving that it was indeed pleasure.

—◊—

A training schedule order. Lois hadn't had one of those in a long time. It was simple, clear, and she had no doubt who was behind it.

*Simulator #3 – 1700 hours – report to Master Sergeant Jake Hamlin*

She wanted to tell Kendall to go to hell. They'd been lovers for a month, and he'd kept asking her if she wanted to go up for a real flight in an actual Hawk. Kept asking until she'd shut him down hard. It was the closest they'd come to a fight; his impossible calm only making her fears all the worse. She'd shut him down so hard that he'd never brought it up again. Which was good because every mention of flying, especially in her beloved Black Hawk, had cut at her like a knife.

She tried to track him down to tell him to go to hell, but obviously he'd guessed that's what she'd do. His cell phone went straight to voice mail, and if he was anywhere on post, she sure wasn't finding him.

But the damned training schedule wasn't a request; it was an order. You didn't refuse an order, no matter how much it pissed you off. That would get her out of the service far faster than the slow-moving Physical Eval Board process. She'd be out on her ass with a dishonorable discharge mere minutes after her court-martial was done and over.

Fine!

At 1659 hours, U.S. Army Captain Lois Lang was sitting in the "up next" chair in the simulator building wearing her ACU fatigues and carrying her scuffed and scratched helmet with the big red "S" on a field of yellow in an irregular pentagon on the side.

Jake climbed down along with some other trainee he'd just put through the wringer. He sauntered over to her, started to smile, and then thought better of it.

For maybe the first time in her life, he straightened up into rigid attention and gave her a parade ground salute. "We're ready when you are, Captain."

She rose and returned the salute as formally as it had been given. "I'm so not, Jake. And I want to apologize beforehand for the civilian blood I'm going to be spilling all over the inside of your nice simulator when I get up there. Clark is toast."

"Don't worry, ma'am. Be glad to clean it up. But I would note one thing before you commit murder."

"Fire away." She pulled on her helmet and began cinching it down.

"Listen to him first. He's as good at what he does as you are at what you do."

"Did. Past tense, Jake."

This time he smiled down at her.

"And?"

"Go get him, Superwoman."

And she would. She climbed the stairs, Jake again riding safety behind her—though she felt far less need for it this time—and settled in just as she would for any training flight.

"What's the scenario?" She snapped out as a greeting. Nothing said she had to be polite to a civilian, even if he was sharing her bed and made her feel like Venus despite her missing limb.

"You have a choice of two, Captain." Kendall kept it formal, too. He was never stupid and would know full well just how pissed she was. "We have a standard Jake torture test."

Jake's Tortures, as they were known far and wide, were notorious. Not many pilots survived those. The simulator had six major categories of weather and eighteen of failures; some of which had dozens of options. There were technical and moral challenges. Engine fires and very hot targets, copilot bleeding out versus terrorist getting away with it. You never knew what was coming, and there was always something new.

"The second one?"

"It's one that I designed, Lois. Just for you. Based on a real flight tape." The tone of his voice got to her. He knew her so well, had gotten past every shield she'd ever had, ever thrown up. Over the last month, he'd convinced her that maybe, just maybe, she could find a way to live in the "new life" without hating it so much. Without having to work every day to find the positive, the upside.

*Designed it just for me.* In the soft, personal tone that he didn't use when they had exhausted each other by pushing the bounds of sex to new limits. No, it was that quiet, gentle tone each time she awoke from the nightmare, and he held her and told her everything would be all right.

*Damn him!*

She took a deep breath, dropped her hands on the controls, and let the breath out slowly. Then a nod to, "Bring it on." She didn't trust herself to speak.

*NSDQ. NSDQ. Night Stalkers Don't Quit. NSD—*

Unholy hell was breaking out all around her. Her helmet's tactical display reported a dozen sources of gunfire. The covering fire from the DAP Hawk circling above them wouldn't be enough for much longer.

A technical came around the far side of the crashed Little Bird, clearing a boulder in a four-wheel slide that was the only reason the gunner couldn't get a bead on her fast enough. She could see in her night vision the big twin barrels of a Russian ZU-23 anti-aircraft gun mounted on the truck's bed slowly swinging to aim at her cockpit. It fired one-inch shells that would punch through the Hawk's armor as if it wasn't even there.

Even as she cried out his name and the direction, Hi-Gear took it out, gunner, gun, and then the vehicle. The fireball was blinding through the windscreen, the night-vision gear temporarily overloaded.

"Ten," one of the medics called out from the Little Bird.

Still blinking hard, she couldn't see anything yet, she began counting down the seconds. At five, she pulled the collective up to get a low hover. It would also raise the blade tips almost two feet, making the medic's passage beneath the spinning disk that much safer.

At zero, everyone was aboard and at plus-three-seconds she got the signal and she was gone.

Punching out through her own dust cloud, her adrenaline pumping high and hot, she slammed into the first turn.

Then she saw it.

This time, before the warning systems, before she had in reality, Lois spotted the spark of heat from the RPG's firing. Even if she'd seen it that early in reality, the only way to save her Black Hawk would have been to roll right and up.

If she did, the RPG would have blown into the rear cargo bay, killing her entire crew. Next, they'd have rammed head-on into the canyon wall. Had she seen it in time, her answer would have been the same: to hold the turn.

It played out, but she was no longer connected, no longer in control. She simply watched the chopper's recorder play out the sequence of events.

The hit to engine one.

Kendall pulling the Fire Suppress T-handle at the same moment Dusty had.

She could have belly flopped into the rocks, killed most of her crew and possibly—she looked again at the rocks—probably walked away.

But her decision, the only real choice—at least for her—was to turn her own side of the chopper into the cliff wall and to keep her foot down on the right pedal to kick the tail and the rear cargo bay up into the air, over that deadly line of boulders. She did so again, not that it would change how the tape played out.

Again, she watched as the chopper nosed in and tumbled. Could feel the searing pain once again in her right leg. Could remember pushing and pushing against the pain as they rolled, even after there was no longer any pedal to push against or any foot to push with.

The video came to a stop. The chopper rocking once, twice, and then dying from the abuse.

Dusty must have pulled the recorder cartridge during the evac.

She'd never seen it before, hadn't thought about it. The review board had exonerated her long before she was out of the drugs enough to care. She'd awoken to a Purple Heart and a Silver Star Medal for valor. She'd known why, she just didn't know how anyone else knew. This probably meant her crew knew, and that's why they stayed in such close touch. She'd saved their lives at such a cost to herself.

"It was the only choice." Her voice was hoarse and scratchy as she confirmed what she'd always known.

"It was the damned bravest thing I've ever seen,"

Jake Hamlin said gruffly from behind them. "An honor and a privilege, Captain. An honor and a privilege." Once again, he left her alone with Kendall in the cockpit of the simulator.

Her heart was calm. The adrenaline comedown wasn't bad as such things went.

"Hell of a risk there, Clark. Sending your girlfriend back on that flight."

"Hell of a risk," he agreed quietly, "to do that to the woman you love." He'd said he loved her before, but never with that roughness of honesty she couldn't deny.

"Why? I mean we had a good thing going. Why risk it? Trying to cure me of my nightmares?" And she did love him back. But that didn't mean she could say it.

"No. Trying to cure you of your stupid-ass idea of leaving the service. Your heart would die without it. Look at how much you have to give. Just because you can't fly combat, doesn't mean you can't train others to make those hard choices when they have to."

She kept her silence. It was a big idea. A huge one, and it would take a bit of getting used to.

He filled the silence that she couldn't. "I've been flying training missions in this box and through the Pacific Northwest for five years now. Maybe one in fifty could have done that maneuver even if they tried. Maybe one in a thousand would have made that choice. You saved your entire crew and all three casualties, Lois. Every one of them. You really are Superwoman, and you've got to know that's worth teaching."

Lois began shutting down the flight controls, resetting the simulator so that it was no longer a crashed chopper on a field of boulders half a world away.

Kendall was right. She was going to have to sit down with Clara and get her foot in the door with AW2, so to speak.

"You really love me enough to risk losing me? For my own good?"

"I do."

Lois pulled off her helmet and rested it on the joystick of the cyclic, brushing at the scuffs and scratches across the Superwoman logo. She turned to look at Kendall for the first time since she'd entered the simulator. Saw that, as Superman always would, he spoke absolute truth.

"Of course, I had an ace in the hole." His deep voice was a caress.

"What was that?"

He tapped her helmet. Not the logo, but the heavy block letters she'd had painted beneath it.

How could she help but be madly in love with a man who understood her better than she understood herself? Well, if he'd risk that much for her, she could do no less for him.

Lois now knew that Kendall deserved only one answer. An answer that she would give gladly, now and on the altar.

It was a promise to last them a lifetime.

"NSDQ."

This story is dedicated to "CNN Top 10 Hero of 2013" Dale Beatty and his battle buddy John Gallina. After volunteers built a home for double-amputee Dale, they cofounded Purple Heart Homes—a nonprofit organization that has built or remodeled dozens of homes for disabled veterans. More information at: www.purplehearthomesusa.org

# ABOUT THE AUTHOR

**M.L. Buchman** has over thirty novels in print. His military romantic suspense books have been named among the "Top 5 of the Year" for Barnes & Noble and NPR and "Top 10 of the Year" for *Booklist*. In addition to romance, he also writes thrillers, fantasy, and science fiction.

In among his career as a corporate project manager, he has rebuilt and single-handed a fifty-foot sailboat, both flown and jumped out of airplanes, designed and built two houses, and bicycled solo around the world. He is now making his living as a full-time writer on the Oregon Coast with his beloved wife. He is constantly amazed at what you can do with a degree in geophysics. You may keep up with his writing by subscribing to his newsletter at www.mlbuchman.com.

# SEALED
## WITH PASSION

## ANNE ELIZABETH

# CHAPTER 1

HIS INDEX FINGER FLEXED LIKE IT NEEDED TO PULL A trigger. He took a slow deep breath and forced himself to relax. It was hard to calm that reflex after months on the job.

The drive up to Julian from Coronado, California, was a long meandering one, full of twists and turns and no passing zones. After months of driving in a hot desert where there were no roads or rules, only crazy drivers with junker cars and way too many enemies with guns perched in odd places, it felt good to be back in the U.S.A. His mind and body needed the break. Tough to stay on alert for extended periods of time, the tension wreaked havoc on...everything.

Navy SEAL LT CMDR Jonah Melo scratched his chin, grateful to be free of the whiskers that had plagued him. Nothing felt better than smooth-shaven skin. Being part of a SEAL Team meant he had to go native at times. Since he had been home, he'd shaved twice and already showered four times, and his boots had only been on the ground for two days. It was relaxing to be in a place where water was bountiful and the heat didn't fry his genitals when he had to take a leak.

He wasn't complaining. Hell, he loved his job and would never trade it in. But being in Africa had been tough, the overall mission fraught with complications. His Team had come at their objective from five different angles and still couldn't get the results they wanted. At that point, Command had rolled up shop and shipped them all home. There had been more injuries in his group on this deployment than had been counted for the entire year for all the Teams combined.

Sometimes, shit just went down that way. No matter what anyone did, it was determined to go sideways. A better approach would present itself, and then they'd get another chance or someone else would.

*Damn, I hope it's me. I've got an ax to grind with those bastards.* He slapped the steering wheel.

His eyes strayed to the chicken farm he sped by on his left. With his car windows open, he could smell the stink, and it was oddly comforting. This was one of his favorite routes up the mountain, and he had driven it at least a thousand times over the years.

He took a slow, deep breath of the acrid stench. His olfactory sense might have objected, but his body released the tension by at least a few more degrees.

Command had been adamant about the entire Team taking time off. *Spending time with their roots*, they'd called it. He'd rather be getting his feet wet on the next available operation, but this frogman was going to follow orders.

R&R for him meant working, so he was on his way up to Julian to find out the progress of his best friend's— Kevin Toms—house, which happened to be a part of the Wounded Warrior Project in conjunction with the Wounded Warrior Housing Project. He'd contributed sweat to many of their building projects, but this one was particularly special. It was for a man who had been his buddy for a long, long time. If Kevin were up there, his arrival would be a surprise. Even his family didn't know he was going to be in town.

Cows stood in the front pastures chewing the long grass, and from the looks of things, he could tell that it had rained recently. This area wasn't known for its rainfall, but the wetness would keep the dreaded wildfires away.

A mile down the road, the camel farm came into sight. He smiled briefly at the child pointing to the large animal and jumping up and down with excitement. They sold camel milk and cheese there. Having been forced to ingest it upon occasion, he was happy to stick with cow or goat if circumstances allowed a preference.

His mind went into overdrive as a camper pulled over to allow him to pass, and he drove the rest of the way up the mountain. When he pulled his old Ford truck onto the curb in front of the Tomses' house, his eyes assessed the vision before him. This was indeed a brand-new home that was complete on the outside and, by the looks of the paint cans stacked outside, nearly done on the inside.

Putting the truck in park, he turned off the engine and got out of Big Berta. The vehicle had been in his family for years and pretty much lived on the Naval Amphibious Base in Coronado. He preferred this beauty to any speedster on the road when he was on the West Coast. Nothing beat the dependability, although she could probably use some paint where the salt air had been tough on her.

He grabbed his toolbox and closed the truck door quietly, a matter of habit, and took his time admiring the house.

Walking up the recently laid front path, he waved to

a few of the guys he knew. This spot was special to him.
They had all bought it together after graduate school and
whoever married first was going to be the happy recipient. Jonah had made sure it was Kevin. The man's life
had been rough, and he wanted the best for him.

Spotting his buddy's van in the dirt driveway, he
grinned to himself. His showing up here was going to
be one helluva surprise.

Placing his hand on the knob, he turned it and walked
inside where his enthusiasm fizzled out like a warm beer
on a hot day.

Nothing prepared him for the sight that greeted him
as he stood in the open doorway. Seeing *her* was like
driving a Ka-Bar straight into his heart—voluntarily!
Since that wasn't something he would normally do,
Jonah realized that he probably should have checked
to see if the devastatingly gorgeous Alisha Winters,
Interior Decorator Extraordinaire, was going to be at the
Tomses' new home.

"In or out!" yelled a frustrated voice.

He cringed. Not a chance he was standing on cer-
emony. He knew that sound all too well. Alisha was
Julie's best friend, and Julie was the wife of his buddy
Kevin. Alisha was also the, ah, maid of honor he had
slept with once and hadn't seen in over five years. If
he'd been thinking, it wouldn't have surprised him that
Alisha would be here.

"Hurry up! You're ruining the light," shouted the
petite woman whose current annoyance didn't squash
her buoyant personality.

His feet were like lead as he just stood there and stared
at her. Alisha hadn't changed one bit, except perhaps she

was even more beautiful than he remembered, as if she had grown into her charms.

"Seriously! I'm talking to you." She looked over her shoulder. Her eyes went wide with shock and then she was tumbling off the ladder.

He dumped the toolbox he was holding, and before the lot even hit the ground, was there to intercept what gravity was dropping into his waiting arms. Catching her weight to him, he cuddled her close. The smell of her perfume was intoxicating, much nicer than the strong paint fumes, and a memory flashed in this mind of her guiding him to her neck and asking him to follow his nose…

A part of him responded instantly, like his instincts knew she was his. It was impossible to ignore the past; her, her presence, and the bliss of her body called to him. Not a pretty sight when a big man like him could be felled by a small thunderclap like her.

Soft strands of her hair caressed his skin, and he barely resisted the urge to bury his nose in her beautiful long mane.

Large eyes with thick lashes batted at him. They didn't look happy. Peeved was probably the emotion he would have chosen to describe that look.

His brain flipped through conversation starters. He'd never been at a loss for words. But, it was her. She was an anomaly. After several long seconds, he said, "Are you okay?"

She turned her head to the side slightly, as if she were getting a better view of him. Her gaze softened briefly, becoming almost dewy, and he had an overwhelming urge to kiss her.

"Alisha," he murmured. Leaning in, he decided to give in to the wish...

In the space of two breaths, her demeanor changed back to brittle. Her hands pushed on his chest, and she demanded, "Put me down!"

He sighed and relinquished his hold on her. Placing the woman on her feet was a serious buzzkill.

She shook her head and then rubbed her fingers over her clothes as if smoothing away imaginary wrinkles. When she finally looked up at him again, her eyes were bright with fire. "Jonah."

He struggled not to grin. She was working so hard to keep a lid on her anger, and though he had no interest in becoming the recipient of those flames, he knew the emotion was bound to burst out. "Alisha." He paused, allowing his eyes to travel the length of her before settling on her steely gaze. "You look well."

She took a tiny step closer to him, her hands settling on her hips. "You can't show up here and pretend it was yesterday." Her shoulders squared. The timbre of her voice dropped to a whisper. "We need to talk."

His left eyebrow lifted. "Oh, I'm looking forward to it."

A voice came from the other room. "Hey! Is that my mellow bud?"

Jonah couldn't resist caressing her skin with his hand as he skirted by her to greet Kevin. The frown she sent in his direction only made his smile grow. *Oh yes, he was definitely going to enjoy talking to her.*

# CHAPTER 2

"YOU UGLY SOB! WHY DIDN'T YOU TELL ME YOU were back?" teased Kevin as he reached up from his wheelchair to embrace Jonah. Both of the men had large shoulders and thick necks, but what was housed above those necks was very different in Alisha's opinion. Kevin was open, forthright, and very compassionate, and Jonah was secretive, manipulative, and too handsome for his own good.

"Seems like the ugly parade would have alerted you to my presence considering that you're their king," replied Jonah with a grin.

Alisha crossed her arms over her chest. No woman liked being ignored, but what these guys did was just short of a bromance. One more moment of the two of them giving each other another line of baloney was more than she could stand. Taking a few steps backward, she reversed course and made a great show of organizing her color-coded *To Do* chart that covered half a wall.

Frowning at the list, she realized that if she stayed all night and part of the next day, the projects *might* be completed on time. Julie and Kevin planned an open house the next day at noon to thank everyone who had participated in the build. She wanted everything to be perfect!

"You're the man, Kev," laughed Jonah as he high-fived his buddy about some asinine story regarding a launch from a submarine. Who would want to be in a torpedo tube while it was filled with water? She shivered.

Just then Julie rounded the corner with an armful of new paintbrushes and roller pans that she promptly dropped on the floor as she ran toward Jonah with a squeal of delight. "You're here! Oh, I knew you'd come. Somehow, I just knew." She threw her arms around him for a huge hug.

Didn't anyone understand how hard this was for her? The answer was a resounding N.O., as the Tomses and Jonah joked around. It was as if she wasn't even there.

Alisha was dismayed. The havoc that Jonah had wrought in her life was enormous, and Julie knew it. Not that Alisha was willing to admit that she still carried a torch for the SEAL. Why did men have to be so infuriating?

Opening up the can, she stirred the celery-colored paint. Sweet. This was going to be a gorgeous trim for the bright yellow walls of the kitchen, and it would complement the pastel dreamland of wildflowers in the mosaic tiles of the backsplash behind the stove. Julie understood her artistic palette, and she wasn't afraid of allowing Alisha to demonstrate her love of the rainbow on these walls.

"Alisha," said Julie. "Are you hungry?"

Alisha glanced over her shoulder at her best friend.

Julie gestured for her to come over.

Shaking her head in the negative, she went back to what she was doing. *Yep*, Alisha told herself, *I do have to stand by as my best friend Julie hugs and chats amicably with Jonah*. She wanted to shout "traitor," but that would get her exactly nowhere.

Picking up the proper sized brush from the pileup on the floor, she walked past the chatty bunch and into the kitchen. The trim only needed to be painted in a few spots, and then it would be her version of a Van Gogh. Well, if Van Gogh had been an interior designer.

She could hear the happy camaraderie from the other room.

"I know what Alisha likes. Pick up the fettuccine Alfredo with a Greek salad and dressing on the side, and I'll have the same. Why don't you two go pick up the food, and I'll help Alisha finish up in the kitchen? I know she has a lot to finish before the night is over." Julie sounded upbeat, happy even.

Alisha gritted her teeth. *I wish that didn't sound delicious, but it does. Will I have the stomach to eat with him?* She put the paint down and looked at her friends. She wanted to interrupt and offer them money. They'd never take it. But, she wasn't taking a cent for her materials and time either. That's what friends did…watched out for each other. So, why did Kevin befriend Jonah? Was there something she didn't know about him?

"I'm kinda tired. How about I stay here, and you two go," said Kevin.

Julie nodded. "Of course. Let me get my purse." She leaned down and kissed her husband.

"How are you doing?" asked Jonah, his tone serious.

"I'm going to need another surgery. Julie doesn't want to talk about it. The wives of the guys from my support group seem to be helping her out some. Mostly, she relies on Alisha. I don't know what we'd do without her." Kevin's voice was low.

"She's something special," Jonah agreed.

Alisha had ducked back behind the doorway. They hadn't seen her, and she didn't want to let on that she was there. She was trying not to listen, but they weren't exactly whispering.

"Are you going to talk to her...about that night?" asked Kevin.

Jonah sighed. "I don't know. How can I tell her how much I like her in one breath and why that was precisely the reason I abandoned her in the next."

"Seriously, man, chicks dig that stuff. It's called romance."

"Riiiiiiiggghhhht," Jonah scoffed. "If she 'dug' me, I'd have heard from her over the years instead of me holding some damn torch for her Highness."

"I'm ready," said Julie, coming abruptly back into the room. "Let's go. I'm starved."

"Get the antipasto, too," added Kevin.

"On it," said Jonah as they headed out the front door.

# CHAPTER 3

CLOUDS FILLED THE SKY. THE WIND HAD PICKED UP, swirling dust and debris into the air, and the temperature had cooled, making it look as if it might rain at any minute. But, the weather genie in Julian was fickle, and it didn't storm unless the winds stilled and then, and only then, would a deluge occur.

"Have you seen your family?" asked Julie.

"Nope. They don't even know I'm here yet."

"Oh, God, your sisters are going to freak when they find out you're in town. You grew up here, right?"

"Yep, and I couldn't wait to run away. Funny thing is…when I really grew up…I couldn't wait to come back." Jonah held open the passenger door of his truck. "Your husband spent most of his holiday breaks here with me and fell in love with the town."

"I've heard the stories enough times to recite them by heart." Julie hopped inside. "Thanks," she said, before he closed the door behind her.

He walked around the truck. His eyes strayed to the large front picture window where he could see Alisha and Kevin talking.

His lips drew into a thin line. Alisha. She was passion personified, and the woman drove him bonkers!

Opening the driver's side door, he slid behind the wheel, fastened his seat belt, and turned on the truck. As he pulled onto the empty road, he noticed that Julie was staring at him.

"Don't look at me like that! You know I'll stop by and see my folks and siblings tonight or tomorrow. My priority is to spend time with you and Kevin. Okay?"

"I appreciate it. He does, too. Things…are better when you're here. It's hard…at times." Julie admitted.

"I'm always just an email away. The minute I get it, or can get away from what I'm doing, I'd be here for you both. There are times I go dark, but Kevin has the emergency contact. I can be reached…eventually."

"Thanks. We know that." Julie hesitated. "I don't want to bring it up, but you know I'm going to…"

"What?" he asked.

"You like her. Why are you such a dick to her?"

His shoulders tensed. "Seriously! A dick? Thanks for the feedback."

She smiled. "Maybe that word is too harsh. Those three weeks we all spent together before the wedding, that's when it happened, you fell for her."

"Do we have to rehash this?" He knew his face betrayed the wealth of emotion he had for Alisha.

She clapped her hands together. "I knew it! Another point for my intuition. That's great, Jonah!"

"No, it isn't," grumbled Jonah. No man wanted his heart to be worn on his sleeve for the whole world to see. It was simpler and much safer to keep those emotions hidden.

"Don't be like that," said Julie. "I've known you for a lot of years, and not once have I ever heard you talk about a lady. And now I know why."

He rolled his eyes. "Drop it, will ya? I didn't come up here to deal with Alisha."

"Whatever! I'm poking at this bear until he growls.

Ah, let's see what else can I find out." She grinned at him.

Jonah frowned. That was the problem with military wives, the good ones knew when someone was running a line of bullshit and they were determined to get to the truth and make that stream run clear. *Shit!* If Alisha ever learned to read him that well, he was doomed. "You're not going to be happy unless I bare my soul, are you?"

She nodded her head, and Julie's smile could light up San Diego. "I'll tell you what; we can make a trade. You can ask me any question about Alisha, but I get to do the same in return."

He sighed. He knew when he was cornered, but maybe he could delay revealing anything too personal. And, if he played it right, he just might get some good Intel out of Julie.

---

"I got it." Kevin snapped the phone shut and smiled at Alisha. "Sorry to interrupt our chat, but that was one of the best phone calls of my life."

"No worries," said Alisha. "What did you get?"

"Hug me, first." He opened his arms.

She leapt into them and hugged him enthusiastically and then stood back up and waited. To her, Kevin was the brother she had always wanted growing up. Now, with all of her family gone, the relationship with Julie and Kevin was even more precious.

"Alisha, that's the best thing. You're willing to celebrate without even knowing why." Kevin tipped his chair back slightly and spun around.

Alisha sat down on a box full of books, so Kevin

wouldn't have to tilt his neck back at an uncomfortable angle. "Stop with crap-tastic stuff, and tell me about it. I'm not waiting until the rest of them get back to hear this big news. Your smile is practically taking up your whole face."

He nodded. "Okay. So, you know how I've been going to support meetings sponsored by the Wounded Warrior Project. Well, some sponsors from Southern California got together and set up a job fair for the men and women in the programs. One of the companies had an opening. And, it's not just any job, but the position I've been dreaming about with an aerospace company that's working on an advanced return flight craft that is both space and seaworthy. Alisha, this is exactly what I've been looking for! It's less than an hour from here driving on back roads, so the commute is easy, too."

"Oh my goodness, what fun!" exclaimed Alisha. "You must be thrilled."

"I am," said Kevin with a nod. "Jonah is going to be green with envy."

"Why?" Alisha shifted her weight. Every time Jonah's name came up she wanted to scream and yell, and yet at the same time, she craved information. Why couldn't she forget about this man in all these years? She knew she didn't want to answer that question.

Kevin chuckled. "As you know, we went to engineering school together. It was the best and worst experience at the same time. Labs at seven in the morning and professors who enjoyed making us sweat—worse than boot camp. Then, we were forced to devise something unique to develop a master's thesis on; in this day and age when practically everything has been done to death, too." He sighed. "I'm glad school's over, nothing could convince me to get a doctorate."

"So, why will Jonah be jealous?"

"Because he's a huge Jacques Cousteau fan, and that's one of the main reasons he wanted to be a SEAL. He loves marine life, conservation, and…this is the most important part…he felt there was a link between outer space and water. I bet he'd give his eye teeth to be a part of this project." Kevin did a wheelie. "Dang, I can hardly wait 'til they get back."

"Cool!" she said. The need for more information had questions tripping off her tongue. Besides, Kevin loved retelling his stories. "Did you both get a master's degree from…?"

"MIT for the master's and we both went to Stanford for undergrad."

"Wow." Now, that *was* impressive. "Brainiacs."

"Yeah, well, we were the two scholarship kids. I went into the Marine Corps to pay for my education, and Jonah joined the Navy, but only after we'd both gotten exactly what we wanted out of our educations. Ultimately, both of us wanted to be astronauts and go into space or be deep sea divers and work in the ocean." Kevin took off his left glove and rubbed his hand. "Hey, I'm going to head out to the car and get my water bottle."

Alisha could see how raw his fingers were from all the extra work he'd done. She stood up quickly. "No way! I'll get it." She'd do anything for him.

"It's in the cup holder," he shouted after her, before she disappeared out the door.

She was back in a flash. She handed him the water

bottle and watched him take a long drink before clearing her throat. "Um, can you tell me more about…Jonah?"

Kevin's gaze locked on hers. He raised his eyebrows. "Caught your interest, huh? I knew it. Thought there was some chemistry during the wedding. But you never asked anything. Why now?"

"I don't know," she scoffed. "The wedding was like…years ago. I just was wondering what has been going on with him. You know, to have a friendly conversation with him." *Friendly! What possessed me to say that! Truthfully, I want to kick him in the ass.*

"Right," he said skeptically. "Let's see…"

---

Jonah could barely contain his laughter. The stories Julie was sharing about Alisha were a riot. He loaded the food from Romano's into his truck and then pulled out of the parking space, taking the short way out of town toward home. As much as he wanted to keep pumping Julie for info, cold food was no fun.

"The house was supposed to be a light periwinkle, and she painted the walls bright Barney purple. The owners had a fit. You should have heard them yelling, but none of that fazed Alisha. She just hustled them out of the house. Told them that they needed to wait until her whole vision was complete, and if they hated it then, she would completely redo it." Julie took several short breaths. "I nearly lost it when they came back two days later and congratulated her on a job well done. Seriously, Alisha pulled off Barney-colored walls, and these people ended up loving it."

"She really found her niche. Seems like the past few

years have been good for her." Jonah turned down a side road.

Julie quieted. "Sort of. I mean, professionally, yeah, she's been great. The happiest I've ever seen her. But personally, no."

"In terms of relationships…" He hated asking that question. Honestly, he didn't want to know. He'd rather think Alisha had been celibate for all the years they'd been apart. She was a beauty, though, and there was no doubt in his mind that she'd had plenty of suitors knocking at her door.

"I shouldn't tell you this," she said flatly. "Her past few boyfriends have been a disaster. Beyond the worst of the worst, and now she doesn't even want to date anymore. I think part of her has been holding out for you."

"I'm sorry to hear that," said Jonah. And yet, he wasn't. On one hand he wanted her happy, but he also wanted her with him. But could it really work? The reason he left her that night had to do with his job—she said that she didn't want to be with a military guy, and he wasn't leaving his career. He knew the core of him would forever be a SEAL—that wasn't ever going away whether he was active duty or retired. How did one get past a major roadblock like that? In his mind, you didn't.

―――

"Well, Jonah's a good guy. I've known him for years. He's the one who talked me into going to the Wounded Warriors and the Housing Project for help. He's been involved with both of them for a long time. Seems a friend of his, Declan Swifton, Master Chief from Team FIVE, needed help modifying his house and consulted the groups. Now, a lot of the Team guys contribute some muscle on their downtime or vacations. I've gotten a bunch of my Marine Corps friends involved, too."

Kevin took a long, slow breath. "It makes a difference, knowing that other people want to see you heal and succeed. I've got a lot of pride, and I didn't think I'd be able to handle reaching out for help, but what I learned is that a strong person reaches and a coward stays locked away and silent."

Alisha leaned over and hugged him. "I'm glad you reached out. Otherwise, the two of you would still be renting and it would be FOR-EVER before I could decorate a place for you. Speaking of which, I just need ten more minutes and then the kitchen is done. I'd like to check it off my list before they get back."

"Go for it, my sister," egged Kevin. "I'm going to make a few calls, if you need me."

"Righto," said Alisha cheerily as she went back to her kitchen tasks. She was glad that they'd talked. Speaking with Kevin had been enlightening. She wondered what had prevented her from doing this sooner.

Her mind shouted an answer. *Ego, my dear. It always comes back to ego.*

Alisha sighed as she picked up the paintbrush and went back to completing the celery trim. *So true.*

# CHAPTER 4

DINNER HAD BEEN RELAXING. IN ESSENCE, IT WAS A replay of years ago, before that fateful night when Jonah and Alisha had hooked up. All of them were laughing and enjoying each other's company so much that it took some doing on both of their parts to get Kevin and Julie out the door so the house projects could be completed. Reminding the happy couple that tomorrow was moving day as well as a celebration for the volunteers had made Julie stress out, and she willingly dragged Kevin back to their rental.

The silence after the Tomses left was almost deafening, and Jonah wanted to be the bigger person and break it. "I'm sorry," he said to Alisha as they cleaned up the empty plates and containers from dinner.

She stilled. "For what?"

"Damn," he said. "You're not going to make this easy, are you?"

"I thought, 'The only easy day was yesterday,' if I'm quoting the SEAL adage correctly." Alisha wiped her hands on a napkin and put it in the bag with the rest of the trash.

"You are." He took the bag from her and put it on the ground. "Give me a break here. I'm trying."

She sat down. "I'm listening."

He followed suit, sitting across from her. The box threatened to give way beneath him, but he balanced himself so it wouldn't. "Here are all my cards. Meeting you. Spending time with you…that was an important time for me."

"Not more important than whatever dragged you away from me," she said.

"Alisha, I left because you said that you only wanted a man who could give you his sole focus. You told Julie's mother that it was a nine-to-five man or nothing. I was devastated. I'm not that! I'll never be that. Even when I retire, I'll probably do something else that has me on the go 24/7. I can't stop being me." Jonah hadn't meant to state it that way, to put the onus on her, but bottled emotion expressed passionately had a way of becoming greater in the heat of the moment.

Her mouth was hanging open. "You…you weren't meant to hear that. How…did you?"

"Julie sent me to find you. She needed help with her dress; something about the maid of honor has a bathroom duty or something like that. When I heard what you said, I didn't know what to think or how to react." Jonah wavered between anger and sadness. He knew what he'd wanted to happen that night, but none of it had been possible after those words.

Alisha stood up. "So you decided to screw me and leave me, was that it?"

His nostrils flared. "I made love to you, and I hope you never forget it, lady." He stood up to leave. He didn't have to take this. Having no idea what her game plan was, he didn't feel up for any more conversation. This emotion was very real to him. He took a step toward the door.

"I didn't." Her words were very soft.

"What?" He turned back.

Her eyes were filled with tears. "I didn't forget. You are the measuring stick that all men have to live up to, Jonah Melo. There's never been anyone else." She wiped her sleeve over her eyes. "I didn't mean to hurt you that night. For that, I will always be sorry." Grabbing a clean napkin off the makeshift table, she blew her nose. "I said those words to appease Julie's mother, because *she* was upset that her daughter married a Marine and *she* was scared about the kind of life her daughter would have. Those words were for her…no one else."

Standing up, she walked toward him. Her hand touched his arm tenderly. "I respect the military. I wish…I wish you had told me your reason. I thought…it was me. That was the reason you left. Maybe I was bad in bed, or you decided you didn't like me or something like that."

He looked up, beckoning strength, because the hurt in her voice was crushing him. "Never. Ali, I could only see you." Drawing her into his arms, he kissed her. It was like drinking from a heavenly spring, and he didn't want to stop.

"Jonah…" Her hands drew him closer, pulling at his clothes.

He wanted nothing more than to get naked with her, but not if it meant either one of them ran away afterward. "Wait. Let's promise. We both stick past tonight. We work this out, a way to be together."

"I agree," she said, eagerly undoing the straps of her overalls and pulling her T-shirt over her head.

His shirt and pants hit the floor just as quickly. He hadn't worn underwear since the third grade, so he didn't have to worry about that. Seeing Alisha in her underthings was a treat, and his admiration was making itself very evident.

～～～

Her fingers ran over his taut frame. She loved watching the muscles dance. If someone had told her an hour ago that she'd be getting naked with Jonah again, she would have laughed in his face and made a snide comment. Now that she knew the truth, nothing was going to keep her from being with him again. Only a man who a woman loved could make her that angry, and this was definitely the case for her.

She knew in her heart of hearts that she loved Jonah Melo, and she wanted to be his girlfriend and someday his wife. Would that scare him off? If he were the man she thought he was, probably not. Her guess was…that he loved her, too.

Regardless, she was going to live in the moment and enjoy being alive. Hadn't Kevin and Julie been telling her for years that she needed to be spontaneous? Well, here goes.

Alisha did a risqué striptease with her bra and panties and then launched herself at him.

Jonah put on a condom, caught her to him, wrapping her legs around his waist, and walked them to the wall. He balanced them against the deep red backdrop with the bright blue crown molding and kissed her.

Alisha had never felt a kiss like his. It transported her. Filling her with such intense need and passion that she clawed at him until he was there, pushing himself gently inside her.

Her wetness and heat beckoned him, and with one thrust he was seated to the hilt.

Spasms of pleasure washed through her senses. She could climax from his size alone—he filled her completely. She held on to him for dear life as her body drew on his for satiation.

But he wasn't done, and neither was she.

Jonah tilted her head toward his, so they were looking at each other as they made love. Slowly, deliberately, and passionately, they moved as one until the intensity was too much for either of them, and they came together, crying out each other's name.

# CHAPTER 5

BEING CARRIED TO THE MASTER BATH WAS RIGHT OUT of a fantasy. Alisha felt like a newlywed as Jonah perched her on the edge of the bamboo bathing seat, closed the door to the tub, and flipped on the taps. "Don't you think we're going too far?" asked Alisha, uncomfortable with the practice of trying out Kevin and Julie's specialty step-in tub. "What if we break it?"

"Hey, we need to make sure this thing doesn't leak," Jonah said with a grin. "Besides, I'm curious about the inner workings. I'd like to be able to tell Kevin that he's 'good to go' with some hanky-panky in here with Julie. He'd thank me for this."

"You wouldn't dare tell him!" She was incredulous. "Kevin's like a brother to me."

"Good. Glad you feel that way about him. But, I don't feel that way about you."

Alisha kicked her feet, splashing water at him. "I'm getting out."

"No way," he said, catching her to him. "You promised to stick this night out. Now, before we have to get back to work and finish your checklist, let's get clean and then…talk."

"Your smirk is much too smug, Mr. Melo."

He handed her the bar of soap, and they made quick work of washing up. The tub really was superb. Julie and Kevin were going to love it.

Jonah helped her out of the tub and onto a pile of paint tarps and brand-new towels. Jonah slid underneath her and balanced her on top of him. "Unless you want to, ah, do other things now."

His tongue snaked out and licked a large drop of water off her neck, and he watched her eyes mirror her delight as her body leaned toward his for more attention. When he pulled back, she followed his lead.

She kissed the top of his nose. "You're right. We need to talk, to clear the air. So, you go first. I'd like to know how you feel about me."

"Okay." He took a deep breath. "Me first. Honestly, I've never felt this way with anyone." His statement made his face scrunch up, like it pained him.

She elbowed him. "That bad."

"No, your knee is pushing on a delicate spot."

She shifted her weight. "Sorry about that. Thanks for being honest. I like you, too."

"Only like?" he asked. There was mirth in his eyes.

"I'm not feeding your ego. I'm attempting to be honest, you jerk!"

He gathered her closer. "I know. I'm sorry. I agree. You've…always been the ideal, my wish for a mate. I just…always thought there would be more time. And, that we'd be able to date and court and move our relationship along in a normal way. Now that I know you like military men and are not opposed to moving forward, I'd like to. But, we still might need to make it a bit accelerated."

She made a derisive noise. "As if…anything about you is normal." She shrugged. "You know, normal is overrated." Turning her face toward his, she reached forward for his lips.

He leaned in and kissed her. "Sweet, succulent kisses. No one kisses like you."

"Thanks." She leaned back. "Wait! Why would it need to be accelerated?"

"I'm back on duty in a couple weeks. I have a new assignment, and since the base is secure, only wives can accompany." Jonah said this very nonchalantly.

"Duty? Where?"

"Well, I can't give out all the details. But, I'm competing to go into space."

"No way! Haven't you seen *Gravity*? I don't want you out there, now that I finally have you." She wasn't cool with this. Space! Really?

"Alisha, do you like being an interior designer? If I asked you never to do it again…"

She held up her hands. "Okay. I get it. Point almost taken. It's not like I can get stranded and suffocate in a fabric warehouse, or get shot to death with a glue gun. It's not exactly an equivalent situation we're talking about here."

He kissed her, a long, deep, languorous kiss. "None of us knows what is on the next horizon. Look at Kevin and Julie. Would they have tied the knot if they had been afraid of the future? No. What changed it for them? Facing it together."

His hands stroked over her flesh. He distracted her from the conversation. But, she was tuned in enough to finally, really see the truth.

A blush rose in her cheeks. "I understand. Life is full of stolen moments, times that you value like pearls to tuck in the treasure box of your heart." Her hand patted his chest. "I think I was angry with you.

I wanted something that wasn't real, a fantasy in my brain; when in reality, true life is better than anything I could ever imagine."

"Are you saying what I think you're saying?" He was hopeful. He didn't want to let his heart go there, but nothing could rescue his spirit from feeling connected to hers. From the moment they had met, he'd known she was perfect for him. He was an idiot to have waited for the ideal time to be with her. That moment was now. If he didn't embrace the moment and put his heart on the line, then he knew he would regret it.

Her smile was a ray of sunshine, a light that made his own smile grow. "Yes."

"I need to hear…the words."

She put her chin on his chest, grinning up at him. "I love you, Jonah. It's always been you."

The vise that had been gripping his heart released. He tumbled her gently onto her back and then kissed her—a long, slow, tender, languorous kiss. Against her lips, he murmured, "I love you, Alisha. I love you."

He could feel her smile against his lips as her fingers sank into his hair.

She rubbed her breasts against his chest, the luscious tips of her nipples teasing his flesh.

A growl climbed up his throat, possessive and hungry. She was his.

"It's my turn," she stated, her eyes flashing with emotion.

He released his hold on her. He wasn't going to argue, even though every fiber in his being wanted to take her now.

Alisha rolled him onto his back. This was a woman

who knew what she wanted. She pushed his arms over his head. Her fingers stroking the tender flesh around his wrist, down his forearm, and up his bicep. Then, she grabbed his jaw and slowly lowered her face to his. All the while her eyes were teasing him, asking him how long he could relinquish control.

For this kind of torture, he was all game. She didn't know that he'd go to the very edge of want and then even further to make her happy. But, she would learn what a giving soul he was.

When her lips touched his, he wanted to wrap his arms around her…lose himself in the kiss. Her soft lips were the stuff of sirens and legends, and they were undoing his mighty hold on control. "No fair," he murmured.

"Every move is fair on the game board of love." Her voice was thick with want. He knew that sound, and he could feel her body rubbing on his.

His body responded, craving her, needing her. He gritted his teeth, trying to deny the effect she had on him.

Her fingernails trailed over his nipples, gently teasing and inciting.

Her hips lifted, and she rubbed that most tender part of herself over him.

He stopped her and put on a condom.

She smiled at him and then went back to her toying.

His body tightened, hardened further until she could guide him to the exact place she wanted him.

How could he deny the pleasure of that inner sanctum? For anyone else, he could keep his control intact, but not with her. Alisha had always been his undoing. Maybe that was why he hadn't pushed a relationship with her so long ago. She was the kind of woman who could suck his focus away if he wasn't careful.

Did women know they had that kind of power? The right person for the right person was a game changer for an entire lifetime. He hoped not! Otherwise, his little vixen was going to be on the winning end of all arguments in their home.

As he slid inside her, every thought in his brain ceased. This was heaven, the absolute peacefulness of pure bliss, and as she lifted his arms and placed them on her hips, her eyes caught his. She rocked gently back and forth until they were moving in rhythm together. The passion grew with every movement and each stroke, until he was holding on by a mere thread of control.

Her fingernails scraped gently over his stomach as she tormented him. Her hands moved up her own body to cup her breasts.

He licked his lips, wanting so badly to touch her.

She lifted his hands, placed them over her breasts, and wrapped her hands around his.

His thumbs stroked in unison, gently over her nipples.

Her eyes widened as she quickened her pace.

"Yes," he murmured as her back arched and she came. Again and again, her body tightened over his until his precious waiting was over, and he gave himself completely to her.

He cried out. "Alisha." It was a plea, a thank-you, and a rallying cry that released his need and brought him even closer to her, the woman he loved. The feeling of being connected at the physical root of each other along with the spiritual connection was so palpable that he felt he could reach out and touch her soul. Could she feel his?

He lifted himself up to her. They kissed, a loving lock of lips that had him feeling like they were wrapped in a cocoon together. Alone. And that no one else in the world existed.

When they pulled apart, he could see tears in her eyes. "Hey, what's this about?"

She shook her head. "I…I've never felt so connected with anyone but you." Her hands fluttered between them. "I was prepared to make this into a contest or game, so that I wouldn't get hurt. But, when you're here, I cannot stop my heart from connecting with yours. I'm naked in front of you."

"What's wrong with that? Both figuratively and literally," he asked. "I could change the tone and mood of the conversation. Do you want me to punctuate it with… this is how it is and you can take it or leave it?"

Alisha sat up. Her back was ramrod straight. "That turns this discussion into a power struggle. After that incredible moment, is this what you want?"

"Maybe. Make-up sex is a great way to go."

Her hand slapped at his chest. "Jonah! Be serious."

"No, my love, this isn't what *I* want. I'd prefer laying all the cards on the table and finding the best medium. We both need to bend, and we both need to lead. Right now, I'm following your lead. Tell me…what *you* want."

She laughed. Her outburst turned into a fit of giggles. When she finally stopped and laid her head on his chest, he nuzzled his chin against her head. To an outsider, it might appear that Alisha was unhinged, but he knew her better. This was her process. She was a creative person, an artist, and thus had a lot of emotional depth.

"I get it. You're right." Her voice was resigned but

not unhappy. Instead, it sounded like she had come to terms with something important inside of herself. "*This* is the way it's going to be, toe-to-toe on every issue in our lives. Equals, who will occasionally have to duke it out before we reach a compromise. True?"

"Isn't that what you want?" He raised an eyebrow. How could she want anything else, anything less than a man who was her match?

She pursed her lips, considering his words. "Certainly, I want a man who rocks my world with passion and excitement, and then steadies it again with his love and compassion. Yes, it is what I want." Her words were firm. He liked that definitiveness. "It explains a lot. Why I usually went for either simpering men or ones who were overly domineering to the point of possession. Neither worked out."

"Good, because that's what I'm offering, a lifetime of this…of me."

Her head snapped up. "Are you proposing to me now? Here?"

He chortled. "Of course! We've christened a good part of our best friends' house, why not have the most important memory here, too?" It did seem right, oddly perfect. Could the Tomses have arranged it? Seemed unlikely. No one knew he was coming up here today… or did they?

Alisha groaned. "Jonah! Julie's practically my shadow! How am I going to tell her about the proposal? When a story starts with…hey, so we were lying naked on the floor of your new house… Oh, God!" She laughed. "Help me think up a better story, quick!"

He joined in on the laughter, until there were tears

streaming down both of their faces. "Tell you what. I will propose to you in a bunch of places, and you can pick your favorite one."

Her face was suddenly serious. "Jonah, this will always be 'the' spot. If it weren't for this house and the whole project, how would we have come back into each other's life?"

He gathered her close and hugged her. "I would have found a way. Alisha, you've always been the ideal, the person I measure every woman against, and all of them were lacking, because they weren't you."

"Jonah," she sighed as her fingers caressed his chest. "I'm sorry I ever let you go."

"For the record, you demanded I leave."

"I remember." She looked up at him. "I'm sorry I hurt you. I thought…I was going to be another notch on your belt."

"You could never be that." He could feel her breathing change. Her heart rate sped up.

Her lips flattened and then slowly pulled into a smile. He smiled right back and couldn't resist a little teasing. "Are you going to be happy with a man who makes you—what are your words—more angry than you thought possible?"

She nodded her head. "Only if we can make time to become more happy than we deserve to be."

"Roger that. Priority One," he breathed as he kissed her. The touch of their mouths was like a wildfire, igniting passion that ran hot instantly and consumed all of his attention. He wanted her again. How would he ever be able to get enough of her and get this house finished?

# CHAPTER 6

THE DIAL ON HIS LUMINOX DIVE WATCH READ ONE IN the morning. "C'mon, Alisha, we've got to get moving."

They'd made a bed on the floor with towels and catching a few hours sleep made a big difference in his book. If only they had time to make love again before they worked their way through the checklist.

*Nah*, he told himself. *If I open that door, we won't get anything done tonight.* He threw back the towel covering him and scooped up his naked lady. Felt funny to call her that, but she was. This was a good time to be labeling their status.

Her hand batted at him. "Stop. I want to sleep."

He moved quickly through the house until he was at the pile of their clothes. As he placed her on her feet he asked, "Do you want to face Kevin and Julie in four hours when they show up at 0500 and this house isn't finished, or do you want to get moving while I follow all of your instructions?"

Alisha bit the corner of her thumb playfully. "Pfftttt." She stuck her tongue out at him with a proper raspberry and rubbed the sleep out of her eyes. "You know I choose Kevin and Julie. Let's get after it. But I want to discuss that 'follow all my instructions' idea once we're done for the day."

He blew her an air kiss. "As you wish."

Jonah was genuinely amazed at how organized

Alisha was as they went through the list. It was going to be close, but they could make this happen. He picked up a tool belt, adjusted it to fit, and then secured it around his hips. Reviewing the list, he indicated two items and said, "I'm on it." And with that, they both went to work.

―◦◦◦―

Alisha came up behind him and put her arms around his body.

"Yyyyyesssss," he said in a low voice. "How can I help you?"

"My mind is spinning with questions," she admitted, coming around to face him.

"Like…"

She put her hands on her hips. "What now? What about tomorrow?"

"We get married and move to support my next assignment, or we get married and you stay here and I come back on my open weekends." Jonah spoke as if he were ordering pizza, like this conversation was the most normal thing in the world.

Jonah put down the hammer and picked up the piece of art and hung it on the wall.

"Am I what you want? What do you truly want from us?"

"I need to be able to communicate with you," she replied quickly. "The sex is electric. That's never been a factor for us, but we barely stay put to talk. We have to make that work, and when we argue we have to promise to stick with it until we get to that common ground."

"You're talking about 'Rules of Engagement.' I'm good with that. Let's pound them out now and add to them as we need to." Jonah put out his hand. "My word is my bond."

"As is mine." Her spirit settled into the comfort of his as they figured out the details of what they each needed. She shook his hand and then reached up for his kiss. This item topped the list of her personal "needs" list.

# CHAPTER 7

A WEIGHT WAS LIFTED FROM BOTH OF THEIR SHOULDERS AS they went back to work. They had made fast work of a good portion of the checklist by the time Kevin's van pulled into the driveway at nine a.m. There was still a serious amount to be done, but they had a few hours before the party at noon.

"You're late. We were expecting you at 0500," said Jonah as Kevin entered the room.

"Blame my wife. She needed bagels from her favorite shop, and that meant driving several hours out of our way, both there and back." Kevin yawned. "We could have been doing something more fun, hon."

"Trust me, that was fun," said Julie, kissing her husband. "I'll make it up to you. I promise."

"Coffee! Julie, you are an angel," said Jonah, taking the proffered cup of steaming caffeine. "If this is how you greet a man, I know why Kevin married you."

"It better be for more than that," said Julie with a wink. "Where's Alisha?"

"In the kitchen, unpacking," said Jonah, holding off on raiding the bagels until Alisha was done with her task. He liked the idea of them eating together. Damn, he had it bad for her.

"Hey, man, I thought about last night…leaving you here with Alisha. I was up all fucking night thinking about you and her here. She's like family, a sister. Tell me that you two didn't knock boots."

Jonah didn't say a word. The man said not to tell him. He went back to unpacking the ram's head fixture. The wires were in a plastic packet, and they were tangled. Wonderful! His fingers worked through the mess of wires.

"Well, crap! I'm such a jerk to leave her with you." Kevin looked pained.

"Thanks, Kev. Love you, too." Jonah leaned in. "You know how I feel about her. She's incredible. I'd rather hurt myself than bring her pain." Jonah finally got the electrical wires untangled and threaded through the fixture.

"Appreciate that. She's precious," admitted Kevin. He coughed and then cleared his throat...twice.

"Whatever it is...spit it out. Sounds like you're choking on a duck." Jonah looked up at his friend, pausing in his task and giving his full attention to Kevin.

"Since we're alone, the ladies are otherwise occupied and stuff, I, ah, I'm sorry about our last phone call. I knew you were busy, and I didn't want to bring shit up, but you needed to know what'd happened..."

Jonah nodded his head. "No worries. I get it. There are things you need to say in person."

Kevin shook his head. "Man, we've been friends for a long time, and I shouldn't have been an asshole, but I needed you and didn't want to ask for help, especially with you across the planet doing God knows what. The timing was wrong and the thing is...the mind is tricky. For months, I couldn't remember anything leading up to the explosion. I didn't even know my feet had been blown off until I hit the ground and I couldn't get up again." He ran his hands through his hair, scrubbing his scalp. "Without those memories, it was like doubt ran through my brain like wildfire, and I couldn't count on myself or contain the inferno."

"What changed?" Jonah's voice was low and calm as his hands continued pulling the wires until he reached the end and then he picked up another one and followed the same procedure. He didn't need to look to know what needed to be done.

"My wife. That lady fights like a lioness protecting her cubs. She was fierce with the doctors and harsh with some of the things she said to me, to put me back on track. The best part was…she didn't give up. She pulled me out of darkness and forced me to interact with her and others." He laughed. "Man, I never want to be on the wrong side of her."

"She's quite a lady. You're blessed."

"I am." The rough sound of Kevin's voice filled the room. "That's why…during that call I yelled like a maniac at you. We had just lost a baby, only a couple months into the pregnancy. Our first. It was hard…to keep fighting. Julie wouldn't let me back away…from anything." He patted his legs. "So, I picked myself up and I did a lot of soul searching. And, I took those freaking PTSD classes; even did some regression therapy, too, and other shit like that. It surprised me that those Wounded Warrior programs helped…a lot. The hardest part was talking, but once I started, just jawing with other guys who had experienced similar stuff and were going through the same things with a desire to reach the other side…it was easier. Like we shouldered the weight for each other. It's like you've got this choice: either sit still and dwell in this infinite loop of hellish turmoil or you get moving, go for the gold and grab life by the balls."

"Yeah, you've always been a ball-grabber," Jonah joked.

"Look who's fucking calling me that!" Kevin laughed and then he scratched his chin. "No, but seriously, thanks for hanging…you know, sticking in there, even when I was a bastard."

"Kevin, we've been brothers from another mother for a long time. I even tried to marry you into the family, but noooooooooo! You had to meet Miss Perfect Julie and get married. None of my eight sisters were good enough." Jonah winked at his buddy, and then he put down the wall sconce and looked at his friend. "Seriously, Kev, I would have taken the pain for you if I could have."

"I know. Thanks for that. I had to figure this out on my own." Kevin patted Jonah on the back. "Look at me now…the wife is happy and I'm fucking employed and I'm moving into a gorgeous house! Shit happens and then you move on. Hey, when I was in the Corps, Julie and I almost had the divorce-me conversation. You know eighty percent of marriages at Camp Pendleton fail. That's a crappy number, and we were on our way to becoming a statistic, and then this happened. It forced us to communicate, really talk to each other, and stuff changed. None of it was overnight. We had to put in the work, but this experience, in all its horror, did actually bring us closer. Not that I would have ever chosen this particular path."

"No shit," said Jonah. "Glad the marriage is better. You deserve the happiness and the great job, too."

"Thanks, man. Working on the space-to-water vehicle is going to be mind-blowing." Kevin smiled proudly. "The engineers have a special building less than an hour away and then the main facility is up the coast on the water."

"Bastard," said Jonah, slapping Kevin's hand in a high five. "You are definitely a lucky man."

"Yeah, well, now it's your turn to find happiness and tie the fucking knot," teased Kevin. "You'll get to see the pluses and minuses of what all married men know."

"Yup, that's the plan." Jonah picked up his task and began wiring another wall sconce.

"Ha! I knew it. I saw you looking at Alisha. Pretty hot lady…" Kevin baited him.

"Yup…" Jonah said, nonplussed. He had it so bad it was showing all over the place. Well, he did like Alisha as well as love her. There was something about her pluck, her joy, and her energy that intrigued him. He wanted to learn more about her…and show her what he loved about life. Damn, that was corny, but he'd never had the urge to share his innermost experiences with someone before and yet, it was easy to talk to her; and the way she kissed made his body react like a race car engine going from 0 to 200 in seconds. If heat were fuel, this lady could fill all the tanks at NASCAR.

"Excuse me, you're like a dog on the hunt, and that lady is the juicy bone," Kevin joked.

"Nice." Jonah frowned. "A little more class, please. That's the woman I love."

"Oh! I touched a nerve! You really do love her. Good to know the truth! I've always known you'd hit it off." Kevin lifted his water bottle and took a long drink.

"Man, I wish this was a Longboard Lager. I could use a cold one."

"You and me both, brother," agreed Jonah. "You and me both."

―――∿∿∿―――

Alisha blushed. He loved her. Her stomach did several flips. She loved him, too.

The reaction of her body was a surge of heat, remembering last night's kisses. His hands caressing her body and the way she fit perfectly against him. Like they were made for each other…

Julie came out of the bathroom looking pale. "I'm never going to get used to morning sickness. Probably because it comes out of nowhere at any time of the day. Thank God, Kevin is oblivious."

"Why haven't you told Kevin about, ahem, you know?" Alisha nodded to the woman's slim belly. "Not that you're showing. How can you be five and a half months along and be that tiny?"

"Because I had twenty pounds on me when it all started." She smiled. The expression melted from her face as a memory struck. "You know how hard it was when we lost our daughter. Kevin was destroyed. I just want to reach the six-month mark, and then I'll say something. I…have to be sure."

"Should I finish the, ah, baby's room? Or wait?" Alisha hoped she could complete it. The crib and additional furnishings were in the back of her hybrid, and she was eager to play with it. Hopefully, Julie would let her do it before the party, but she could wait if they wanted it to be private.

As if her friend had been eavesdropping on her brain, Julie said, "Before the party, we'll do it. The cravings are getting worse, and I know I'm going to have to admit it soon. Maybe the room will tip him off to the news that I'm scared to share."

"You're going to love it! He's going to adore it!" Alisha hugged her. "A boy's room is so much fun to decorate."

"I'm sure it will be. Now, Kevin Jr. and I need more food. I'm thinking fudge. Let them know I'm heading to town. How much do I love that the gas station opens at oh-dark-nothing and has homemade fudge and jams?" Julie grabbed her phone and purse as she headed out the back door. Her friend was a woman on a mission, and that mission was chocolate. Being pregnant was ruling her world. She was surprised Kevin hadn't caught on, yet. Men!

Alisha had to get moving. She pushed away from the counter she'd been leaning on and got into gear. Unpacking the boxes and scrambling to get things in place before everyone arrived was a serious race, not to mention the long night of lovemaking had already exhausted her. No rest for the weary! She still had her hands full, unwrapping the dangling crystals that would make up the dining room chandelier, too. Busy, busy, busy. She pushed herself into overdrive.

The trays for the party would be here at ten a.m. and then it would be time to set up for the party…and for the baby reveal. She was crossing her fingers that it all went as planned.

# CHAPTER 8

ALISHA DISTRACTED KEVIN WHILE JONAH double-timed his actions putting the crib together and setting up the baby room. The SEAL had looked like a grinning monkey when she had shared the news. She had punched him in the stomach and told him not to get any ideas, and then she had passed over the keys to her car and urged Jonah to hurry. Then, she maneuvered Kevin into the kitchen to help her with the process of putting together the kitchen table and chairs.

Honestly, she could have done it herself, but the busywork was keeping the father-to-be distracted. The problem was, he was doing it all too fast.

"Are you sure there aren't any more screws?" asked Kevin.

"Let me see," said Alisha, feeling around on the floor behind her. "Oh, yeah, here are a few more."

Kevin scratched his ear. "So, are you going to tell me what's going on?"

"What do you mean?"

"I've known you for years, Alisha, and I've seen you put stuff like this together in twenty minutes flat. We've been in here for about a half an hour. And, where's Julie?" Kevin picked up his phone and texted.

A phone binged from the other room.

"Well, I guess she's back." Kevin was fast. He was on the go and out of the kitchen before she could stop him.

"Wait!" she shouted. But the man was gone.

She ran out of the kitchen and stopped in the doorway of the nursery.

Jonah was blocking her way. His voice was a low, rumbling whisper. "Give them a minute."

"No, I want to see."

His forefinger touched her chin.

She lifted her lips to his. The kiss was succulent. Its tenderness wrapped around her heart like a warm hug. Reluctantly, she pulled away. "Please."

He nodded, stepping aside.

The sight that greeted her was humbling and soul sweet. Kevin was hugging his wife, who was curled up on his lap. Tears were streaming down both their faces.

Kevin looked up at them. "A boy. We're having a boy."

Her eyes sought Jonah's, and the emotion on his face was mirrored in her own. They had that in common, wanting only happiness for their friends.

"May you have as many babies as my parents did," said Jonah as he stepped forward and patted Kevin on the back and then kissed the top of Julie's head. Then he walked to the door and took Alisha's hand.

It felt good to hold his hand. To be connected in this special moment.

He led her from the room, leaving the lovebirds alone together. When they got back into the kitchen, he pulled her into his arms and held her. "I love you, Alisha. It's always been you. You are my passion."

Her heart sang with those words. "I love you, too."

"You better love me more," said a female voice from the door.

A twinge of jealousy pierced her.

Two more females chimed in. "Jonah's my favorite, and I'm his." They started to argue.

Jonah cleared his throat loudly. "Alisha, I'd like you to meet my sisters."

"Your sisters. Ah, hi." The jealousy melted like snow in the sun. "Good to meet you."

"This is my fiancée, though I'm going to redo that title in some kind of fancy, memorable way." Jonah explained, hugging her close. He whispered in her ear. "I'm one of ten. Don't be intimidated, just hold your own. Okay?"

She nodded her agreement, and seeing all those bodies, knew exactly what to do. "Ladies, we need your help to finish organizing the house. Can we count on you?"

The answer was a resounding, "Yes!" as they sprung into action. Jonah's sisters finished putting the table and chairs together. Cleaned the counters. Unpacked groceries and put out the trays. One of them even ran to town for the appetizers, pizzas, and beer. It might not have been fancy in some people's opinion, but it was exactly the kind of party that made everyone in this hometown feel loved.

Pretty soon the house was overflowing with guests. New neighbors. Old friends. House builders. Engineers. Architects. The local priest blessed the house, and platters of food covered every surface, welcoming the Tomses to Julian. The mountains were graced this day with family and friends and a celebration of the spirit.

# ABOUT THE AUTHOR

*New York Times* and *USA Today* bestselling author **Anne Elizabeth** is an award-winning romance author and comic creator of the teen-rated PULSE Series. With a BS in business and MS in communications from Boston University, she is a regular presenter at conventions, as well as a member of The Authors Guild and Romance Writers of America. AE lives with her husband, a retired Navy SEAL, in the mountains above San Diego. They are very active in the West Coast SEAL Community and volunteer for the California Parks. For more information, visit AnneElizabeth.net.

*Timeline: This Troubleshooters story takes place in January 2010, about eight months after the end of* Breaking the Rules.

# HOME FIRE INFERNO

## (Burn, baby, burn!)

### A Troubleshooters Novella

# SUZANNE BROCKMANN

# CHAPTER 1

## JENN

JENNILYN GILLMAN'S WATER BROKE.

At first she'd thought it was some kind of horrific pregnancy-induced incontinence. For a few short seconds she'd actually been *glad* that she'd gotten out of her sister-in-law Eden's car and was standing at the side of the road.

But she—and Eden, too—were standing there because the car had broken down on a lightly traveled stretch of highway in the butt-ugly desert, north and east of San Diego, far, *far* from civilization.

"Oh, my God," Jenn said as she realized that the pain that had nearly doubled her over was a labor contraction and that she hadn't just peed her giant maternity underpants.

No, she was going to give birth. Right here. Right now.

"You okay?" Danny's voice echoed bizarrely over her cell phone, as if her Navy SEAL husband had called her from Mars instead of the Philippines. It was twice as strange that the call from his international cell phone had gotten through, when just moments before neither she nor Eden could get either of their phones to work. Even now, Jenn had maybe half a bar of signal, at the most. And yet Dan's voice, although distant with that odd echo, was clear.

"Yes," Jenn told him, working hard to keep her voice even. Despite her attempt, she sounded raggedly out of breath, still reeling from the shock of that sharp pain. "I'm fine. Cramp."

It wasn't a lie. Labor contractions *were* cramps, of sorts. And she was fine. Or rather, she was going to be fine.

Dan, however, was going to be full-on, steam-out-of-his-ears pissed when he got the news that she'd given birth to his baby daughter in a ditch at the side of Obsidian Springs Road.

He would've been pissed that she'd even agreed to go on this little road trip through the mountains to the tiny desert "resort" town of Obsidian Springs, even if the trip had been completely uneventful and car-trouble-free.

This was their first pregnancy, and Dan was more stressed out about it than Jenn. Not about the having-a-kid part. He was more than okay with that, happily helping to set up their nursery, and even bringing home a collection of adorable stuffed animals in varying shades of pink. No, it was Jenn who was freaked about her lack of experience with infants, and her imminent responsibility for the life of this completely helpless human being that she was about to drop onto the searing hot asphalt.

Danny's issue was all about Jenn's health. This baby they'd made was already ginormous. It was a full-on mystery to both of them exactly how their daughter was going to emerge from Jenn's womb without medical intervention. If it were up to Danny, Jenn would stay in their apartment, feet up, in their bed, 24/7, until their little girl was born.

So yeah, the fact that Jenn had gone on this road trip

with Eden was going to create some noise when Dan found out about it.

But there was one thing of which she was certain. He wasn't going to find out about it from her, not right now, anyway. Nope.

Eden had opened the hood to glare at her car's engine, but when Jenn had squeaked out that *Oh, my God*, she'd glanced up. Now she looked from the expression on Jenn's face to the liquid still splashing on the pavement between her swollen ankles and sensible sneakers, and her eyes widened. "Oh, my *God*," she echoed in a much higher octave, at a much louder volume. "Seriously?"

Yes, Jenn agreed that this seemed like a bad joke, because there was *no way* this was supposed to be happening. She was only eight months along. First babies were always late and never early—or so everyone had told her, over and over. It was part of the rationale she'd used in order to convince Eden that it was okay that she ride along with her today.

Meanwhile, Dan had heard his sister and was now asking, "Wait, is that Eden?"

"Dan," Jenn managed to gasp, "I gotta…" She started over, forcing her voice to sound less squeezed and stressed. "I'm sorry, Danny, I'll call you back. I love you! Everything's fine!" She cut the connection as Eden came toward her.

Incredulity mixed with the concern on her sister-in-law's face. "*I'm* sorry, but everything's, like, the *opposite* of fine! Why would you tell Danny that? I mean, even without *this* magic"—she gestured to the puddle on the asphalt—"we need a tow truck at the very least."

"His status—the SEAL Team's status—is mission ready." That was all Jenn had to say.

Eden nodded, instantly sober. She got it. Her own husband, Izzy Zanella, was also a Navy SEAL. He was one of Dan's teammates, which meant that *Izzy* was currently mission ready, too. The last thing a SEAL needed was to go into a combat situation distracted by problems from back home. It was a hard and fast rule when sending emails or during these rare phone calls. Everything was *always* fine. It had to be.

"Still, this *might* be an exception to the rule," Eden pointed out.

"Childbirth is completely natural," Jenn countered.

"In four-billion-degree heat?" Eden shot back, gesturing around them to a landscape that looked like the surface of the moon. "With a bottle and a half of water between the two of us...?"

Jenn looked down the empty road, in both directions. Nothing moved. Nothing real, that is. It was unnaturally hot for January, and heat mirages shimmered and danced. "This is California. Someone'll drive by. We'll flag 'em down—"

"No one passed us on this road when we were heading north," Eden dourly pointed out. "The only traffic was down on Route 78, which is at least five miles in that direction."

Which meant that Obsidian Springs, with its single still-open gas station, was five miles back in the *other* direction.

"Well, they say you're supposed to walk while in labor...?" But not even Jenn could manage to sound optimistic about a five mile hike in this heat.

"Yeah," Eden said. "To *make* the baby come *faster*. I don't think that's what we want here."

"Maybe this was just a freak thing," Jenn said. "I know the fact that my water broke is not good and I need to get to a hospital relatively soon, but there was only just that one contraction—" As she said it, her body proved her to be a liar, another pain hitting her so hard that she had to sit down, right there in the dusty road.

"Come on." Eden looped Jenn's arm around her neck and lifted the larger woman up. "Let's start by getting you back into the car and out of the sun."

"Oh, my God," Jenn gasped again. She knew from experience that Eden was much stronger and tougher than she looked, with her skinny jeans, her clingy pink top, and her high-heeled sandals.

Eden had, after all, just identified the body of Greg Fortune, her wicked stepfather, at the Obsidian Springs morgue. What the man had been doing in the ghost-town-ish "resort" was unclear, but he'd had a massive heart attack while watching porn on pay-per-view at the Lantern Inn Motor Lodge.

Eden hadn't flinched as the woman in the white lab coat pulled back the sheet to reveal her stepfather's mottled face. She'd just quietly nodded and signed the paperwork. She'd even settled up his motel bill—which was more than Jenn would've done, had their roles been reversed.

"I love you dearly," Eden told her now as she checked both her and Jenn's phones for a signal, "but I am *not* delivering your baby all alone in the back of my car, in the middle of nowhere. How *did* Danny's call come through…? I've tried calling Tracy, I've tried calling Jay, I've tried calling Ben"—all of whom were in San Diego—"I've tried the county sheriff in Obsidian Springs, I just tried 9-1-1, but I get nothing. Even my texts won't send. Maybe an overseas call uses a different cell tower or satellite…?"

"No! I love you dearly, too," Jenn said, reaching out to grab Eden's arm, her fingers tightening as yet another contraction ripped through her—God, that last one hadn't even ended and a new one was starting. It didn't seem fair. She tried to talk through it, and her words came out half-shout, half-snarl, "but you are *not* calling Dan. Or Izzy. They are. Mission. *Ready!*"

Eden gazed back at Jenn with those movie-star gorgeous dark brown eyes that were so like Dan's—except for the fact that she was remarkably unperturbed by Jenn's outburst. It was possible that with everything Eden had been through in her short life, she was incapable of being frightened by anything or anyone.

She was, after all, married to Izzy Zanella.

"I'm not calling either of them," she informed Jenn matter-of-factly as she finished dialing a number and brought her phone up to her ear. "I'm trying the senior chief. Maybe *he* can call Jay Lopez, who can then call Obsidian Springs to get you an ambulance to the nearest hospital."

*Where* was *the nearest hospital*, Jenn wanted to ask, but as the contraction gripped her harder, all she could do was moan, "Don't let him tell Dan! I'm gonna be fine…"

# CHAPTER 2

## IZZY

"*I'M HAVING YOUR BABY!*" NAVY SEAL IZZY ZANELLA sang in his best falsetto. "*I'm a woman in love, and I love what it's doing to me!*"

Dan and Jenk were both on their burner cell phones, talking to their wives—both of whom were pregnant. Mark Jenkins gave Izzy a rueful eye-roll before turning away. Danny just completely ignored him, instead frowning down at his phone as if he'd maybe lost his connection.

And although Danny's wife, Jenn, was farther along in her baby-making journey, it was Marky-Mark's wife, Lindsey, who was the biggest cause for concern. She'd miscarried last year and was playing this current pregnancy super-safe, at least while still in her first trimester.

And, yeah, the fact that words like *trimester* were front and center in Izzy's working vocabulary was proof that conversations with both Danny and Jenk had become rather narrowly focused of late.

Izzy knew that Jenn's biggest issue was backaches and swollen ankles, while Lindsey was still actively riding the morning sickness train. Like it or not, he and his other SEAL teammates were getting a crash course in Pregnant Wife 101.

Most of it was not new to Iz, who'd been the youngest

in his family. He'd grown up with a pack of much older brothers who'd regularly knocked up their girlfriends and/or wives. Starting in his tweens, there was nearly always someone pregnant in the house, sifting through his fridge, searching for the pickles to top her mint chocolate chip ice cream.

It was essential, always, to have salt-free soda crackers at hand. And the sympathetic words, *I know you feel exhausted/nauseous/awful/homicidal. I'm so sorry, baby. How can I help?* were also good to keep near the tip of one's baby-making tongue.

But both crackers and placating words—along with other gifts like takeout for dinner or voluntarily vacuuming the house or folding the laundry—were impossible to provide from the other side of the vast Pacific Ocean.

Right now, Izzy and Danny and Jenk were sitting in the airport in Manila, moments from being given the *go* to participate in the takedown of a commercial cargo vessel that had been hijacked by pirates from a tiny, neighboring island nation.

Alleged pirates. Rumblings from the intel community had made Izzy rather certain that the nameless tiny island nation's current ass-hat dictator was only *calling* them pirates, and claiming that the cargo ship had been hijacked so as to bring down the full wrath of the U.S. Navy onto their heads. Other rumblings implied that said pirates were, in fact, representatives from the opposition party, meeting illegally to discuss an impending election that would move the country toward democracy.

Another quirky thing about this sitch was that the SEALs hadn't been briefed for this mission in some covert ready room at the nearby U.S. military base. In fact, they'd barely been briefed at all.

Instead, Izzy's team of SEALs, led by the very stern and scary looking Lt. Commander Jazz Jacquette, had trooped through Manila's commercial airport in full battle gear—sans only their weaponry. Which, had they'd been wearing, would've been rattling loudly—sabers and HKs alike. The only thing missing from their ultra-dramatic public display of force had been a neon sign flashing red, white, and blue, reading *U.S. Navy SEALs*, while it pointed directly at them in all their military tough-guy glory.

Izzy was pretty damn certain that his SEAL Team wasn't going anywhere—that that *go* command wasn't coming—at least not today. He and his SEAL brothers were, instead, an exclamation point on whatever diplomacy was happening. They were the unspoken *or else* in a message about democracy that was no doubt being delivered to Dictator Ass-Hat.

It wouldn't surprise him one bit if they marched through the airport a few more times before the stand-down order came through, sometime after midnight tonight.

HoboMofo, who was sitting beside Izzy, was thinking the same thing. "I missed Bree's meet-my-dad day at school for *this*?"

The fact that a SEAL who'd been given the most awesome nickname of not just *Mofo*, but *HoboMofo* was the single dad of a girl in the fifth grade, was pretty mind-bending. Izzy didn't know 'Fo all that well, but if he'd been playing a round of Two Truths and a Lie with the other SEAL, and the three statements about the guy had been (1) Wrestles lions for fun; (2) Born on the dark side of the moon; and (3) Lives with his mom and his ten-year-old ballet-dancing daughter named Brianna… Well, Izzy would've picked number three as the blatant, flat-out, had-to-be lie.

Mofo, or Mohf for even shorter, could be best described by someone saying, *Picture the scariest serial killer you can imagine, with a build like a no-neck monster with hams for hands, give him dead, soulless eyes, a buzz cut that makes his blond hair look oddly colorless and even gray, and then make him twice as huge-large and terrifying… Bingo!*

The SEAL even had the requisite bodies-buried-in-the-back-forty Louisiana bayou drawl.

It was kinda fun imagining him in a "World's Best Daddy" apron, cooking pancakes with mouse ears and dancing with his kid to the soundtrack from *The Little Mermaid*. *Unda dah sea…* Yeah, that worked for Izzy in a dangerously perfect way. But he swallowed his laughter, because Mohf was clearly bumming at missing his daughter's whatever-it-was at school.

"Didn't I hear you tell Jenkie that Lopez was gonna fill in for you?" Izzy asked. Their teammate, Jay Lopez, had been Left Behind for this current op, after fucking up his knee during a HAHO training jump. He was still hobbling around on crutches, wearing one of those really stupid knee braces that made it so you couldn't bend your leg. But he'd hobble his way into little Brianna's class and flash his perfect smile, and give his super-special G-rated *I am a Navy SEAL* talk.

Most of the little boys and some of the girls in the class would want to grow up to be him. The rest would want to marry him.

Izzy tried to imagine Mohf speaking publicly, even to a bunch of kids, and got a searing vision of sweat pouring off the big man as he attempted to explain the duties of an E-7 SEAL without mentioning the importance of delivering double pops to a terrorist's head to absofuckinglutely make sure they were not just dead, but motherfucking dead.

Yeah.

But whatever Mohf was thinking, it wasn't *Thank you Jesus and Jay Lopez, for saving me from that travesty.* In fact, at the mention of Lopez's name, Mohf shook his head and laughed the way a man might laugh when finding out that his house's sewage line had backed up into the bathtub.

"Yeah," Mohf said, shooting Izzy a decidedly dark look. "Great. That was actually Jenkin's idea. Lopez. *Fuck.*"

*Lopez. Fuck.* The words didn't make all that much sense. On top of being charismatic and handsome, Lopez was, like HoboMofo, a hospital corpsman—the Navy's version of a medic. He was hands down *the* nicest guy Izzy had ever met, not just in the Teams, but in the entire U.S. Navy. He was sincerely, honestly kind. His name, Jay, was even short for Jesus.

He was great with kids, women fainted when they met him and…

*Oh.*

*There* it was. The reason for HoboMofo's heartfelt *Lopez. Fuck.*

"So how's the school year going?" Izzy asked, trying to sound conversational. "For Brianna. Everything okay? She like her teacher…Missus…or maybe *Miz*…?"

Hobe was a SEAL, which meant that, even as scary and gene-deficient as he looked, he was far from an idiot. He knew exactly what Izzy was fishing for, and he gave Izzy his famous deadeye look. "Yeah," he drawled as he pushed his massive frame up and out of his seat. "She likes her teacher just fine."

As HoboMofo walked away, Izzy reached for his phone. He could at least leave a message for Lopez. *Back slowly away from the hot fifth-grade teacher…*

But before he could dial, Danny Gillman plopped his lanky frame into 'Fo's still-warm seat.

"I need you to call Eden," his teammate, former best-frenemy and still relatively new brother-in-law through Izzy's marriage to Dan's little sister announced. "Something weird is up with Jenn."

# CHAPTER 3

## LOPEZ

JAY LOPEZ WAS HAVING A BAD WEEK. HIS INJURED knee had forced him to remain in San Diego while the rest of his SEAL Team went wheels up.

He worked hard to keep the word *hate* out of his vocabulary, but he had to admit that he vehemently disliked being left behind at times like these. And it didn't help his mood this morning when the doctor told him he'd need to keep this brace in place for a few more days, after which *We'll see*. In the medical world, *We'll see* was code for *Yep, you're going to need surgery*, which was disheartening to say the least.

So when Jay walked into the fifth-grade classroom of the daughter of the SEAL known as HoboMofo, and was greeted by a teacher who could've played an elf princess in *LOTR*, he was ready for his luck to change.

"You must be Chief Lopez," she said, with a warm, wide grin that worked astonishingly well with her elfin features. Pointy chin, freckle-adorned nose, hazel eyes with long, dark lashes... She was alone in a brightly decorated room that was filled with desks.

His first thought was that he was going to be in town for quite a while—a month and a half, maybe two. Surgery, recovery, physical therapy... It was the perfect time to begin a relationship.

"I am," he told the pretty teacher with his warmest smile, balancing on his crutches so he could hold out his hand to shake. "Although the uniform is probably a pretty large clue."

Her eyes sparkled. "I'm Carol Redmond." Her hand was cool and slender, with short-trimmed nails, and just like that, with that otherwise unremarkable skin-to-skin connection, Jay fell completely in love. "Thank you so much for filling in for Hugh today. I can't tell you how much it means to Brianna to have you here to talk about her dad's work. What can I get you? Would you like to sit down? Hugh told me you blew out your knee—that sounds terrible."

Jay winced. It *did* sound terrible, when put in those words. Especially since a blown-out knee generally required surgery. "No, I'm okay, thanks. It's easier to stay standing." His big question, however, had to do with all of those *Hughs*.

The puzzlement must've shown on his face, because she laughed again, even as she gently pulled her hand free. "Hugh told me he had a rather complicated Navy SEAL nickname." Her eyes actually danced. "But for some reason, he wouldn't tell me what it is."

"Bert," Jay managed. "I'm sorry, but his name is Bert Bickles." Wasn't it? "I *am* in the right place, aren't I?"

"You are. His full name is Hubert," she corrected him. "He told me he prefers *Hugh*."

"I didn't know that," Jay admitted. "I mean, I haven't worked with him all that much. And even then, we mostly call him..." He stopped himself.

But now Carol's eyes were lit up in anticipation.

"He really didn't tell you?" Jay asked.

"He's a little shy," the teacher said.

Shy? Mohf? *Shy*. Huh. "And you couldn't get it out of Brianna?"

Carol shook her head. "I'm pretty sure she doesn't know. When I asked, she said she thought it had something to do with...Motown?"

Jay laughed. "That's, um...correct."

The elf princess didn't buy it. But she looked around to make sure the coast was clear and lowered her voice before leaning in to ask, "Mo*fo*?"

Jay lifted both hands in surrender. "You've seen him. You really want me to risk his wrath?"

Her smile was genuinely amused. "He's a marshmallow."

"Yeah, now I *know* I'm in the wrong classroom."

The very lovely Carol Redmond once again laughed, but then a bell rang. "You ready for this?" she asked. "They're coming in from gym, so there'll be a lot of extra energy, combined with the fact that it's the very end of the day. If you want, I can give 'em a spelling test, or maybe a pop quiz on this morning's math lesson. That'll put 'em in a stupor..."

She was kidding. "I got this," Jay said.

"I believe that you do." Her smile was warm and held promises of many wonderful candlelit dinners over the next few months.

Jay felt his phone buzz as a text message came in, but he ignored it—preferring to smile back into Carol's eyes as the first wave of fifth graders came storming into the room.

# CHAPTER 4

## IZZY

SOMETHING WEIRD WAS UP WITH JENN.

Or at least that was what Danny had just stated as an irrevocable truth. Dude believed it, too. While his body language was all slouchy and playing-it-cool as he sat beside Izzy in the hard plastic airport chairs, Dan couldn't disguise the fact that he was wearing his trying-not-to-freak face.

Izzy sighed, because, Jesus. Jenn's ninth and please-gods-final month of baby-cooking was going to be one long, trying endurance test for all of them.

Danny being Danny, Izzy's tiny little barely-there exhale pissed him off. "Look, I was talking to her," Dan said, heavy on the affronted. "And something was definitely up. She just suddenly had to go. And she hasn't called me back."

"Maybe she had to pee," Izzy suggested, while across the waiting area Senior Chief Wolchonok turned to scan the group of SEALs as if he were counting heads. His patience was much like that of a kindergarten teacher or a den mother, only he was far more world-weary and grim. He saw that Izzy was looking at him and as their eyes met, Izzy realized the senior was holding his phone to his ear.

Izzy was just about to leap to his feet and say, *You need sump'n, Senior…?* But Wolchonok's gaze shifted to Gillman, and then back, and then the man shook his head, just a little, like a pitcher shaking off a signal from his catcher. Hmmm. So instead, Izzy kept his convo with Dan-bo going—what were they talking about? Ah, yes. Urination. "Pregnant women frequently have to—"

"She would've told me." Dan cut him off, completely oblivious to Izzy's and the senior's little charades game. "*I have to pee*. Or she would've just taken her phone with her into the bathroom."

"Maybe it was number two," Izzy said as he watched the senior chief pull the phone from his ear and gave it his best death glare, after which he pointed at Jenkins and made a *come here* gesture. Jenk snapped to it. "Women can definitely be all private and weird about doing number two while on the phone and—"

"I'm pretty sure she's with Eden," Dan interrupted again. "First Jenn goes *Oh, my God*, and then someone else—Eden—goes *Oh, my God*, and suddenly Jenn has to hang up."

Yeah, something was definitely up. Across the room, Senior and Marky-Mark were in a deep discussion, and now Mark had *his* phone out, too. Right in front of the senior.

Even though they weren't supposed to bring personal cells on a mission, the SEALs nearly almost all did it anyway, carrying international phones with SIM cards— because they subscribed to the Navy SEAL adage "Two is one and one is none."

As Izzy watched, their XXL CO joined them, and then *he* got his phone out, as well.

But Danny hadn't noticed—he was in his own oblivious, miserable world.

"*Oh, my God* is an appropriate exclamation," Izzy pointed out, "for everything from an apocalyptic mega-earthquake to finding an awesome deal on a newborn-sized *Star Trek* uniform onesie. With Ben coming home from school with an A on his latest English paper somewhere in the middle there."

Dan and Eden's younger brother Ben was still in high school. Izzy and Eden shared custody of the kid with Danny and Jenn. It worked out nicely, with Ben bouncing between their two apartments, and Eden, Jenn, and Ben hanging together for extra home-fires-burning support when the SEALs were out in the world, doing their sea-air-and-land thing.

"And there has *not* been an earthquake," Izzy quickly continued as he realized he'd put a bad idea into Dan's already too-noisy head. "At least not the Big One. We would've heard about it by now—it'd be all over Twitter. Seriously, bro, what's the absolute worst that this weirdness could be? That Jenn's gone into labor, right? *Oh, my God, I'm having this massively giant Gillbaby, right—aaahhh!—now—uuuhhh!* Well, if that's the case, then good news! *Some*one's with her. It's definitely not Eden, though. I got an email, said she's driving out to the desert today, to some wannabe resort town called something appropriately silly like Idiot Springs, to check out some potential wedding reception site for Tracy and Deck. And frankly? *I* should be the one yowling about weirdness. Whatever's up with Jennilyn, at least she's not doing the bridesmaid thing for one of your exes."

Long before Izzy had met Eden, he'd briefly collided with the somewhat ditzy but surprisingly tough-as-nails Tracy, who had finally found a forever home with former

SEAL chief Larry Decker. They were planning a big wedding, and Tracy had asked Eden to be a bridesmaid.

"That *is* weird," Mark Jenkins agreed, sitting down on the other side of Danny. Somehow he'd made it across the room without Izzy noticing. But, yup. The senior and the CO were still leaning against the far wall, still working their phones. And the tadpole, Tony Vlachic, had just joined them, his phone out, too.

Curiouser and curiouser.

Izzy turned his attention to Mark, who was purposely mimicking Dan's faux-whatever body language. He looked equally loose and relaxed. And barely legal, with his golly-gee freckles, boyish face, compact frame, and lean build. One of these days, dude was gonna Ron-Howard. He'd pull off his hat, be balding underneath, and suddenly look his age. But until that day, probably well into his forties, Mark Jenkins would continue to get carded.

"Senior wants you, Zanella," Mark told Izzy, managing to keep his tenor sounding calm and matter-of-fact. But he opened his eyes, just a millimeter wider, shooting Izzy a message-filled look while Dan's head was down.

Ruh-roh.

Izzy answered with a questioning narrowing of his own eyes, to which Mark responded with a tip of his not-quite-red head, complete with a pointed look at the senior, as if to say, *All your questions will be answered, douchebag, if you simply stand up and cross the room*.

So Izzy stood up and crossed the room, leaving Marky-Mark to distract Danny with some scintillating pregnancy-related topic. "Lindsey's having these crazy erratic swings regarding food," he heard Mark say as if he really gave half a shat. "She gets these cravings, but in the time it takes me to cook dinner, the thing she was craving now completely grosses her out."

"Take her out to eat," Izzy heard Dan recommend. "Or get to-go and order two very different meals. Then be ready to give her yours when the food comes. Switch plates again, halfway through. Works like a charm."

Meanwhile, the muscle was jumping in Senior Chief Wolchonok's very square jaw. In true senior chief manner, he cut through the bullshit and got to the point. "I got a phone call from Eden," the senior said, and Izzy swallowed the surprised urge to say *My Eden?* Because really, it wasn't as if they knew a dozen different Edens. His wife's name was relatively unique.

Instead, as Izzy instantly did the math and realized that Danny was probably right and Eden *was* with Jenn, the senior chief confirmed that.

"She's with Jennilyn Gillman. Her car broke down, they're out of town somewhere in the desert, they're having some kind of weird heat wave, and Jenn's gone into labor."

Izzy turned inappropriate surprised laughter into a cough that didn't fool Wolchonok.

"Before your wife could tell me where they are," the senior grimly continued, "the signal broke up. I haven't been able to resume contact with her. I'm hoping you can help."

"Eden told me she was going out to Obsidian Springs," Izzy said. "But with Tracy, not Jenn. FYI, it's a Palm Springs wannabe, not far from Borrego Springs, and even less successful." At his words, the rest of the telethon team sprang into action, including the senior. They all started barking orders into their phones.

Izzy got out his own phone and speed-dialed Eden.

"Come on, come on, come on," he said as the thing first searched for a signal, and then went straight to his wife's voice mail.

# CHAPTER 5

## LOPEZ

"EVERY MEMBER OF A SEAL TEAM HAS A SPECIFIC JOB," Jay told the roomful of wide-eyed ten- and eleven-year-olds, and one very attractive twentysomething—after he'd explained to them exactly how he'd gotten injured. He knew they wouldn't be able to focus until he got that story out of the way, and it had eaten into much of his time. He now had maybe twenty minutes left before school ended for the day.

But that was great. He'd leave 'em wanting more—especially the twentysomething.

"Every SEAL has a specific area of expertise," he continued, "in addition to being able to handle explosives, fire weapons, swim, run, jump out of planes—these are skills that all SEALs have, right? But we each also have a few talents that are unique, that we bring to the team, that make the team stronger. And when our COs—commanding officers—and our senior chiefs are deciding who to send on a mission, they take that into account. For example, I'm a hospital corpsman. Who knows what that means?"

Carol Redmond was smiling—*she* clearly knew what it meant. It was, to be honest, Jay's deal-closer. He knew exactly what he looked like. With his dark hair, brown eyes, handsome face, and trim physique, he knew he had the ability to catch a pretty woman's eye. His being a SEAL helped out in that department, too. But women liked men who saved lives, and it was the fact that he was a hospital corpsman that got him the non-hesitating *yes* when he asked a woman out to dinner.

But that was a question for later.

Right now, several hands shot up around the room, but Jay called on HoboMofo's daughter, Brianna, who looked almost shockingly like her gigantic father, with the same thick blond hair and wide blue eyes. With her redwood-tree-like build, Bree already towered over her teacher. Although unlike her dad's angry ogre affect, the girl's default expression was a charming, quicksilver smile that transformed her completely. She was pure strapping milkmaid—with an easygoing manner that was sweet and friendly.

"A hospital corpsman is like a paramedic." Brianna turned to speak to the entire class. "You know, when you call an ambulance, paramedics are the ones who show up and perform first aid and save everyone's life."

"That's right," Jay said. "And why do you think Hobo...*Bert*!" He cleared his throat. "Excuse me, *Hu*bert, Brianna's dad, and I—why do you think we rarely serve together on the same team?"

"Because you're both hospital corpsmen," Brianna answered triumphantly.

"That's right," Jay said, smiling back at the girl, aware that her teacher was watching and smiling, too. Yes, he *was* very good with kids, thanks. "And most seven or eight men SEAL Teams need only one. Because they also need a radio man, an explosives expert, a point man—he's the guy who goes first when you go into dark and scary places—that's an important job." He ticked them off on his fingers. "A sniper, a commanding officer—can't forget him, he's in charge." The classroom door opened, and an older woman poked her head in. As Jay kept talking, he watched Carol cross toward her. "And depending on the mission, we might need a languages expert, or a computer expert, or a variety of other types of experts."

Brianna raised her hand, and Jay called on her again as, heads together, the two women spoke. "I can think of an op where the CO would want an entire SEAL Team of hospital corpsmen," she said. "If there was an earthquake, and a hospital got destroyed…?"

"For humanitarian efforts, yes. Good one." From the corner of his eyes, Jay saw both Carol and the other woman turn and look directly at him.

Something was definitely up. "I'm guessing I shouldn't have set my phone on silent," he said as he balanced on his crutches to pull it out of his pocket. He flicked it on and…

Holy crap. Twenty missed calls, and a whole slew of texts that said…Danny's wife Jenn had gone into labor, *where*?

"I'm sorry," he said, already hobbling his way toward the door. "I have to run."

But the look on little Brianna's face made him realize that he'd frightened her. She'd leapt to the conclusion that if a SEAL with an injured knee was being called in, something terrible had happened to the SEALs—like her father—who were already out in the world.

"Everything's fine," he told her, told the whole class. "But a bunch of my friends are overseas on an op with

Bree's dad, and another of my friends is going to have a baby—right now. And I need to go help her, because her car broke down out in the desert, about an hour outside of town."

As the words left his lips, Jay realized that he didn't actually have any way to help Jenn. Because of his knee, he wasn't driving his car. He'd gotten dropped off at the school by his teammate Tony V's fiancé, Adam, who was an actor. Adam was currently filming an indie movie down by the Del, on the beach in Coronado, and he wasn't going to be able to swing by to pick Jay up until after four. At the earliest. Jay's plan had been to hang at the nearby library until Adam returned.

Now, Jay looked at Carol Redmond. "I don't suppose you have a car that I can borrow. Maybe…?" His teammate Izzy Zanella had a song for every occasion, and the irreverent SEAL's voice echoed in Jay's head. *Hey, I just met you. And this is crazy…*

Carol laughed her surprise. "Can you even drive? I mean, with the…" She gestured to his brace.

He nodded. "I'll take it off."

"Won't that hurt?"

Yes, but at least he'd be able to help Jenn. "I'll be fine. I'm sorry to ask, I know you don't really know me, but—"

"No, it's okay." Carol hurried to the big desk positioned at the front of the room, pulling an enormous, slouchy bag from the bottom drawer. She put it over her shoulder as she began sifting through it, hopefully searching for her car keys.

"Brianna's dad, Hugh Bickles, called the office, hoping to reach you," the older woman said. "Apparently there's been a major accident north of Borrego Springs, and all emergency vehicles are tied up."

"Dawn, this is Chief Jay Lopez. Jay, Dawn—Mrs. Breckenridge—is the school principal." Carol threw out a quick introduction as she pulled out her keys. But she clearly was hesitating to just hand them over to Jay, instead looking at the other woman. "I don't have bus duty today," she started.

The principal nodded. "Go ahead. Drive the chief where he needs to go. The bell's going to ring in a few minutes. I've got your class until then."

"Thank you, Mrs. B.," Carol said, and Jay echoed her.

She led the way out of the room, and broke into a run in the empty corridor. "Follow me out this door," she called, pointing ahead of her. "I'll get the car, pull it around!"

Carol was kind, beautiful, *and* a quick-thinker while under pressure. If Jay hadn't already fallen hard for her, he'd now be total toast.

# CHAPTER 6

## EDEN

"First-time mothers are always late. There's no way this baby's ready to make the scene. Certainly not today." That's what Jenn had told Eden, in order to let her ride shotgun on this mission of misery.

Freakin' Greg. Eden's stepfather was still making life hard for her, even from beyond the grave.

Late last night, when she'd gotten the call from her too-pathetic mother telling her that Greg was dead, Eden's friend Tracy had immediately volunteered to go with. But that was before Tracy had a three a.m. visit from the Food Poisoning Fairy, and spent the wee hours of the morning sharing intimate secrets with her new porcelain BFF. And shortly after *that* was when Jenn proclaimed that she, instead, would keep Eden company, because *always, no way, certainly not today*…

Famous last words, Alex, for three hundred.

"Right about now I'm regretting not letting Ben come with us," Eden said to Jenn as she helped her into the backseat of the car. Her little brother had gone pale at the news of nasty Greg's passing, and yet he'd asked to come along. But only one of the Gillman siblings was needed for this unpleasant task, and since Danny was out of the country with SEAL Team Sixteen, it had fallen on Eden's shoulders.

"Believe me," she'd told Ben when she and Jenn had dropped him at the high school, "if Danny were home, I'd skip this magic show, too."

"I was just thinking *thank God he's* not *here*," Jenn admitted, soggy and sweating and out of breath from that contraction.

Truth be told, it was almost as hot inside the car as it was out on the road. Eden opened up the other two doors, hoping for a cross breeze that didn't come. She now took inventory of everything in the car's glove compartment and trunk. The only useful items were an old beach blanket and a small bottle of hand sanitizer. And that was going with a very generous definition of the word *useful*.

"I mean, Ben would want to go get help," Jenn continued breathlessly as Eden scanned the road, hoping for an approaching car but coming up empty. "And then we'd have to worry that he was alone on the side of the road, and that he'd bump into some motorcycle gang of white supremacist survivalist skinheads, except wait. *He* could stay with me while *you* went to get help…" At Eden's look, she added, "Well, obviously, in any fight between you and survivalist skinheads, *you'd* win."

It was nice to know that Jenn had that much faith in her. But as another contraction started, and Jenn grabbed hold of Eden's hand and attempted to breathe through it, Eden was hit with a massive wave of overwhelm that she quickly hid.

She knew she could help Jenn deliver this baby, even here in the back of the car. Her sister-in-law was healthy and strong, with nice wide, womanly hips. This baby would probably pop out of her easily—piece of cake. Eden hoped.

But Eden also knew that sometimes babies were born needing immediate medical aid, and she was full-on screaming terrified that this roadside delivery would turn into a horror show, with that baby gasping for air in her arms, God help her. Because there'd be nothing Eden could do to save it.

Her.

This baby was a girl—Jenn and Dan had found that out months ago when they'd had their ultrasound.

Eden let Jenn hang on to one of her hands as she used her other to try dialing her phone again. She'd gotten through to the senior chief once, surely she could do it again. But she couldn't connect and she couldn't connect. So she focused on Jenn and the fact that Senior Chief Wolchonok was a very smart—if slightly scary—man.

Still, if anyone had the brainpower to track them here, it was Izzy. And Eden found herself wishing she'd broken the rule and dialed her husband instead.

# CHAPTER 7

## LOPEZ

JAY HAD THE FRONT PASSENGER SEAT PUSHED ALL THE way back and reclined, so that he could sit in the front with his knee brace on.

As Carol Redmond drove, he worked the GPS on his phone, not only trying to find the most direct road to Obsidian Springs but also attempting to figure out the route that Jenn and Eden might've taken. Luckily, there just weren't that many ways to get there and back, so they weren't going to have to crisscross the county, searching for the disabled car.

Also, he knew where Eden and Dan's little brother Ben went to school. Odds were good the two women had headed east directly after dropping him that morning. Which meant they would have taken Route 78 for quite a few miles, before heading north on Obsidian Springs Road.

As they barreled east, as the last remnants of the San Diego suburbs fell behind them and the landscape became desolate and harsh, Carol put her little hybrid into warp drive. She was an excellent driver—confident and sure—and clearly unafraid to push the speed limit. She glanced over at Jay, no doubt because she felt him looking at her, and smiled.

"You ever deliver a baby before?" he asked her.

She shook her head as she turned back to the road. "No. You?"

"No," he admitted. "I've stood by—assisted, but…"

"Not a whole lot of opportunities to practice delivering a baby for a Navy SEAL hospital corpsman," she noted.

"Nope," he agreed. "So, it's been a while."

Carol glanced at him again. "You scared?"

Jay laughed at her directness. "A little, yeah. This baby's about a month early. So yes, scared and worried and a little freaked out pretty much covers it."

Carol nodded. "So our plan should be to get her into the car immediately—get us all moving toward the nearest hospital." She paused. "Where *is* the nearest hospital? It'd be good to know that going in."

Jay was already using his phone's GPS to find that information—but it was rough going because they were already in some kind of cellphone hell-zone. "Are you sure you're not secretly a SEAL chief?" he asked.

"Nope," she said. "But I've got a kind of major crush on one, so…"

Oh, be still his wildly pounding heart! "The feeling is quite, *quite* mutual," he said.

"Really? Oh! Oh my God," Carol said, but he didn't get to hear the rest of whatever she was going to tell him, because his phone rang.

Caller ID presented him with a number he didn't recognize, and he answered it hoping whoever was on the other end would have more information as to Jenn and Eden's whereabouts. Coordinates. Coordinates would be nice. "Lopez." He punched the speaker, so Carol could hear, too.

"Chief!" The voice on the other end echoed oddly, but otherwise was clear. "It's Jules Cassidy. Where are you?"

"Heading east on 78," Jay reported, leaning down to scan the sky out both the front and back windshield. "Where are *you*, sir? And please say in a helo soon-to-be over my head."

Jules Cassidy was an upper echelon FBI team leader who had quite a few friends in the SpecWar community. If anyone could get a helicopter on short notice, it was Cassidy.

"Sorry, I'm in DC," Cassidy said. "But I have access to, uh"—he cleared his throat—"well, let's just say certain communications satellites, and leave it at that. I haven't quite reached Jenn and Eden yet, but I'm working on it. There *is* a helo—a commercial one—headed your way, but we don't have a doctor or even a medic on board."

Jay checked his GPS and rattled off their current coordinates. "We're already in the middle of nowhere, still about twenty miles west of the turn off to Obsidian Springs." He shifted in his seat as he scanned the area. "Plenty of room for a helo to land—the only wires are along the state road."

"I'll tell Adam," Cassidy came back. "What color's your car?"

"Blue Honda Civic," Jay reported. "We'll be the ones pulled over, waving our arms." He realized what Cassidy had said. "*Adam's* in the helo?"

"Yup," Cassidy said. "Someone—Tony probably—got through to him on set, out in Coronado. They were filming some kind of aerial shot, and Adam commandeered the helicopter—hang on." Cassidy was talking on more than one phone at once, and his voice was muffled as he spoke to someone else, probably Adam in the helo.

"Adam's an actor," Jay lowered his voice to explain to Carol. "A movie star, really. He's engaged to be married to one of my teammates, Tony."

"Gay married?" she asked.

"Yeah, well, I guess… But we just call it, you know, *married*."

"Of course," Carol said quickly. "Right. I wasn't…I was just checking to see if maybe I misunderstood and there was a *female* SEAL named Toni in your team, because, frankly, that would be pretty great, too." She pointed in the rearview mirror. "Is that…?"

Jay turned to look out the back. That little dot on the horizon was indeed the helo. It was a larger bird than he expected, and he could tell just from looking that it was capable of moving pretty fast.

"Pull over," he said, but Carol had already signaled and was slowing. "I hate to just abandon you out here," he started, but she cut him off as she put her car into park.

"Nope," she said as they both climbed out of the car. She opened the back to extract his crutches. "Don't worry about me. I'll be fine. Besides, I don't want to leave my car on the side of the road, *and* I don't want to take up any extra space on the helicopter. Also…" She made a face. "I'm kind of a wimp when it comes to flying."

"Uh-oh," Jay said as he tucked his crutches under his arms. "That might be a relationship deal-breaker."

"About that," she said, but the helo was already coming in for a landing. Not only did its huge blades make it impossible to talk, but they also kicked up a crapload of dust and dirt.

"I'm kidding," Jay told her as he gently pushed her back into the driver's seat. "Thank you again. I'll call you with an update." His crutches made it impossible to bury his face in the crook of one elbow, so he simply squinted and tried not to breathe in the dust as he hobbled out to where the helo was gently touching down.

Adam slid open the door and was crouched there inside. He took Jay's crutches and helped him up and into the cabin. Jay waved one last time to Carol right before the door slid closed, and they were off.

Adam was shouting something about how Jules—he was on a first name basis with FBI Team Leader Cassidy—still hadn't gotten through to Eden or Jenn, but that the helo pilot was going to follow the road all the way to Obsidian Springs, if necessary.

"Is there a first aid kit on board?" Jay shouted, and Adam pointed toward the back of the cabin.

The medical kit was far from military grade—geared more toward sprains, breaks, burns, and lacerations. It did, however, include a blood pressure cuff, along with tubing and equipment necessary to set up an IV, if one was needed. Other than that, if things went south with either Jenn or the baby, Jay would have to improvise.

But he could do this. He *would* do this. Dan was counting on him. He took a deep breath in and exhaled hard.

It wasn't until then that Jay realized his epic fail. He'd forgotten to get Carol Redmond's phone number. But just as quickly, he realized that wouldn't be a problem.

He could always get her number from HoboMofo. She was, after all, the Mohf's daughter's fifth-grade teacher.

The SEAL chief probably had her on his VIP contacts list.

Jay gently pushed the teacher out of his mind as he went to the windows to help Adam and the pilot scan the shoulder of the road for Eden's car.

# CHAPTER 8

## EDEN

A TRUCK WENT BY, BUT DIDN'T STOP.

Eden chased the damn thing, waving her arms and shouting—screaming after it—at the top of her lungs. But whoever was driving was too busy or too frightened to pull over.

"*Son* of a bitch!" she said, hands on her knees as she caught her breath. "*Son* of a *bitch*!"

The heat was brain-melting, reflecting up off the road in an oven-worthy wave as she heard Jenn call out for her. "Eden…?"

She ran back to the car. "I'm right here!" she called. "Asshole didn't stop."

"I think…something's…buzzing?" Jenn exhaled hard, which meant she was feeling the start of another contraction. They were coming closer together now, and lasting longer.

Eden held out her hand for Jenn to grab. "Buzzing?" The moment she said the word, she realized that she'd set her phone to vibrate when they'd gone into the morgue. And she hadn't turned the ringer back on.

Damn it!

Keeping her grasp on Jenn's hand, she reached into the front where she'd put her phone into the plastic cup holder. She touched the screen and… God, there were about fifteen missed calls. All from the same number.

She quickly hit *return call* and put the phone to her ear, but nothing happened. She tried again as Jenn panted the word *shit* from between clenched teeth. Again, nothing.

But then Jenn said, "Uh-oh," and Eden looked down to see a tinge of red staining her sister-in-law's maternity skirt. Oh, God! That was *blood*.

"I think that's normal," Eden lied as another contraction gripped Jenn, and she did what she promised Jenn she wouldn't do—she dialed Danny's cell.

# CHAPTER 9

## IZZY

Izzy was heading over to where Mark Jenkins was still babysitting Dan when it happened.

He wasn't close enough to hear, but he saw Danny shifting slightly in his seat in order to pull his phone out of his pocket. He saw Dan frown, and then Izzy read Dan's lips as he said, "That's weird. It's Eden."

Izzy started running as Dan put the phone to his ear.

"Hey, Eden, is everything okay?" Dan said, but then pulled the phone away to look at it as Izzy skidded to a stop in front of him. "Huh. Maybe she butt-dialed me."

# CHAPTER 10

## EDEN

EDEN WAS INCREDULOUS. JENN HAD BATTED THE phone out of her hand.

"It was working," she said. "I finally had a connection!" But when she picked it up, it was back to zero bars. "Damn it!"

"I'm fine," Jenn snarled. "*I'm. Fine.*"

"Yeah, you're not," Eden told this woman who, after Izzy, was her very best friend in the entire blessed world. "I was lying about the blood, Jenni. It's not okay, and I no longer give a shit about *mission ready*."

"But I do."

"I get that," Eden said. "But I need you to think, just for a moment, about the possibility that you're *not* okay. You're *not* fine. And I want you to think about Dan, coming home, and you not being there to meet him."

Jenn was shaking her head.

"This," Eden continued, gesturing toward Jenn, "is now officially a life-and-death emergency. And if, for whatever reason, we can randomly get through to Dan's overseas burner phone out in Wherever-the-hell-he-is, then that's what we're going to do."

It was then that Eden saw it—movement. A car. Way in the distance. Approaching along the shimmering heat of the road.

Except it was moving faster than a car. And it wasn't on the road, it was above it.

"Chopper!" Eden said, but then realized she'd used the Army nickname. "Oh my God, Jenn, it's a helo."

For some reason, the Navy called helicopters *helos*, and this helo that was approaching was definitely courtesy of members of the U.S. Navy. Thank you, *thank you*, Senior Chief Wolchonok!

As Jenn pushed herself up to look out the back window, Eden's phone rang. It was that same number— that one that had tried over and over to call her when her phone was stupidly set on silent.

"Thank you so much," she said, uncaring as to who was on the other end. "The helo is here."

"Hey, Eden. It's Jules. Cassidy. I guess Adam and Jay found you. About time you answered your phone, sweetie."

"Jay Lopez is really on that helo?" Eden had to shout above the rapid-fire sound of the blades as it landed in the desert, sending clouds of dust into the air. She quickly closed the car doors on that side, so that Jenn wouldn't choke.

"He is," Jules said, and Eden quickly relayed that to Jenn who nodded forcefully through another contraction, even as Eden put the beach blanket up and around Jenn's head. "We've got both an OB-GYN and a pediatric specialist standing by to assist him via phone, in case that baby doesn't want to wait for you to get to the hospital."

"Thank you, but I need both hands free," Eden said and cut the connection, jamming the phone into her pocket.

Jenn was already pushing herself out of the car, but Eden held her back. "We're gonna carry you to the helo," she told her friend. "Don't want to accidentally dump the baby out onto the desert."

"That would be my preference, too." They both looked up to see Jay. He was wearing his beige chief's working uniform and his usual air of cool, calm confidence and authority.

Eden knew that Jay Lopez hadn't been thrilled when Izzy married her, and she still thought that he didn't like her very much. Whenever he showed up to a party or dinner out with the gang, her heart always sank, just a little, and she tried not to sit too close to him. But right now, she'd never been more glad to see *anyone* in her entire life. "Thank God you're here!" she said.

"Before we get Jenn to the helo," Jay said, "let's see what's going on in the baby zone."

"Oh, *this* isn't awkward at all." Jenn laughed, her sense of humor still intact despite everything. "When we're telling this story to Danny, let's skip this part, okay? We can focus on the helo rescue, and then just have the baby magically appear in my arms."

"You want *me* to look? Would that be less awkward?"

Eden realized that Adam Wyndham, partner to Navy SEAL Tony Vlachic, had gotten off the helo with Jay. He was, oddly enough, dressed only in a bathing suit and flip-flops.

There was a woman behind him—the pilot, come to help carry Jenn since Jay was on crutches.

"She's only dilated a little bit," Eden told them all. "The only way the baby's falling out is if she has some massive contraction while she's walking to the helo.

That's why I thought we should carry her. I'd like to get her to the hospital, ASAP."

Jay glanced up at Eden as he caught sight of the blood on Jenni's skirt, and she nodded.

"Let's do this," he said, and Eden thrust both hers and Jenn's handbags into Jay's arms before helping Jenn up and out of the car.

But before they could create a six-armed, three-person sling, a car pulled up and then a truck and another car.

It was the cavalry, so to speak—friends, coworkers, and family of Izzy's SEAL teammates, all of whom had apparently leaped into action and raced to Eden's and Jenn's rescue when they'd received the senior chief's long-distance distress call.

Kelly Paoletti—a pediatrician, thank God—came racing out of the first car, followed more slowly by Lindsey, Navy SEAL Mark Jenkins's also-pregnant wife, who'd been driving.

Lindsey had to lean against the car for a moment. She didn't so much as have morning sickness as every-moment-of-the-day-and-night sickness, but despite that, Eden wasn't surprised that she'd volunteered to come.

"You okay?" Kelly's husband Tom, who was the former CO of SEAL Team Sixteen and the current head of the private security firm, Troubleshooters Inc., had been right behind them in that truck. He stopped to make sure Lindsey, who was one of his top operatives, wasn't going to faint.

"I'm great," Lindsey lied. "It's Jenn who needs help."

But Tom stayed close until Eden's friend Tracy, looking pale from last night's run-in with food poisoning, emerged from the third vehicle along with Eden's brother Ben. Tracy was still moving slowly, so she hung back to make sure Lindsey really was okay while Tom and Ben both ran over to assist Kelly.

But Kelly had already taken command. "Hi, Jenni! Hey, Eden!" Kelly said with her usual good cheer, "Oh, good, Jay, I'm glad you're here. Let's get you into the helo, Jenn, get you to the hospital as quickly as possible, okay?"

Everyone rushed to carry Jenn, and it was easy with so much help.

"Ben, why don't you take my seat on the helo," Adam offered. "I'll stay with Eden's car and wait for the tow truck."

"Thank you so much," Eden told him and all of their friends, as both she and Ben climbed into the helo behind Jenn and Kelly and Jay.

The pilot got in, the others backed off, the doors slid shut, and just like that they were in the air.

Ben's eyes were wide, his teenage ennui on a temporary hold. "Is Jenni gonna be okay?" he whispered to Eden.

She hugged her brother as they belted themselves in. "Yes," she answered, and for the first time in hours, she truly believed it. "And the baby, too. They both, absolutely, will be okay."

# CHAPTER 11

## IZZY

I ZZY WAS SITTING NEXT TO D AN WHEN THE CALL came in.

He was watching for it—hoping hard it would come soon and be good news. So he caught the sudden movement when Senior Chief Wolchonok straightened up, then looked at his phone and brought it to his ear.

The senior was not prone to dramatics. Dude was steadfast, particularly in the face of tragedy—at least when he was on duty. And he was one of those stoically manly men, some years older than Izzy, who considered himself on duty the moment he stepped away from his family and out of his house.

His wife, a former Coast Guard pilot named Teri, had had more than her share of miscarriages as they'd attempted to start a family. She'd nearly died while giving birth, and they'd adopted their second and third kids.

But if Senior was feeling any sort of flashback to the night he'd nearly lost his wife and eldest child, he didn't let it show.

At least not until after that phone call. As Izzy watched, Wolchonok went limp with what could only be relief—just for a fraction of a nanosecond—before he clenched his fist and made the international gesture for *yes*, complete with three implied exclamation points.

Both his relief and that *yes* happened so quickly that if Izzy had blinked, he wouldn't've seen it.

"Petty Officer Gillman," Wolchonok intoned as he strode across the waiting area toward Danny.

Dan stood up, because you always stood when the senior came at you like that. Izzy and Jenk stood, too, on either side of him. It was clear Dan was clueless, because he shot both of them an *Uh-oh, what did we do now* look.

But Senior held out his hand and said "Congratulations, son," and Dan automatically took it and shook, still confused until Wolchonok added, "You're a father, Dan. Jennilyn and the baby are both healthy and doing fine."

Dan laughed his surprise. "Wait. *What*?"

Lieutenant Commander Jacquette, the team's CO, was right behind the senior chief, and he, too, shook Dan's hand, delivering his congrats in his *basso profundo*. Then the rest of the team surrounded them.

"Jenn had the baby," Dan realized, and he turned to hug Izzy and then Jenkins.

Izzy took the opportunity to sit down. Thank God thank God *thank God*.

But Danny was not an idiot, and he soon realized... "You knew! She went into labor and everyone knew?" He aimed his accusation at the entire team—officer and enlisted alike. Although—again, because he was not an idiot—he waited until both the CO and the senior were well out of range.

Dan turned and punched Izzy in the shoulder.

"Ow! Why do I get punched?" Izzy asked.

But Dan was already extracting the details from Jenk, who'd admitted, without any punching, that Jenn had gone into labor while on an impromptu road trip with Eden, because apparently Tracy got food poisoning...?

That didn't make sense, because the whole purpose of the trip was to check out some potential wedding reception site, so why go without the bride-to-be?

Izzy felt his phone rattle in his pants, and he pulled it out to see that Eden had sent him several photos via email. The subject header was "Stealth Penis."

That was...interesting.

"Callista," Izzy heard Dan say, as he opened the email and the photo slowly uploaded. "Callie, for short. Yeah, no, we picked out that name as soon as we found out we were having a daughter. Holy shit, you guys, I have a *daughter*."

Izzy looked at the first picture—it was a selfie of Eden smiling, her head next to Jenn's. Jenn was in a hospital bed, looking exhausted but happy, with an equally exhausted tiny baby in her arms. The baby was wrapped in a white blanket, with a little blue hat on its head and...

Wait a minute... *Stealth penis*...?

Izzy scrolled to the next shot, which was of Dr. Kelly Paoletti, holding a naked and yowling baby, a big smile on her face. And sure enough...

"Whoa, check out these pictures, Danny," Izzy said. "Eden sent them. Dude! Congratulations! Your daughter has a penis!"

Danny grabbed Izzy's phone, and as he looked for himself he started to laugh. "Holy shit, it's a boy. I have a son—with a million pink toys."

"He's a baby, what does he care?" Izzy said.

But Dan stopped on the photo of Jenn in that bed with their baby in her arms, and the expression of gratefulness and love on his face was so private that Izzy turned away.

And found the senior chief heading toward him, on yet another mission. At their eye contact, Senior motioned for Izzy to step away from the crowd.

"'Sup, S?" Izzy asked, quickly adding, "and that S stands for Senior not Stan because even though I know that's your name, I'd never call you Stan, Senior."

The senior spoke over him as he handed Izzy a piece of paper. It looked like a short list of airlines, flight numbers, departure times, and gates. The first was a nonstop to Los Angeles. The second went to San Diego, with a stop in Tokyo. The third did the same.

"I just received our stand-down order," Senior told Izzy quietly, "but we won't get a military transport flight out of here until Thursday at the earliest." He pointed to the list. "All of these flights are filled, but these airlines are willing to rebook passengers onto later flights—if you can get anyone to volunteer to give up their seat for Dan."

"Whoa, this first one's boarding in ten minutes," Izzy realized. It was two gates down. He'd made note of the fact, during one of their walks through the airport, that most of the passengers there were American.

This could work.

"I thought maybe you could go over there and quietly see what you could do," the senior said.

"Thank you, Senior Chief."

Senior caught Izzy's arm before he could go. "See if you can't get yourself a seat, too," he said. "Your wife and Jennilyn went up to the morgue in Obsidian Springs to ID the body of her—Eden's—stepfather."

"Oh, God," Izzy said.

"I know you've had trouble with him in the past," the senior continued, "but that couldn't've been easy for her."

Izzy had to agree. "Still, let me get Danny home, first."

Senior smacked him on the same shoulder that Dan had punched, but this time Izzy didn't say *ow*. Especially when the senior said, "You're a good man, Zanella. Get it done."

Izzy went to the gate, and yes, he was right. The passengers here were mostly Americans. He went right to the counter at the front, near the boarding door, and climbed up to stand on top of it.

"May I have your attention please?" he said, using his outdoor voice. "My fellow Americans, my name is Irving Zanella, and I'm a member of your military fighting force. I'm here with about a dozen of my Navy SEAL brothers-in-arms, and one of us, my dear friend Danny, just found that his son—his first child—was born about an hour ago, in a hospital not that far from San Diego. So if anyone here is not in a screaming rush to get back to the States, this very generous airline will put you on a later flight, and let Danny use your seat so he can go home and meet his beautiful, *beautiful* newborn son."

A young woman in the back had stood up when Izzy said the word *born*, and she and what looked like two friends made their way toward him. "We're on vacation," she said. "We'll give you our seats, but we're traveling together, and there're three of us."

Izzy jumped down. "Thank you so much. Three seats would be incredible. Wait here, I'm gonna get my senior chief." He dashed back to where the team was hunkered down.

The senior was shaking his head. "That was you being quiet?" he asked rhetorically as he went to handle the details with both the volunteers and the airline. Dan went with him, still holding Izzy's phone, no doubt eager to start showing off pictures of his shiny new baby.

Izzy sat down next to Mark Jenkins. "Hey, I know you're in a hurry to get home, too, but would you mind very much if I gave the third seat to Hobe?"

"HoboMofo?" Mark asked, as if there was more than one *Hobe* in the team.

"Yeah," Izzy said. "We accidentally introduced Lopez to his daughter's fifth-grade teacher. His daughter's *single* fifth-grade teacher, that 'Fo was hoping to get to know a little better…?"

"Aw, shit!" Mark said. "Yeah, give him the seat, and tell him I'm sorry. *Damn* it."

"Thanks, bro," Izzy said, and went to gather up the 'Fo, who was happy to go home early.

And after they joined Dan at the gate, Izzy took his phone back and emailed his wife.

I love you, he wrote in response to her "Stealth Penis" email. I'll see you soon. Keep those home fires burning.

# CHAPTER 12

## LOPEZ

Jay was at the hospital when Dan, Izzy, and HoboMofo—the SEAL whose real name was Hugh Bickles—arrived.

They must've rented a car at LAX and driven directly here, after their fourteen-hour flight.

Dan came into Jenn's hospital room like a man on fire, and Eden shooed Jay and Ben out into the hallway lobby area, so the two of them—three Gillmans, now—had privacy.

"We have a son," Jay heard Jenn tell Dan. "Are you disappointed? I know you wanted a girl."

"I only wanted a healthy baby," Dan said. "And for you to be okay, too. God, Jenni, I love you so much—"

The door closed on them as Izzy, meanwhile, didn't feel the need for any privacy to soul-kiss his wife. "You okay?" he asked Eden, his hands around her face, their foreheads together.

Eden's eyes welled with tears—it was the first time Jay had seen her come anywhere close to crying. She'd been Jennilyn Gillman's staunchest ally and greatest friend—holding her hand and breathing with her—essentially cheerleading the way throughout what had been an arduous and frightening delivery.

But even now, Eden nodded, *yes*. She *was* okay, and clearly very glad Izzy was safely home.

"Daddy!" Jay turned to see Brianna Bickles fling herself into Hobo's—Hugh's—giant arms. The big SEAL lifted up his daughter as if she weighed next to nothing, as he grinned his ass off with a smile that was a lot like his daughter's. It transformed him from angry ogre to… Wow, kinda ruggedly handsome, enormously jacked guy.

Where had Brianna come from? Jay leaned forward in his chair to look down the hall, and sure enough the door opened and there she was.

Carol Redmond.

She'd come out to the hospital, apparently giving a ride to Hugh's mom and Bree.

Jay waved to her, but she didn't see him, her smile was aimed at…

Hobo…*Mofo*.

Really?

*Really?*

Now Hobe was smiling at Carol—and damned if that didn't make him look freaking adorable.

What was it that Carol had told him in the car? That she had a kind of a major crush on a Navy SEAL chief…?

Hubert Bickles, a.k.a. HoboMofo, was a Navy SEAL chief.

Wow, *that* would've been really not okay—Jay's hitting on a woman that one of his SEAL brothers liked, or, God, maybe even loved.

What was there *not* to love about Carol Redmond?

Jay felt a pang of regret—a brief little burst of sorrow for what was not-to-be. But it faded quickly as he watched Carol smile up at Hobe—Hugh—her pleasure at seeing him evident in her body language.

"I really wanted to come talk to the class," Hugh was saying, as Brianna danced off to join her grandmother. "I'm sorry I had to send a substitute."

"Oh, Chief Lopez was *very* good," Carol told him earnestly. "The kids loved him, he was so sweet with Bree, and then he led me on quite the adventure." She laughed. "It was…educational."

As Jay watched, Hugh winced. "Well, great. That's… great. He's, um, here if you, you know, want to say *hi*."

He pointed over at Jay.

"Oh, hi, Jay," Carol said as she looked over at him with so much nothing in her eyes, that he almost laughed aloud. She returned her attention to Hubert, even as she moved toward Jay.

He didn't know how she did it, but she managed, without taking Hugh's hand, to pull him with her as she told Jay, "Congratulations. I assume you had something to do with Jenn's and the baby's good health." He was about to stand, but she stopped him. "Oh, no, don't get up."

"I got lucky," Jay admitted. "We have another friend, Dr. Kelly Paoletti—she managed to drive out to where Jenn and Eden were stuck. She took over, so I just assisted, which was fine with me."

"It was the most amazing thing," Carol told Hugh. "After Jay got into the chopper, I decided to keep going. I thought I could help by staying with Eden's car or…I don't know. But when I got there, there were all these people who'd already come to the rescue. Tom and Adam and Lindsey and Tracy. They just dropped everything, because Dan—and you—were overseas."

"That's how it works," Hugh said. "Kinda like Jay filling in for me in a pinch."

"It's so impressive," Carol said. "And you know, if I've seemed at all hesitant, it's because it scared me. The idea of a relationship with someone who's not only got a dangerous job, but who's also always…kind of…gone. But it was great to see how it works. Starting with Jay's amazing generosity and ending with a random group of people all coming to Jenn's rescue—except they weren't random. They're family. They're *more* than family."

Jay could see that Hugh was struggling to understand, and he knew all the big SEAL had heard was "Jay's amazing."

"It really was nice to see that," Carol said again.

"I have an idea," Jay said, because it was so obvious that Hugh was stuck in some terrible parallel universe where he'd returned from the mission to find Jay and Carol already engaged to be married. And unlike that brief pang of regret that Jay had felt when he'd seen Carol smile at Hugh, Hugh's suffering was deep and intense. *Someone* had to put the man out of his misery. "Why don't we go out sometime, like on a double date." He looked at Carol. "You and Hugh, and me and…" He cleared his throat and lied. "Well, there's a woman I've been dying to ask out, and… This'll give me a reason to. Ask her."

"I'd like that," Carol said, looking up at Hugh.

"Um, *wow. Yeah*," he said, light finally dawning. "I'd like that, too. Very much. Thank you." The smile he shot Jay was definitely adorable.

"We could go tonight," Jay said, but then slapped his forehead. "Wait, no, I can't make it, not tonight. But *you* could go. Right?"

"I'm free," Carol told Hugh as Jay found his crutches, and pulled himself up, and slowly backed away.

"Ooh," Hugh said, making an *I don't know* face. "First night back always belongs to Bree."

And it was beyond obvious from the look on Carol's face that those words made her love Hugh all the more.

"We could all go out," she suggested. "Bree and your mom, and…you and me."

"Oh, Jesus, 'Fo," Izzy Zanella said from where he was sitting, his arm around Eden. "Will you just grab her and kiss her already?"

Hugh laughed.

And did just that.

And Carol kissed him back.

# ABOUT THE AUTHOR

After childhood plans to become the captain of a starship didn't pan out, **Suzanne Brockmann** took her fascination with military history, her respect for the men and women who serve, her reverence for diversity, and her love of storytelling, and explored brave new worlds as a *New York Times* bestselling romance author. Over the past twenty years, she has written fifty-five novels, including her award-winning Troubleshooters series about Navy SEAL heroes and the women—and sometimes men—who win their hearts. In addition to writing books, Suzanne Brockmann has co-written and co-produced a feature-length movie, the award-winning romantic comedy *The Perfect Wedding*. She has also co-written a YA novel, *Night Sky*, with her daughter Melanie. Find Suz on Facebook at www.facebook .com/SuzanneBrockmannBooks, follow her on Twitter @SuzBrockmann, and visit her website at www.SuzanneBrockmann.com.

# Read More!

- To find more books by the authors in this anthology
- Read excerpts of forthcoming titles, and
- Learn how you can support wounded veterans

**VISIT**

www.wayofthewarriorromance.com

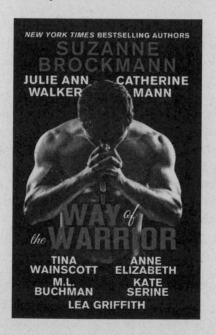

READ ON FOR A PREVIEW OF
THE NEW DEEP SIX SERIES, COMING SOON

# Hell or High Water

### JULIE ANN WALKER

*Present day*
*10:52 p.m....*

"AND THE *SANTA CRISTINA* AND HER BRAVE CREW AND captain were sucked down into Davy Jones's locker, lost to the world. That is...until now..."

Leo "the Lion" Anderson, known to his friends as LT—a nod to his former Naval rank—let his last words hang in the air before glancing around at the four faces illuminated by the flickering beach bonfire. Rapt expressions stared back at him. He fought the grin curving his lips.

*Bingo, bango, bongo.* His listeners had fallen under a spell as deep and fathomless as the great oceans themselves. It happened anytime he recounted the legend of the *Santa Cristina*. Not that he could blame his audience. The story of the ghost galleon, the holy grail of sunken Spanish shipwrecks, had fascinated *him* ever since he'd been old enough to understand the tale while bouncing on his father's knee. And that lifelong fascination might account for why he was now determined to do what so many before him—his dearly departed father included—had been unable to do. Namely, locate and excavate the mother lode of the grand ol' ship.

Of course, he reckoned the romance and mystery of discovering her waterlogged remains were only *part* of the reason he'd spent the last two months and a huge portion of his savings—as well as huge portions of the savings of the others—refurbishing his father's decrepit, leaking salvage boat. The rest of the story as to why he was here now? Why they were *all* here now? Well, that didn't bear dwelling on.

*At least not on a night like tonight.* When a million glittering stars and a big half-moon reflected off the dark, rippling waters of the lagoon on the southeast side of the private speck of jungle, mangrove forest, and sand in the Florida Keys. When the sea air was soft and warm, caressing his skin and hair with gentle, salt-tinged fingers. When there was so much…*life* to enjoy.

That had been his vow—*their* vow—had it not? To grab life by the balls and really *live* it? To suck the marrow from its proverbial bones?

His eyes were automatically drawn to the skin on the inside of his left forearm where scrolling, tattooed lettering read: *For RL.* He ran a thumb over the pitch-black ink.

*This one's for you, you stubborn sonofagun*, he pledged, flipping the lid on the cooler sunk deep into the sand beside his lawn chair. Grabbing a bottle of Budweiser and twisting off the cap, he let his gaze run down the long dock to where his uncle's catamaran was moored. The clips on the sailboat's rigging lines clinked rhythmically against its metal mast, adding to the harmony of softly shushing waves, quietly crackling fire, and the high-pitched *peesy, peesy, peesy* call of a nearby black-and-white warbler.

Then he turned his eyes to the open ocean past the underwater reef surrounding the side of Wayfarer Island, where his father's old salvage ship bobbed lazily with the tide. Up and down. Side to side. Her newly painted hull and refurbished anchor chain gleamed dully in the moonlight. Her name, *Wayfarer-I*, was clearly visible thanks to the new, bright-white lettering.

As he dragged in a deep breath, the smell of burning driftwood and suntan lotion tunneled up his nose, and he did his best to appreciate the calmness of the evening and the comforting thought that the vessel looked, if not necessarily sexy, then at least seaworthy. *Which is a hell of an improvement.*

*Hot damn*, he was proud of all the work he and his men had done on her, and—

His men…

He reminded himself for the one hundred zillionth time that he wasn't supposed to think of them that way. Not anymore. Not since those five crazy-assed SEALs waved their farewells to the Navy in order to join him on his quest for high-seas adventure and the discovery of untold riches. Not since they were now, officially, *civilians*.

"But why you guys?" The blond who was parked beneath Spiro "Romeo" Delgado's arm yanked Leo from his thoughts. "What makes you different from all those who've already tried and failed to find her?"

# Night Sky

## SUZANNE BROCKMANN
## AND MELANIE BROCKMANN

I HAD NOT BEEN UNDER THE IMPRESSION THAT TROPHY wives owned guns.

Of course, my impression of a lot of things had been changing lately, so the idea of a homicidal contortionist with a designer handbag and a vanity license plate that read DRSWIFEY was, surprisingly, not very surprising at all.

"What's up with Little Miss Sunshine?" Calvin mumbled to me, tapping my forearm with his hand as we made our way to the front doors of the Sav'A'Buck supermarket. He motioned with his head for me to look behind him, and I glanced over at the lady. Huge, fake-looking boobs and even larger sunglasses. I doubted she needed them at nine o'clock at night…the sunglasses, that is. It *was* September in Florida, but come on.

"Dunno," I answered, picking up my pace a little bit. I was eager to get inside the store. Even without the sun, the humidity made the air feel like it was about ninety thousand degrees. I had a bad case of swamp butt, and my jean shorts were sticking to my backside uncomfortably.

Calvin laughed as I fixed my wedgie with an apparently less-than-discreet swipe. "Could you fix mine too? It's really bad. Horrible," he said, lifting himself halfway off the seat of his electric wheelchair.

I socked him once in the bicep. "Punk."

The linoleum floors of the Sav'A'Buck were sticky, and the place smelled like pig grease and stale cigarettes. But that's what we got for venturing outside our pristine gated community and driving across the proverbial tracks into neighboring Harrisburg to the only place open after nine.

"Man, you really want to buy *food* from here?" Calvin grumbled, while two small kids whisked in front of us, barefoot, their faces coated with melted purple ice pop. The woman working register four turned around, her disastrous mullet matched only by the disapproving frown she offered Calvin and me as we strolled by.

Neither of us accepted it.

"We're making s'mores," I insisted, my resolve strong. It had been a hellish week, and I wanted something chocolate. We had driven all the way out here; we weren't turning back now.

Calvin rolled his eyes. "Come on," he said, steering himself sharply toward the right. "Cookies and crackers. Aisle seven."

I followed behind him, breaking into a trot to keep up with his chair.

But Calvin pressed his brake and we nearly collided. "There she is again," he hissed, tapping my hand furiously. "Doesn't she creep you out, even a little?"

Little Miss Sunshine, as Calvin had called her, was busy inspecting the nutrition information on the backs of two different bags of corn chips. Her long, blond hair was swept up in an elegant French chignon. She hadn't bothered to take off her sunglasses.

I scooped up a box of graham crackers and left the aisle. Calvin followed me this time.

Once the woman was out of earshot, I told him, "The only weird thing about her is that she looks like she's rolling in dough, unlike most Sav'A'Buck customers." I shrugged. "But we probably stick out here too." I found the aisle for candy and grabbed a humongous bag of chocolate. "So give her a break."

Calvin acknowledged his two-hundred-dollar polo shirt and shrugged. "Eh, you're right," he replied, and popped his collar.

"That's lame, by the way," I said, and found an empty basket to dump my purchases into.

"What?" Calvin replied, his expression one of mock offense. "Girl, you are just jealous because you can't pull off the look."

"Sooo jealous," I replied sarcastically. I was perfectly happy in my jean shorts and plain black tank top. Nobody needed to know my mom had spent a fortune for both articles of clothing. If it were up to me, I'd wear clothes from the local consignment shop, thank you very much. People were going hungry these days, and obviously many of them were right here in Harrisburg. That was way creepier, IMO, than Little Miss Sunshine jonesing for cheap, salty grease.

Calvin poked his nose into my basket. "Would you mind telling me exactly how white girls from the north make s'mores? Where I come from, we use marshmallows."

"Dammit!" I'd forgotten to grab a bag when we were in the candy aisle.

"Come on," Calvin replied, and reached for my basket. He set it atop his lap and followed me as I sprinted back toward aisle eight.

"Skylar, slow your ass down!" Calvin whined, but when I did, he zoomed past me, laughing.

"Oh, it's on," I said, pushing to keep up. "I could totally beat you in a race."

It was Calvin's turn to roll his eyes when we both had to slow for oncoming traffic. "Oh, yeah? How much you wanna bet?"

"I'll have to think about it," I answered, and that's when the screaming started.

# Free Fall

## CATHERINE MANN

EVEN AS THE YAWNING ENTRANCE TO THE CAVE CAME into sight, Stella refused to relax her guard. She pulled back on the throttle. Entering slowly, she scanned while her quiet companions held their MP5s at the ready. Would an Interpol operative, four CIA agents, six SEALs, and two PJs be enough to face anything that waited inside? The low hum of the motor echoed like a growling beast in the cavern, one light strobing forward into the darkness.

Illuminating a waiting U.S. fishing boat.

Her final contingency.

Her plan had to work; otherwise, she would screw up her hard-earned chance of working in Africa before the mission barely got off the ground. She flung open the door to the small forward cabin of her speedboat. The clang of metal hitting metal echoed in her mind like the closing of her mother's coffin. Melanie Carson's daughter would not give up on day one.

Digging around in the hull, Stella pulled out small

duffel bags, one after the other, tossing them to each of the men in wet suits.

"Change, gentlemen. We're about to become American tourists on a sightseeing excursion. Mr. Jones," who could blend in best with the locals and even spoke a regional dialect thanks to his mother, "will be our guide. We're swapping boats, then splitting up at the dock. Blend into the crowds. Report at the embassy. You've got a duress code if you need to call in. Any questions?"

Only the sound of oxygen tanks and gear hitting the deck answered her.

"Good." Her heart rate started to return to something close to normal again.

The sound of zippers sent her spinning on her heels to take care of her own transformation. She unrolled a colorful rectangular cloth, an East African kanga, complete with the standard intricate border and message woven into the red and orange pattern.

It would be hot as hell over her black pants, top, and bulletproof vest. But a little dehydration was a small price to pay for an extra layer of anonymity.

"Need help?"

She turned and there were those coffee dark eyes again. Static-like awareness snapped when she looked back at the intense gaze that had held her's earlier as he'd lifted his face mask. Except now he was more than eyes and a wet suit. He was a lean, honed man in a pair of fitted swim trunks he must have worn under the diving gear. He was glistening bronze with a body trained for survival anyplace, anytime.

The boat rocked under her feet from a rogue wave. At least she thought it was a wave.

"Uh, no, I'm good. Thanks. You should get dressed. We need to haul butt out of here." And his current state of undress definitely didn't qualify as "low profile."

"I meant, do you need help with the cut on your temple?" He gestured to the left side of her face, almost touching. "You brought along two PJs for a reason, ma'am."

Her skin hummed with a sting that her brain must have pushed aside earlier for survival's sake. She tapped the side of her forehead gingerly.

"Ouch!" Her fingertips were stained with blood as murky red as her hair.

"A bullet must have grazed you," he said with a flat Midwestern accent. A no-accent really, just pure masculine rumble. "Could have been much worse. This was your lucky day, ma'am."

"Stella." For right now she could be more than Miss Lucky Smith.

"They call me Cuervo."

Call him.

Call signs.

No real name from him for now. Understandable and a reality check to get her professional groove back on: "Do I need stitches?"

He tugged a small kit from his gear, a waterproof pack of some sort. "Antiseptic and butterfly bandages should hold you until we can get someplace where I'll have time to treat you more fully."

*We.*

Her brain hitched on the word, the answer to who she would be partnering with as they escaped into the crowd. She wasn't saying good-bye to him—to Cuervo—at the dock. Irrational relief flooded her, followed by a bolt of excitement.

"Thanks, Cuervo. Blood dripping down my face would definitely draw undue attention at an inopportune time." She forced a smile.

Still, his face, those eyes, they held her, and while she wasn't a mystical person, she couldn't miss the connection. Attraction? Sure, but she understood how to compartmentalize on the job. This was something that felt elemental. Before she could stop the thought, the words *soul mate* flashed through her head.

And God, that was crazy and irrational when she was always, always logical. Her brothers called her a female version of Spock from *Star Trek*.

Still, as those fingers cleaned her wound, smoothed ointment over her temple, and stretched butterfly bandages along her skin, she couldn't stop thinking about spending the rest of the day with him as they melded into the port city and made their way back to the embassy.

Damn it, she could not waste the time or emotional energy on romance or even a fling. Right now, she could only focus on working with the Mr. Smiths and Mr. Browns of her profession. She needed to make peace with her past, *then* move on with her life. Then, and only then, she would find Mr. *Right* and shift from the field to a desk job so she could settle down into that real family dream she'd missed out on.

Yet those brown eyes drew her into a molten heat and she had the inescapable sense that Mr. Right had arrived ahead of schedule.

**The Elite Force series by Catherine Mann**

*Cover Me*
*Hot Zone*
*Under Fire*
*Free Fall*

# Bring On the Dusk

### M.L. BUCHMAN

THERE WERE FEW TIMES THAT COLONEL MICHAEL Gibson of Delta Force appreciated the near-psychotic level of commitment displayed by terrorists, but this was one of those times. If they hadn't been so rigid in even their attire, his disguise would have been much more difficult.

The al-Qaeda terrorist training camp deep in the Yemeni desert required that all of their hundred new trainees dress in white with black headdresses that left only the eyes exposed. The thirty-four trainers were dressed similarly but wholly in black, making them easy to distinguish. They were also the only ones armed, which was a definite advantage.

The camp's dress code made for a perfect cover. The four men of his team wore loose-fitting black robes like the trainers. Lieutenant Bill Bruce used dark contacts to hide his blue eyes, and they all had rubbed a dye onto their hands and wrists, the only other uncovered portion of their bodies.

Michael and his team had parachuted into the deep

desert the night before and traveled a quick ten kilome-
ters on foot before burying themselves in the sand along
the edges of the main training grounds. Only their faces
were exposed, each carefully hidden by a thorn bush.

The midday temperatures had easily blown through
110 degrees. It felt twice that inside the heavy clothing
and lying under a foot of hot sand, but uncomfortable
was a way of life in "The Unit," as Delta Force called
itself, so this was of little concern. They'd dug deep
enough so that they weren't simply roasted alive, even
if it felt that way by the end of the motionless day.

It was three minutes to sunset, three minutes until the
start of Maghrib, the fourth scheduled prayer of the five
that were performed daily.

At the instant of sunset, the muezzin began chanting
*adhan*, the call to prayer.

Thinking themselves secure in the deep desert of
the Abyan province of southern Yemen, every one of
the trainees and the trainers knelt and faced northwest
toward Mecca.

After fourteen motionless hours—fewer than a dozen
steps from a hundred and thirty terrorists—moving
smoothly and naturally was a challenge as Michael rose
from his hiding place. He shook off the sand and swung
his AK-47 into a comfortable position. The four of them
approached the prostrate group in staggered formation
from the southeast over a small hillock.

The Delta operators interspersed themselves among
the other trainers and knelt, blending in perfectly.
Of necessity, they all spoke enough Arabic to pass
if questioned.

Michael didn't check the others because that might

draw attention. If they hadn't made it cleanly into place, an alarm would have been raised and the plan would have changed drastically. All was quiet, so he listened to the muezzin's words and allowed himself to settle into the peace of the prayer.

*Bismi-llāhi r-raḥmāni r-raḥīm…*

*In the name of Allah, the most compassionate, the most merciful…*

He sank into the rhythm and meaning of it—not as these terrorists twisted it in the name of murder and warfare, but as it was actually stated. Moments like this one drove home the irony of his long career to become the most senior field operative in Delta while finding an inner quiet in the moment before dealing death.

Perhaps in their religious fervor, the terrorists found the same experience. But what they lacked was flexibility. They wound themselves up to throw away their lives, if necessary, to complete their preprogrammed actions exactly as planned.

For Michael, an essential centering in self allowed perfect adaptability when situations went kinetic— Delta's word for the shit unexpectedly hitting the fan.

That was Delta's absolute specialty.

Starting with zero preconceptions in either energy or strategy allowed for the perfect action that fit each moment in a rapidly changing scenario. Among the team, they'd joke sometimes about how Zen, if not so Buddhist, the moment before battle was.

And, as always, he accepted the irony of that with no more than a brief smile at life's whimsy.

Dealing death was one significant part of what The Unit did.

U.S. SFOD-D, Special Forces Operational Detachment-Delta, went where no other fighting force could go and did what no one else could do.

Today, it was a Yemeni terrorist training camp.

Tomorrow would take care of itself.

They were the U.S. Army's Tier One asset and no one, except their targets, would ever know they'd been here. One thing for certain, had The Unit been unleashed on bin Laden, not a soul outside the command structure would know who'd been there. SEAL Team Six had done a top-notch job, but talking about it wasn't something a Delta operator did. But Joint Special Operations Command's leader at the time was a former STS member, so the SEALs had gone in instead.

Three more minutes of prayer.

Then seven minutes to help move the trainees into their quarters where they would be locked in under guard for the night, as they were still the unknowns.

Or so the trainers thought.

Three more minutes to move across the compound through the abrupt fall of darkness in the equatorial desert to where the commanders would meet for their evening meal and evaluation of the trainees.

After that the night would get interesting.

*Bismi-llāhi r-raḥmāni r-raḥīm...*

*In the name of Allah, the most compassionate, the most merciful...*

## Also by M.L. Buchman

### The Night Stalkers
*The Night Is Mine*
*I Own the Dawn*
*Wait Until Dark*
*Take Over at Midnight*
*Light Up the Night*
*Bring On the Dusk*

### The Firehawks
*Pure Heat*
*Full Blaze*
*Hot Point*

READ ON FOR A PREVIEW OF THE NEXT
WEST COAST NAVY SEALS ROMANCE

# A SEAL Forever

## ANNE ELIZABETH

MASTER CHIEF DECLAN SWIFTON OF SEAL TEAM FIVE rolled over the side of the Rigid-Hulled Inflatable Boat and slid soundlessly into the Pacific Ocean. The RIB took off without even a comment from the operator, leaving Declan to sink further into the drink.

The temperature cooled as he swam away from the surface. Fish skirted the edges of his thighs, small shimmers of movement against his skin. He scissor-kicked his way forward. The ocean currents caught him, dragging him in the direction they wanted to go, toward shore. He lay with his arms at his sides, frog-kicking only. Above him, he could see the afternoon sunlight glistening and frothy foam chasing away the glassy surface. Down here, things were different…calmer. Peaceful in a way few souls would understand, and yet, he knew that even he would have to surface soon.

His lungs would start to ache and burn, his gut would begin to feel as if it would cave in, and that would force him to either head topside or drink in the salt water.

But there was still time. This was the water in front of Imperial Beach and the apartment he lived in. He knew it very well.

Scanning the ocean floor, he gauged it would be about thirty seconds until he reached one of the many rocky sand bars out here. He'd have to pull up before then or the force of the current would smack him against the side. As his body began to complain, he used both arms and legs to draw himself upward. Breaking the surface, he opened his mouth and drew in air like a thirsty man.

The waves bounced him like a buoy. The tide was coming in and the wind was picking up momentum. Looking at the sky to the east, he could see a storm was likely. Dec took a long, slow breath and appreciated the sunset. The colors were extraordinary; orange and gold dappled the horizon as the blazing ball of light attempted to sink before the moon lifted higher in the sky.

His hands flexed, cupping the water. It had been a warm day and the sun's rays had heated the top of the water, making the surface feel like a warm bath, loosening his muscles. Three months ago, he'd been in waters so frigid, there were actual ice caps; the memory still made him cold. But here, the Pacific Ocean off California's Imperial Beach was a slice of heaven.

Coming in from the east were some nasty-looking cumulus-nimbus clouds. Seeing the lightning arc way off toward the distant desert, he decided it was time to go in and right on cue, here came a perfect wave.

Swimming at top speed, Declan pushed his way through the changing current, one that sought to drag him into faster-moving waters. He went over a sand bar, having no intention of going to Mexico today, and increased the reach of his stroke. With single-mindedness, he worked his way into the more placid surf as he homed in on a large stretch of beach.

He felt a few sea lions swimming around him; one nosed him in the gut and another in his back a few times, assessing whether or not he'd play. *Not this time, my friends*. He continued swimming without engaging. If he stopped to play, he'd be out there for hours.

Switching to the breaststroke, his arms protested. His Platoon had switched their training this month to desert warfare techniques, and he'd been sweating his balls off in the heat. He'd managed to learn a thing or two, even now, after all his years in the Teams. But it felt good to be back in the ocean, his element. He'd live in the deep blue like a Jules Verne character if he could.

Taking in a mouthful of water, he swished it around and spat it out. *Salt water, nature's peroxide*.

Pausing to focus in on the beach, he saw two sun-bathers to the left, apparently arguing, and a handful of children at the other end packing up their sand castle gear. The area abutted some nasty terrain where even the tweakers and druggies didn't venture.

Dec bodysurfed the rest of the way to shore. With the cool, sandy bottom beneath his feet, he walked up onto the beach, leaving behind the water's warmth. The wind ruffled the tops of the waves, blowing hard from east to west.

Taking one more glance at the sunset, he noted the time. He needed to keep moving to stay on schedule. A certain lovely lady would be having his undivided attention later this evening.

# West Coast Navy SEALs by Anne Elizabeth

*A SEAL at Heart*
*Once a SEAL*
*A SEAL Forever*

# Endgame Ops

### LEA GRIFFITH

*Douala International Airport*
*Cameroon, Africa*

QUINN FEARED SHE WASN'T GOING TO MAKE HER
flight and damn, she really needed to be on that plane.
She weaved through the throngs of people in the main
terminal, trying not to knock down anyone who refused
to the get the hell out of her way.

"Final call for Air France flight 1701 to Paris, boarding now," the gate hostess said in a lilting, accented
voice over the intercom.

Quinn pushed her heavy blond hair out of her face,
breathed deeply, and smiled at the woman as she handed
her the boarding pass. The woman shooed her through.
*One step closer to home.* Exhilaration pumped through
Quinn's body. She pulled her carry-on behind her down
the loading ramp. The *tick, tick, splat* of rain on the
dock's tin roof reminded her that it was monsoon season
in Cameroon. She definitely wouldn't miss the rain. The

people were a different story. She'd miss the hell out of them. But she'd be back.

She stepped into the plane and nodded at an attendant.

"Welcome aboard, *mademoiselle*," the flight attendant said with a smile.

Visions of manicures, pedicures, and McDonald's French fries danced in her head as she practically skipped down the aisle of the 747.

Quinn found her seat, pushed down the handle of her carry-on, and lifted it to the overhead compartment. She struggled for several moments, cursing, before she got it situated. Her gaze fell as she closed the compartment door and her breath stuck in her throat. In the row behind her sat a lone man.

Quite possibly the hottest man she'd ever seen. He was looking out the window and she stood there in awe as she took in his mink-brown, wavy hair. High cheekbones balanced a square jaw darkened by a five o'clock shadow.

She took in the strong column of his neck and the breadth of his chest. Then she slammed right into his gaze and Quinn almost swallowed her tongue. His eyes were the green of an Irish hillside, and his lips curved at her perusal.

His eyes smoldered then he blinked. That single instant of reprieve allowed her to get her shit together—okay, almost together. She sat quickly in her aisle seat. She tried to concentrate on breathing evenly. The sexy bastard in the row behind her had stolen the oxygen from her lungs. Quinn wasn't a believer in insta-love, but insta-lust? Very possible.

"We'll be leaving shortly. Please make sure all

carry-on luggage is stowed carefully in the assigned compartments," a flight attendant said over the speaker.

Quinn was flying to Paris and then catching a flight to D.C. Home was at least eighteen hours away—if everything connected properly.

Quinn closed her eyes and focused on her go-to fantasy—McDonald's French fries. Yeah, the Golden Arches had some thirty thousand locations worldwide, but not one McD's graced the country where she'd spent the last three years. She took a deep breath and smelled evergreens and mint. Her body tightened and she looked up.

"Excuse me," said Mr. Hotness. "I think I had the wrong seat," he said in a deep baritone that seriously rearranged pieces inside Quinn's abdomen.

"Uh, well, okay?" She was a mess in the face of all that hotness.

He smiled, which was possibly the most beautiful thing she'd ever seen on any man, ever.

"I think what I'm asking," he began and sighed patiently, "is do you want the aisle or the window?"

She stared up at him and his brows lowered. Then it hit her. "Oh! Aisle is fine, thanks," she murmured as she started to stand so he could sit down.

He brushed by her and there it was—the holy grail of backside views.

Quinn shook her head and sat down. But when her arm brushed against his (which was damn near impossible to avoid because the dude was huge) Quinn jerked her arm away and felt more than saw his chest rising and falling.

He was laughing at her.

Quinn drowned it out by closing her eyes again and

thinking of McDonald's fries. She was lost to the dream of salty goodness, trying hard to get Mr. Hotness off her mind, and so the *rat-a-tat-tat* took her by surprise.

A strong hand pushed her head down. "Don't move!" he bit out.

"Hey," she objected but it was directed to her knees. She tried lifting her head but his grip on the back of her neck was solid.

"We've got trouble. I need you to keep your head down, 'kay?" he whispered in her ear.

Trouble? *Understatement*, she thought. Shots fired were a *bit* more than trouble.

More *rat-a-tat-tat-tat*, and it was definitely automatic weapons fire. Children and adults were screaming, and over it all, a hard voice demanded that everyone sit down.

*Well shit*. "All I wanted was a mani/pedi and some hot McDonald's fries," she muttered.

"What?" he asked.

Then every single thought left her brain as a woman screamed. Quinn's instincts kicked in and she reached for his hand to remove it from her neck.

"I said to stay down," he bit out.

She twisted his hand in a move her father had taught her and he released her immediately. She lifted her head and her gaze found chaos.

At least five men holding AK47s were shouting orders to people in heavily accented, broken English interspersed with...*Arabic*?

"Where is the woman?" one of them yelled as he shoved his gun in the face of a stewardess.

Oh, damn. This was so not good.

**If you enjoyed *Beauty and the Marine*,
you'll also love these titles by Tina Wainscott**

READ ON FOR A PREVIEW OF BOOK ONE IN THE HOT
NEW ROMANTIC SUSPENSE SERIES

# Protect and Serve

## KATE SERINE

KYLE DAWSON'S HEART WAS IN HIS THROAT. HE AND
his brothers arrived at the house to find two sheriff's
vehicles and three Oakdale police cars parked out front.
The door was standing open and two of the Oakdale
officers were walking the perimeter, shining their flash-
lights along the hedges.

"Abby!" Kyle cried as he jumped out of Gabe's
department Tahoe, not even bothering to close
the door behind him as he sprinted toward the
house. "Abby!"

An Oakdale officer met him at the door, barring his
entrance. "I'm sorry, you can't come in here."

Kyle had the sudden urge to throat-punch the guy,
but instead, he reached into the back pocket of his jeans
and produced his ID. "Agent Kyle Dawson," he said,
flashing his badge. "I received a call from someone at
this residence."

"It's okay, Mike," Gabe said, coming up behind him,
Tom and Joe in tow. "He's our brother. Let him in."

Officer "Mike" did a double-take at Kyle, then stepped aside. "Sure. Sorry. Come on in."

Kyle squeezed by before the guy was even out of the doorway, rushing into the dark house. *Why the hell weren't there any lights, by the way?*

His father was barking orders in the semidarkness. As Kyle headed in the direction of his father's voice, he felt a brief spike of apprehension at the thought of walking headlong into the same room as the Old Man, but his concern for Abby overrode his instinct to turn around and walk away.

"Abby!" he called out again as he reached the entrance to what appeared to be the living room. A man in what looked like a security guard's uniform sat on a couch with an ice pack on the crown of his head, apparently having taken a blow to the back of the head.

Frantic, he looked for Abby, his gaze taking in the entire room at a glance. His throat went tight when he caught sight of her sitting on the couch, her shoulders slightly hunched, her gorgeous blond hair a tangled mess. Her gray T-shirt was rumpled, a small tear near the collar, and her white capris had a smudge of dirt on the knee, but she was in far better condition than he'd feared he would find her. Sitting next to her was her nephew Tyler. The boy's wide blue eyes, so very similar to Abby's, turned their attention to the doorway where he stood.

For a long, heavy moment, Abby's gaze met Kyle's, her expression unreadable. And for a few agonizing seconds, Kyle thought maybe she was in shock and didn't recognize him. But then she launched to her feet and rushed toward him, a strangled sob escaping her as he moved forward to meet her.

And then she was throwing herself into his arms, squeezing him around the neck so hard he could hardly breathe. He gathered her close, holding her as his heart pounded with relief and joy at finding her alive. And it was almost as if they'd never been apart, as if there'd never been any harsh words or misunderstandings. *Almost.* But then Abby's hold on him suddenly loosened and she was pushing out of their embrace.

She wiped at her cheeks in a quick swipe as if embarrassed by her tears and took a step back. "Sorry. I shouldn't have—I mean, I didn't realize…" Her words trailed off as a frown brought her fair brows together. "What are you doing here? How did you know?"

"You called me," Kyle explained, trying to recover his composure and not let on how much he'd enjoyed having her back in his arms again—even if for just a few short moments—and how much it killed him to let her go. "I heard what was happening and got here as soon as I could."

She cocked her head to one side, clearly confused. "But…I thought you were in New Orleans."

"In case you failed to notice, this happens to be a crime scene," his father interrupted. "And while I appreciate the FBI's concern, I'm sure their illustrious agents have more important business to attend to than a *humble* little B&E. I have no doubt that we small-town cops can handle even a case like this without your assistance."

Kyle tried his damnedest not to roll his eyes. He should've known the first encounter with Mac would be like this after the way the last one had ended. And he wasn't surprised one bit to hear his own angry words thrown back in his face. But it still pissed him off.

He sent an exasperated glance his dad's way, then turned his attention back at Abby. "Breaking and entering?"

An almost imperceptible flush rose to her cheeks. "Yes."

*She was lying. Why?*

"Perhaps you misunderstood me," Mac said, his voice louder. "We currently do not have need of your services, *Agent* Dawson."

Kyle turned to finally peg the Old Man with an exasperated look. His father hadn't changed a bit. Tall, powerfully built, Mac Dawson was just as imposing a figure as he'd ever been and as full of piss and vinegar as Kyle remembered. And he was looking at his youngest son like he was an intruder, an outsider who had no business there.

Hell, maybe he was right. But Kyle had never given him the satisfaction of an easy victory, so why start today?